Leave It to Psmith

Leave It
to
Psmith

P. G. Wodehouse

Vintage Books
A Division of Random House, Inc.
New York

SECOND VINTAGE BOOKS EDITION, APRIL 2005

Library of Congress Cataloging-in-Publication Data
Wodehouse, Pelham Grenville, 1881–1975.
Leave it to Psmith.
I. Title.
[PZ3.W817Le7]   [PR6045.O53]   823'.9'12   75-13377

ISBN 1-4000-7960-8

Book design by Georgia Küng

www.vintagebooks.com

Printed in the United States of America
10 9 8 7 6 5 4 3 2 1

To

MY DAUGHTER LEONORA

Queen of her species.

CONTENTS

Leave It to Psmith

§ 1

A T the open window of the great library of Blandings Castle, drooping like a wet sock, as was his habit when he had nothing to prop his spine against, the Earl of Emsworth, that amiable and boneheaded peer, stood gazing out over his domain.

It was a lovely morning and the air was fragrant with gentle summer scents. Yet in his lordship's pale blue eyes there was a look of melancholy. His brow was furrowed, his mouth peevish. And this was all the more strange in that he was normally as happy as only a fluffy-minded man with excellent health and a large income can be. A writer, describing Blandings Castle in a magazine article, had once said: 'Tiny mosses have grown in the cavities of the stones, until, viewed near at hand, the place seems shaggy with vegetation.' It would not have been a bad description of the proprietor. Fifty-odd years of serene and unruffled placidity had given Lord Emsworth a curiously moss-covered look. Very few things had the power to disturb him. Even his younger son, the Hon. Freddie Threepwood, could only do it occasionally.

Yet now he was sad. And – not to make a mystery of it any longer – the reason of his sorrow was the fact that he had mislaid his glasses and without them was as blind, to use his own neat simile, as a bat. He was keenly aware of the sunshine that poured down on his gardens, and was yearning to pop out and potter among the flowers he loved. But no man, pop he never so wisely, can hope to potter with any good result if the world is a mere blur.

The door behind him opened, and Beach the butler entered, a dignified procession of one.

'Who's that?' inquired Lord Emsworth, spinning on his axis.

'It is I, your lordship – Beach.'

'Have you found them?'

'Not yet, your lordship,' sighed the butler.

'You can't have looked.'

'I have searched assiduously, your lordship, but without avail. Thomas and Charles also announce non-success. Stokes has not yet made his report.'

'Ah!'

'I am re-despatching Thomas and Charles to your lordship's bedroom,' said the Master of the Hunt. 'I trust that their efforts will be rewarded.'

Beach withdrew, and Lord Emsworth turned to the window again. The scene that spread itself beneath him – though he was unfortunately not able to see it – was a singularly beautiful one, for the castle, which is one of the oldest inhabited houses in England, stands upon a knoll of rising ground at the southern end of the celebrated Vale of Blandings in the county of Shropshire. Away in the blue distance wooded hills ran down to where the Severn gleamed like an unsheathed sword; while up from the river rolling park-land, mounting and dipping, surged in a green wave almost to the castle walls, breaking on the terraces in a many-coloured flurry of flowers as it reached the spot where the province of Angus McAllister, his lordship's head gardener, began. The day being June the thirtieth, which is the very high-tide time of summer flowers, the immediate neighbour-hood of the castle was ablaze with roses, pinks, pansies, carna-tions, hollyhocks, columbines, larkspurs, London pride, Canterbury bells, and a multitude of other choice blooms of which only Angus could have told you the names. A conscien-tious man was Angus; and in spite of being a good deal hampered by Lord Emsworth's amateur assistance, he showed excellent results in his department. In his beds there was much at which to point with pride, little to view with concern.

Scarcely had Beach removed himself when Lord Emsworth was called upon to turn again. The door had opened for the second time, and a young man in a beautifully-cut suit of grey flannel was standing in the doorway. He had a long and vacant face topped by shining hair brushed back and heavily brillian-tined after the prevailing mode, and he was standing on one leg. For Freddie Threepwood was seldom completely at his ease in his parent's presence.

'Hallo, guv'nor.'

'Well, Frederick?'

It would be paltering with the truth to say that Lord Emsworth's greeting was a warm one. It lacked the note of true affection. A few weeks before he had had to pay a matter of five hundred pounds to settle certain racing debts for his offspring; and, while this had not actually dealt an irretrievable blow at his bank account, it had undeniably tended to diminish Freddie's charm in his eyes.

'Hear you've lost your glasses, guv'nor.'

'That is so.'

'Nuisance, what?'

'Undeniably.'

'Ought to have a spare pair.'

'I have broken my spare pair.'

'Tough luck! And lost the other?'

'And, as you say, lost the other.'

'Have you looked for the bally things?'

'I have.'

'Must be somewhere, I mean.'

'Quite possibly.'

'Where,' asked Freddie, warming to his work, 'did you see them last?'

'Go away!' said Lord Emsworth, on whom his child's conversation had begun to exercise an oppressive effect.

'Eh?'

'Go away!'

'Go away?'

'Yes, go away!'

'Right ho!'

The door closed. His lordship returned to the window once more.

He had been standing there some few minutes when one of those miracles occurred which happen in libraries. Without sound or warning a section of books started to move away from the parent body and, swinging out in a solid chunk into the room, showed a glimpse of a small, study-like apartment. A young man in spectacles came noiselessly through and the books returned to their place.

The contrast between Lord Emsworth and the new-comer, as they stood there, was striking, almost dramatic. Lord Emsworth was so acutely spectacle-less; Rupert Baxter, his secretary, so pronouncedly spectacled. It was his spectacles that struck you first as you saw the man. They gleamed efficiently at you. If you had a guilty conscience, they pierced you through and through; and even if your conscience was one hundred per cent. pure you could not ignore them. 'Here,' you said to yourself, 'is an efficient young man in spectacles.'

In describing Rupert Baxter as efficient, you did not overestimate him. He was essentially that. Technically but a salaried subordinate, he had become by degrees, owing to the limp amiability of his employer, the real master of the house. He was the Brains of Blandings, the man at the switch, the person in charge, and the pilot, so to speak, who weathered the storm. Lord Emsworth left everything to Baxter, only asking to be allowed to potter in peace; and Baxter, more than equal to the task, shouldered it without wincing.

Having got within range, Baxter coughed; and Lord Emsworth, recognising the sound, wheeled round with a faint flicker of hope. It might be that even this apparently insoluble problem of the missing pince-nez would yield before the other's efficiency.

'Baxter, my dear fellow, I've lost my glasses. My glasses. I have mislaid them. I cannot think where they can have gone to. You haven't seen them anywhere by any chance?'

'Yes, Lord Emsworth,' replied the secretary, quietly equal to the crisis. 'They are hanging down your back.'

'Down my back? Why, bless my soul!' His lordship tested the statement and found it – like all Baxter's statements – accurate. 'Why, bless my soul, so they are! Do you know, Baxter, I really believe I must be growing absent-minded.' He hauled in the slack, secured the pince-nez, adjusted them beamingly. His irritability had vanished like the dew off one of his roses. 'Thank you, Baxter, thank you. You are invaluable.'

And with a radiant smile Lord Emsworth made buoyantly for the door, en route for God's air and the society of McAllister. The movement drew from Baxter another cough – a sharp, peremptory cough this time; and his lordship paused, reluctantly, like a dog whistled back from the chase. A cloud fell over the sunniness of his mood. Admirable as Baxter was in so many respects, he had a tendency to worry him at times; and something told Lord Emsworth that he was going to worry him now.

'The car will be at the door,' said Baxter with quiet firmness, 'at two sharp.'

'Car? What car?'

'The car to take you to the station.'

'Station? What station?'

Rupert Baxter preserved his calm. There were times when he found his employer a little trying, but he never showed it.

'You have perhaps forgotten, Lord Emsworth, that you arranged with Lady Constance to go to London this afternoon.'

'Go to London!' gasped Lord Emsworth, appalled. 'In weather like this? With a thousand things to attend to in the garden? What a perfectly preposterous notion! Why should I go to London? I hate London.'

'You arranged with Lady Constance that you would give Mr McTodd lunch to-morrow at your club.'

'Who the devil is Mr McTodd?'

'The well-known Canadian poet.'

'Never heard of him.'

'Lady Constance has long been a great admirer of his work. She wrote inviting him, should he ever come to England, to pay a visit to Blandings. He is now in London and is to come down to-morrow for two weeks. Lady Constance's suggestion was that, as a compliment to Mr McTodd's eminence in the world of literature, you should meet him in London and bring him back here yourself.'

Lord Emsworth remembered now. He also remembered that this positively infernal scheme had not been his sister Constance's in the first place. It was Baxter who had made the suggestion, and Constance had approved. He made use of the recovered pince-nez to glower through them at his secretary; and not for the first time in recent months was aware of a feeling that this fellow Baxter was becoming a dashed infliction. Baxter was getting above himself, throwing his weight about, making himself a confounded nuisance. He wished he could get rid of the man. But where could he find an adequate successor? That was the trouble. With all his drawbacks, Baxter *was* efficient. Nevertheless, for a moment Lord Emsworth toyed with the pleasant dream of dismissing him. And it is possible, such was his exasperation, that he might on this occasion have done something practical in that direction, had not the library door at this moment opened for the third time, to admit yet another intruder – at the sight of whom his lordship's militant mood faded weakly.

'Oh – hallo, Connie!' he said, guiltily, like a small boy caught in the jam cupboard. Somehow his sister always had this effect upon him.

Of all those who had entered the library that morning the new arrival was the best worth looking at. Lord Emsworth was tall and lean and scraggy, Rupert Baxter thick-set and handicapped by that vaguely grubby appearance which is presented by swarthy young men of bad complexion, and even Beach, though dignified, and Freddie, though slim, would never have got far in a beauty competition. But Lady Constance Keeble really took the eye. She was a strikingly handsome woman in the middle forties. She had a fair, broad brow, teeth of a perfect even whiteness, and the carriage of an empress. Her eyes were large and grey, and gentle – and incidentally misleading, for gentle was hardly the adjective which anybody who knew her would have applied to Lady Constance. Though genial enough when she got her way, on the rare occasions when people attempted to thwart her she was apt to comport herself in a manner reminiscent of Cleopatra on one of the latter's bad mornings.

'I hope I am not disturbing you,' said Lady Constance with a bright smile. 'I just came in to tell you to be sure not to forget, Clarence, that you are going to London this afternoon to meet Mr McTodd.'

'I was just telling Lord Emsworth,' said Baxter, 'that the car would be at the door at two.'

'Thank you, Mr Baxter. Of course I might have known that you would not forget. You are so wonderfully capable. I don't know what in the world we would do without you.'

The Efficient Baxter bowed. But, though gratified, he was not overwhelmed by the tribute. The same thought had often occurred to him independently.

'If you will excuse me,' he said, 'I have one or two things to attend to . . .'

'Certainly, Mr Baxter.'

The Efficient One withdrew through the door in the bookshelf. He realised that his employer was in fractious mood, but knew that he was leaving him in capable hands.

Lord Emsworth turned from the window, out of which he had been gazing with a plaintive detachment.

'Look here, Connie,' he grumbled feebly. 'You know I hate literary fellows. It's bad enough having them in the house, but when it comes to going to London to fetch 'em . . .'

He shuffled morosely. It was a perpetual grievance of his, this practice of his sister's of collecting literary celebrities and dumping them down in the home for indeterminate visits. You never knew when she was going to spring another on you. Already since the beginning of the year he had suffered from a round dozen of the species at brief intervals; and at this very moment his life was being poisoned by the fact that Blandings was sheltering a certain Miss Aileen Peavey, the mere thought of whom was enough to turn the sunshine off as with a tap.

'Can't stand literary fellows,' proceeded his lordship. 'Never could. And, by Jove, literary females are worse. Miss Peavey...' Here words temporarily failed the owner of Blandings. 'Miss Peavey....' he resumed after an eloquent pause. 'Who *is* Miss Peavey?'

'My dear Clarence,' replied Lady Constance tolerantly, for the fine morning had made her mild and amiable, 'if you do not know that Aileen is one of the leading poetesses of the younger school, you must be very ignorant.'

'I don't mean that. I know she writes poetry. I mean who *is* she? You suddenly produced her here like a rabbit out of a hat,' said his lordship, in a tone of strong resentment. 'Where did you find her?'

'I first made Aileen's acquaintance on an Atlantic liner when Joe and I were coming back from our trip round the world. She was very kind to me when I was feeling the motion of the vessel.... If you mean what is her family, I think Aileen told me once that she was connected with the Rutlandshire Peaveys.'

'Never heard of them!' snapped Lord Emsworth. 'And, if they're anything like Miss Peavey, God help Rutlandshire!'

Tranquil as Lady Constance's mood was this morning, an ominous stoniness came into her grey eyes at these words, and there is little doubt that in another instant she would have discharged at her mutinous brother one of those shattering come-backs for which she had been celebrated in the family from nursery days onward; but at this juncture the Efficient Baxter appeared again through the bookshelf.

'Excuse me,' said Baxter, securing attention with a flash of his spectacles. 'I forgot to mention, Lord Emsworth, that, to suit everybody's convenience, I have arranged that Miss Halliday shall call to see you at your club to-morrow after lunch.'

'Good Lord, Baxter!' The harassed peer started as if he had been bitten in the leg. 'Who's Miss Halliday? Not another literary female?'

'Miss Halliday is the young lady who is coming to Blandings to catalogue the library.'

'Catalogue the library? What does it want cataloguing for?'

'It has not been done since the year 1885.'

'Well, and look how splendidly we've got along without it,' said Lord Emsworth acutely.

'Don't be so ridiculous, Clarence,' said Lady Constance, annoyed. 'The catalogue of a great library like this must be brought up to date.' She moved to the door. 'I do wish you would try to wake up and take an interest in things. If it wasn't for Mr Baxter, I don't know what would happen.'

And with a beaming glance of approval at her ally she left the room. Baxter, coldly austere, returned to the subject under discussion.

'I have written to Miss Halliday suggesting two-thirty as a suitable hour for the interview.'

'But look here . . .'

'You will wish to see her before definitely confirming the engagement.'

'Yes, but look here, I wish you wouldn't go tying me up with all these appointments.'

'I thought that as you were going to London to meet Mr McTodd . . .'

'But I'm not going to London to meet Mr McTodd,' cried Lord Emsworth with weak fury. 'It's out of the question. I can't possibly leave Blandings. The weather may break at any moment. I don't want to miss a day of it.'

'The arrangements are all made.'

'Send the fellow a wire . . . "unavoidably detained".'

'I could not take the responsibility for such a course myself,' said Baxter coldly. 'But possibly if you were to make the suggestion to Lady Constance . . .'

'Oh, dash it!' said Lord Emsworth unhappily, at once realising the impossibility of the scheme. 'Oh, well, if I've got to go, I've got to go,' he said after a gloomy pause. 'But to leave my garden and stew in London at this time of the year . . .'

There seemed nothing further to say on the subject. He took off his glasses, polished them, put them on again, and shuffled to the door. After all, he reflected, even though the car was coming for him at two, at least he had the morning, and he proposed to make the most of it. But his first careless rapture at the prospect of pottering among his flowers was dimmed, and would not be recaptured. He did not entertain any project so mad as the idea of defying his sister Constance, but he felt extremely bitter about the whole affair. Confound Constance! . . . Dash Baxter! . . . Miss Peavey . . .

The door closed behind Lord Emsworth.

§ 2

Lady Constance meanwhile, proceeding downstairs, had reached the big hall, when the door of the smoking-room opened and a head popped out. A round, grizzled head with a healthy pink face attached to it.

'Connie!' said the head.

Lady Constance halted.

'Yes, Joe?'

'Come in here a minute,' said the head. 'Want to speak to you.'

Lady Constance went into the smoking-room. It was large and cosily book-lined, and its window looked out on to an Italian garden. A wide fire-place occupied nearly the whole of one side of it, and in front of this, his legs spread to an invisible blaze, Mr Joseph Keeble had already taken his stand. His manner was bluff, but an acute observer might have detected embarrassment in it.

'What is it, Joe?' asked Lady Constance, and smiled pleasantly at her husband. When, two years previously, she had married this elderly widower, of whom the world knew nothing beyond the fact that he had amassed a large fortune in South African diamond mines, there had not been wanting cynics to set the match down as one of convenience, a purely business arrangement by which Mr Keeble exchanged his money for Lady Constance's social position. Such was not the case. It had been a genuine marriage of affection on both sides. Mr Keeble worshipped his wife, and she was devoted to him, though never foolishly indulgent. They were a happy and united couple.

Mr Keeble cleared his throat. He seemed to find some difficulty in speaking. And when he spoke it was not on the subject which he had intended to open, but on one which had already been worn out in previous conversations.

'Connie, I've been thinking about that necklace again.'

Lady Constance laughed.

'Oh, don't be silly, Joe. You haven't called me into this stuffy room on a lovely morning like this to talk about that for the hundredth time.'

'Well, you know, there's no sense in taking risks.'

'Don't be absurd. What risks can there be?'

'There was a burglary over at Winstone Court, not ten miles from here, only a day or two ago.'

'Don't be so fussy, Joe.'

'That necklace cost nearly twenty thousand pounds,' said Mr Keeble, in the reverent voice in which men of business traditions speak of large sums.

'I know.'

'It ought to be in the bank.'

'Once and for all, Joe,' said Lady Constance, losing her amiability and becoming suddenly imperious and Cleopatrine, 'I will *not* keep that necklace in a bank. What on earth is the use of having a beautiful necklace if it is lying in the strong-room of a bank all the time? There is the County Ball coming on, and the Bachelors' Ball after that, and . . . well, I *need* it. I will send the thing to the bank when we pass through London on our way to Scotland, but not till then. And I do wish you would stop worrying me about it.'

There was a silence. Mr Keeble was regretting now that his unfortunate poltroonery had stopped him from tackling in a straightforward and manly fashion the really important matter which was weighing on his mind: for he perceived that his remarks about the necklace, eminently sensible though they were, had marred the genial mood in which his wife had begun this interview. It was going to be more difficult now than ever to approach the main issue. Still, ruffled though she might be, the thing had to be done: for it involved a matter of finance, and in matters of finance Mr Keeble was no longer a free agent. He and Lady Constance had a mutual banking account, and it was she who supervised the spending of it. This was an arrangement, subsequently regretted by Mr Keeble, which had been come to in the early days of the honeymoon, when men are apt to do foolish things.

Mr Keeble coughed. Not the sharp, efficient cough which we have heard Rupert Baxter uttering in the library, but a feeble, strangled thing like the bleat of a diffident sheep.

'Connie,' he said. 'Er – Connie.'

And at the words a sort of cold film seemed to come over Lady Constance's eyes: for some sixth sense told her what subject it was that was now about to be introduced.

'Connie, I – er – had a letter from Phyllis this morning.'

Lady Constance said nothing. Her eyes gleamed for an instant, then became frozen again. Her intuition had not deceived her.

Into the married life of this happy couple only one shadow had intruded itself up to the present. But unfortunately it was a shadow of considerable proportions, a kind of super-shadow; and its effect had been chilling. It was Phyllis, Mr Keeble's step-daughter, who had caused it – by the simple process of jilting the rich and suitable young man whom Lady Constance had attached to her (rather in the manner of a conjurer forcing a card upon his victim) and running off and marrying a far from rich and quite unsuitable person of whom all that seemed to be known was that his name was Jackson. Mr Keeble, whose simple creed was that Phyllis could do no wrong, had been prepared to accept the situation philosophically; but his wife's wrath had been deep and enduring. So much so that the mere mentioning of the girl's name must be accounted to him for a brave deed, Lady Constance having specifically stated that she never wished to hear it again.

Keenly alive to this prejudice of hers, Mr Keeble stopped after making his announcement, and had to rattle his keys in his pocket in order to acquire the necessary courage to continue. He was not looking at his wife, but he knew just how forbidding her expression must be. This task of his was no easy, congenial task for a pleasant summer morning.

'She says in her letter,' proceeded Mr Keeble, his eyes on the carpet and his cheeks a deeper pink, 'that young Jackson has got the chance of buying a big farm . . . in Lincolnshire, I think she said . . . if he can raise three thousand pounds.'

He paused, and stole a glance at his wife. It was as he had feared. She had congealed. Like some spell, the name Jackson had apparently turned her to marble. It was like the Pygmalion and Galatea business working the wrong way round. She was presumably breathing, but there was no sign of it.

'So I was just thinking,' said Mr Keeble, producing another *obbligato* on the keys, 'it just crossed my mind . . . it isn't as if the thing were a speculation . . . the place is apparently coining money . . . present owner only selling because he wants to go abroad . . . it occurred to me . . . and they would pay good interest on the loan . . .'

'What loan?' inquired the statue icily, coming to life.

'Well, what I was thinking . . . just a suggestion, you know . . . what struck me was that if you were willing we might . . . good investment, you know, and nowadays it's deuced hard to find good investments … I was thinking that we might lend them the money.'

He stopped. But he had got the thing out and felt happier. He rattled his keys again, and rubbed the back of his head against the mantelpiece. The friction seemed to give him confidence.

'We had better settle this thing once and for all, Joe,' said Lady Constance. 'As you know, when we were married, I was ready to do everything for Phyllis. I was prepared to be a mother to her. I gave her every chance, took her everywhere. And what happened?'

'Yes, I know. But …'

'She became engaged to a man with plenty of money…'

'Shocking young ass,' interjected Mr Keeble, perking up for a moment at the recollection of the late lamented, whom he had never liked. 'And a rip, what's more. I've heard stories.'

'Nonsense! If you are going to believe all the gossip you hear about people, nobody would be safe. He was a delightful young man and he would have made Phyllis perfectly happy. Instead of marrying him, she chose to go off with this – Jackson.' Lady Constance's voice quivered. Greater scorn could hardly have been packed into two syllables. 'After what has happened, I certainly intend to have nothing more to do with her. I shall not lend them a penny, so please do not let us continue this discussion any longer. I hope I am not an unjust woman, but I must say that I consider, after the way Phyllis behaved …'

The sudden opening of the door caused her to break off. Lord Emsworth, mould-stained and wearing a deplorable old jacket, pottered into the room. He peered benevolently at his sister and his brother-in-law, but seemed unaware that he was interrupting a conversation.

'"Gardening as a Fine Art",' he murmured. 'Connie, have you seen a book called "Gardening as a Fine Art"? I was reading it in here last night. "Gardening as a Fine Art". That is the title. Now, where can it have got to?' His dreamy eye flitted to and fro. 'I want to show it to McAllister. There is a passage in it that directly refutes his anarchistic views on . . .'

'It is probably on one of the shelves,' said Lady Constance shortly.

'On one of the shelves?' said Lord Emsworth, obviously impressed by this bright suggestion. 'Why, of course, to be sure.'

Mr Keeble was rattling his keys moodily. A mutinous expression was on his pink face. These moments of rebellion did not come to him very often, for he loved his wife with a dog-like affection and had grown accustomed to being ruled by her, but now resentment filled him. She was unreasonable, he considered. She ought to have realised how strongly he felt about poor little Phyllis. It was too infernally cold-blooded to abandon the poor child like an old shoe simply because . . .

'Are you going?' he asked, observing his wife moving to the door.

'Yes. I am going into the garden,' said Lady Constance. 'Why? Was there anything else you wanted to talk to me about?'

'No,' said Mr Keeble despondently. 'Oh, no.'

Lady Constance left the room, and a deep masculine silence fell. Mr Keeble rubbed the back of his head meditatively against the mantelpiece, and Lord Emsworth scratched among the book-shelves.

'Clarence!' said Mr Keeble suddenly. An idea – one might almost say an inspiration – had come to him.

'Eh?' responded his lordship absently. He had found his book and was turning its pages, absorbed.

'Clarence, can you . . .'

'Angus McAllister,' observed Lord Emsworth bitterly, 'is an obstinate, stiff-necked son of Belial. The writer of this book distinctly states in so many words . . .'

'Clarence, can you lend me three thousand pounds on good security and keep it dark from Connie?'

Lord Emsworth blinked.

'Keep something dark from Connie?' He raised his eyes from his book in order to peer at this visionary with a gentle pity. 'My dear fellow, it can't be done.'

'She would never know. I will tell you just why I want this money . . .'

'Money?' Lord Emsworth's eye had become vacant again. He was reading once more. 'Money? Money, my dear fellow? Money? Money? What money? If I have said once,' declared Lord Emsworth, 'that Angus McAllister is all wrong on the subject of hollyhocks, I've said it a hundred times.'

'Let me explain. This three thousand pounds . . .'

'My dear fellow, no. No, no. It was like you,' said his lordship with a vague heartiness, 'it was like you – good and generous – to make this offer, but I have ample, thank you, ample. I don't *need* three thousand pounds.'

'You don't understand. I . . .'

'No, no. No, no. But I am very much obliged, all the same. It was kind of you, my dear fellow, to give me the opportunity. Very kind. Very, very, very kind,' proceeded his lordship, trailing to the door and reading as he went. 'Oh, very, very, very . . .'

The door closed behind him.

'Oh, *damn!*' said Mr Keeble.

He sank into a chair in a state of profound dejection. He thought of the letter he would have to write to Phyllis. Poor little

Phyllis ... he would have to tell her that what she asked could not be managed. And why, thought Mr Keeble sourly, as he rose from his seat and went to the writing-table, could it not be managed? Simply because he was a weak-kneed, spineless creature who was afraid of a pair of grey eyes that had a tendency to freeze.

'*My dear Phyllis,*' he wrote.

Here he stopped. How on earth was he to put it? What a letter to have to write! Mr Keeble placed his head between his hands and groaned aloud.

'Hallo, Uncle Joe!'

The letter-writer, turning sharply, was aware – without pleasure – of his nephew Frederick, standing beside his chair. He eyed him resentfully, for he was not only exasperated but startled. He had not heard the door open. It was as if the smooth-haired youth had popped up out of a trap.

'Came in through the window,' explained the Hon. Freddie. 'I say, Uncle Joe.'

'Well, what is it?'

'I say, Uncle Joe,' said Freddie, 'can you lend me a thousand quid?'

Mr Keeble uttered a yelp like a pinched Pomeranian.

§ 3

As Mr Keeble, red-eyed and overwrought, rose slowly from his chair and began to swell in ominous silence, his nephew raised his hand appealingly. It began to occur to the Hon. Freddie that he had perhaps not led up to his request with the maximum of smooth tact.

'Half a jiffy!' he entreated. 'I say, don't go in off the deep end for just a second. I can explain.'

Mr Keeble's feelings expressed themselves in a loud snort. 'Explain!'

'Well, I can. Whole trouble was, I started at the wrong end. Shouldn't have sprung it on you like that. The fact is, Uncle Joe, I've got a scheme. I give you my word that, if you'll only put off having apoplexy for about three minutes,' said Freddie, scanning his fermenting relative with some anxiety, 'I can shove you on to a good thing. Honestly I can. And all I say is, if this scheme I'm talking about is worth a thousand quid to you, will you slip it across? I'm game to spill it and leave it to your honesty to cash up if the thing looks good to you.'

'A thousand pounds!'

'Nice round sum,' urged Freddie ingratiatingly.

'Why,' demanded Mr Keeble, now somewhat recovered, 'do you want a thousand pounds?'

'Well, who doesn't, if it comes to that?' said Freddie. 'But I don't mind telling you my special reason for wanting it at just this moment, if you'll swear to keep it under your hat as far as the guv'nor is concerned.'

'If you mean that you wish me not to repeat to your father anything you may tell me in confidence, naturally I should not dream of doing such a thing.'

Freddie looked puzzled. His was no lightning brain.

'Can't quite work that out,' he confessed. 'Do you mean you will tell him or you won't?'

'I will not tell him.'

'Good old Uncle Joe!' said Freddie, relieved. 'A topper! I've always said so. Well, look here, you know all the trouble there's been about my dropping a bit on the races lately?'

'I do.'

'Between ourselves, I dropped about five hundred of the best. And I just want to ask you one simple question. *Why* did I drop it?'

'Because you were an infernal young ass.'

'Well, yes,' agreed Freddie, having considered the point, 'you might put it that way, of course. But why was I an ass?'

'Good God!' exclaimed the exasperated Mr Keeble. 'Am I a psycho-analyst?'

'I mean to say, if you come right down to it, I lost all that stuff simply because I was on the wrong side of the fence. It's a mug's game betting on horses. The only way to make money is to be a bookie, and that's what I'm going to do if you'll part with that thousand. Pal of mine, who was up at Oxford with me, is in a bookie's office, and they're game to take me in too if I can put up a thousand quid. Only I must let them know quick, because the offer's not going to be open for ever. You've no notion what a deuce of a lot of competition there is for that sort of job.'

Mr Keeble, who had been endeavouring with some energy to get a word in during this harangue, now contrived to speak.

'And do you seriously suppose that I would . . . But what's the use of wasting time talking? I have no means of laying my hands on the sum you mention. If I had,' said Mr Keeble wistfully. 'If I had . . .' And his eye strayed to the letter on the desk, the letter which had got as far as 'My dear Phyllis' and stuck there.

Freddie gazed upon him with cordial sympathy.

'Oh, I know how you're situated, Uncle Joe, and I'm dashed sorry for you. I mean, Aunt Constance and all that.'

'What!' Irksome as Mr Keeble sometimes found the peculiar condition of his financial arrangements, he had always had the consolation of supposing that they were a secret between his wife and himself. 'What do you mean?'

'Well, I know that Aunt Constance keeps an eye on the doubloons and checks the outgoings pretty narrowly. And I think it's a dashed shame that she won't unbuckle to help poor old Phyllis. A girl,' said Freddie, 'I always liked. Bally shame! Why the dickens shouldn't she marry that fellow Jackson? I mean, love's love,' said Freddie, who felt strongly on this point.

Mr Keeble was making curious gulping noises.

'Perhaps I ought to explain,' said Freddie, 'that I was having a quiet after-breakfast smoke outside the window there and heard the whole thing. I mean, you and Aunt Constance going to the mat about poor old Phyllis and you trying to bite the guv'nor's ear and so forth.'

Mr Keeble bubbled for a while.

'You – you listened!' he managed to ejaculate at length.

'And dashed lucky for you,' said Freddie with a cordiality unimpaired by the frankly unfriendly stare under which a nicer-minded youth would have withered; 'dashed lucky for you that I did. Because I've got a scheme.'

Mr Keeble's estimate of his young relative's sagacity was not a high one, and it is doubtful whether, had the latter caught him in a less despondent mood, he would have wasted time in inquiring into the details of this scheme, the mention of which had been playing in and out of Freddie's conversation like a will-o'-the-wisp. But such was his reduced state at the moment that a reluctant gleam of hope crept into his troubled eye.

'A scheme? Do you mean a scheme to help me out of – out of my difficulty?'

'Absolutely! You want the best seats, we have 'em. I mean,' Freddie went on in interpretation of these peculiar words, 'you want three thousand quid, and I can show you how to get it.'

'Then kindly do so,' said Mr Keeble; and, having opened the door, peered cautiously out, and closed it again, he crossed the room and shut the window.

'Makes it a bit fuggy, but perhaps you're right,' said Freddie, eyeing these manœuvres. 'Well, it's like this, Uncle Joe. You remember what you were saying to Aunt Constance about some bird being apt to sneak up and pinch her necklace?'

'I do.'

'Well, why not?'

'What do you mean?'

'I mean, why don't you?'

Mr Keeble regarded his nephew with unconcealed astonishment. He had been prepared for imbecility, but this exceeded his expectations.

'Steal my wife's necklace!'

'That's it. Frightfully quick you are, getting on to an idea. Pinch Aunt Connie's necklace. For, mark you,' continued Freddie, so far forgetting the respect due from a nephew as to tap his uncle sharply on the chest, 'if a husband pinches anything from a wife, it isn't stealing. That's law. I found that out from a movie I saw in town.'

The Hon. Freddie was a great student of the movies. He could tell a super-film from a super-super-film at a glance, and what he did not know about erring wives and licentious clubmen could have been written in a sub-title.

'Are you insane?' growled Mr Keeble.

'It wouldn't be hard for you to get hold of it. And once you'd got it everybody would be happy. I mean, all you'd have to do would be to draw a cheque to pay for another one for Aunt

Connie – which would make her perfectly chirpy, as well as putting you one up, if you follow me. Then you would have the other necklace, the pinched one, to play about with. See what I mean? You could sell it privily and by stealth, ship Phyllis her three thousand, push across my thousand, and what was left over would be a nice little private account for you to tuck away somewhere where Aunt Connie wouldn't know anything about it. And a dashed useful thing,' said Freddie, 'to have up your sleeve in case of emergencies.'

'Are you . . . ?'

Mr Keeble was on the point of repeating his previous remark when suddenly there came the realisation that, despite all preconceived opinions, the young man was anything but insane. The scheme, at which he had been prepared to scoff, was so brilliant, yet simple, that it seemed almost incredible that its sponsor could have worked it out for himself.

'Not my own,' said Freddie modestly, as if in answer to the thought. 'Saw much the same thing in a movie once. Only there the fellow, if I remember, wanted to do down an insurance company, and it wasn't a necklace that he pinched but bonds. Still, the principle's the same. Well, how do we go, Uncle Joe? How about it? Is that worth a thousand quid or not?'

Even though he had seen in person to the closing of the door and the window, Mr Keeble could not refrain from a conspirator-like glance about him. They had been speaking with lowered voices, but now words came from him in an almost inaudible whisper.

'Could it really be done? Is it feasible?'

'Feasible? Why, dash it, what the dickens is there to stop you? You could do it in a second. And the beauty of the whole thing is that, if you were copped, nobody could say a word, because husband pinching from wife isn't stealing. Law.'

The statement that in the circumstances indicated nobody could say a word seemed to Mr Keeble so at variance with the facts that he was compelled to challenge it.

'Your aunt would have a good deal to say,' he observed ruefully.

'Eh? Oh, yes, I see what you mean. Well, you would have to risk that. After all, the chances would be dead against her finding out.'

'But she might.'

'Oh, well, if you put it like that, I suppose she might.'

'Freddie, my boy,' said Mr Keeble weakly, 'I daren't do it!'

The vision of his thousand pounds slipping from his grasp so wrought upon Freddie that he expressed himself in a manner far from fitting in one of his years towards an older man.

'Oh, I say, don't be such a rabbit!'

Mr Keeble shook his head.

'No,' he repeated, 'I daren't.'

It might have seemed that the negotiations had reached a deadlock, but Freddie, with a thousand pounds in sight, was in far too stimulated a condition to permit so tame an ending to such a promising plot. As he stood there, chafing at his uncle's pusillanimity, an idea was vouchsafed to him.

'By Jove! I'll tell you what!' he cried.

'Not so loud!' moaned the apprehensive Mr Keeble. 'Not so loud!'

'I'll tell you what,' repeated Freddie in a hoarse whisper. 'How would it be if *I* did the pinching?'

'What!'

'How would it . . .'

35

'Would you?' Hope, which had vanished from Mr Keeble's face, came flooding back. 'My boy, would you really?'

'For a thousand quid you bet I would.'

Mr Keeble clutched at his young relative's hand and gripped it feverishly.

'Freddie,' he said, 'the moment you place that necklace in my hands, I will give you not a thousand but two thousand pounds.'

'Uncle Joe,' said Freddie with equal intensity, 'it's a bet!'

Mr Keeble mopped at his forehead.

'You think you can manage it?'

'Manage it?' Freddie laughed a light laugh. 'Just watch me!'

Mr Keeble grasped his hand again with the utmost warmth.

'I must go out and get some air,' he said. 'I'm all upset. May I really leave this matter to you, Freddie?'

'Rather!'

'Good! Then to-night I will write to Phyllis and say that I may be able to do what she wishes.'

'Don't say "may",' cried Freddie buoyantly. 'The word is "will". Bally will! What ho!'

§ 4

Exhilaration is a heady drug; but, like other drugs, it has the disadvantage that its stimulating effects seldom last for very long. For perhaps ten minutes after his uncle had left him, Freddie Threepwood lay back in his chair in a sort of ecstasy. He felt strong, vigorous, alert. Then by degrees, like a chilling wind, doubt began to creep upon him – faintly at first, then more and more insistently, till by the end of a quarter of an hour he was in a state of pronounced self-mistrust. Or, to put it with less elegance, he was suffering from an exceedingly severe attack of cold feet.

The more he contemplated the venture which he had undertaken, the less alluring did it appear to him. His was not a keen imagination, but even he could shape with a gruesome clearness a vision of the frightful bust-up that would ensue should he be detected stealing his Aunt Constance's diamond necklace. Common decency would in such an event seal his lips as regarded his Uncle Joseph's share in the matter. And even if – as might conceivably happen – common decency failed at the crisis, reason told him that his Uncle Joseph would infallibly disclaim any knowledge of or connection with the rash act. And then where would he be? In the soup, undoubtedly. For Freddie could not conceal it from himself that there was nothing in his previous record to make it seem inconceivable to his nearest and dearest that he should steal the jewellery of a female relative for purely personal ends. The verdict in the event of detection would be one of uncompromising condemnation.

And yet he hated the idea of meekly allowing that two thousand pounds to escape from his clutch...

A young man's cross-roads.

* * * * *

The agony of spirit into which these meditations cast him had brought him up with a bound from the comfortable depths of his arm-chair and had set him prowling restlessly about the room. His wanderings led him at this point to collide somewhat painfully with the long table on which Beach the butler, a tidy soul, was in the habit of arranging in a neat row the daily papers, weekly papers, and magazines which found their way into the castle. The shock had the effect of rousing him from his stupor, and in an absent way he clutched the nearest daily paper, which happened to be the *Morning Globe*, and returned to his chair in the hope of quieting his nerves with a perusal of the racing intelligence. For, though far removed now from any practical share in the doings of the racing world, he still took a faint melancholy interest in ascertaining what Captain Curb, the Head Lad, Little Brighteyes, and the rest of the newspaper experts fancied for the day's big event. He lit a cigarette and unfolded the journal.

The next moment, instead of passing directly, as was his usual practice, to the last page, which was devoted to sport, he was gazing with a strange dry feeling in his throat at a certain advertisement on page one.

It was a well-displayed advertisement, and one that had caught the eye of many other readers of the paper that morning. It was worded to attract attention, and it had achieved its object. But where others who read it had merely smiled and marvelled idly how anybody could spend good money putting nonsense like this in the paper, to Freddie its import was wholly serious. It read to him like the Real Thing. His motion-picture-trained mind accepted this advertisement at its face-value.

It ran as follows:—

LEAVE IT TO PSMITH!
Psmith Will Help You
Psmith Is Ready For Anything
DO YOU WANT
Someone To Manage Your Affairs?
Someone To Handle Your Business?
Someone To Take The Dog For A Run?
Someone To Assassinate Your Aunt?

PSMITH WILL DO IT
CRIME NOT OBJECTED TO
Whatever Job You Have To Offer
(Provided It Has Nothing To Do With Fish)
LEAVE IT TO PSMITH!
Address Applications To 'R. Psmith, Box 365'
LEAVE IT TO PSMITH!

Freddie laid the paper down with a deep intake of breath. He picked it up again, and read the advertisement a second time. Yes, it sounded good.

More, it had something of the quality of a direct answer to prayer. Very vividly now Freddie realised that what he had been wishing for was a partner to share the perils of this enterprise which he had so rashly undertaken. In fact, not so much to share them as to take them off his shoulders altogether. And such a partner he was now in a position to command. Uncle Joe was going to give him two thousand if he brought the thing off. This advertisement fellow would probably be charmed to come in for a few hundred...

* * * * *

Two minutes later, Freddie was at the writing-desk, scribbling a letter. From time to time he glanced furtively over his shoulder at the door. But the house was still. No footsteps came to interrupt him at his task.

§ 5

Freddie went out into the garden. He had not wandered far when from somewhere close at hand there was borne to him on the breeze a remark in a high voice about Scottish obstinacy, which could only have proceeded from one source. He quickened his steps.

'Hallo, guv'nor.'

'Well, Frederick?'

Freddie shuffled.

'I say, guv'nor, do you think I might go up to town with you this afternoon?'

'What!'

'Fact is, I ought to see my dentist. Haven't been to him for a deuce of a time.'

'I cannot see the necessity for you to visit a London dentist. There is an excellent man in Shrewsbury, and you know I have the strongest objection to your going to London.'

'Well, you see, this fellow understands my snappers. Always been to him, I mean to say. Anybody who knows anything about these things will tell you greatest mistake go buzzing about to different dentists.'

Already Lord Emsworth's attention was wandering back to the waiting McAllister.

'Oh, very well, very well.'

'Thanks awfully, guv'nor.'

'But on one thing I insist, Frederick. I cannot have you loafing about London the whole day. You must catch the twelve-fifty train back.'

'Right ho. That'll be all right, guv'nor.'

'Now, listen to reason, McAllister,' said his lordship. 'That is all I ask you to do – listen to reason . . .'

§ 1

AT about the hour when Lord Emsworth's train, whirling him and his son Freddie to London, had reached the half-way point in its journey, a very tall, very thin, very solemn young man, gleaming in a speckless top hat and a morning-coat of irreproachable fit, mounted the steps of Number Eighteen, Wallingford Street, West Kensington, and rang the front-door bell. This done, he removed the hat; and having touched his forehead lightly with a silk handkerchief, for the afternoon sun was warm, gazed about him with a grave distaste.

'A scaly neighbourhood!' he murmured.

The young man's judgment was one at which few people with an eye for beauty would have cavilled. When the great revolution against London's ugliness really starts and yelling hordes of artists and architects, maddened beyond endurance, finally take the law into their own hands and rage through the city burning and destroying, Wallingford Street, West Kensington, will surely not escape the torch. Long since it must have been marked down for destruction. For, though it possesses certain merits of a low practical kind, being inexpensive in the matter of rents and handy for the buses and the Underground, it is a peculiarly beastly little street. Situated in the middle of one of those districts where London breaks out into a sort of eczema of red brick, it consists of two parallel rows of semi-detached villas, all exactly alike, each guarded by a ragged evergreen hedge, each with coloured glass of an extremely regrettable nature let into the panels of the front door; and sensitive young impressionists from the artists' colony up Holland Park way may sometimes be seen stumbling through it with hands over their eyes, muttering between clenched teeth 'How long? How long?'

A small maid-of-all-work appeared in answer to the bell, and stood transfixed as the visitor, producing a monocle, placed it in his right eye and inspected her through it.

'A warm afternoon,' he said cordially.

'Yes, sir.'

'But pleasant,' urged the young man. 'Tell me, is Mrs Jackson at home?'

'No, sir.'

'Not at home?'

'No, sir.'

The young man sighed.

'Ah well,' he said, 'we must always remember that these disappointments are sent to us for some good purpose. No doubt they make us more spiritual. Will you inform her that I called? The name is Psmith. P-smith.'

'Peasmith, sir?'

'No, no. P-s-m-i-t-h. I should explain to you that I started life without the initial letter, and my father always clung ruggedly to the plain Smith. But it seemed to me that there were so many Smiths in the world that a little variety might well be introduced. Smythe I look on as a cowardly evasion, nor do I approve of the too prevalent custom of tacking another name on in front by means of a hyphen. So I decided to adopt the Psmith. The p, I should add for your guidance, is silent, as in phthisis, psychic, and ptarmigan. You follow me?'

'Y-yes, sir.'

'You don't think,' he said anxiously, 'that I did wrong in pursuing this course?'

'N-no, sir.'

'Splendid!' said the young man, flicking a speck of dust from his coat-sleeve. 'Splendid! Splendid!'

And with a courteous bow he descended the steps and made his way down the street. The little maid, having followed him with bulging eyes till he was out of sight, closed the door and returned to her kitchen.

Psmith strolled meditatively on. The genial warmth of the afternoon soothed him. He hummed lightly – only stopping when, as he reached the end of the street, a young man of his own age, rounding the corner rapidly, almost ran into him.

'Sorry,' said the young man. 'Hallo, Smith.'

Psmith gazed upon him with benevolent affection.

'Comrade Jackson,' he said, 'this is well met. The one man of all others whom I would have wished to encounter. We will pop off somewhere, Comrade Jackson, should your engagements permit, and restore our tissues with a cup of tea. I had hoped to touch the Jackson family for some slight refreshment, but I was informed that your wife was out.'

Mike Jackson laughed.

'Phyllis isn't out. She . . .'

'Not out? Then,' said Psmith, pained, 'there has been dirty work done this day. For I was turned from the door. It would not be exaggerating to say that I was given the bird. Is this the boasted Jackson hospitality?'

'Phyllis is giving a tea to some of her old school pals,' explained Mike. 'She told the maid to say she wasn't at home to anybody else. I'm not allowed in myself.'

'Enough, Comrade Jackson!' said Psmith agreeably. 'Say no more. If you yourself have been booted out in spite of all the loving, honouring, and obeying your wife promised at the altar, who am I to complain? And possibly, one can console oneself by reflecting, we are well out of it. These gatherings of old girls'-school chums are not the sort of function your man of affairs wants to get lugged into. Capital company as we are, Comrade Jackson, we should doubtless have been extremely in the way. I suppose the conversation would have dealt exclusively with reminiscences of the dear old school, of tales of surreptitious cocoa-drinking in the dormitories and what the deportment mistress said when Angela was found chewing tobacco in the shrubbery. Yes, I fancy we have not missed a lot. . . . By the way, I don't think much of the new home. True, I only saw it from the outside, but . . . no, I don't think much of it.'

'Best we can afford.'

'And who,' said Psmith, 'am I to taunt my boyhood friend with his honest poverty? Especially as I myself am standing on the very brink of destitution.'

'You?'

'I in person. That low moaning sound you hear is the wolf bivouacked outside my door.'

'But I thought your uncle gave you rather a good salary.'

'So he did. But my uncle and I are about to part company. From now on he, so to speak, will take the high road and I'll take the low road. I dine with him to-night, and over the nuts and wine I shall hand him the bad news that I propose to resign my position in the firm. I have no doubt that he supposed he was doing me a good turn by starting me in his fish business, but even what little experience I have had of it has convinced me that it is not my proper sphere. The whisper flies round the clubs "Psmith has not found his niche!"

'I am not,' said Psmith, 'an unreasonable man. I realise that humanity must be supplied with fish. I am not averse from a bit of fish myself. But to be professionally connected with a firm that handles the material in the raw is not my idea of a large life-work. Remind me to tell you some time what it feels like to sling yourself out of bed at four a.m. and go down to toil in Billings-gate Market. No, there is money in fish – my uncle has made a pot of it – but what I feel is that there must be other walks in life for a bright young man. I chuck it to-night.'

'What are you going to do, then?'

'That, Comrade Jackson, is more or less on the knees of the gods. To-morrow morning I think I will stroll round to an employment agency and see how the market for bright young men stands. Do you know a good one?'

'Phyllis always goes to Miss Clarkson's in Shaftesbury Avenue. But . . .'

'Miss Clarkson's in Shaftesbury Avenue. I will make a note of it. . . . Meanwhile, I wonder if you saw the *Morning Globe* to-day?'

'No. Why?'

'I had an advertisement in it, in which I expressed myself as willing – indeed, eager – to tackle any undertaking that had nothing to do with fish. I am confidently expecting shoals of replies. I look forward to winnowing the heap and selecting the most desirable.'

'Pretty hard to get a job these days,' said Mike doubtfully.

'Not if you have something superlatively good to offer.'

'What have you got to offer?'

'My services,' said Psmith with faint reproach.

'What as?'

'As anything. I made no restrictions. Would you care to take a look at my manifesto? I have a copy in my pocket.'

Psmith produced from inside his immaculate waistcoat a folded clipping.

'I should welcome your opinion of it, Comrade Jackson. I have frequently said that for sturdy common sense you stand alone. Your judgment should be invaluable.'

The advertisement, which some hours earlier had so electrified the Hon. Freddie Threepwood in the smoking-room at Blandings Castle, seemed to affect Mike, whose mind was of the stolid and serious type, somewhat differently. He finished his perusal and stared speechlessly.

'Neat, don't you think?' said Psmith. 'Covers the ground adequately? I think so, I think so.'

'Do you mean to say you're going to put drivel like that in the paper?' asked Mike.

'I *have* put it in the paper. As I told you, it appeared this morning. By this time to-morrow I shall no doubt have finished sorting out the first batch of replies.'

Mike's emotion took him back to the phraseology of school days.

'You *are* an ass!'

Psmith restored the clipping to his waistcoat pocket.

'You wound me, Comrade Jackson,' he said. 'I had expected a broader outlook from you. In fact, I rather supposed that you would have rushed round instantly to the offices of the journal and shoved in a similar advertisement yourself. But nothing that you can say can damp my buoyant spirit. The cry goes round Kensington (and district) "Psmith is off!" In what direction the cry omits to state: but that information the future will supply. And now, Comrade Jackson, let us trickle into yonder tea-shop and drink success to the venture in a cup of the steaming. I had a particularly hard morning to-day among the whitebait, and I need refreshment.'

§ 2

After Psmith had withdrawn his spectacular person from it, there was an interval of perhaps twenty minutes before anything else occurred to brighten the drabness of Wallingford Street. The lethargy of afternoon held the thoroughfare in its grip. Occasionally a tradesman's cart would rattle round the corner, and from time to time cats appeared, stalking purposefully among the evergreens. But at ten minutes to five a girl ran up the steps of Number Eighteen and rang the bell.

She was a girl of medium height, very straight and slim; and her fair hair, her cheerful smile, and the boyish suppleness of her body all contributed to a general effect of valiant gaiety, a sort of golden sunniness – accentuated by the fact that, like all girls who looked to Paris for inspiration in their dress that season, she was wearing black.

The small maid appeared again.

'Is Mrs Jackson at home?' said the girl. 'I think she's expecting me. Miss Halliday.'

'Yes, miss.'

A door at the end of the narrow hall had opened.

'Is that you, Eve?'

'Hallo, Phyl, darling.'

Phyllis Jackson fluttered down the passage like a rose-leaf on the wind, and hurled herself into Eve's arms. She was small and fragile, with great brown eyes under a cloud of dark hair. She had a wistful look, and most people who knew her wanted to pet her. Eve had always petted her, from their first days at school together.

'Am I late or early?' asked Eve.

'You're the first, but we won't wait. Jane, will you bring tea into the drawing-room.'

'Yes'm.'

'And, remember, I don't want to see anyone for the rest of the afternoon. If anybody calls, tell them I'm not at home. Except Miss Clarkson and Mrs McTodd, of course.'

'Yes'm.'

'Who is Mrs McTodd?' inquired Eve. 'Is that Cynthia?'

'Yes. Didn't you know she had married Ralston McTodd, the Canadian poet? You knew she went out to Canada?'

'I knew that, yes. But I hadn't heard that she was married. Funny how out of touch one gets with girls who were one's best friends at school. Do you realise it's nearly two years since I saw you?'

'I know. Isn't it awful! I got your address from Elsa Wentworth two or three days ago, and then Clarkie told me that Cynthia was over here on a visit with her husband, so I thought how jolly it would be to have a regular reunion. We three were such friends in the old days.... You remember Clarkie, of course? Miss Clarkson, who used to be English mistress at Wayland House.'

'Yes, of course. Where did you run into her?'

'Oh, I see a lot of her. She runs a Domestic Employment Agency in Shaftesbury Avenue now, and I have to go there about once a fortnight to get a new maid. She supplied Jane.'

'Is Cynthia's husband coming with her this afternoon?'

'No. I wanted it to be simply us four. Do you know him? But of course you don't. This is his first visit to England.'

'I know his poetry. He's quite a celebrity. Cynthia's lucky.'

They had made their way into the drawing-room, a gruesome little apartment full of all those antimacassars, wax flowers, and china dogs inseparable from the cheaper type of London furnished house. Eve, though the exterior of Number Eighteen should have prepared her for all this, was unable to check a slight shudder as she caught the eye of the least prepossessing of the dogs, goggling at her from the mantelpiece.

'Don't look at them,' recommended Phyllis, following her gaze. 'I try not to. We've only just moved in here, so I haven't had time to make the place nice. Here's tea. All right, Jane, put it down there. Tea, Eve?'

Eve sat down. She was puzzled and curious. She threw her mind back to the days at school and remembered the Phyllis of that epoch as almost indecently opulent. A millionaire stepfather there had been then, she recollected. What had become of him now, that he should allow Phyllis to stay in surroundings like this? Eve scented a mystery, and in her customary straightforward way went to the heart of it.

'Tell me all about yourself,' she said, having achieved as much comfort as the peculiar structure of her chair would permit. 'And remember that I haven't seen you for two years, so don't leave anything out.'

'It's so difficult to know where to start.'

'Well, you signed your letter "Phyllis Jackson". Start with the mysterious Jackson. Where does he come in? The last I heard about you was an announcement in the *Morning Post* that you were engaged to – I've forgotten the name, but I'm certain it wasn't Jackson.'

'Rollo Mountford.'

'Was it? Well, what has become of Rollo? You seem to have mislaid him. Did you break off the engagement?'

'Well, it – sort of broke itself off. I mean, you see, I went and married Mike.'

'Eloped with him, do you mean?'

'Yes.'

'Good heavens!'

'I'm awfully ashamed about that, Eve. I suppose I treated Rollo awfully badly.'

'Never mind. A man with a name like that was made for suffering.'

'I never really cared for him. He had horrid swimmy eyes...'

'I understand. So you eloped with your Mike. Tell me about him. Who is he? What does he do?'

'Well, at present he's master at a school. But he doesn't like it. He wants to get back to the country again. When I met him, he was agent on a place in the country belonging to some people named Smith. Mike had been at school and Cambridge with the son. They were very rich then and had a big estate. It was the next place to the Edgelows. I had gone to stay with Mary Edgelow – I don't know if you remember her at school? I met Mike first at a dance, and then I met him out riding, and then – well, after that we used to meet every day. And we fell in love right from the start and we went and got married. Oh, Eve, I wish you could have seen our darling little house. It was all over ivy and roses, and we had horses and dogs and...'

Phyllis's narrative broke off with a gulp. Eve looked at her sympathetically. All her life she herself had been joyously impecunious, but it had never seemed to matter. She was strong and adventurous, and revelled in the perpetual excitement of trying to make both ends meet. But Phyllis was one of those sweet porcelain girls whom the roughnesses of life bruise instead of stimulating. She needed comfort and pleasant surroundings. Eve looked morosely at the china dog, which leered back at her with an insufferable good-fellowship.

'We had hardly got married,' resumed Phyllis, blinking, 'when poor Mr Smith died and the whole place was broken up. He must have been speculating or something, I suppose, because he hardly left any money, and the estate had to be sold. And the people who bought it – they were coal people from Wolverhampton – had a nephew for whom they wanted the agent job, so Mike had to go. So here we are.'

Eve put the question which she had been waiting to ask ever since she had entered the house.

'But what about your stepfather? Surely, when we were at school, you had a rich stepfather in the background. Has he lost his money, too?'

'No.'

'Well, why doesn't he help you, then?'

'He would, I know, if he was left to himself. But it's Aunt Constance.'

'What's Aunt Constance? And who *is* Aunt Constance?'

'Well, I call her that, but she's really my stepmother – sort of. I suppose she's really my step-stepmother. My stepfather married again two years ago. It was Aunt Constance who was so furious when I married Mike. She wanted me to marry Rollo. She has never forgiven me, and she won't let my stepfather do anything to help us.'

'But the man must be a worm!' said Eve indignantly. 'Why doesn't he insist? You always used to tell me how fond he was of you.'

'He isn't a worm, Eve. He's a dear. It's just that he has let her boss him. She's rather a terror, you know. She can be quite nice, and they're awfully fond of each other, but she is as hard as nails sometimes.' Phyllis broke off. The front door had opened, and there were footsteps in the hall. 'Here's Clarkie. I hope she has brought Cynthia with her. She was to pick her up on her way. Don't talk about what I've been telling you in front of her, Eve, there's an angel.'

'Why not?'

'She's so motherly about it. It's sweet of her, but . . .'

Eve understood.

'All right. Later on.'

The door opened to admit Miss Clarkson.

The adjective which Phyllis had applied to her late schoolmistress was obviously well chosen. Miss Clarkson exuded motherliness. She was large, wholesome, and soft, and she swooped on Eve like a hen on its chicken almost before the door had closed.

'Eve! How nice to see you after all this time! My dear, you're looking perfectly lovely! And *so* prosperous. What a beautiful hat!'

'I've been envying it ever since you came, Eve,' said Phyllis. 'Where did you get it?'

'Madeleine Sœurs, in Regent Street.'

Miss Clarkson, having acquired and stirred a cup of tea, started to improve the occasion. Eve had always been a favourite of hers at school. She beamed affectionately upon her.

'Now doesn't this show – what I always used to say to you in the dear old days, Eve – that one must never despair, however black the outlook may seem? I remember you at school, dear, as poor as a church mouse, and with no prospects, none whatever. And yet here you are – rich . . .'

Eve laughed. She got up and kissed Miss Clarkson. She regretted that she was compelled to strike a jarring note, but it had to be done.

'I'm awfully sorry, Clarkie dear,' she said, 'but I'm afraid I've misled you. I'm just as broke as I ever was. In fact, when Phyllis told me you were running an Employment Agency, I made a note to come and see you and ask if you had some attractive billet to dispose of. Governess to a thoroughly angelic child would do. Or isn't there some nice cosy author or something who wants his letters answered and his press-clippings pasted in an album?'

'Oh, my dear!' Miss Clarkson was deeply concerned. 'I did hope . . . That hat . . . !'

'The hat's the whole trouble. Of course I had no business even to think of it, but I saw it in the shop-window and coveted it for days, and finally fell. And then, you see, I had to live up to it – buy shoes and a dress to match. I tell you it was a perfect orgy, and I'm thoroughly ashamed of myself now. Too late, as usual.'

'Oh, dear! You always were such a wild, impetuous child, even at school. I remember how often I used to speak to you about it.'

'Well, when it was all over and I was sane again, I found I had only a few pounds left, not nearly enough to see me through till the relief expedition arrived. So I thought it over and decided to invest my little all.'

'I hope you chose something safe?'

'It ought to have been. The *Sporting Express* called it "To-day's Safety Bet". It was Bounding Willie for the two-thirty race at Sandown last Wednesday.'

'Oh, dear!'

'That's what I said when poor old Willie came in sixth. But it's no good worrying, is it? What it means is that I simply must find something to do that will carry me through till I get my next quarter's allowance. And that won't be till September.... But don't let's talk business here. I'll come round to your office, Clarkie, to-morrow.... Where's Cynthia? Didn't you bring her?'

'Yes, I thought you were going to pick Cynthia up on your way, Clarkie,' said Phyllis.

If Eve's information as to her financial affairs had caused Miss Clarkson to mourn, the mention of Cynthia plunged her into the very depths of woe. Her mouth quivered and a tear stole down her cheek. Eve and Phyllis exchanged bewildered glances.

'I say,' said Eve after a moment's pause and a silence broken only by a smothered sob from their late instructress, 'we aren't being very cheerful, are we, considering that this is supposed to be a joyous reunion? Is anything wrong with Cynthia?'

So poignant was Miss Clarkson's anguish that Phyllis, in a flutter of alarm, rose and left the room swiftly in search of the only remedy that suggested itself to her – her smelling-salts.

'Poor dear Cynthia!' moaned Miss Clarkson.

'Why, what's the matter with her?' asked Eve. She was not callous to Miss Clarkson's grief, but she could not help the tiniest of smiles. In a flash she had been transported to her school-days, when the other's habit of extracting the utmost tragedy out of the slimmest material had been a source of ever-fresh amusement to her. Not for an instant did she expect to hear any worse news of her old friend than that she was in bed with a cold or had twisted her ankle.

'She's married, you know,' said Miss Clarkson.

'Well, I see no harm in that, Clarkie. If a few more Safety Bets go wrong, I shall probably have to rush out and marry someone myself. Some nice, rich, indulgent man who will spoil me.'

'Oh, Eve, my dear,' pleaded Miss Clarkson, bleating with alarm, 'do please be careful whom you marry. I never hear of one of my girls marrying without feeling that the worst may happen and that, all unknowing, she may be stepping over a grim precipice!'

'You don't *tell* them that, do you? Because I should think it would rather cast a damper on the wedding festivities. Has Cynthia gone stepping over grim precipices? I was just saying to Phyllis that I envied her, marrying a celebrity like Ralston McTodd.'

Miss Clarkson gulped.

'The man must be a *fiend*!' she said brokenly. 'I have just left poor dear Cynthia in floods of tears at the Cadogan Hotel – she has a very nice quiet room on the fourth floor, though the carpet does not harmonise with the wall-paper. . . . She was broken-hearted, poor child. I did what I could to console her, but it was useless. She always was so highly strung. I must be getting back to her very soon. I only came on here because I did not want to disappoint you two dear girls . . .'

'Why?' said Eve with quiet intensity. She knew from experience that Miss Clarkson, unless firmly checked, would pirouette round and round the point for minutes without ever touching it.

'Why?' echoed Miss Clarkson, blinking as if the word was something solid that had struck her unexpectedly.

'Why was Cynthia in floods of tears?'

'But I'm telling you, my dear. That man has left her!'

'Left her!'

'They had a quarrel, and he walked straight out of the hotel. That was the day before yesterday, and he has not been back since. This afternoon the curtest note came from him to say that he never intended to return. He had secretly and in a most underhand way arranged for his luggage to be removed from the hotel to a District Messenger office, and from there he has taken it no one knows where. He has completely disappeared.'

Eve stared. She had not been prepared for news of this momentous order.

'But what did they quarrel about?'

'Cynthia, poor child, was too overwrought to tell me!'

Eve clenched her teeth.

'The beast!...Poor old Cynthia....Shall I come round with you?'

'No, my dear, better let me look after her alone. I will tell her to write and let you know when she can see you. I must be going, Phyllis dear,' she said, as her hostess re-entered, bearing a small bottle.

'But you've only just come!' said Phyllis, surprised.

'Poor old Cynthia's husband has left her,' explained Eve briefly. 'And Clarkie's going back to look after her. She's in a pretty bad way, it seems.'

'Oh, no!'

'Yes, indeed. And I really must be going at once,' said Miss Clarkson.

Eve waited in the drawing-room till the front door banged and Phyllis came back to her. Phyllis was more wistful than ever. She had been looking forward to this tea-party, and it had not been the happy occasion she had anticipated. The two girls sat in silence for a moment.

'What brutes some men are!' said Eve at length.

'Mike,' said Phyllis dreamily, 'is an angel.'

Eve welcomed the unspoken invitation to return to a more agreeable topic. She felt very deeply for the stricken Cynthia, but she hated aimless talk, and nothing could have been more aimless than for her and Phyllis to sit there exchanging lamentations concerning a tragedy of which neither knew more than the bare outlines. Phyllis had her tragedy, too, and it was one where Eve saw the possibility of doing something practical and helpful. She was a girl of action, and was glad to be able to attack a living issue.

'Yes, let's go on talking about you and Mike,' she said. 'At present I can't understand the position at all. When Clarkie came in, you were just telling me about your stepfather and why he wouldn't help you. And I thought you made out a very poor case for him. Tell me some more. I've forgotten his name, by the way.'

'Keeble.'

'Oh? Well, I think you ought to write and tell him how hard-up you are. He may be under the impression that you are still living in luxury and don't need any help. After all, he can't know unless you tell him. And I should ask him straight out to come to the rescue. It isn't as if it was your Mike's fault that you're broke. He married you on the strength of a very good position which looked like a permanency, and lost it through no fault of his own. I should write to him, Phyl. Pitch it strong.'

'I have. I wrote to-day. Mike's just been offered a wonderful opportunity. A sort of farm place in Lincolnshire. You know. Cows and things. Just what he would like and just what he would do awfully well. And we only need three thousand pounds to get it. . . . But I'm afraid nothing will come of it.'

'Because of Aunt Constance, you mean?'

'Yes.'

'You must *make* something come of it.' Eve's chin went up. She looked like a Goddess of Determination. 'If I were you, I'd haunt their doorstep till they had to give you the money to get rid of you. The idea of anybody doing that absurd driving-into-the-snow business in these days! Why *shouldn't* you marry the man you were in love with? If I were you, I'd go and chain myself to their railings and howl like a dog till they rushed out with cheque-books just to get some peace. Do they live in London?'

'They are down in Shropshire at present at a place called Blandings Castle.'

Eve started.

'Blandings Castle? Good gracious!'

'Aunt Constance is Lord Emsworth's sister.'

'But this is the most extraordinary thing. I'm going to Blandings myself in a few days.'

'No!'

'They've engaged me to catalogue the castle library.'

'But, Eve, were you only joking when you asked Clarkie to find you something to do? She took you quite seriously.'

'No, I wasn't joking. There's a drawback to my going to Blandings. I suppose you know the place pretty well?'

'I've often stayed there. It's beautiful.'

'Then you know Lord Emsworth's second son, Freddie Threepwood?'

'Of course.'

'Well, he's the drawback. He wants to marry me, and I certainly don't want to marry him. And what I've been wondering is whether a nice easy job like that, which would tide me over beautifully till September, is attractive enough to make up for the nuisance of having to be always squelching poor Freddie. I ought to have thought of it right at the beginning, of course, when he wrote and told me to apply for the position, but I was so delighted at the idea of regular work that it didn't occur to me. Then I began to wonder. He's such a persevering young man. He proposes early and often.'

'Where did you meet Freddie?'

'At a theatre party. About two months ago. He was living in London then, but he suddenly disappeared and I had a heart-broken letter from him, saying that he had been running up debts and things and his father had snatched him away to live at Blandings, which apparently is Freddie's idea of the Inferno. The world seems full of hard-hearted relatives.'

'Oh, Lord Emsworth isn't really hard-hearted. You will love him. He's so dreamy and absent-minded. He potters about the garden all the time. I don't think you'll like Aunt Constance much. But I suppose you won't see a great deal of her.'

'Whom *shall* I see much of – except Freddie, of course?'

'Mr Baxter, Lord Emsworth's secretary, I expect. I don't like him at all. He's a sort of spectacled caveman.'

'He doesn't sound attractive. But you say the place is nice?'

'It's gorgeous. I should go, if I were you, Eve.'

'Well, I had intended not to. But now you've told me about Mr Keeble and Aunt Constance, I've changed my mind. I'll have to look in at Clarkie's office to-morrow and tell her I'm fixed up and shan't need her help. I'm going to take your sad case in hand, darling. I shall go to Blandings, and I will dog your stepfather's footsteps.... Well, I must be going. Come and see me to the front door, or I'll be losing my way in the miles of stately corridors.... I suppose I mayn't smash that china dog before I go? Oh, well, I just thought I'd ask.'

Out in the hall the little maid-of-all-work bobbed up and intercepted them.

'I forgot to tell you, mum, a gentleman called. I told him you was out.'

'Quite right, Jane.'

'Said his name was Smith, 'm.'

Phyllis gave a cry of dismay.

'Oh, no! What a shame! I particularly wanted you to meet him, Eve. I wish I'd known.'

'Smith?' said Eve. 'The name seems familiar. Why were you so anxious for me to meet him?'

'He's Mike's best friend. Mike worships him. He's the son of the Mr Smith I was telling you about – the one Mike was at school and Cambridge with. He's a perfect darling, Eve, and you would love him. He's just your sort. I do wish we had known. And now you're going to Blandings for goodness knows how long, and you won't be able to see him.'

'What a pity,' said Eve, politely uninterested.

'I'm so sorry for him.'

'Why?'

'He's in the fish business.'

'Ugh!'

'Well, he hates it, poor dear. But he was left stranded like all the rest of us after the crash, and he was put into the business by an uncle who is a sort of fish magnate.'

'Well, why does he stay there, if he dislikes it so much?' said Eve with indignation. The helpless type of man was her pet aversion. 'I hate a man who's got no enterprise.'

'I don't think you could call him unenterprising. He never struck me like that. . . . You simply must meet him when you come back to London.'

'All right,' said Eve indifferently. 'Just as you like. I might put business in his way. I'm very fond of fish.'

WHAT strikes the visitor to London most forcibly, as he enters
the heart of that city's fashionable shopping district, is the
almost entire absence of ostentation in the shop-windows,
the studied avoidance of garish display. About the front of the
premises of Messrs Thorpe & Briscoe, for instance, who sell
coal in Dover Street, there is as a rule nothing whatever to
attract fascinated attention. You might give the place a glance
as you passed, but you would certainly not pause and stand
staring at it as at the Sistine Chapel or the Taj Mahal. Yet at
ten-thirty on the morning after Eve Halliday had taken tea
with her friend Phyllis Jackson in West Kensington, Psmith,
lounging gracefully in the smoking-room window of the Drones
Club, which is immediately opposite the Thorpe & Briscoe
establishment, had been gazing at it fixedly for a full five minutes. One would have said that the spectacle enthralled him. He
seemed unable to take his eyes off it.

There is always a reason for the most apparently inexplicable
happenings. It is the practice of Thorpe (or Briscoe) during the
months of summer to run out an awning over the shop. A quiet,
genteel awning, of course, nothing to offend the eye – but an
awning which offers a quite adequate protection against those
sudden showers which are such a delightfully piquant feature of

the English summer: one of which had just begun to sprinkle the West End of London with a good deal of heartiness and vigour. And under this awning, peering plaintively out at the rain, Eve Halliday, on her way to the Ada Clarkson Employment Bureau, had taken refuge. It was she who had so enchained Psmith's interest. It was his considered opinion that she improved the Thorpe & Briscoe frontage by about ninety-five per cent.

Pleased and gratified as Psmith was to have something nice to look at out of the smoking-room window, he was also somewhat puzzled. This girl seemed to him to radiate an atmosphere of wealth. Starting at farthest south and proceeding northward, she began in a gleam of patent-leather shoes. Fawn stockings, obviously expensive, led up to a black crêpe frock. And then, just as the eye was beginning to feel that there could be nothing more, it was stunned by a supreme hat of soft, dull satin with a black bird of Paradise feather falling down over the left shoulder. Even to the masculine eye, which is notoriously to seek in these matters, a whale of a hat. And yet this sumptuously upholstered young woman had been marooned by a shower of rain beneath the awning of Messrs Thorpe & Briscoe. Why, Psmith asked himself, was this? Even, he argued, if Charles the chauffeur had been given the day off or was driving her father the millionaire to the City to attend to his vast interests, she could surely afford a cab-fare? We, who are familiar with the state of Eve's finances, can understand her inability to take cabs, but Psmith was frankly perplexed.

Being, however, both ready-witted and chivalrous, he perceived that this was no time for idle speculation. His not to reason why; his obvious duty was to take steps to assist Beauty in distress. He left the window of the smoking-room, and, having made his way with a smooth dignity to the club's cloak-room, proceeded to submit a row of umbrellas to a close inspection. He was not easy to satisfy. Two which he went so far as to pull out of the rack he returned with a shake of the head. Quite good umbrellas, but not fit for this special service. At length, however, he found a beauty, and a gentle smile flickered across his solemn face. He put up his monocle and gazed searchingly at this umbrella. It seemed to answer every test. He was well pleased with it.

'Whose,' he inquired of the attendant, 'is this?'

'Belongs to the Honourable Mr Walderwick, sir.'

'Ah!' said Psmith tolerantly.

He tucked the umbrella under his arm and went out.

* * * * *

Meanwhile Eve Halliday, lightening up the sombre austerity of Messrs Thorpe & Briscoe's shop-front, continued to think hard thoughts of the English climate and to inspect the sky in the hope of detecting a spot of blue. She was engaged in this cheerless occupation when at her side a voice spoke.

'Excuse me!'

A hatless young man was standing beside her, holding an umbrella. He was a striking-looking young man, very tall, very thin, and very well dressed. In his right eye there was a monocle, and through this he looked down at her with a grave friendliness. He said nothing further, but, taking her fingers, clasped them round the handle of the umbrella, which he had obligingly opened, and then with a courteous bow proceeded to dash with long strides across the road, disappearing through the doorway of a gloomy building which, from the number of men who had gone in and out during her vigil, she had set down as a club of some sort.

A good many surprising things had happened to Eve since first she had come to live in London, but nothing quite so surprising as this. For several minutes she stood where she was without moving, staring round-eyed at the building opposite. The episode was, however, apparently ended. The young man did not reappear. He did not even show himself at the window. The club had swallowed him up. And eventually Eve, deciding that this was not the sort of day on which to refuse umbrellas even if they dropped inexplicably from heaven, stepped out from under the awning, laughing helplessly, and started to resume her interrupted journey to Miss Clarkson's.

* * * * *

The offices of the Ada Clarkson International Employment Bureau ('Promptitude – Courtesy – Intelligence') are at the top of Shaftesbury Avenue, a little way past the Palace Theatre. Eve, closing the umbrella, which had prevented even a spot of rain falling on her hat, climbed the short stair leading to the door and tapped on the window marked 'Enquiries'.

'Can I see Miss Clarkson?'

'What name, please?' responded Enquiries promptly and with intelligent courtesy.

'Miss Halliday.'

Brief interlude, involving business with speaking-tube.

'Will you go into the private office, please,' said Enquiries a moment later, in a voice which now added respect to the other advertised qualities, for she had had time to observe and digest the hat.

Eve passed in through the general waiting-room with its magazine-covered table, and tapped at the door beyond marked 'Private'.

'Eve, dear!' exclaimed Miss Clarkson the moment she had entered, 'I don't know how to tell you, but I have been looking through my books and I have nothing, simply nothing. There is not a single place that you could possibly take. What *is* to be done?'

'That's all right, Clarkie.'

'But . . .'

'I didn't come to talk business. I came to ask after Cynthia. How is she?'

Miss Clarkson sighed.

'Poor child, she is still in a dreadful state, and no wonder. No news at all from her husband. He has simply deserted her.'

'Poor darling! Can't I see her?'

'Not at present. I have persuaded her to go down to Brighton for a day or two. I think the sea air will pick her up. So much better than mooning about in a London hotel. She is leaving on the eleven o'clock train. I gave her your love, and she was most grateful that you should have remembered your old friendship and be sorry for her in her affliction.'

'Well, I can write to her. Where is she staying?'

'I don't know her Brighton address, but no doubt the Cadogan Hotel would forward letters. I think she would be glad to hear from you, dear.'

Eve looked sadly at the framed testimonials which decorated the wall. She was not often melancholy, but it was such a beast of a day and all her friends seemed to be having such a bad time.

'Oh, Clarkie,' she said, 'what a lot of trouble there is in the world!'

'Yes, yes!' sighed Miss Clarkson, a specialist on this subject.

'All the horses you back finish sixth and all the girls you like best come croppers. Poor little Phyllis! weren't you sorry for her?'

'But her husband, surely, is most devoted?'

'Yes, but she's frightfully hard up, and you remember how opulent she used to be at school. Of course, it must sound funny hearing me pitying people for having no money. But somehow other people's hard-upness always seems so much worse than mine. Especially poor old Phyl's, because she really isn't fit to stand it. I've been used to being absolutely broke all my life. Poor dear father always seemed to be writing an article against time, with creditors scratching earnestly at the door.' Eve laughed, but her eyes were misty. 'He was a brick, wasn't he? I mean, sending me to a first-class school like Wayland House when he often hadn't enough money to buy tobacco, poor angel. I expect he wasn't always up to time with fees, was he?'

'Well, my dear, of course I was only an assistant mistress at Wayland House and had nothing to do with the financial side, but I did hear sometimes...'

'Poor darling father! Do you know, one of my earliest recollections – I couldn't have been more than ten – is of a ring at the front-door bell and father diving like a seal under the sofa and poking his head out and imploring me in a hoarse voice to hold the fort. I went to the door and found an indignant man with a blue paper. I prattled so prettily and innocently that he not only went away quite contentedly but actually patted me on the head and gave me a penny. And when the door had shut father crawled out from under the sofa and gave me twopence, making threepence in all – a good morning's work. I bought father a diamond ring with it at a shop down the street, I remember. At least I thought it was a diamond. They may have swindled me, for I was very young.'

'You have had a hard life, dear.'

'Yes, but hasn't it been a lark! I've loved every minute of it. Besides, you can't call me really one of the submerged tenth. Uncle Thomas left me a hundred and fifty pounds a year, and mercifully I'm not allowed to touch the capital. If only there were no hats or safety bets in the world, I should be smugly opulent.... But I mustn't keep you any longer, Clarkie dear. I expect the waiting-room is full of dukes who want cooks and cooks who want dukes, all fidgeting and wondering how much longer you're going to keep them. Good-bye, darling.'

And, having kissed Miss Clarkson fondly and straightened her hat, which the other's motherly embrace had disarranged, Eve left the room.

MEANWHILE, at the Drones Club, a rather painful scene had been taking place. Psmith, regaining the shelter of the building, had made his way to the wash-room, where, having studied his features with interest for a moment in the mirror, he smoothed his hair, which the rain had somewhat disordered, and brushed his clothes with extreme care. He then went to the cloak-room for his hat. The attendant regarded him as he entered with the air of one whose mind is not wholly at rest.

'Mr Walderwick was in here a moment ago, sir,' said the attendant.

'Yes?' said Psmith, mildly interested. 'An energetic, bustling soul, Comrade Walderwick. Always somewhere. Now here, now there.'

'Asking about his umbrella, he was,' pursued the attendant with a touch of coldness.

'Indeed? Asking about his umbrella, eh?'

'Made a great fuss about it, sir, he did.'

'And rightly,' said Psmith with approval. 'The good man loves his umbrella.'

'Of course I had to tell him that you had took it, sir.'

'I would not have it otherwise,' assented Psmith heartily. 'I like this spirit of candour. There must be no reservations, no subterfuges between you and Comrade Walderwick. Let all be open and above-board.'

'He seemed very put out, sir. He went off to find you.'

'I am always glad of a chat with Comrade Walderwick,' said Psmith. 'Always.'

He left the cloak-room and made for the hall, where he desired the porter to procure him a cab. This having drawn up in front of the club, he descended the steps and was about to enter it, when there was a hoarse cry in his rear, and through the front door there came bounding a pinkly indignant youth, who called loudly:

'Here! Hi! Smith! Dash it!'

Psmith climbed into the cab and gazed benevolently out at the new-comer.

'Ah, Comrade Walderwick!' he said. 'What have we on our mind?'

'Where's my umbrella?' demanded the pink one. 'The cloak-room waiter says you took my umbrella. I mean, a joke's a joke, but that was a dashed good umbrella.'

'It was, indeed,' Psmith agreed cordially. 'It may be of interest to you to know that I selected it as the only possible one from among a number of competitors. I fear this club is becoming very mixed, Comrade Walderwick. You with your pure mind would hardly believe the rottenness of some of the umbrellas I inspected in the cloak-room.'

'Where is it?'

'The cloak-room? You turn to the left as you go in at the main entrance and . . .'

'My umbrella, dash it! Where's my umbrella?'

'Ah, there,' said Psmith, and there was a touch of manly regret in his voice, 'you have me. I gave it to a young lady in the street. Where she is at the present moment I could not say.'

The pink youth tottered slightly.

'You gave my umbrella to a girl?'

'A very loose way of describing her. You would not speak of her in that light fashion if you had seen her. Comrade Walderwick, she was wonderful! I am a plain, blunt, rugged man, above the softer emotions as a general thing, but I frankly confess that she stirred a chord in me which is not often stirred. She thrilled my battered old heart, Comrade Walderwick. There is no other word. Thrilled it!'

'But, dash it! . . .'

Psmith reached out a long arm and laid his hand paternally on the other's shoulder.

'Be brave, Comrade Walderwick!' he said. 'Face this thing like a man! I am sorry to have been the means of depriving you of an excellent umbrella, but as you will readily understand I had no alternative. It was raining. She was over there, crouched despairingly beneath the awning of that shop. She wanted to be elsewhere, but the moisture lay in wait to damage her hat. What could I do? What could any man worthy of the name do but go down to the cloak-room and pinch the best umbrella in sight and take it to her? Yours was easily the best. There was absolutely no comparison. I gave it to her, and she has gone off with it, happy once more. This explanation,' said Psmith, 'will, I am sure, sensibly diminish your natural chagrin. You have lost your umbrella, Comrade Walderwick, but in what a cause! In what a cause, Comrade Walderwick! You are now entitled to rank with Sir Philip Sidney and Sir Walter Ralegh. The latter is perhaps the closer historical parallel. He spread his cloak to keep a queen from wetting her feet. You – by proxy – yielded up your umbrella to save a girl's hat. Posterity will be proud of you, Comrade Walderwick. I shall be vastly surprised if you do not go down in legend and song. Children in ages to come will cluster about their grandfather's knees, saying, "Tell us how the great Walderwick lost his umbrella, grandpapa!" And he will tell them, and they will rise from the recital better, deeper, broader children. . . . But now, as I see that the driver has started his meter, I fear I must conclude this little chat – which I, for one, have heartily enjoyed. Drive on,' he said, leaning out of the window. 'I want to go to Ada Clarkson's International Employment Bureau in Shaftesbury Avenue.'

The cab moved off. The Hon. Hugo Walderwick, after one passionate glance in its wake, realised that he was getting wet and went back into the club.

* * * * *

Arriving at the address named, Psmith paid his cab and, having mounted the stairs, delicately knuckled the ground-glass window of Enquiries.

'My dear Miss Clarkson,' he began in an affable voice, the instant the window had shot up, 'if you can spare me a few moments of your valuable time . . .'

'Miss Clarkson's engaged.'

Psmith scrutinised her gravely through his monocle.

'Aren't *you* Miss Clarkson?'

Enquiries said she was not.

'Then,' said Psmith, 'there has been a misunderstanding, for which,' he added cordially, 'I am to blame. Perhaps I could see her anon? You will find me in the waiting-room when required.'

He went into the waiting-room, and, having picked up a magazine from the table, settled down to read a story in *The Girl's Pet* – the January number of the year 1919, for Employment Agencies, like dentists, prefer their literature of a matured vintage. He was absorbed in this when Eve came out of the private office.

Psmith rose courteously as she entered.

'My dear Miss Clarkson,' he said, 'if you can spare me a moment of your valuable time...'

'Good gracious!' said Eve. 'How extraordinary!'

'A singular coincidence,' agreed Psmith.

'You never gave me time to thank you for the umbrella,' said Eve reproachfully. 'You must have thought me awfully rude. But you took my breath away.'

'My dear Miss Clarkson, please do not...'

'Why do you keep calling me that?'

'Aren't *you* Miss Clarkson either?'

'Of course I'm not.'

'Then,' said Psmith, 'I must start my quest all over again. These constant checks are trying to an ardent spirit. Perhaps you are a young bride come to engage her first cook?'

'No. I'm not married.'

'Good!'

Eve found his relieved thankfulness a little embarrassing. In the momentary pause which followed his remark, Enquiries entered alertly.

'Miss Clarkson will see you now, sir.'

'Leave us,' said Psmith with a wave of his hand. 'We would be alone.'

Enquiries stared; then, awed by his manner and general appearance of magnificence, withdrew.

'I suppose really,' said Eve, toying with the umbrella, 'I ought to give this back to you.' She glanced at the dripping window. 'But it *is* raining rather hard, isn't it?'

'Like the dickens,' assented Psmith.

'Then would you mind very much if I kept it till this evening?'

'Please do.'

'Thanks ever so much. I will send it back to you to-night if you will give me the name and address.'

Psmith waved his hand deprecatingly.

'No, no. If it is of any use to you, I hope that you will look on it as a present.'

'A present!'

'A gift,' explained Psmith.

'But I really can't go about accepting expensive umbrellas from people. Where shall I send it?'

'If you insist, you may send it to the Hon. Hugo Walderwick, Drones Club, Dover Street. But it really isn't necessary.'

'I won't forget. And thank you very much, Mr Walderwick.'

'Why do you call me that?'

'Well, you said . . .'

'Ah, I see. A slight confusion of ideas. No, I am not Mr Walderwick. And between ourselves I should hate to be. His is a very C3 intelligence. Comrade Walderwick is merely the man to whom the umbrella belongs.'

Eve's eyes opened wide.

'Do you mean to say you gave me somebody else's umbrella?'

'I had unfortunately omitted to bring my own out with me this morning.'

'I never heard of such a thing!'

'Merely practical Socialism. Other people are content to talk about the Redistribution of Property. I go out and do it.'

'But won't he be awfully angry when he finds out it has gone?'

'He *has* found out. And it was pretty to see his delight. I explained the circumstances, and he was charmed to have been of service to you.'

The door opened again, and this time it was Miss Clarkson in person who entered. She had found Enquiries' statement over the speaking-tube rambling and unsatisfactory, and had come to investigate for herself the reason why the machinery of the office was being held up.

'Oh, I must go,' said Eve, as she saw her. 'I'm interrupting your business.'

'I'm so glad you're still here, dear,' said Miss Clarkson. 'I have just been looking over my files, and I see that there *is* one vacancy. For a nurse,' said Miss Clarkson with a touch of the apologetic in her voice.

'Oh, no, that's all right,' said Eve. 'I don't really need anything. But thanks ever so much for bothering.'

She smiled affectionately upon the proprietress, bestowed another smile upon Psmith as he opened the door for her, and went out. Psmith turned away from the door with a thoughtful look upon his face.

'Is that young lady a nurse?' he asked.

'Do you want a nurse?' inquired Miss Clarkson, at once the woman of business.

'I want that nurse,' said Psmith with conviction.

'She is a delightful girl,' said Miss Clarkson with enthusiasm. 'There is no one in whom I would feel more confidence in recommending to a position. She is a Miss Halliday, the daughter of a very clever but erratic writer, who died some years ago. I can speak with particular knowledge of Miss Halliday, for I was for many years an assistant mistress at Wayland House, where she was at school. She is a charming, warm-hearted, impulsive girl. . . . But you will hardly want to hear all this.'

'On the contrary,' said Psmith, 'I could listen for hours. You have stumbled upon my favourite subject.'

Miss Clarkson eyed him a little doubtfully, and decided that it would be best to reintroduce the business theme.

'Perhaps, when you say you are looking for a nurse, you mean you need a hospital nurse?'

'My friends have sometimes suggested it.'

'Miss Halliday's greatest experience has, of course, been as a governess.'

'A governess is just as good,' said Psmith agreeably.

Miss Clarkson began to be conscious of a sensation of being out of her depth.

'How old are your children, sir?' she asked.

'I fear,' said Psmith, 'you are peeping into Volume Two. This romance has only just started.'

'I am afraid,' said Miss Clarkson, now completely fogged, 'I do not quite understand. What exactly are you looking for?'

Psmith flicked a speck of fluff from his coat-sleeve.

'A job,' he said.

'A job!' echoed Miss Clarkson, her voice breaking in an amazed squeak.

Psmith raised his eyebrows.

'You seem surprised. Isn't this a job emporium?'

'This *is* an Employment Bureau,' admitted Miss Clarkson.

'I knew it, I knew it,' said Psmith. 'Something seemed to tell me. Possibly it was the legend "Employment Bureau" over the door. And those framed testimonials would convince the most sceptical. Yes, Miss Clarkson, I want a job, and I feel somehow that you are the woman to find it for me. I have inserted an advertisement in the papers, expressing my readiness to undertake any form of employment, but I have since begun to wonder if after all this will lead to wealth and fame. At any rate, it is wise to attack the great world from another angle as well, so I come to you.'

'But you must excuse me if I remark that this application of yours strikes me as most extraordinary.'

'Why? I am young, active, and extremely broke.'

'But your – er – your clothes . . .'

Psmith squinted, not without complacency, down a faultlessly fitting waistcoat, and flicked another speck of dust off his sleeve.

'You consider me well dressed?' he said. 'You find me natty? Well, well, perhaps you are right, perhaps you are right. But consider, Miss Clarkson. If one expects to find employment in these days of strenuous competition, one must be neatly and decently clad. Employers look askance at a baggy trouser-leg. A zippy waistcoat is more to them than an honest heart. This beautiful crease was obtained with the aid of the mattress upon which I tossed feverishly last night in my attic room.'

'I can't take you seriously.'

'Oh, don't say that, please.'

'You really want me to find you work?'

'I prefer the term "employment".'

Miss Clarkson produced a notebook.

'If you are really not making this application just as a joke . . .'

'I assure you, no. My entire capital consists, in specie, of about ten pounds.'

'Then perhaps you will tell me your name.'

'Ah! Things are beginning to move. The name is Psmith. P-smith. The p is silent.'

'Psmith?'

'Psmith.'

Miss Clarkson brooded over this for a moment in almost pained silence, then recovered her slipping grip of affairs.

'I think,' she said, 'you had better give me a few particulars about yourself.'

'There is nothing I should like better,' responded Psmith warmly. 'I am always ready – I may say eager – to tell people the story of my life, but in this rushing age I get little encouragement. Let us start at the beginning. My infancy. When I was but a babe, my eldest sister was bribed with sixpence an hour by my nurse to keep an eye on me and see that I did not raise Cain. At the end of the first day she struck for a shilling, and got it. We now pass to my boyhood. At an early age I was sent to Eton, everybody predicting a bright career for me. Those were happy days, Miss Clarkson. A merry, laughing lad with curly hair and a sunny smile, it is not too much to say that I was the pet of the place. The old cloisters. . . . But I am boring you. I can see it in your eye.'

'No, no,' protested Miss Clarkson. 'But what I meant was . . . I thought you might have had some experience in some particular line of . . . In fact, what sort of work . . . ?'

'Employment.'

'What sort of employment do you require?'

'Broadly speaking,' said Psmith, 'any reasonably salaried position that has nothing to do with fish.'

'Fish!' quavered Miss Clarkson, slipping again. 'Why fish?'

'Because, Miss Clarkson, the fish trade was until this morning my walk in life, and my soul has sickened of it.'

'You are in the *fish* trade?' squeaked Miss Clarkson, with an amazed glance at the knife-like crease in his trousers.

'These are not my working clothes,' said Psmith, following and interpreting her glance. 'Yes, owing to a financial upheaval in my branch of the family, I was until this morning at the beck and call of an uncle who unfortunately happens to be a Mackerel Monarch or a Sardine Sultan, or whatever these merchant princes are called who rule the fish market. He insisted on my going into the business to learn it from the bottom up, thinking, no doubt, that I would follow in his footsteps and eventually work my way to the position of a Whitebait Wizard. Alas! he was too sanguine. It was not to be,' said Psmith solemnly, fixing an owl-like gaze on Miss Clarkson through his eyeglass.

'No?' said Miss Clarkson.

'No. Last night I was obliged to inform him that the fish business was all right, but it wouldn't do, and that I proposed to sever my connection with the firm for ever. I may say at once that there ensued something in the nature of a family earthquake. Hard words,' sighed Psmith. 'Black looks. Unseemly wrangle. And the upshot of it all was that my uncle washed his hands of me and drove me forth into the great world. Hence my anxiety to find employment. My uncle has definitely withdrawn his countenance from me, Miss Clarkson.'

'Dear, dear!' murmured the proprietress sympathetically.

'Yes. He is a hard man, and he judges his fellows solely by their devotion to fish. I never in my life met a man so wrapped up in a subject. For years he has been practically a monomaniac on the subject of fish. So much so that he actually looks like one. It is as if he had taken one of those auto-suggestion courses and had kept saying to himself, "Every day, in every way, I grow more and more like a fish." His closest friends can hardly tell now whether he more nearly resembles a halibut or a cod. . . . But I am boring you again with this family gossip?'

He eyed Miss Clarkson with such a sudden and penetrating glance that she started nervously.

'No, no,' she exclaimed.

'You relieve my apprehensions. I am only too well aware that, when fairly launched on the topic of fish, I am more than apt to weary my audience. I cannot understand this enthusiasm for fish. My uncle used to talk about an unusually large catch of pilchards in Cornwall in much the same awed way as a right-minded curate would talk about the spiritual excellence of his bishop. To me, Miss Clarkson, from the very start, the fish business was what I can only describe as a wash-out. It nauseated my finer feelings. It got right in amongst my fibres. I had to rise and partake of a simple breakfast at about four in the morning, after which I would make my way to Billingsgate Market and stand for some hours knee-deep in dead fish of every description. A jolly life for a cat, no doubt, but a bit too thick for a Shropshire Psmith. Mine, Miss Clarkson, is a refined and poetic nature. I like to be surrounded by joy and life, and I know nothing more joyless and deader than a dead fish. Multiply that dead fish by a million, and you have an environment which only a Dante could contemplate with equanimity. My uncle used to tell me that the way to ascertain whether a fish was fresh was to peer into its eyes. Could I spend the springtime of life staring into the eyes of dead fish? No!' He rose. 'Well, I will not detain you any longer. Thank you for the unfailing courtesy and attention with which you have listened to me. You can understand now why my talents are on the market and why I am compelled to state specifically that no employment can be considered which has anything to do with fish. I am convinced that you will shortly have something particularly good to offer me.'

'I don't know that I can say that, Mr Psmith.'

'The p is silent, as in pshrimp,' he reminded her. 'Oh, by the way,' he said, pausing at the door, 'there is one other thing before I go. While I was waiting for you to be disengaged, I chanced on an instalment of a serial story in *The Girl's Pet* for January, 1919. My search for the remaining issues proved fruitless. The title was "Her Honour at Stake", by Jane Emmeline Moss. You don't happen to know how it all came out in the end, do you? Did Lord Eustace ever learn that, when he found Clarice in Sir Jasper's rooms at midnight, she had only gone there to recover some compromising letters for a girl friend? You don't know? I feared as much. Well, good morning, Miss Clarkson, good morning. I leave my future in your hands with a light heart.'

'I will do my best for you, of course.'

'And what,' said Psmith cordially, 'could be better than Miss Clarkson's best?'

He closed the door gently behind him, and went out. Struck by a kindly thought, he tapped upon Enquiries' window, and beamed benevolently as her bobbed head shot into view.

'They tell me,' he said, 'that Aspidistra is much fancied for the four o'clock race at Birmingham this afternoon. I give the information without prejudice, for what it is worth. Good day!'

§ 1

T H E rain had stopped when Psmith stepped out into the street, and the sun was shining again in that half blustering, half apologetic manner which it affects on its reappearance after a summer shower. The pavements glistened cheerfully, and the air had a welcome freshness. Pausing at the corner, he pondered for a moment as to the best method of passing the hour and twenty minutes which must elapse before he could reasonably think of lunching. The fact that the offices of the *Morning Globe* were within easy strolling distance decided him to go thither and see if the first post had brought anything in the shape of answers to his advertisements. And his energy was rewarded a few minutes later when Box 365 on being opened yielded up quite a little budget of literary matter. No fewer than seven letters in all. A nice bag.

What, however, had appeared at first sight evidence of a pleasing ebullition of enterprise on the part of the newspaper-reading public turned out on closer inspection, when he had retired to a corner where he could concentrate in peace, a hollow delusion. Enterprising in a sense though the communications were – and they certainly showed the writers as men of considerable ginger and business push – to Psmith they came as a disappointment. He had expected better things. These letters were not at all what he had paid good money to receive. They missed the point altogether. The right spirit, it seemed to him, was entirely absent.

The first envelope, attractive though it looked from the outside, being of an expensive brand of stationery and gaily adorned with a somewhat startling crest, merely contained a pleasantly-worded offer from a Mr Alistair MacDougall to advance him any sum from ten to fifty thousand pounds on his note of hand only. The second revealed a similar proposal from another Scot named Colin MacDonald. While in the third Mr Ian Campbell was prepared to go as high as one hundred thousand. All three philanthropists had but one stipulation to make – they would have no dealings with minors. Youth, with all its glorious traditions, did not seem to appeal to them. But they cordially urged Psmith, in the event of his having celebrated his twenty-first birthday, to come round to the office and take the stuff away in a sack.

Keeping his head well in the midst of this shower of riches, Psmith dropped the three letters with a sigh into the waste-paper basket, and opened the next in order. This was a bulky envelope, and its contents consisted of a printed brochure entitled, 'This Night Shall Thy Soul be Required of Thee' – while, by a curious and appropriate coincidence, Number Five proved to be a circular from an energetic firm of coffin-makers offering to bury him for eight pounds ten. Number Six, also printed, was a manifesto from one Howard Hill, of Newmarket, recommending him to apply without delay for 'Hill's Three-Horse Special', without which – ('Who,' demanded Mr Hill in large type, 'gave you Wibbly-Wob for the Jubilee Cup?') – no sportsman could hope to accomplish the undoing of the book-makers.

Although by doing so he convicted himself of that very lack of enterprise which he had been deploring in the great public, Psmith placed this communication with the others in the waste-paper basket. There now remained only Number Seven, and a slight flicker of hope returned to him when he perceived that this envelope was addressed by hand and not in typescript. He opened it.

Beyond a doubt he had kept the pick of the bunch to the last. Here was something that made up for all those other disappointments. Written in a scrawly and apparently agitated hand, the letter ran as follows:

'If R. Psmith will meet the writer in the lobby of the Piccadilly Palace Hotel at twelve sharp, Friday, July 1, business may result if business meant and terms reasonable. R. Psmith will wear a pink chrysanthemum in his buttonhole, and will say to the writer, "There will be rain in Northumberland to-morrow," to which the writer will reply, "Good for the crops." Kindly be punctual.'

A pleased smile played about Psmith's solemn face as he read this communication for the second time. It was much more the sort of thing for which he had been hoping. Although his closest friend, Mike Jackson, was a young man of complete ordinariness, Psmith's tastes when he sought companionship lay as a rule in the direction of the bizarre. He preferred his humanity eccentric. And 'the writer', to judge him by this specimen of his correspondence, appeared to be eccentric enough for the most exacting taste. Whether this promising person turned out to be a ribald jester or an earnest crank, Psmith felt no doubt whatever as to the advisability of following the matter up. Whichever he might be, his society ought to afford entertainment during the interval before lunch. Psmith glanced at his watch. The hour was a quarter to twelve. He would be able to secure the necessary chrysanthemum and reach the Piccadilly Palace Hotel by twelve sharp, thus achieving the businesslike punctuality on which the unknown writer seemed to set such store.

* * * * *

It was not until he had entered a florist's shop on the way to the tryst that it was borne in upon him that the adventure was going to have its drawbacks. The first of these was the chrysanthemum. Preoccupied with the rest of the communication, Psmith, when he had read the letter, had not given much thought to the decoration which it would be necessary for him to wear; and it was only when, in reply to his demand for a chrysanthemum, the florist came forward, almost hidden, like the army at Dunsinane, behind what looked like a small shrubbery, that he realised what he, a correct and fastidious dresser, was up against.

'Is that a chrysanthemum?'

'Yes, sir. Pink chrysanthemum.'

'One?'

'Yes, sir. One pink chrysanthemum.'

Psmith regarded the repellent object with disfavour through his eyeglass. Then, having placed it in his buttonhole, he proceeded on his way, feeling like some wild thing peering through the undergrowth. The distressing shrub completely spoiled his walk.

Arrived at the hotel and standing in the lobby, he perceived the existence of further complications. The lobby was in its usual state of congestion, it being a recognised meeting-place for those who did not find it convenient to go as far east as that traditional rendezvous of Londoners, the spot under the clock at Charing Cross Station; and 'the writer', while giving instructions as to how Psmith should ornament his exterior, had carelessly omitted to mention how he himself was to be recognised. A rollicking, slap-dash conspirator, was Psmith's opinion.

It seemed best to take up a position as nearly as possible in the centre of the lobby and stand there until 'the writer', lured by the chrysanthemum, should come forward and start something. This he accordingly did, but when at the end of ten minutes nothing had happened beyond a series of collisions with perhaps a dozen hurrying visitors to the hotel, he decided on a more active course. A young man of sporting appearance had been standing beside him for the last five minutes, and ever and anon this young man had glanced with some impatience at his watch. He was plainly waiting for someone, so Psmith tried the formula on him.

'There will be rain,' said Psmith, 'in Northumberland to-morrow.'

The young man looked at him, not without interest, certainly, but without that gleam of intelligence in his eye which Psmith had hoped to see.

'What?' he replied.

'There will be rain in Northumberland to-morrow.'

'Thanks, Zadkiel,' said the young man. 'Deuced gratifying, I'm sure. I suppose you couldn't predict the winner of the Goodwood Cup as well?'

He then withdrew rapidly to intercept a young woman in a large hat who had just come through the swing doors. Psmith was forced to the conclusion that this was not his man. He was sorry on the whole, for he had seemed a pleasant fellow.

As Psmith had taken up a stationary position and the population of the lobby was for the most part in a state of flux, he was finding himself next to someone new all the time; and now he decided to accost the individual whom the re-shuffle had just brought elbow to elbow with him. This was a jovial-looking soul with a flowered waistcoat, a white hat, and a mottled face. Just the man who might have written that letter.

The effect upon this person of Psmith's meteorological remark was instantaneous. A light of the utmost friendliness shone in his beautifully-shaven face as he turned. He seized Psmith's hand and gripped it with a delightful heartiness. He had the air of a man who has found a friend, and what is more, an old friend. He had a sort of journeys-end-in-lovers'-meeting look.

'My dear old chap!' he cried. 'I've been waiting for you to speak for the last five minutes. Knew we'd met before somewhere, but couldn't place you. Face familiar as the dickens, of course. Well, well, well! And how are they all?'

'Who?' said Psmith courteously.

'Why, the boys, my dear chap.'

'Oh, the boys?'

'The dear old boys,' said the other, specifying more exactly. He slapped Psmith on the shoulder. 'What times those were, eh?'

'Which?' said Psmith.

'The times we all used to have together.'

'Oh, *those*?' said Psmith.

Something of discouragement seemed to creep over the other's exuberance, as a cloud creeps over the summer sky. But he persevered.

'Fancy meeting you again like this!'

'It is a small world,' agreed Psmith.

'I'd ask you to come and have a drink,' said the jovial one, with the slight increase of tensity which comes to a man who approaches the core of a business deal, 'but the fact is my ass of a man sent me out this morning without a penny. Forgot to give me my note-case. Damn' careless! I'll have to sack the fellow.'

'Annoying, certainly,' said Psmith.

'I wish I could have stood you a drink,' said the other wistfully.

'Of all sad words of tongue or pen, the saddest are these, "It might have been",' sighed Psmith.

'I'll tell you what,' said the jovial one, inspired. 'Lend me a fiver, my dear old boy. That's the best way out of the difficulty. I can send it round to your hotel or wherever you are this evening when I get home.'

A sweet, sad smile played over Psmith's face.

'Leave me, comrade!' he murmured.

'Eh?'

'Pass along, old friend, pass along.'

Resignation displaced joviality in the other's countenance.

'Nothing doing?' he inquired.

'Nothing.'

'Well, there was no harm in trying,' argued the other.

'None whatever.'

'You see,' said the now far less jovial man confidentially, 'you look such a perfect mug with that eyeglass that it tempts a chap.'

88

'I can quite understand how it must!'

'No offence.'

'Assuredly not.'

The white hat disappeared through the swing doors, and Psmith returned to his quest. He engaged the attention of a middle-aged man in a snuff-coloured suit who had just come within hail.

'There will be rain in Northumberland to-morrow,' he said.

The man peered at him inquiringly.

'Hey?' he said.

Psmith repeated his observation.

'Huh?' said the man.

Psmith was beginning to lose the unruffled calm which made him such an impressive figure to the public eye. He had not taken into consideration the possibility that the object of his search might be deaf. It undoubtedly added to the embarrassment of the pursuit. He was moving away, when a hand fell on his sleeve.

Psmith turned. The hand which still grasped his sleeve belonged to an elegantly dressed young man of somewhat nervous and feverish appearance. During his recent vigil Psmith had noticed this young man standing not far away, and had had half a mind to include him in the platoon of new friends he was making that morning.

'I say,' said this young man in a tense whisper, 'did I hear you say that there would be rain in Northumberland to-morrow?'

'If,' said Smith, 'you were anywhere within the radius of a dozen yards while I was chatting with the recent deaf adder, I think it is possible that you did.'

'Good for the crops,' said the young man. 'Come over here where we can talk quietly.'

§ 2

'So you're R. Psmith?' said the young man, when they had made their way to a remote corner of the lobby, apart from the throng.

'The same.'

'I say, dash it, you're frightfully late, you know. I told you to be here at twelve sharp. It's nearly twelve past.'

'You wrong me,' said Psmith. 'I arrived here precisely at twelve. Since when, I have been standing like Patience on a monument...'

'Like what?'

'Let it go,' said Psmith. 'It is not important.'

'I asked you to wear a pink chrysanthemum. So I could recognise you, you know.'

'I *am* wearing a pink chrysanthemum. I should have imagined that that was a fact that the most casual could hardly have overlooked.'

'That thing?' The other gazed disparagingly at the floral decoration. 'I thought it was some kind of cabbage. I meant one of those little what-d'you-may-call-its that people do wear in their button-holes.'

'Carnation, possibly?'

'Carnation! That's right.'

Psmith removed the chrysanthemum and dropped it behind his chair. He looked at his companion reproachfully.

'If you had studied botany at school, comrade,' he said, 'much misery might have been averted. I cannot begin to tell you the spiritual agony I suffered, trailing through the metropolis behind that shrub.'

Whatever decent sympathy and remorse the other might have shown at these words was swept away in the shock resultant on a glance at his watch. Not for an instant during this brief return of his to London had Freddie Threepwood been unmindful of his father's stern injunction to him to catch the twelve-fifty train back to Market Blandings. If he missed it, there would be the deuce of a lot of unpleasantness, and unpleasantness in the home was the one thing Freddie wanted to avoid nowadays; for, like a prudent convict in a prison, he hoped by exemplary behaviour to get his sentence of imprisonment at Blandings Castle reduced for good conduct.

'Good Lord! I've only got about five minutes. Got to talk quick.... About this thing. This business. That advertisement of yours.'

'Ah, yes. My advertisement. It interested you?'

'Was it on the level?'

'Assuredly. We Psmiths do not deceive.'

Freddie looked at him doubtfully.

'You know, you aren't a bit like I expected you'd be.'

'In what respect,' inquired Psmith, 'do I fall short of the ideal?'

'It isn't so much falling short. It's – oh, I don't know... Well, yes, if you want to know, I thought you'd be a tougher specimen altogether. I got the impression from your advertisement that you were down and out and ready for anything, and you look as if you were on your way to a garden-party at Buckingham Palace.'

'Ah!' said Psmith, enlightened. 'It is my costume that is causing these doubts in your mind. This is the second time this morning that such a misunderstanding has occurred. Have no misgivings. These trousers may sit well, but, if they do, it is because the pockets are empty.'

'Are you really broke?'

'As broke as the Ten Commandments.'

'I'm hanged if I can believe it.'

'Suppose I brush my hat the wrong way for a moment?' said Psmith obligingly. 'Would that help?'

His companion remained silent for a few moments. In spite of the fact that he was in so great a hurry and that every minute that passed brought nearer the moment when he would be compelled to tear himself away and make a dash for Paddington Station, Freddie was finding it difficult to open the subject he had come there to discuss.

'Look here,' he said at length, 'I shall have to trust you, dash it.'

'You could pursue no better course.'

'It's like this. I'm trying to raise a thousand quid . . .'

'I regret that I cannot offer to advance it to you myself. I have, indeed, already been compelled to decline to lend a gentleman who claimed to be an old friend of mine so small a sum as a fiver. But there is a dear, obliging soul of the name of Alistair MacDougall who . . .'

'Good Lord! You don't think I'm trying to touch you?'

'That impression did flit through my mind.'

'Oh, dash it, no. No, but – well, as I was saying, I'm frightfully keen to get hold of a thousand quid.'

'So am I,' said Psmith. 'Two minds with but a single thought. How do *you* propose to start about it? For my part, I must freely confess that I haven't a notion. I am stumped. The cry goes round the chancelleries, "Psmith is baffled!"'

'I say, old thing,' said Freddie plaintively, 'you couldn't talk a bit less, could you? I've only got about two minutes.'

'I beg your pardon. Proceed.'

'It's so dashed difficult to know how to begin the thing. I mean, it's all a bit complicated till you get the hang of it. . . . Look here, you said in your advertisement that you had no objection to crime.'

Psmith considered the point.

'Within reason – and if undetected – I see no objection to two-pennorth of crime.'

'Well, look here...look here...Well, look here,' said Freddie, 'will you steal my aunt's diamond necklace?'

Psmith placed his monocle in his eye and bent gravely toward his companion.

'Steal your aunt's necklace?' he said indulgently.

'Yes.'

'You do not think she might consider it a liberty from one to whom she has never been introduced?'

What Freddie might have replied to this pertinent question will never be known, for at this moment, looking nervously at his watch for the twentieth time, he observed that the hands had passed the half-hour and were well on their way to twenty-five minutes to one. He bounded up with a cry.

'I must go! I shall miss that damned train!'

'And meanwhile ... ?' said Psmith.

The familiar phrase – the words 'And meanwhile' had occurred at least once in every film Freddie had ever seen – had the effect of wrenching the latter's mind back to the subject in hand for a moment. Freddie was not a clear-thinking young man, but even he could see that he had not left the negotiations suspended at a very satisfactory point. Nevertheless, he had to catch that twelve-fifty.

'Write and tell me what you think about it,' panted Freddie, skimming through the lobby like a swallow.

'You have unfortunately omitted to leave a name and address,' Psmith pointed out, following him at an easy jog-trot.

In spite of his hurry, a prudence born of much movie-seeing restrained Freddie from supplying the information asked for. Give away your name and address and you never knew what might happen.

'I'll write to you,' he cried, racing for a cab.

'I shall count the minutes,' said Psmith courteously.

'Drive like blazes!' said Freddie to the chauffeur.

'Where?' inquired the man, not unreasonably.

'Eh? Oh, Paddington.'

The cab whirled off, and Psmith, pleasantly conscious of a morning not ill-spent, gazed after it pensively for a moment. Then, with the feeling that the authorities of Colney Hatch or some kindred establishment had been extraordinarily negligent, he permitted his mind to turn with genial anticipation in the direction of lunch. For, though he had celebrated his first day of emancipation from Billingsgate Fish Market by rising late and breakfasting later, he had become aware by now of that not unpleasant emptiness which is the silent luncheon-gong of the soul.

§ 3

The minor problem now presented itself of where to lunch; and with scarcely a moment's consideration he dismissed those large, noisy, and bustling restaurants which lie near Piccadilly Circus. After a morning spent with Eve Halliday and the young man who was going about the place asking people to steal his aunt's necklace, it was imperative that he select some place where he could sit and think quietly. Any food of which he partook must be consumed in calm, even cloistral surroundings, unpolluted by the presence of a first violin who tied himself into

94

knots and an orchestra in whose lexicon there was no such word as *piano*. One of his clubs seemed indicated.

In the days of his prosperity, Psmith's father, an enthusiastic clubman, had enrolled his son's name on the list of several institutions: and now, although the lean years had arrived, he was still a member of six, and would continue to be a member till the beginning of the new year and the consequent call for fresh subscriptions. These clubs ranged from the Drones, frankly frivolous, to the Senior Conservative, solidly worthy. Almost immediately Psmith decided that for such a mood as was upon him at the moment, the latter might have been specially constructed.

Anybody familiar with the interior of the Senior Conservative Club would have applauded his choice. In the whole of London no better haven could have been found by one desirous of staying his interior with excellently-cooked food while passing his soul under a leisurely examination. They fed you well at the Drones, too, no doubt: but there Youth held carnival, and the thoughtful man, examining his soul, was apt at any moment to have his meditations broken in upon by a chunk of bread, dexterously thrown by some bright spirit at an adjoining table. No horror of that description could possibly occur at the Senior Conservative. The Senior Conservative has six thousand one hundred and eleven members. Some of the six thousand one hundred and eleven are more respectable than the others, but they are all respectable – whether they be numbered among the oldest inhabitants like the Earl of Emsworth, who joined as a country member in 1888, or are among the recent creations of the last election of candidates. They are bald, reverend men, who look as if they are on their way to the City to preside at directors' meetings or have dropped in after conferring with the Prime

Minister at Downing Street as to the prospects at the coming by-election in the Little Wabsley Division.

With the quiet dignity which atoned for his lack in years in this stronghold of mellow worth, Psmith mounted the steps, passed through the doors which were obligingly flung open for him by two uniformed dignitaries, and made his way to the coffee-room. Here, having selected a table in the middle of the room and ordered a simple and appetising lunch, he gave himself up to thoughts of Eve Halliday. As he had confessed to his young friend Mr Walderwick, she had made a powerful impression upon him. He was tearing himself from his day-dreams in order to wrestle with a mutton chop, when a foreign body shot into his orbit and blundered heavily against the table. Looking up, he perceived a long, thin, elderly gentleman of pleasantly vague aspect, who immediately began to apologise.

'My dear sir, I am extremely sorry. I trust I have caused no damage.'

'None whatever,' replied Psmith courteously.

'The fact is, I have mislaid my glasses. Blind as a bat without them. Can't see where I'm going.'

A gloomy-looking young man with long and disordered hair, who stood at the elderly gentleman's elbow, coughed suggestively. He was shuffling restlessly, and appeared to be anxious to close the episode and move on. A young man, evidently, of highly-strung temperament. He had a sullen air.

The elderly gentleman started vaguely at the sound of the cough.

'Eh?' he said, as if in answer to some spoken remark. 'Oh, yes, quite so, quite so, my dear fellow. Mustn't stop here chatting, eh? Had to apologise, though. Nearly upset this gentleman's table.

Can't see where I'm going without my glasses. Blind as a bat. Eh? What? Quite so, quite so.'

He ambled off, doddering cheerfully, while his companion still preserved his look of sulky aloofness. Psmith gazed after them with interest.

'Can you tell me,' he asked of the waiter, who was rallying round with the potatoes, 'who that was?'

The waiter followed his glance.

'Don't know who the young gentleman is, sir. Guest here, I fancy. The old gentleman is the Earl of Emsworth. Lives in the country and doesn't often come to the club. Very absent-minded gentleman, they tell me. Potatoes, sir?'

'Thank you,' said Psmith.

The waiter drifted away, and returned.

'I have been looking at the guest-book, sir. The name of the gentleman lunching with Lord Emsworth is Mr Ralston McTodd.'

'Thank you very much. I am sorry you had the trouble.'

'No trouble, sir.'

Psmith resumed his meal.

§ 4

The sullen demeanour of the young man who had accompanied Lord Emsworth through the coffee-room accurately reflected the emotions which were vexing his troubled soul. Ralston McTodd, the powerful young singer of Saskatoon ('Plumbs the depths of human emotion and strikes a new note' – *Montreal Star*. 'Very readable' – *Ipsilanti Herald*), had not enjoyed his lunch. The pleasing sense of importance induced by the fact that for the first time in his life he was hob-nobbing with a genuine earl had given way after ten minutes of his host's society to a mingled despair and irritation which had grown steadily deeper as the meal proceeded. It is not too much to say that by the time the fish course arrived it would have been a relief to Mr McTodd's feelings if he could have taken up the butter-dish and banged it down, butter and all, on his lordship's bald head.

A temperamental young man was Ralston McTodd. He liked to be the centre of the picture, to do the talking, to air his views, to be listened to respectfully and with interest by a submissive audience. At the meal which had just concluded none of these reasonable demands had been permitted to him. From the very beginning, Lord Emsworth had collared the conversation and held it with a gentle, bleating persistency against all assaults. Five times had Mr McTodd almost succeeded in launching one of his best epigrams, only to see it swept away on the tossing flood of a lecture on hollyhocks. At the sixth attempt he had managed to get it out, complete and sparkling, and the old ass opposite him had taken it in his stride like a hurdle and gone galloping off about the mental and moral defects of a creature named Angus McAllister, who appeared to be his head gardener or something of the kind. The luncheon, though he was a hearty feeder and as a rule appreciative of good cooking, had turned to ashes in Mr McTodd's mouth, and it was a soured and chafing Singer of Saskatoon who dropped scowlingly into an arm-chair by the window of the lower smoking-room a few moments later. We introduce Ralston McTodd to the reader, in short, at a moment when he is very near the breaking-point. A little more provocation, and goodness knows what he may not do. For the time being, he is merely leaning back in his chair and scowling. He has a faint hope, however, that a cigar may bring some sort of relief, and he is waiting for one to be ordered for him.

The Earl of Emsworth did not see the scowl. He had not really seen Mr McTodd at all from the moment of his arrival at the club, when somebody, who sounded like the head porter, had informed him that a gentleman was waiting to see him and had led him up to a shapeless blur which had introduced itself as his expected guest. The loss of his glasses had had its usual effect on Lord Emsworth, making the world a misty place in which indefinite objects swam dimly like fish in muddy water. Not that this mattered much, seeing that he was in London, for in London there was never anything worth looking at. Beyond a vague feeling that it would be more comfortable on the whole if he had his glasses – a feeling just strong enough to have made him send off a messenger boy to his hotel to hunt for them – Lord Emsworth had not allowed lack of vision to interfere with his enjoyment of the proceedings.

And, unlike Mr McTodd, he had been enjoying himself very much. A good listener, this young man, he felt. Very soothing, the way he had constituted himself a willing audience, never interrupting or thrusting himself forward, as is so often the deplorable tendency of the modern young man. Lord Emsworth was bound to admit that, much as he had disliked the idea of going to London to pick up this poet or whatever he was, the thing had turned out better than he had expected. He liked Mr McTodd's silent but obvious interest in flowers, his tacit but warm-hearted sympathy in the matter of Angus McAllister. He was glad he was coming to Blandings. It would be agreeable to conduct him personally through the gardens, to introduce him to Angus McAllister and allow him to plumb for himself the black abysses of that outcast's mental processes.

Meanwhile, he had forgotten all about ordering that cigar...

'In large gardens where ample space permits,' said Lord Emsworth, dropping cosily into his chair and taking up the conversation at the point where it had been broken off, 'nothing is more desirable than that there should be some places, or one at least, of quiet greenery alone, without any flowers whatever. I see that you agree with me.'

Mr McTodd had not agreed with him. The grunt which Lord Emsworth had taken for an exclamation of rapturous adhesion to his sentiments had been merely a sort of bubble of sound rising from the tortured depths of Mr McTodd's suffering soul – the cry, as the poet beautifully puts it, 'of some strong smoker in his agony'. The desire to smoke had now gripped Mr McTodd's very vitals; but, as some lingering remains of the social sense kept him from asking point-blank for the cigar for which he yearned, he sought in his mind for a way of approaching the subject obliquely.

'In no other way,' proceeded Lord Emsworth, 'can the brilliancy of flowers be so keenly enjoyed as by...'

'Talking of flowers,' said Mr McTodd, 'it is a fact, I believe, that tobacco smoke is good for roses.'

'...as by pacing for a time,' said Lord Emsworth, 'in some cool, green alley, and then passing on to the flowery places. It is partly, no doubt, the unconscious working out of some optical law, the explanation of which in everyday language is that the eye...'

'Some people say that smoking is bad for the eyes. I don't agree with them,' said Mr McTodd warmly.

'...being, as it were, saturated with the green colour, is the more attuned to receive the others, especially the reds. It was probably some such consideration that influenced the designers

LORD EMSWORTH MEETS A POET

of the many old gardens of England in devoting so much attention to the cult of the yew tree. When you come to Blandings, my dear fellow, I will show you our celebrated yew alley. And, when you see it, you will agree that I was right in taking the stand I did against Angus McAllister's pernicious views.'

'I was lunching in a club yesterday,' said Mr McTodd, with the splendid McTodd doggedness, 'where they had no matches on the tables in the smoking-room. Only spills. It made it very inconvenient...'

'Angus McAllister,' said Lord Emsworth, 'is a professional gardener. I need say no more. You know as well as I do, my dear fellow, what professional gardeners are like when it is a question of moss...'

'What it meant was that, when you wanted to light your after-luncheon cigar, you had to get up and go to a gas-burner on a bracket at the other end of the room...'

'Moss, for some obscure reason, appears to infuriate them. It rouses their basest passions. Nature intended a yew alley to be carpeted with a mossy growth. The mossy path in the yew alley at Blandings is in true relation for colour to the trees and grassy edges yet will you credit it that that soulless disgrace to Scotland actually wished to grub it all up and have a rolled gravel path staring up from beneath those immemorial trees! I have already told you how I was compelled to give in to him in the matter of the hollyhocks – head gardeners of any ability at all are rare in these days and one has to make concessions – but this was too much. I was perfectly friendly and civil about it. "Certainly, McAllister," I said, "you may have your gravel path if you wish it. I make but one proviso, that you construct it over my dead body. Only when I am weltering in my blood on the threshold of that yew alley shall you disturb one inch of my beautiful moss. Try to remember, McAllister," I said, still quite cordially, "that you are not laying out a recreation ground in a Glasgow suburb – you are proposing to make an eyesore of what is possibly the most beautiful nook in one of the finest and oldest gardens in the United Kingdom." He made some repulsive Scotch noise at the back of his throat, and there the matter rests.... Let me, my dear fellow,' said Lord Emsworth, writhing down into the depths of his chair like an aristocratic snake until his spine rested snugly against the leather, 'let me describe for you the Yew Alley at Blandings. Entering from the west...'

Mr McTodd gave up the struggle and sank back, filled with black and deleterious thoughts, into a tobacco-less hell. The smoking-room was full now, and on all sides fragrant blue clouds arose from the little groups of serious thinkers who were discussing what Gladstone had said in '78. Mr McTodd, as he watched them, had something of the emotions of the Peri excluded from Paradise. So reduced was he by this time that he would have accepted gratefully the meanest straight-cut cigarette in place of the Corona of his dreams. But even this poor substitute for smoking was denied him.

Lord Emsworth droned on. Having approached from the west, he was now well inside the yew alley.

'Many of the yews, no doubt, have taken forms other than those that were originally designed. Some are like turned chessmen; some might be taken for adaptations of human figures, for one can trace here and there a hat-covered head or a spreading petticoat. Some rise in solid blocks with rounded roof and stemless mushroom finial. These have for the most part arched recesses, forming arbours. One of the tallest... Eh? What?'

Lord Emsworth blinked vaguely at the waiter who had sidled up. A moment before he had been a hundred odd miles away, and it was not easy to adjust his mind immediately to the fact that he was in the smoking-room of the Senior Conservative Club.

'Eh? What?'

'A messenger boy has just arrived with these, your lordship.'

Lord Emsworth peered in a dazed and woolly manner at the proffered spectacle-case. Intelligence returned to him.

'Oh, thank you. Thank you very much. My glasses. Capital! Thank you, thank you, thank you.'

He removed the glasses from their case and placed them on his nose: and instantly the world sprang into being before his eyes, sharp and well-defined. It was like coming out of a fog.

'Dear me!' he said in a self-congratulatory voice.

Then abruptly he sat up, transfixed. The lower smoking-room at the Senior Conservative Club is on the street level, and Lord Emsworth's chair faced the large window. Through this, as he raised his now spectacled face, he perceived for the first time that among the row of shops on the opposite side of the road was a jaunty new florist's. It had not been there at his last visit to the metropolis, and he stared at it raptly, as a small boy would stare at a saucer of ice-cream if such a thing had suddenly descended from heaven immediately in front of him. And, like a small boy in such a situation, he had eyes for nothing else. He did not look at his guest. Indeed, in the ecstasy of his discovery, he had completely forgotten that he had a guest.

Any flower shop, however small, was a magnet to the Earl of Emsworth. And this was a particularly spacious and arresting flower shop. Its window was gay with summer blooms. And Lord Emsworth, slowly rising from his chair, 'pointed' like a dog that sees a pheasant.

'Bless my soul!' he murmured.

If the reader has followed with the closeness which it deserves the extremely entertaining conversation of his lordship recorded in the last few paragraphs, he will have noted a reference to hollyhocks. Lord Emsworth had ventilated the hollyhock question at some little length while seated at the luncheon table. But, as we had not the good fortune to be present at that enjoyable meal, a brief résumé of the situation must now be given and the intelligent public allowed to judge between his lordship and the uncompromising McAllister.

Briefly, the position was this. Many head gardeners are apt to favour in the hollyhock forms that one cannot but think have for their aim an ideal that is a false and unworthy one. Angus McAllister, clinging to the head-gardeneresque standard of beauty and correct form, would not sanction the wide outer petal. The flower, so Angus held, must be very tight and very round, like the uniform of a major-general. Lord Emsworth, on the other hand, considered this view narrow, and claimed the liberty to try for the very highest and truest beauty in hollyhocks. The loosely-folded inner petals of the hollyhock, he considered, invited a wonderful play and brilliancy of colour; while the wide outer petal, with its slightly waved surface and gently frilled edge . . . well, anyway, Lord Emsworth liked his hollyhocks floppy and Angus McAllister liked them tight, and bitter warfare had resulted, in which, as we have seen, his lordship had been compelled to give way. He had been brooding on this defeat ever since, and in the florist opposite he saw a possible sympathiser, a potential ally, an intelligent chum with whom he could get together and thoroughly damn Angus McAllister's Glaswegian obstinacy.

You would not have suspected Lord Emsworth, from a casual glance, of having within him the ability to move rapidly; but it is a fact that he was out of the smoking-room and skimming down the front steps of the club before Mr McTodd's jaw, which had fallen at the spectacle of his host bounding out of his horizon of vision like a jack-rabbit, had time to hitch itself up again. A moment later, Mr McTodd, happening to direct his gaze out of the window, saw him whiz across the road and vanish into the florist's shop.

It was at this juncture that Psmith, having finished his lunch, came downstairs to enjoy a quiet cup of coffee. The room was rather crowded, and the chair which Lord Emsworth had vacated offered a wide invitation. He made his way to it.

'Is this chair occupied?' he inquired politely. So politely that Mr McTodd's reply sounded by contrast even more violent than it might otherwise have done.

'No, it isn't!' snapped Mr McTodd.

Psmith seated himself. He was feeling agreeably disposed to conversation.

'Lord Emsworth has left you then?' he said.

'Is he a friend of yours?' inquired Mr McTodd in a voice that suggested that he was perfectly willing to accept a proxy as a target for his wrath.

'I know him by sight. Nothing more.'

'Blast him!' muttered Mr McTodd with indescribable virulence.

Psmith eyed him inquiringly.

'Correct me if I am wrong,' he said, 'but I seem to detect in your manner a certain half-veiled annoyance. Is anything the matter?'

Mr McTodd barked bitterly.

'Oh, no. Nothing's the matter. Nothing whatever, except that that old beaver – ' – here he wronged Lord Emsworth, who, whatever his faults, was not a bearded man – 'that old beaver invited me to lunch, talked all the time about his infernal flowers, never let me get a word in edgeways, hadn't the common civility to offer me a cigar, and now has gone off without a word of apology and buried himself in that shop over the way. I've never been so insulted in my life!' raved Mr McTodd.

'Scarcely the perfect host,' admitted Psmith.

'And if he thinks,' said Mr McTodd, rising, 'that I'm going to go and stay with him at his beastly castle after this, he's mistaken. I'm supposed to go down there with him this evening. And perhaps the old fossil thinks I will! After this!' A horrid laugh rolled up from Mr McTodd's interior. 'Likely! I see myself! After being insulted like this... Would *you*?' he demanded.

Psmith gave the matter thought.

'I am inclined to think no.'

'And so am I damned well inclined to think no!' cried Mr McTodd. 'I'm going away now, this very minute. And if that old total loss ever comes back, you can tell him he's seen the last of me.'

And Ralston McTodd, his blood boiling with justifiable indignation and pique to a degree dangerous on such a warm day, stalked off towards the door with a hard, set face. Through the door he stalked to the cloak-room for his hat and cane; then, his lips moving silently, he stalked through the hall, stalked down the steps, and passed from the scene, stalking furiously round the corner in quest of a tobacconist's. At the moment of his disappearance, the Earl of Emsworth had just begun to give the sympathetic florist a limpid character-sketch of Angus McAllister.

* * * * *

Psmith shook his head sadly. These clashings of human temperament were very lamentable. They disturbed the after-luncheon repose of the man of sensibility. He ordered coffee, and endeavoured to forget the painful scene by thinking of Eve Halliday.

§ 5

The florist who had settled down to ply his trade opposite the Senior Conservative Club was a delightful fellow, thoroughly sound on the hollyhock question and so informative in the matter of delphiniums, achilleas, coreopsis, eryngiums, geums, lupines, bergamot and early phloxes that Lord Emsworth gave himself up whole-heartedly to the feast of reason and the flow of soul; and it was only some fifteen minutes later that he remembered that he had left a guest languishing in the lower smoking-room and that this guest might be thinking him a trifle remiss in the observance of the sacred duties of hospitality.

'Bless my soul, yes!' said his lordship, coming out from under the influence with a start.

Even then he could not bring himself to dash abruptly from the shop. Twice he reached the door and twice pottered back to sniff at flowers and say something he had forgotten to mention about the Stronger Growing Clematis. Finally, however, with one last, longing, lingering look behind, he tore himself away and trotted back across the road.

Arrived in the lower smoking-room, he stood in the doorway for a moment, peering. The place had been a blur to him when he had left it, but he remembered that he had been sitting in the middle window and, as there were only two seats by the window, that tall, dark young man in one of them must be the guest he had deserted. That he could be a changeling never occurred to Lord Emsworth. So pleasantly had the time passed in the shop across the way that he had the impression that he had only been gone a couple of minutes or so. He made his way to where the young man sat. A vague idea came into his head that the other had grown a bit in his absence, but it passed.

'My dear fellow,' he said genially, as he slid into the other chair, 'I really must apologise.'

It was plain to Psmith that the other was under a misapprehension, and a really nice-minded young man would no doubt have put the matter right at once. The fact that it never for a single instant occurred to Psmith to do so was due, no doubt, to some innate defect in his character. He was essentially a young man who took life as it came, and the more inconsequently it came the better he liked it. Presently, he reflected, it would become necessary for him to make some excuse and steal quietly out of the other's life; but meanwhile the situation seemed to him to present entertaining possibilities.

'Not at all,' he replied graciously. 'Not at all.'

'I was afraid for a moment,' said Lord Emsworth, 'that you might – quite naturally – be offended.'

'Absurd!'

'Shouldn't have left you like that. Shocking bad manners. But, my dear fellow, I simply had to pop across the street.'

'Most decidedly,' said Psmith. 'Always pop across streets. It is the secret of a happy and successful life.'

Lord Emsworth looked at him a little perplexedly, and wondered if he had caught the last remark correctly. But his mind had never been designed for the purpose of dwelling closely on problems for any length of time, and he let it go.

'Beautiful roses that man has,' he observed. 'Really an extraordinarily fine display.'

'Indeed?' said Psmith.

'Nothing to touch mine, though. I wish, my dear fellow, you could have been down at Blandings at the beginning of the month. My roses were at their best then. It's too bad you weren't there to see them.'

'The fault no doubt was mine,' said Psmith.

'Of course you weren't in England then.'

'Ah! That explains it.'

'Still, I shall have plenty of flowers to show you when you are at Blandings. I expect,' said Lord Emsworth, at last showing a host-like disposition to give his guest a belated innings, 'I expect you'll write one of your poems about my gardens, eh?'

Psmith was conscious of a feeling of distinct gratification. Weeks of toil among the herrings of Billingsgate had left him with a sort of haunting fear that even in private life there clung to him the miasma of the fish market. Yet here was a perfectly unprejudiced observer looking squarely at him and mistaking him for a poet – showing that in spite of all he had gone through there must still be something notably spiritual and unfishy about his outward appearance.

'Very possibly,' he said. 'Very possibly.'

'I suppose you get ideas for your poetry from all sorts of things,' said Lord Emsworth, nobly resisting the temptation to collar the conversation again. He was feeling extremely friendly towards this poet fellow. It was deuced civil of him not to be put out and huffy at being left alone in the smoking-room.

'From practically everything,' said Psmith, 'except fish.'

'Fish?'

'I have never written a poem about fish.'

'No?' said Lord Emsworth, again feeling that a pin had worked loose in the machinery of the conversation.

'I was once offered a princely sum,' went on Psmith, now floating happily along on the tide of his native exuberance, 'to write a ballad for the *Fishmonger's Gazette* entitled, "Herbert the Turbot". But I was firm. I declined.'

'Indeed?' said Lord Emsworth.

'One has one's self-respect,' said Psmith.

'Oh, decidedly,' said Lord Emsworth.

'It was painful, of course. The editor broke down completely when he realised that my refusal was final. However, I sent him on with a letter of introduction to John Drinkwater, who, I believe, turned him out quite a good little effort on the theme.'

At this moment, when Lord Emsworth was feeling a trifle dizzy, and Psmith, on whom conversation always acted as a mental stimulus, was on the point of plunging even deeper into the agreeable depths of light persiflage, a waiter approached.

'A lady to see you, your lordship.'

'Eh? Ah, yes, of course, of course. I was expecting her. It is a Miss—what is the name? Holliday? Halliday. It is a Miss Halliday,' he said in explanation to Psmith, 'who is coming down to Blandings to catalogue the library. My secretary, Baxter, told her to call here and see me. If you will excuse me for a moment, my dear fellow?'

'Certainly.'

As Lord Emsworth disappeared, it occurred to Psmith that the moment had arrived for him to get his hat and steal softly out of the other's life for ever. Only so could confusion and embarrassing explanations be avoided. And it was Psmith's guiding rule in life always to avoid explanations. It might, he felt, cause

Lord Emsworth a momentary pang when he returned to the smoking-room and found that he was a poet short, but what is that in these modern days when poets are so plentiful that it is almost impossible to fling a brick in any public place without damaging some stern young singer. Psmith's view of the matter was that, if Lord Emsworth was bent on associating with poets, there was bound to be another one along in a minute. He was on the point, therefore, of rising, when the laziness induced by a good lunch decided him to remain in his comfortable chair for a few minutes longer. He was in one of those moods of rare tranquillity which it is rash to break.

He lit another cigarette, and his thoughts, as they had done after the departure of Mr McTodd, turned dreamily in the direction of the girl he had met at Miss Clarkson's Employment Bureau. He mused upon her with a gentle melancholy. Sad, he felt, that two obviously kindred spirits like himself and her should meet in the whirl of London life, only to separate again – presumably for ever – simply because the etiquette governing those who are created male and female forbids a man to cement a chance acquaintanceship by ascertaining the lady's name and address, asking her to lunch, and swearing eternal friendship. He sighed as he gazed thoughtfully out of the lower smoking-room window. As he had indicated in his conversation with Mr Walderwick, those blue eyes and that cheerful, friendly face had made a deep impression on him. Who was she? Where did she live? And was he ever to see her again?

He was. Even as he asked himself the question, two figures came down the steps of the club, and paused. One was Lord Emsworth, without his hat. The other – and Psmith's usually orderly heart gave a spasmodic bound at the sight of her – was the very girl who was occupying his thoughts. There she stood, as blue-eyed, as fair-haired, as indescribably jolly and charming as ever.

Psmith rose from his chair with a vehemence almost equal to that recently displayed by Mr McTodd. It was his intention to add himself immediately to the group. He raced across the room in a manner that drew censorious glances from the local grey-beards, many of whom had half a mind to write to the committee about it.

But when he reached the open air the pavement at the foot of the club steps was empty. The girl was just vanishing round the corner into the Strand, and of Lord Emsworth there was no sign whatever.

By this time, however, Psmith had acquired a useful working knowledge of his lordship's habits, and he knew where to look. He crossed the street and headed for the florist's shop.

'Ah, my dear fellow,' said his lordship amiably, suspending his conversation with the proprietor on the subject of delphiniums, 'must you be off? Don't forget that our train leaves Paddington at five sharp. You take your ticket for Market Blandings.'

Psmith had come into the shop merely with the intention of asking his lordship if he happened to know Miss Halliday's address, but these words opened out such a vista of attractive possibilities that he had abandoned this tame programme immediately. He remembered now that among Mr McTodd's remarks on things in general had been one to the effect that he had received an invitation to visit Blandings Castle – of which invitation he did not propose to avail himself; and he argued that if he had acted as substitute for Mr McTodd at the club, he might well continue the kindly work by officiating for him at Blandings. Looking at the matter altruistically, he would prevent his kind host much disappointment by taking this course;

and, looking at it from a more personal viewpoint, only by going to Blandings could he renew his acquaintance with this girl. Psmith had never been one of those who hang back diffidently when Adventure calls, and he did not hang back now.

'At five sharp,' he said. 'I will be there.'

'Capital, my dear fellow,' said his lordship.

'Does Miss Halliday travel with us?'

'Eh? No, she is coming down in a day or two.'

'I shall look forward to meeting her,' said Psmith.

He turned to the door, and Lord Emsworth with a farewell beam resumed his conversation with the florist.

§ 1

THE five o'clock train, having given itself a spasmodic jerk, began to move slowly out of Paddington Station. The platform past which it was gliding was crowded with a number of the fauna always to be seen at railway stations at such moments, but in their ranks there was no sign of Mr Ralston McTodd: and Psmith, as he sat opposite Lord Emsworth in a corner seat of a first-class compartment, felt that genial glow of satisfaction which comes to the man who has successfully taken a chance. Until now, he had been half afraid that McTodd, having changed his mind, might suddenly appear with bag and baggage – an event which must necessarily have caused confusion and discomfort. His mind was now tranquil. Concerning the future he declined to worry. It would, no doubt, contain its little difficulties, but he was prepared to meet them in the right spirit; and his only trouble in the world now was the difficulty he was experiencing in avoiding his lordship's legs, which showed a disposition to pervade the compartment like the tentacles of an octopus. Lord Emsworth rather ran to leg, and his practice of reclining when at ease on the base of his spine was causing him to straddle, like Apollyon in Pilgrim's Progress, 'right across the way'. It became manifest that in a journey lasting several hours his society was likely to prove irksome. For the time being, however, he endured it, and listened with polite attention to his host's remarks on the subject of the Blandings gardens. Lord Emsworth, in a train moving in the direction of home, was behaving like a horse heading for his stable. He snorted eagerly, and spoke at length and with emotion of roses and herbaceous borders.

'It will be dark, I suppose, by the time we arrive,' he said regretfully, 'but the first thing to-morrow, my dear fellow, I must take you round and show you my gardens.'

'I shall look forward to it keenly,' said Psmith. 'They are, I can readily imagine, distinctly oojah-cum-spiff.'

'I beg your pardon?' said Lord Emsworth with a start.

'Not at all,' said Psmith graciously.

'Er – what did you say?' asked his lordship after a slight pause.

'I was saying that, from all reports, you must have a very nifty display of garden-produce at your rural seat.'

'Oh, yes. Oh, most,' said his lordship, looking puzzled. He examined Psmith across the compartment with something of the peering curiosity which he would have bestowed upon a new and unclassified shrub. 'Most extraordinary!' he murmured. 'I trust, my dear fellow, you will not think me personal, but, do you know, nobody would imagine that you were a poet. You don't look like a poet, and, dash it, you don't talk like a poet.'

'How should a poet talk?'

'Well...' Lord Emsworth considered the point. 'Well, Miss Peavey... But of course you don't know Miss Peavey... Miss Peavey is a poetess, and she waylaid me the other morning while I was having a most important conference with McAllister on the subject of bulbs and asked me if I didn't think that it was fairies' tear-drops that made the dew. Did you ever hear such dashed nonsense?'

'Evidently an aggravated case. Is Miss Peavey staying at the castle?'

'My dear fellow, you couldn't shift her with blasting-powder. Really this craze of my sister Constance for filling the house with these infernal literary people is getting on my nerves. I can't stand these poets and what not. Never could.'

'We must always remember, however,' said Psmith gravely, 'that poets are also God's creatures.'

'Good heavens!' exclaimed his lordship, aghast. 'I had forgotten that you were one. What will you think of me, my dear fellow! But, of course, as I said a moment ago, you are different. I admit that when Constance told me that she had invited you to the house I was not cheered, but, now that I have had the pleasure of meeting you . . .'

The conversation had worked round to the very point to which Psmith had been wishing to direct it. He was keenly desirous of finding out why Mr McTodd had been invited to Blandings and – a still more vital matter – of ascertaining whether, on his arrival there as Mr McTodd's understudy, he was going to meet people who knew the poet by sight. On this latter point, it seemed to him, hung the question of whether he was about to enjoy a delightful visit to a historic country house in the society of Eve Halliday – or leave the train at the next stop and omit to return to it.

'It was extremely kind of Lady Constance,' he hazarded, 'to invite a perfect stranger to Blandings.'

'Oh, she's always doing that sort of thing,' said his lordship. 'It didn't matter to her that she'd never seen you in her life. She had read your books, you know, and liked them: and when she heard that you were coming to England, she wrote to you.'

'I see,' said Psmith, relieved.

'Of course, it is all right as it has turned out,' said Lord Emsworth handsomely. 'As I say, you're different. And how you came to write that . . . that . . .'

'Bilge?' suggested Psmith.

'The very word I was about to employ, my dear fellow. . . . No, no, I don't mean that. . . . I – I . . . Capital stuff, no doubt, capital stuff . . . but . . .'

'I understand.'

'Constance tried to make me read the things, but I couldn't. I fell asleep over them.'

'I hope you rested well.'

'I – er – the fact is, I suppose they were beyond me. I couldn't see any sense in the things.'

'If you would care to have another pop at them,' said Psmith agreeably, 'I have a complete set in my bag.'

'No, no, my dear fellow, thank you very much, thank you a thousand times. I – er – find that reading in the train tries my eyes.'

'Ah! You would prefer that I read them aloud?'

'No, no.' A look of hunted alarm came into his lordship's speaking countenance at the suggestion. 'As a matter of fact, I generally take a short nap at the beginning of a railway journey. I find it refreshing and – er – in short, refreshing. You will excuse me?'

'If you think you can get to sleep all right without the aid of my poems, certainly.'

'You won't think me rude?'

'Not at all, not at all. By the way, am I likely to meet any old friends at Blandings?'

'Eh? Oh no. There will be nobody but ourselves. Except my sister and Miss Peavey, of course. You said you had not met Miss Peavey, I think?'

'I have not had that pleasure. I am, of course, looking forward to it with the utmost keenness.'

Lord Emsworth eyed him for a moment, astonished: then concluded the conversation by closing his eyes defensively. Psmith was left to his reflections, which a few minutes later were interrupted by a smart kick on the shin, as Lord Emsworth, a jumpy sleeper, began to throw his long legs about. Psmith moved to the other end of the seat, and, taking his bag down from the rack, extracted a slim volume bound in squashy mauve. After gazing at this in an unfriendly manner for a moment, he opened it at random and began to read. His first move on leaving Lord Emsworth at the florist's had been to spend a portion of his slender capital on the works of Ralston McTodd in order not to be taken at a disadvantage in the event of questions about them at Blandings: but he speedily realised, as he dipped into the poems, that anything in the nature of a prolonged study of them was likely to spoil his little holiday. They were not light summer reading.

'Across the pale parabola of Joy...'

A gurgling snort from the other end of the compartment abruptly detached his mind from its struggle with this mystic line. He perceived that his host had slipped even further down on to his spine and was now lying with open mouth in an attitude suggestive of dislocation. And as he looked, there was a whistling sound, and another snore proceeded from the back of his lordship's throat.

Psmith rose and took his book of poems out into the corridor with the purpose of roaming along the train until he should find an empty compartment in which to read in peace.

With the two adjoining compartments he had no luck. One was occupied by an elderly man with a retriever, while the presence of a baby in the other ruled it out of consideration. The third, however, looked more promising. It was not actually empty, but there was only one occupant, and he was asleep. He was lying back in the far corner with a large silk handkerchief draped over his face and his feet propped up on the seat opposite. His society did not seem likely to act as a bar to the study of Mr McTodd's masterpieces. Psmith sat down and resumed his reading.

'Across the pale parabola of Joy...'

Psmith knitted his brow. It was just the sort of line which was likely to have puzzled his patroness, Lady Constance, and he anticipated that she would come to him directly he arrived and ask for an explanation. It would obviously be a poor start for his visit to confess that he had no theory as to its meaning himself. He tried it again.

'Across the pale parabola of Joy...'

A sound like two or three pigs feeding rather noisily in the middle of a thunderstorm interrupted his meditations. Psmith laid his book down and gazed in a pained way across the compartment. There came to him a sense of being unfairly put upon, as towards the end of his troubles it might have come upon Job. This, he felt, was too much. He was being harried.

The man in the corner went on snoring.

* * * * *

There is always a way. Almost immediately Psmith saw what Napoleon would have done in this crisis. On the seat beside the sleeper was lying a compact little suit-case with hard, sharp edges. Rising softly, Psmith edged along the compartment and secured this. Then, having balanced it carefully on the rack above the sleeper's stomach, he returned to his seat to await developments.

These were not long in coming. The train, now flying at its best speed through open country, was shaking itself at intervals in a vigorous way as it raced along. A few seconds later it apparently passed over some points, and shivered briskly down its whole length. The suit-case wobbled insecurely, hesitated, and fell chunkily in the exact middle of its owner's waistcoat. There was a smothered gulp beneath the handkerchief. The sleeper sat up with a jerk. The handkerchief fell off. And there was revealed to Psmith's interested gaze the face of the Hon. Freddie Threepwood.

§ 2

'Goo!' observed Freddie. He removed the bag from his midriff and began to massage the stricken spot. Then suddenly perceiving that he was not alone he looked up and saw Psmith.

'Goo!' said Freddie, and sat staring wildly.

Nobody is more alive than we are to the fact that the dialogue of Frederick Threepwood, recorded above, is not bright. Nevertheless, those were his opening remarks, and the excuse must be that he had passed through a trying time and had just received two shocks, one after the other. From the first of these, the physical impact of the suit-case, he was recovering; but the second had simply paralysed him. When, the mists of sleep having cleared away, he saw sitting but a few feet away from him on the train that was carrying him home the very man with whom he had plotted in the lobby of the Piccadilly Palace Hotel, a cold fear gripped Freddie's very vitals.

Freddie's troubles had begun when he just missed the twelve-fifty train. This disaster had perturbed him greatly, for he could not forget his father's stern injunctions on the subject. But what had really upset him was the fact that he had come within an ace of missing the five o'clock train as well. He had spent the afternoon in a motion-picture palace, and the fascination of the film had caused him to lose all sense of time, so that only the slow fade-out on the embrace and the words 'The End' reminded him to look at his watch. A mad rush had got him to Paddington just as the five o'clock express was leaving the station. Exhausted, he had fallen into a troubled sleep, from which he had been aroused by a violent blow in the waistcoat and the nightmare vision of Psmith in the seat across the compartment. One cannot wonder in these circumstances that Freddie did not immediately soar to the heights of eloquence.

The picture which the Hon. Frederick Threepwood had selected for his patronage that afternoon was the well-known super-super-film, 'Fangs of the Past', featuring Bertha Blevitch and Maurice Heddlestone – which, as everybody knows, is all about blackmail. Green-walled by primeval hills, bathed in the golden sunshine of peace and happiness, the village of Honeydean slumbered in the clear morning air. But off the train from the city stepped A Stranger – (The Stranger –

Maxwell Bannister). He inquired of a passing rustic – (The Passing Rustic – Claude Hepworth) – the way to the great house where Myrtle Dale, the Lady Bountiful of the village ... well, anyway, it is all about blackmail, and it had affected Freddie profoundly. It still coloured his imagination, and the conclusion to which he came the moment he saw Psmith was that the latter had shadowed him and was following him home with the purpose of extracting hush-money.

While he was still gurgling wordlessly, Psmith opened the conversation.

'A delightful and unexpected pleasure, comrade. I thought you had left the Metropolis some hours since.'

As Freddie sat looking like a cornered dormouse a voice from the corridor spoke.

'Ah, there you are, my dear fellow!'

Lord Emsworth was beaming in the doorway. His slumbers, like those of Freddie, had not lasted long. He had been aroused only a few minutes after Psmith's departure by the arrival of the retriever from the next compartment, which, bored by the society of its owner, had strolled off on a tour of investigation and, finding next door an old acquaintance in the person of his lordship, had jumped on the seat and licked his face with such hearty good will that further sleep was out of the question. Being awake, Lord Emsworth, as always when he was awake, had begun to potter.

When he saw Freddie his amiability suffered a shock.

'Frederick! I thought I told you to be sure to return on the twelve-fifty train!'

'Missed it, guv'nor,' mumbled Freddie thickly. 'Not my fault.'

'H'mph!' His father seemed about to pursue the subject, but the fact that a stranger and one who was his guest was present apparently decided him to avoid anything in the shape of family wrangles. He peered from Freddie to Psmith and back again. 'Do you two know each other?' he said.

'Not yet,' said Psmith. 'We only met a moment ago.'

'My son Frederick,' said Lord Emsworth, rather in the voice with which he would have called attention to the presence of a slug among his flowers. 'Frederick, this is Mr McTodd, the poet, who is coming to stay at Blandings.'

Freddie started, and his mouth opened. But, meeting Psmith's friendly gaze, he closed the orifice again without speaking. He licked his lips in an overwrought way.

'You'll find me next door, if you want me,' said Lord Emsworth to Psmith. 'Just discovered that George Willard, very old friend of mine, is in there. Never saw him get on the train. His dog came into my compartment and licked my face. One of my neighbours. A remarkable rose-grower. As you are so interested in flowers, I will take you over to his place some time. Why don't you join us now?'

'I would prefer, if you do not mind,' said Psmith, 'to remain here for the moment and foster what I feel sure is about to develop into a great and lasting friendship. I am convinced that your son and I will have much to talk about together.'

'Very well, my dear fellow. We will meet at dinner in the restaurant-car.'

Lord Emsworth pottered off, and Psmith rose and closed the door. He returned to his seat to find Freddie regarding him with a tortured expression in his rather prominent eyes. Freddie's brain had had more exercise in the last few minutes than in years of his normal life, and he was feeling the strain.

'I say, what?' he observed feebly.

'If there is anything,' said Psmith kindly, 'that I can do to clear up any little difficulty that is perplexing you, call on me. What is biting you?'

Freddie swallowed convulsively.

'I say, he said your name was McTodd!'

'Precisely.'

'But you said it was Psmith.'

'It is.'

'Then why did father call you McTodd?'

'He thinks I am. It is a harmless error, and I see no reason why it should be discouraged.'

'But why does he think you're McTodd?'

'It is a long story, which you may find tedious. But, if you really wish to hear it . . .'

Nothing could have exceeded the raptness of Freddie's attention as he listened to the tale of the encounter with Lord Emsworth at the Senior Conservative Club.

'Do you mean to say,' he demanded at its conclusion, 'that you're coming to Blandings pretending to be this poet blighter?'

'That is the scheme.'

'But why?'

'I have my reasons, Comrade – what is the name? Threepwood? I thank you. You will pardon me, Comrade Threepwood, if I do not go into them. And now,' said Psmith, 'to resume our very interesting chat which was unfortunately cut short this morning, why do you want me to steal your aunt's necklace?'

Freddie jumped. For the moment, so tensely had the fact of his companion's audacity chained his interest, he had actually forgotten about the necklace.

'Great Scott!' he exclaimed. 'Why, of course!'

'You still have not made it quite clear.'

'It fits splendidly.'

'The necklace?'

'I mean to say, the great difficulty would have been to find a way of getting you into the house, and here you are, coming there as this poet bird. Topping!'

'If,' said Psmith, regarding him patiently through his eyeglass, 'I do not seem to be immediately infected by your joyous enthusiasm, put it down to the fact that I haven't the remotest idea what you're talking about. Could you give me a pointer or two? What, for instance, assuming that I agreed to steal your aunt's necklace, would you expect me to do with it, when and if stolen?'

'Why, hand it over to me.'

'I see. And what would you do with it?'

'Hand it over to my uncle.'

'And whom would he hand it over to?'

'Look here,' said Freddie, 'I might as well start at the beginning.'

'An excellent idea.'

The speed at which the train was now proceeding had begun to render conversation in anything but stentorian tones somewhat difficult. Freddie accordingly bent forward till his mouth almost touched Psmith's ear.

'You see, it's like this. My uncle, old Joe Keeble . . .'

'Keeble?' said Psmith. 'Why,' he murmured meditatively, 'is that name familiar?'

'Don't interrupt, old lad,' pleaded Freddie.

'I stand corrected.'

'Uncle Joe has a stepdaughter – Phyllis her name is – and some time ago she popped off and married a cove called Jackson . . .'

Psmith did not interrupt the narrative again, but as it proceeded his look of interest deepened. And at the conclusion he patted his companion encouragingly on the shoulder.

'The proceeds, then, of this jewel-robbery, if it comes off,' he said, 'will go to establish the Jackson home on a firm footing? Am I right in thinking that?'

'Absolutely.'

'There is no danger – you will pardon the suggestion – of you clinging like glue to the swag and using it to maintain yourself in the position to which you are accustomed?'

'Absolutely not. Uncle Joe is giving me – er – giving me a bit for myself. Just a small bit, you understand. This is the scheme. You sneak the necklace and hand it over to me. I push the necklace over to Uncle Joe, who hides it somewhere for the moment. There is the dickens of a fuss, and Uncle Joe comes out strong by telling Aunt Constance that he'll buy her another necklace, just as good. Then he takes the stones out of the necklace, has them reset, and gives them to Aunt Constance. Looks like a new necklace, if you see what I mean. Then he draws a cheque for twenty thousand quid, which Aunt Constance naturally thinks is for the new necklace, and he shoves the money somewhere as a little private account. He gives Phyllis her money, and everybody's happy. Aunt Constance has got her necklace, Phyllis has got her money, and all that's happened is that Aunt Constance's and Uncle Joe's combined bank balance has had a bit of a hole knocked in it. See?'

'I see. It is a little difficult to follow all the necklaces. I seemed to count about seventeen of them while you were talking, but I suppose I was wrong. Yes, I see, Comrade Threepwood, and I may say at once that you can rely on my co-operation.'

'You'll do it?'

'I will.'

'Of course,' said Freddie awkwardly, 'I'll see that you get a bit all right. I mean . . .'

Psmith waved his hand deprecatingly.

'My dear Comrade Threepwood, let us not become sordid on this glad occasion. As far as I am concerned, there will be no charge.'

'What! But look here . . .'

'Any assistance I can give will be offered in a purely amateur spirit. I would have mentioned before, only I was reluctant to interrupt you, that Comrade Jackson is my boyhood chum, and that Phyllis, his wife, injects into my life the few beams of sunshine that illumine its dreary round. I have long desired to do something to ameliorate their lot, and now that the chance has come I am delighted. It is true that I am not a man of affluence – my bank-manager, I am told, winces in a rather painful manner whenever my name is mentioned – but I am not so reduced that I must charge a fee for performing, on behalf of a pal, a simple act of courtesy like pinching a twenty thousand pound necklace.'

'Good Lord! Fancy that!'

'Fancy what, Comrade Threepwood?'

'Fancy your knowing Phyllis and her husband.'

'It is odd, no doubt. But true. Many a whack at the cold beef have I had on Sunday evenings under their roof, and I am much obliged to you for putting in my way this opportunity of repaying their hospitality. Thank you!'

'Oh, that's all right,' said Freddie, somewhat bewildered by this eloquence.

'Even if the little enterprise meets with disaster, the reflection that I did my best for the young couple will be a great consolation to me when I am serving my bit of time in Worm-wood Scrubs. It will cheer me up. The jailers will cluster outside the door to listen to me singing in my cell. My pet rat, as he creeps out to share the crumbs of my breakfast, will wonder why I whistle as I pick the morning's oakum. I shall join in the hymns on Sundays in a way that will electrify the chaplain. That is to say, if anything goes wrong and I am what I believe is technically termed "copped". I say "if",' said Psmith, gazing solemnly at his companion. 'But I do not intend to be copped. I have never gone in largely for crime hitherto, but something tells me I shall be rather good at it. I look forward confidently to making a nice, clean job of the thing. And now, Comrade Threepwood, I must ask you to excuse me while I get the half-nelson on this rather poisonous poetry of good old McTodd's. From the cursory glance I have taken at it, the stuff doesn't seem to mean anything. I think the boy's *non compos*. *You* don't happen to understand the expression "Across the pale parabola of Joy", do you? ... I feared as much. Well, pip-pip for the present, Comrade Threepwood. I shall now ask you to retire into your corner and amuse yourself for a while as you best can. I must concentrate, concentrate.'

And Psmith, having put his feet up on the opposite seat and reopened the mauve volume, began to read. Freddie, his mind still in a whirl, looked out of the window at the passing scenery in a mood which was a nice blend of elation and apprehension.

§ 3

Although the hands of the station clock pointed to several minutes past nine, it was still apparently early evening when the train drew up at the platform of Market Blandings and discharged its distinguished passengers. The sun, taken in as usual by the never-failing practical joke of the Daylight Saving Act, had only just set, and a golden afterglow lingered on the fields as the car which had met the train purred over the two miles of country road that separated the little town from the castle. As they passed in between the great stone gate-posts and shot up the winding drive, the soft murmur of the engines seemed to deepen rather than break the soothing stillness. The air was fragrant with indescribable English scents. Somewhere in the distance sheep-bells tinkled; rabbits, waggling white tails, bolted across the path; and once a herd of agitated deer made a brief appearance among the trees. The only thing that disturbed the magic hush was the fluting voice of Lord Emsworth, on whom the spectacle of his beloved property had acted as an immediate stimulant. Unlike his son Freddie, who sat silent in his corner wrestling with his hopes and fears, Lord Emsworth had plunged into a perfect Niagara of speech the moment the car entered the park. In a high tenor voice, and with wide, excited gestures, he pointed out to Psmith oaks with a history and rhododendrons with a past: his conversation as they drew near the castle and came in sight of the flower-beds taking on an almost lyrical note and becoming a sort of anthem of gladness, through which, like some theme in the minor, ran a series of opprobrious observations on the subject of Angus McAllister.

Beach, the butler, solicitously scooping them out of the car at the front door, announced that her ladyship and Miss Peavey were taking their after-dinner coffee in the arbour by the bowling-green; and presently Psmith, conducted by his lordship, found himself shaking hands with a strikingly handsome woman in whom, though her manner was friendliness itself, he could detect a marked suggestion of the formidable. Æsthetically, he admired Lady Constance's appearance, but he could not conceal from himself that in the peculiar circumstances he would have preferred something rather more fragile and drooping. Lady Constance conveyed the impression that anybody who had the choice between stealing anything from her and stirring up a nest of hornets with a short walking-stick would do well to choose the hornets.

'How do you do, Mr McTodd?' said Lady Constance with great amiability. 'I am so glad you were able to come after all.'

Psmith wondered what she meant by 'after all', but there were so many things about his present situation calculated to tax the mind that he had no desire to probe slight verbal ambiguities. He shook her hand and replied that it was very kind of her to say so.

'We are quite a small party at present,' continued Lady Constance, 'but we are expecting a number of people quite soon. For the moment Aileen and you are our only guests. Oh, I am sorry, I should have . . . Miss Peavey, Mr McTodd.'

The slim and willowy female who during this brief conversation had been waiting in an attitude of suspended animation, gazing at Psmith with large, wistful eyes, stepped forward. She clasped Psmith's hand in hers, held it, and in a low, soft voice, like thick cream made audible, uttered one reverent word.

'*Maître!*'

'I beg your pardon?' said Psmith. A young man capable of bearing himself with calm and dignity in most circumstances, however trying, he found his poise wobbling under the impact of Miss Aileen Peavey.

Miss Peavey often had this effect on the less soulful type of man, especially in the mornings, when such men are not at their strongest and best. When she came into the breakfast-room of a country house, brave men who had been up a bit late the night before quailed and tried to hide behind newspapers. She was the sort of woman who tells a man who is propping his eyes open with his fingers and endeavouring to correct a headache with strong tea, that she was up at six watching the dew fade off the grass, and didn't he think that those wisps of morning mist were the elves' bridal-veils. She had large, fine, melancholy eyes, and was apt to droop dreamily.

'Master!' said Miss Peavey, obligingly translating.

There did not seem to be any immediate come-back to a remark like this, so Psmith contented himself with beaming genially at her through his monocle: and Miss Peavey came to bat again.

'How wonderful that you were able to come – after all!'

Again this 'after all' motive creeping into the theme....

'You know Miss Peavey's work, of course?' said Lady Constance, smiling pleasantly on her two celebrities.

'Who does not?' said Psmith courteously.

'Oh, *do* you?' said Miss Peavey, gratification causing her slender body to perform a sort of ladylike shimmy down its whole length. 'I scarcely hoped that you would know my name. My Canadian sales have not been large.'

'Quite large enough,' said Psmith. 'I mean, of course,' he added with a paternal smile, 'that, while your delicate art may not have a universal appeal in a young country, it is intensely appreciated by a small and select body of the intelligentsia.'

And if that was not the stuff to give them, he reflected with not a little complacency, he was dashed.

'Your own wonderful poems,' replied Miss Peavey, 'are, of course, known the whole world over. Oh, Mr McTodd, you can hardly appreciate how I feel, meeting you. It is like the realisation of some golden dream of childhood. It is like ...'

Here the Hon. Freddie Threepwood remarked suddenly that he was going to pop into the house for a whisky and soda. As he had not previously spoken, his observation had something of the effect of a voice from the tomb. The daylight was ebbing fast now, and in the shadows he had contrived to pass out of sight as well as out of mind. Miss Peavey started like an abruptly awakened somnambulist, and Psmith was at last able to release his hand, which he had begun to look on as gone beyond his control for ever. Until this fortunate interruption there had seemed no reason why Miss Peavey should not have continued to hold it till bedtime.

Freddie's departure had the effect of breaking a spell. Lord Emsworth, who had been standing perfectly still with vacant eyes, like a dog listening to a noise a long way off, came to life with a jerk.

'I'm going to have a look at my flowers,' he announced.

'Don't be silly, Clarence,' said his sister. 'It's much too dark to see flowers.'

'I could smell 'em,' retorted his lordship argumentatively.

It seemed as if the party must break up, for already his lordship had begun to potter off, when a new-comer arrived to solidify it again.

'Ah, Baxter, my dear fellow,' said Lord Emsworth. 'Here we are, you see.'

'Mr Baxter,' said Lady Constance, 'I want you to meet Mr McTodd.'

'Mr McTodd!' said the new arrival, on a note of surprise.

'Yes, he found himself able to come after all.'

'Ah!' said the Efficient Baxter.

It occurred to Psmith as a passing thought, to which he gave no more than a momentary attention, that this spectacled and capable-looking man was gazing at him, as they shook hands, with a curious intensity. But possibly, he reflected, this was merely a species of optical illusion due to the other's spectacles. Baxter, staring through his spectacles, often gave people the impression of possessing an eye that could pierce six inches of harveyised steel and stick out on the other side. Having registered in his consciousness the fact that he had been stared at keenly by this stranger, Psmith thought no more of the matter.

In thus lightly dismissing the Baxterian stare, Psmith had acted injudiciously. He should have examined it more closely and made an effort to analyse it, for it was by no means without its message. It was a stare of suspicion. Vague suspicion as yet, but nevertheless suspicion. Rupert Baxter was one of those men whose chief characteristic is a disposition to suspect their fellows. He did not suspect them of this or that definite crime: he simply suspected them. He had not yet definitely accused Psmith in his mind of any specific tort or malfeasance. He merely had a nebulous feeling that he would bear watching.

Miss Peavey now fluttered again into the centre of things. On the arrival of Baxter she had withdrawn for a moment into the background, but she was not the woman to stay there long. She came forward holding out a small oblong book, which, with a languishing firmness, she pressed into Psmith's hands.

'Could I persuade you, Mr McTodd,' said Miss Peavey pleadingly, 'to write some little thought in my autograph-book and sign it? I have a fountain-pen.'

Light flooded the arbour. The Efficient Baxter, who knew where everything was, had found and pressed the switch. He did this not so much to oblige Miss Peavey as to enable him to obtain a clearer view of the visitor. With each minute that passed

the Efficient Baxter was finding himself more and more doubtful in his mind about this visitor.

'There!' said Miss Peavey, welcoming the illumination.

Psmith tapped his chin thoughtfully with the fountain-pen.
He felt that he should have foreseen this emergency earlier. If
ever there was a woman who was bound to have an autograph-
book, that woman was Miss Peavey.

'Just some little thought...'

Psmith hesitated no longer. In a firm hand he wrote the words
'Across the pale parabola of Joy...' added an unfaltering 'Ralston McTodd', and handed the book back.

'How strange,' sighed Miss Peavey.

'May I look?' said Baxter, moving quickly to her side.

'How strange!' repeated Miss Peavey. 'To think that you
should have chosen that line! There are several of your more
mystic passages that I meant to ask you to explain, but particularly "Across the pale parabola of Joy"...'

'You find it difficult to understand?'

'A little, I confess.'

'Well, well,' said Psmith indulgently, 'perhaps I did put a bit of
top-spin on that one.'

'I beg your pardon?'

'I say, perhaps it is a little obscure. We must have a long chat
about it – later on.'

'Why not now?' demanded the Efficient Baxter, flashing his
spectacles.

'I am rather tired,' said Psmith with gentle reproach, 'after my
journey. Fatigued. We artists...'

'Of course,' said Miss Peavey, with an indignant glance at the
secretary. 'Mr Baxter does not understand the sensitive poetic
temperament.'

'A bit unspiritual, eh?' said Psmith tolerantly. 'A trifle earthy? So I thought, so I thought. One of these strong, hard men of affairs, I shouldn't wonder.'

'Shall we go and find Lord Emsworth, Mr McTodd?' said Miss Peavey, dismissing the fermenting Baxter with a scornful look. 'He wandered off just now. I suppose he is among his flowers. Flowers are very beautiful by night.'

'Indeed, yes,' said Psmith. 'And also by day. When I am surrounded by flowers, a sort of divine peace floods over me, and the rough, harsh world seems far away. I feel soothed, tranquil. I sometimes think, Miss Peavey, that flowers must be the souls of little children who have died in their innocence.'

'What a beautiful thought, Mr McTodd!' exclaimed Miss Peavey rapturously.

'Yes,' agreed Psmith. 'Don't pinch it. It's copyright.'

The darkness swallowed them up. Lady Constance turned to the Efficient Baxter, who was brooding with furrowed brow.

'Charming, is he not?'

'I beg your pardon?'

'I said I thought Mr McTodd was charming.'

'Oh, quite.'

'Completely unspoiled.'

'Oh, decidedly.'

'I am so glad that he was able to come after all. That telegram he sent this afternoon cancelling his visit seemed so curt and final.'

'So I thought it.'

'Almost as if he had taken offence at something and decided to have nothing to do with us.'

'Quite.'

Lady Constance shivered delicately. A cool breeze had sprung up. She drew her wrap more closely about her shapely shoulders, and began to walk to the house. Baxter did not accompany her. The moment she had gone he switched off the light and sat down, chin in hand. That massive brain was working hard.

§ 1

'Miss Halliday,' announced the Efficient Baxter, removing another letter from its envelope and submitting it to a swift, keen scrutiny, 'arrives at about three to-day. She is catching the twelve-fifty train.'

He placed the letter on the pile beside his plate; and, having decapitated an egg, peered sharply into its interior as if hoping to surprise guilty secrets. For it was the breakfast hour, and the members of the house party, scattered up and down the long table, were fortifying their tissues against another day. An agreeable scent of bacon floated over the scene like a benediction.

Lord Emsworth looked up from the seed catalogue in which he was immersed. For some time past his enjoyment of the meal had been marred by a vague sense of something missing, and now he knew what it was.

'Coffee!' he said, not violently, but in the voice of a good man oppressed. 'I want coffee. Why have I no coffee? Constance, my dear, I should have coffee. Why have I none?'

'I'm sure I gave you some,' said Lady Constance, brightly presiding over the beverages at the other end of the table.

'Then where is it?' demanded his lordship clinchingly.

Baxter – almost regretfully, it seemed – gave the egg a clean bill of health, and turned in his able way to cope with this domestic problem.

'Your coffee is behind the catalogue you are reading, Lord Emsworth. You propped the catalogue against your cup.'

'Did I? Did I? Why, so I did! Bless my soul!' His lordship, relieved, took an invigorating sip. 'What were you saying just then, my dear fellow?'

'I have had a letter from Miss Halliday,' said Baxter. 'She writes that she is catching the twelve-fifty train at Paddington, which means that she should arrive at Market Blandings at about three.'

'Who,' asked Miss Peavey, in a low, thrilling voice, ceasing for a moment to peck at her plate of kedgeree, 'is Miss Halliday?'

'The exact question I was about to ask myself,' said Lord Emsworth. 'Baxter, my dear fellow, who is Miss Halliday?'

Baxter, with a stifled sigh, was about to refresh his employer's memory, when Psmith anticipated him. Psmith had been consuming toast and marmalade with his customary languid grace and up till now had firmly checked all attempts to engage him in conversation.

'Miss Halliday,' he said, 'is a very old and valued friend of mine. We two have, so to speak, pulled the gowans fine. I had been hoping to hear that she had been sighted on the horizon.'

The effect of these words on two of the company was somewhat remarkable. Baxter, hearing them, gave such a violent start that he spilled half the contents of his cup: and Freddie, who had been flitting like a butterfly among the dishes on the sideboard and had just decided to help himself to scrambled eggs, deposited a liberal spoonful on the carpet, where it was found and salvaged a moment later by Lady Constance's spaniel.

Psmith did not observe these phenomena, for he had returned to his toast and marmalade. He thus missed encountering perhaps the keenest glance that had ever come through Rupert Baxter's spectacles. It was not a protracted glance, but while it lasted it was like the ray from an oxy-acetylene blowpipe.

'A friend of yours?' said Lord Emsworth. 'Indeed? Of course, Baxter, I remember now. Miss Halliday is the young lady who is coming to catalogue the library.'

'What a delightful task!' cooed Miss Peavey. 'To live among the stored-up thoughts of dead and gone genius!'

'You had better go down and meet her, my dear fellow,' said Lord Emsworth. 'At the station, you know,' he continued, clarifying his meaning. 'She will be glad to see you.'

'I was about to suggest it myself,' said Psmith.

'Though why the library needs cataloguing,' said his lordship, returning to a problem which still vexed his soul when he had leisure to give a thought to it, 'I can't . . . However . . .'

He finished his coffee and rose from the table. A stray shaft of sunlight had fallen provocatively on his bald head, and sunshine always made him restive.

'Are you going to your flowers, Lord Emsworth?' asked Miss Peavey.

'Eh? What? Yes. Oh, yes. Going to have a look at those lobelias.'

'I will accompany you, if I may,' said Psmith.

'Eh? Why, certainly, certainly.'

'I have always held,' said Psmith, 'that there is no finer tonic than a good look at a lobelia immediately after breakfast. Doctors, I believe, recommend it.'

'Oh, I say,' said Freddie hastily, as he reached the door, 'can I have a couple of words with you a bit later on?'

'A thousand if you wish it,' said Psmith. 'You will find me somewhere out there in the great open spaces where men are men.'

He included the entire company in a benevolent smile, and left the room.

'How charming he is!' sighed Miss Peavey. 'Don't you think so, Mr Baxter?'

The Efficient Baxter seemed for a moment to find some difficulty in replying.

'Oh, very,' he said, but not heartily.

'And such a *soul*! It shines on that wonderful brow of his, doesn't it?'

'He has a good forehead,' said Lady Constance. 'But I wish he wouldn't wear his hair so short. Somehow it makes him seem unlike a poet.'

Freddie, alarmed, swallowed a mouthful of scrambled egg.

'Oh, he's a poet all right,' he said hastily.

'Well, really, Freddie,' said Lady Constance, piqued, 'I think we hardly need *you* to tell us that.'

'No, no, of course. But what I mean is, in spite of his wearing his hair short, you know.'

'I ventured to speak to him of that yesterday,' said Miss Peavey, 'and he said he rather expected to be wearing it even shorter very soon.'

'Freddie!' cried Lady Constance with asperity. 'What *are* you doing?'

A brown lake of tea was filling the portion of the tablecloth immediately opposite the Hon. Frederick Threepwood. Like the Efficient Baxter a few minutes before, sudden emotion had caused him to upset his cup.

§ 2

The scrutiny of his lordship's lobelias had palled upon Psmith at a fairly early stage in the proceedings, and he was sitting on the terrace wall enjoying a meditative cigarette when Freddie found him.

'Ah, Comrade Threepwood,' said Psmith, 'welcome to Blandings Castle! You said something about wishing to have speech with me, if I remember rightly?'

The Hon. Freddie shot a nervous glance about him, and seated himself on the wall.

'I say,' he said, 'I wish you wouldn't say things like that.'

'Like what, Comrade Threepwood?'

'What you said to the Peavey woman.'

'I recollect having a refreshing chat with Miss Peavey yesterday afternoon,' said Psmith, 'but I cannot recall saying anything calculated to bring the blush of shame to the cheek of modesty. What observation of mine was it that meets with your censure?'

'Why, that stuff about expecting to wear your hair shorter. If you're going to go about saying that sort of thing – well, dash it, you might just as well give the whole bally show away at once and have done with it.'

Psmith nodded gravely.

'Your generous heat, Comrade Threepwood, is not unjustified. It was undoubtedly an error of judgment. If I have a fault – which I am not prepared to admit – it is a perhaps ungentlemanly desire to pull that curious female's leg. A stronger man than myself might well find it hard to battle against the temptation. However, now that you have called it to my notice, it shall not occur again. In future I will moderate the persiflage. Cheer up, therefore, Comrade Threepwood, and let us see that merry smile of yours, of which I hear such good reports.'

The appeal failed to alleviate Freddie's gloom. He smote morosely at a fly which had settled on his furrowed brow.

'I'm getting as jumpy as a cat,' he said.

'Fight against this unmanly weakness,' urged Psmith. 'As far as I can see, everything is going along nicely.'

'I'm not so sure. I believe that blighter Baxter suspects something.'

'What do you think he suspects?'

'Why, that there's something fishy about you.'

Psmith winced.

'I would be infinitely obliged to you, Comrade Threepwood, if you would not use that particular adjective. It awakens old memories, all very painful. But let us go more deeply into this matter, for you interest me strangely. Why do you think that cheery old Baxter, a delightful personality if ever I met one, suspects me?'

'It's the way he looks at you.'

'I know what you mean, but I attribute no importance to it. As far as I have been able to ascertain during my brief visit, he looks at everybody and everything in precisely the same way. Only last night at dinner I observed him glaring with keen mistrust at about as blameless and innocent a plate of clear soup as was ever dished up. He then proceeded to shovel it down with quite undisguised relish. So possibly you are all wrong about his motive for looking at me like that. It may be admiration.'

'Well, I don't like it.'

'Nor, from an æsthetic point of view, do I. But we must bear these things manfully. We must remind ourselves that it is

Baxter's misfortune rather than his fault that he looks like a dyspeptic lizard.'

Freddie was not to be consoled. His gloom deepened.

'And it isn't only Baxter.'

'What else is on your mind?'

'The whole atmosphere of the place is getting rummy, if you know what I mean.' He bent towards Psmith and whispered pallidly, 'I say, I believe that new housemaid is a detective!'

Psmith eyed him patiently.

'Which new housemaid, Comrade Threepwood? Brooding, as I do, pretty tensely all the time on deep and wonderful subjects, I have little leisure to keep tab on the domestic staff. *Is* there a new housemaid?'

'Yes. Susan, her name is.'

'Susan? Susan? That sounds all right. Just the name a real housemaid would have.'

'Did you ever,' demanded Freddie earnestly, 'see a real housemaid sweep under a bureau?'

'Does she?'

'Caught her at it in my room this morning.'

'But isn't it a trifle far-fetched to imagine that she is a detective? Why should she be a detective?'

'Well, I've seen such a dashed lot of films where the housemaid or the parlourmaid or what not were detectives. Makes a fellow uneasy.'

'Fortunately,' said Psmith, 'there is no necessity to remain in a state of doubt. I can give you an unfailing method by means of which you may discover if she is what she would have us believe her.'

'What's that?'

'Kiss her.'

'Kiss her!'

'Precisely. Go to her and say, "Susan, you're a very pretty girl . . ."'

'But she isn't.'

'We will assume, for purposes of argument, that she is. Go to her and say, "Susan, you are a very pretty girl. What would you do if I were to kiss you?" If she is a detective, she will reply, "How dare you, sir!" or, possibly, more simply, "Sir!" Whereas if she is the genuine housemaid I believe her to be and only sweeps under bureaux out of pure zeal, she will giggle and remark, "Oh, don't be silly, sir!" You appreciate the distinction?'

'How do you know?'

'My grandmother told me, Comrade Threepwood. My advice to you, if the state of doubt you are in is affecting your enjoyment of life, is to put the matter to the test at the earliest convenient opportunity.'

'I'll think it over,' said Freddie dubiously.

Silence fell upon him for a space, and Psmith was well content to have it so. He had no specific need of Freddie's prattle to help him enjoy the pleasant sunshine and the scent of Angus McAllister's innumerable flowers. Presently, however, his companion was off again. But now there was a different note in his voice. Alarm seemed to have given place to something which appeared to be embarrassment. He coughed several times, and his neatly-shod feet, writhing in self-conscious circles, scraped against the wall.

'I say!'

'You have our ear once more, Comrade Threepwood,' said Psmith politely.

'I say, what I really came out here to talk about was something else. I say, are you really a pal of Miss Halliday's?'

'Assuredly. Why?'

'I say!' A rosy blush mantled the Hon. Freddie's young cheek. 'I say, I wish you would put in a word for me, then.'

'Put in a word for you?'

Freddie gulped.

'I love her, dash it!'

'A noble emotion,' said Psmith courteously. 'When did you feel it coming on?'

'I've been in love with her for months. But she won't look at me.'

'That, of course,' agreed Psmith, 'must be a disadvantage. Yes, I should imagine that that would stick the gaff into the course of true love to no small extent.'

'I mean, won't take me seriously, and all that. Laughs at me, don't you know, when I propose. What would you do?'

'I should stop proposing,' said Psmith, having given the matter thought.

'But I can't.'

'Tut, tut!' said Psmith severely. 'And, in case the expression is new to you, what I mean is "Pooh, pooh!" Just say to yourself, "From now on I will not start proposing until after lunch." That done, it will be an easy step to do no proposing during the afternoon. And by degrees you will find that you can give it up altogether. Once you have conquered the impulse for the after-breakfast proposal, the rest will be easy. The first one of the day is always the hardest to drop.'

'I believe she thinks me a mere butterfly,' said Freddie, who had not been listening to this most valuable homily.

Psmith slid down from the wall and stretched himself.

'Why,' he said, 'are butterflies so often described as "mere"? I have heard them so called a hundred times, and I cannot understand the reason.... Well, it would, no doubt, be both interesting and improving to go into the problem, but at this point, Comrade Threepwood, I leave you. I would brood.'

'Yes, but, I say, will you?'

'Will I what?'

'Put in a word for me?'

'If,' said Psmith, 'the subject crops up in the course of the chit-chat, I shall be delighted to spread myself with no little vim on the theme of your fine qualities.'

He melted away into the shrubbery, just in time to avoid Miss Peavey, who broke in on Freddie's meditations a moment later and kept him company till lunch.

§ 3

The twelve-fifty train drew up with a grinding of brakes at the platform of Market Blandings, and Psmith, who had been whiling away the time of waiting by squandering money which he could ill afford on the slot-machine which supplied butter-scotch, turned and submitted it to a grave scrutiny. Eve Halliday got out of a third-class compartment.

'Welcome to our village, Miss Halliday,' said Psmith, advancing.

Eve regarded him with frank astonishment.

'What are you doing here?' she asked.

'Lord Emsworth was kind enough to suggest that, as we were such old friends, I should come down in the car and meet you.'

'Are we old friends?'

'Surely. Have you forgotten all those happy days in London?'

'There was only one.'

'True. But think how many meetings we crammed into it.'

'Are you staying at the castle?'

'Yes. And what is more, I am the life and soul of the party. Have you anything in the shape of luggage?'

'I nearly always take luggage when I am going to stay a month or so in the country. It's at the back somewhere.'

'I will look after it. You will find the car outside. If you care to go and sit in it, I will join you in a moment. And, lest the time hangs heavy on your hands, take this. Butter-scotch. Delicious, and, so I understand, wholesome. I bought it specially for you.'

A few minutes later, having arranged for the trunk to be taken to the castle, Psmith emerged from the station and found Eve drinking in the beauties of the town of Market Blandings.

'What a delightful old place,' she said as they drove off. 'I almost wish I lived here.'

'During the brief period of my stay at the castle,' said Psmith, 'the same thought has occurred to me. It is the sort of place where one feels that one could gladly settle down into a peaceful retirement and grow a honey-coloured beard.' He looked at her with solemn admiration. 'Women are wonderful,' he said.

'And why, Mr Bones, are women wonderful?' asked Eve.

'I was thinking at the moment of your appearance. You have just stepped off the train after a four-hour journey, and you are as fresh and blooming as − if I may coin a simile − a rose. How do you do it? When I arrived I was deep in alluvial deposits, and have only just managed to scrape them off.'

'When did you arrive?'

'On the evening of the day on which I met you.'

'But it's so extraordinary. That you should be here, I mean. I was wondering if I should ever see you again.' Eve coloured a little, and went on rather hurriedly. 'I mean, it seems so strange that we should always be meeting like this.'

'Fate, probably,' said Psmith. 'I hope it isn't going to spoil your visit?'

'Oh, no.'

'I could have done with a trifle more emphasis on the last word,' said Psmith gently. 'Forgive me for criticising your methods of voice production, but surely you can see how much better it would have sounded spoken thus: "Oh, *no!*"'

Eve laughed.

'Very well, then,' she said. 'Oh, *no!*'

'Much better,' said Psmith. 'Much better.'

He began to see that it was going to be difficult to introduce a eulogy of the Hon. Freddie Threepwood into this conversation.

'I'm very glad you're here,' said Eve, resuming the talk after a slight pause. 'Because, as a matter of fact, I'm feeling just the least bit nervous.'

'Nervous? Why?'

'This is my first visit to a place of this size.' The car had turned in at the big stone gates, and they were bowling smoothly up the winding drive. Through an avenue of trees to the right the great bulk of the castle had just appeared, grey and imposing against the sky. The afternoon sun glittered on the lake beyond it. 'Is everything very stately?'

'Not at all. We are very homely folk, we of Blandings Castle. We go about, simple and unaffected, dropping gracious words all over the place. Lord Emsworth didn't overawe you, did he?'

'Oh, he's a dear. And, of course, I know Freddie quite well.'

Psmith nodded. If she knew Freddie quite well, there was naturally no need to talk about him. He did not talk about him, therefore.

'Have you known Lord Emsworth long?' asked Eve.

'I met him for the first time the day I met you.'

'Good gracious!' Eve stared. 'And he invited you to the castle?'
Psmith smoothed his waistcoat.

'Strange, I agree. One can only account for it, can one not, by supposing that I radiate some extraordinary attraction. Have you noticed it?'

'No!'

'No?' said Psmith, surprised. 'Ah, well,' he went on tolerantly, 'no doubt it will flash upon you quite unexpectedly sooner or later. Like a thunderbolt or something.'

'I think you're terribly conceited.'

'Not at all,' said Psmith. 'Conceited? No, no. Success has not spoiled me.'

'Have you had any success?'

'None whatever.' The car stopped. 'We get down here,' said Psmith, opening the door.

'Here? Why?'

'Because, if we go up to the house, you will infallibly be pounced on and set to work by one Baxter – a delightful fellow, but a whale for toil. I propose to conduct you on a tour round the grounds, and then we will go for a row on the lake. You will enjoy that.'

'You seem to have mapped out my future for me.'

'I have,' said Psmith with emphasis, and in the monocled eye that met hers Eve detected so beaming a glance of esteem and admiration that she retreated warily into herself and endeavoured to be frigid.

'I'm afraid I haven't time to wander about the grounds,' she said aloofly. 'I must be going and seeing Mr Baxter.'

'Baxter,' said Psmith, 'is not one of the natural beauties of the place. Time enough to see him when you are compelled to.... We are now in the southern pleasaunce or the west home-park or something. Note the refined way the deer are cropping the grass. All the ground on which we are now standing is of historic interest. Oliver Cromwell went through here in 1550. The record has since been lowered.'

'I haven't time . . .'

'Leaving the pleasaunce on our left, we proceed to the northern messuage. The dandelions were imported from Egypt by the ninth Earl.'

'Well, anyhow,' said Eve mutinously, 'I won't come on the lake.'

'You will enjoy the lake,' said Psmith. 'The newts are of the famous old Blandings strain. They were introduced, together with the water-beetles, in the reign of Queen Elizabeth. Lord Emsworth, of course, holds manorial rights over the mosquito-swatting.'

Eve was a girl of high and haughty spirit, and as such strongly resented being appropriated and having her movements directed by one who, in spite of his specious claims, was almost a stranger. But somehow she found her companion's placid assumption of authority hard to resist. Almost meekly she accompanied him through meadow and shrubbery, over velvet lawns and past gleaming flower-beds, and her indignation evaporated as her eyes absorbed the beauty of it all. She gave a little sigh. If Market Blandings had seemed a place in which one might dwell happily, Blandings Castle was a paradise.

'Before us now,' said Psmith, 'lies the celebrated Yew Alley, so called from the yews which hem it in. Speaking in my capacity of guide to the estate, I may say that when we have turned this next corner you will see a most remarkable sight.'

And they did. Before them, as they passed in under the boughs of an aged tree, lay a green vista, faintly dappled with stray shafts of sunshine. In the middle of this vista the Hon. Frederick Threepwood was embracing a young woman in the dress of a housemaid.

§ 4

Psmith was the first of the little group to recover from the shock of this unexpected encounter, the Hon. Freddie the last. That unfortunate youth, meeting Eve's astonished eye as he raised his head, froze where he stood and remained with his mouth open until she had disappeared, which she did a few moments later, led away by Psmith, who, as he went, directed at his young friend a look in which surprise, pain, and reproof were so nicely blended that it would have been hard to say which predominated. All that a spectator could have said with certainty was that Psmith's finer feelings had suffered a severe blow.

'A painful scene,' he remarked to Eve, as he drew her away in the direction of the house. 'But we must always strive to be charitable. He may have been taking a fly out of her eye, or teaching her jiu-jitsu.'

He looked at her searchingly.

'You seem less revolted,' he said, 'than one might have expected. This argues a sweet, shall we say angelic disposition and confirms my already high opinion of you.'

'Thank you.'

'Not at all. Mark you,' said Psmith, 'I don't think that this sort of thing is a hobby of Comrade Threepwood's. He probably has many other ways of passing his spare time. Remember that before you pass judgment upon him. Also – Young Blood, and all that sort of thing.'

'I haven't any intention of passing judgment upon him. It doesn't interest me what Mr Threepwood does, either in his spare time or out of it.'

'His interest in you, on the other hand, is vast. I forgot to tell you before, but he loves you. He asked me to mention it if the conversation happened to veer round in that direction.'

'I know he does,' said Eve ruefully.

'And does the fact stir no chord in you?'

'I think he's a nuisance.'

'That,' said Psmith cordially, 'is the right spirit. I like to see it. Very well, then, we will discard the topic of Freddie, and I will try to find others that may interest, elevate, and amuse you. We are now approaching the main buildings. I am no expert in architecture, so cannot tell you all I could wish about the façade, but you can see there *is* a façade, and in my opinion – for what it is worth – a jolly good one. We approach by a sweeping gravel walk.'

'I am going in to report to Mr Baxter,' said Eve with decision. 'It's too absurd. I mustn't spend my time strolling about the grounds. I must see Mr Baxter at once.'

Psmith inclined his head courteously.

'Nothing easier. That big, open window there is the library. Doubtless Comrade Baxter is somewhere inside, toiling away among the archives.'

'Yes, but I can't announce myself by shouting to him.'

'Assuredly not,' said Psmith. 'No need for that at all. Leave it to me.' He stooped and picked up a large flower-pot which stood under the terrace wall, and before Eve could intervene had tossed it lightly through the open window. A muffled thud, followed by a sharp exclamation from within, caused a faint smile of gratification to illumine his solemn countenance.

'He *is* in. I thought he would be. Ah, Baxter,' he said graciously, as the upper half of a body surmounted by a spectacled face framed itself suddenly in the window, 'a pleasant, sunny afternoon. How is everything?'

The Efficient Baxter struggled for utterance.

'You look like the Blessed Damozel gazing down from the gold bar of Heaven,' said Psmith genially. 'Baxter, I want to introduce you to Miss Halliday. She arrived safely after a somewhat fatiguing journey. You will like Miss Halliday. If I had a library, I could not wish for a more courteous, obliging, and capable cataloguist.'

This striking and unsolicited testimonial made no appeal to the Efficient Baxter. His mind seemed occupied with other matters.

'Did you throw that flower-pot?' he demanded coldly.

'You will no doubt,' said Psmith, 'wish on some later occasion to have a nice long talk with Miss Halliday in order to give her an outline of her duties. I have been showing her the grounds and am about to take her for a row on the lake. But after that she will – and I know I may speak for Miss Halliday in this matter – be entirely at your disposal.'

'Did you throw that flower-pot?'

'I look forward confidently to the pleasantest of associations between you and Miss Halliday. You will find her,' said Psmith warmly, 'a willing assistant, a tireless worker.'

'Did you . . . ?'

'But now,' said Psmith, 'I must be tearing myself away. In order to impress Miss Halliday, I put on my best suit when I went to meet her. For a row upon the lake something simpler in pale flannel is indicated. I shall only be a few minutes,' he said to Eve. 'Would you mind meeting me at the boat-house?'

'I am not coming on the lake with you.'

'At the boat-house in – say – six and a quarter minutes,' said Psmith with a gentle smile, and pranced into the house like a long-legged mustang.

Eve remained where she stood, struggling between laughter and embarrassment. The Efficient Baxter was still leaning wrathfully out of the library window, and it began to seem a little difficult to carry on an ordinary conversation. The problem of what she was to say in order to continue the scene in an agreeable manner was solved by the arrival of Lord Emsworth, who pottered out from the bushes with a rake in his hand. He stood eyeing Eve for a moment, then memory seemed to wake. Eve's appearance was easier to remember, possibly, than some of the things which his lordship was wont to forget. He came forward beamingly.

'Ah, there you are, Miss...Dear me, I'm really afraid I have forgotten your name. My memory is excellent as a rule, but I cannot remember names...Miss Halliday. Of course, of course. Baxter, my dear fellow,' he proceeded, sighting the watcher at the window, 'this is Miss Halliday.'

'Mr McTodd,' said the Efficient One sourly, 'has already introduced me to Miss Halliday.'

'Has he? Deuced civil of him, deuced civil of him. But where *is* he?' inquired his lordship, scanning the surrounding scenery with a vague eye.

'He went into the house. After,' said Baxter in a cold voice, 'throwing a flower-pot at me.'

'Doing what?'

'He threw a flower-pot at me,' said Baxter, and vanished moodily.

Lord Emsworth stared at the open window, then turned to Eve for enlightenment.

'*Why* did Baxter throw a flower-pot at McTodd?' he said. 'And,' he went on, ventilating an even deeper question, 'where the deuce did he get a flower-pot? There are no flower-pots in the library.'

Eve, on her side, was also seeking information.

'Did you say his name was McTodd, Lord Emsworth?'

'No, no. Baxter. That was Baxter, my secretary.'

'No, I mean the one who met me at the station.'

'Baxter did not meet you at the station. The man who met you at the station,' said Lord Emsworth, speaking slowly, for women are so apt to get things muddled, 'was McTodd. He's staying here. Constance asked him, and I'm bound to say when I first heard of it I was not any too well pleased. I don't like poets as a rule. But this fellow's so different from the other poets I've met. Different altogether. And,' said Lord Emsworth with not a little heat, 'I strongly object to Baxter throwing flower-pots at him. I won't *have* Baxter throwing flower-pots at my guests,' he said firmly; for Lord Emsworth, though occasionally a little vague, was keenly alive to the ancient traditions of his family regarding hospitality.

'Is Mr McTodd a poet?' said Eve, her heart beating.

'Eh? Oh yes, yes. There seems to be no doubt about that. A Canadian poet. Apparently they have poets out there. And,' demanded his lordship, ever a fair-minded man, 'why not? A remarkably growing country. I was there in the year '98. Or was it,' he added, thoughtfully passing a muddy hand over his chin and leaving a rich brown stain, "99? I forget. My memory isn't good for dates....If you will excuse me, Miss – Miss Halliday, of course – if you will excuse me, I must be leaving you. I have to see McAllister, my head gardener. An obstinate man. A Scotchman. If you go into the house, my sister Constance will give you a cup of tea. I don't know what the time is, but I suppose there will be tea soon. Never take it myself.'

'Mr McTodd asked me to go for a row on the lake.'

'On the lake, eh? On the *lake*?' said his lordship, as if this was the last place in the neighbourhood where he would have expected to hear of people proposing to row. Then he brightened. 'Of course, yes, on the lake. I think you will like the lake. I take a dip there myself every morning before break-fast. I find it good for the health and appetite. I plunge in and swim perhaps fifty yards, and then return.' Lord Emsworth suspended the gossip from the training-camp in order to look at his watch. 'Dear me,' he said, 'I must be going. McAllister has been waiting fully ten minutes. Good-bye, then, for the present, Miss – er – good-bye.'

And Lord Emsworth ambled off, on his face that look of tense concentration which it always wore when interviews with Angus McAllister were in prospect – the look which stern warriors wear when about to meet a foeman worthy of their steel.

§ 5

There was a cold expression in Eve's eyes as she made her way slowly to the boat-house. The information which she had just received had come as a shock, and she was trying to adjust her mind to it. When Miss Clarkson had told her of the unhappy conclusion to her old school friend's marriage to Ralston McTodd, she had immediately, without knowing anything of the facts, arrayed herself loyally on Cynthia's side and condemned the unknown McTodd uncompromisingly and without hesitation. It was many years since she had seen Cynthia, and their friendship might almost have been said to have lapsed; but Eve's affection, when she had once given it, was a durable thing, capable of surviving long separation. She had loved Cynthia at school, and she could feel nothing but animosity towards anyone who had treated her badly. She eyed the glittering water of the lake from under lowered brows, and prepared to be frigid and hostile when the villain of the piece should arrive. It was only when she heard footsteps behind her and turned to perceive Psmith hurrying up, radiant in gleaming flannel, that it occurred to her for the first time that there might have been faults on both sides. She had not known Psmith long, it was true, but already his personality had made a somewhat deep impression on her, and she was loath to believe that he could be the callous scoundrel of her imagination. She decided to suspend judgment until they should be out in mid-water and in a position to discuss the matter without interruption.

'I am a little late,' said Psmith, as he came up. 'I was detained by our young friend Freddie. He came into my room and started talking about himself at the very moment when I was tying my tie and needed every ounce of concentration for that delicate task. The recent painful episode appeared to be weighing on his mind to some extent.' He helped Eve into the boat and started to row. 'I consoled him as best I could by telling him that it would probably have made you think all the more highly of him. I ventured the suggestion that girls worship the strong, rough, dashing type of man. And, after I had done my best to convince him that he was a strong, rough, dashing man, I came away. By now, of course, he may have had a relapse into despair; so, if you happen to see a body bobbing about in the water as we row along, it will probably be Freddie's.'

'Never mind about Freddie.'

'I don't if you don't,' said Psmith agreeably. 'Very well, then, if we see a body, we will ignore it.' He rowed on a few strokes. 'Correct me if I am wrong,' he said, resting on his oars and leaning forward, 'but you appear to be brooding about something. If you will give me a clue, I will endeavour to assist you to grapple with any little problem which is troubling you. What is the matter?'

Eve, questioned thus directly, found it difficult to open the subject. She hesitated a moment, and let the water ripple through her fingers.

'I have only just found out your name, Mr McTodd,' she said at length.

Psmith nodded.

'It is always thus,' he said. 'Passing through this life, we meet a fellow-mortal, chat awhile, and part; and the last thing we think of doing is to ask him in a manly and direct way what his label is. There is something oddly furtive and shamefaced in one's attitude towards people's names. It is as if we shrank from probing some hideous secret. We say to ourselves "This pleasant stranger may be a Snooks or a Buggins. Better not inquire." But in my case . . .'

'It was a great shock to me.'

'Now there,' said Psmith, 'I cannot follow you. I wouldn't call McTodd a bad name, as names go. Don't you think there is a sort of Highland strength about it? It sounds to me like something out of "The Lady of the Lake" or "The Lay of the Last Minstrel". "The stag at eve had drunk its fill adoon the glen beyint the hill, and welcomed with a friendly nod old Scotland's pride, young Laird McTodd." You don't think it has a sort of wild romantic ring?'

'I ought to tell you, Mr McTodd,' said Eve, 'that I was at school with Cynthia.'

Psmith was not a young man who often found himself at a loss, but this remark gave him a bewildered feeling such as comes in dreams. It was plain to him that this delightful girl thought she had said something serious, even impressive; but for the moment it did not seem to him to make sense. He sparred warily for time.

'Indeed? With Cynthia? That must have been jolly.'

The harmless observation appeared to have the worst effect upon his companion. The frown came back to her face.

'Oh, don't speak in that flippant, sneering way,' she said. 'It's so cheap.'

Psmith, having nothing to say, remained silent, and the boat drifted on. Eve's face was delicately pink, for she was feeling extraordinarily embarrassed. There was something in the solemn gaze of the man before her which made it difficult for her to go on. But, with the stout-heartedness which was one of her characteristics, she stuck to her task.

'After all,' she said, 'however you may feel about her now, you must have been fond of poor Cynthia at one time, or I don't see why you should have married her.'

Psmith, for want of conversation, had begun rowing again. The start he gave at these remarkable words caused him to skim the surface of the water with the left oar in such a manner as to send a liberal pint into Eve's lap. He started forward with apologies.

'Oh, never mind about that,' said Eve impatiently. 'It doesn't matter. . . . Mr McTodd,' she said, and there was a note of gentleness in her voice, 'I do wish you would tell me what the trouble was.'

Psmith stared at the floor of the boat in silence. He was wrestling with a feeling of injury. True, he had not during their brief conversation at the Senior Conservative Club specifically inquired of Mr McTodd whether he was a bachelor, but somehow he felt that the man should have dropped some hint as to his married state. True, again, Mr McTodd had not asked him to impersonate him at Blandings Castle. And yet, undeniably, he felt that he had a grievance. Psmith's was an orderly mind. He had proposed to continue the pleasant relations which had begun between Eve and himself, seeing to it that every day they became a little pleasanter, until eventually, in due season, they should reach the point where it would become possible to lay heart and hand at her feet. For there was no doubt in his mind that in a world congested to overflowing with girls Eve Halliday stood entirely alone. And now this infernal Cynthia had risen from nowhere to stand between them. Even a young man as liberally endowed with calm assurance as he was might find it awkward to conduct his wooing with such a handicap as a wife in the background.

Eve misinterpreted his silence.

'I suppose you are thinking that it is no business of mine?'

Psmith came out of his thoughts with a start.

'No, no. Not at all.'

'You see, I'm devoted to Cynthia – and I like you.'

She smiled for the first time. Her embarrassment was passing.

'That is the whole point,' she said. 'I do like you. And I'm quite sure that if you were really the sort of man I thought you when I first heard about all this, I shouldn't. The friend who told me about you and Cynthia made it seem as if the whole fault had been yours. I got the impression that you had been very unkind to Cynthia. I thought you must be a brute. And when Lord Emsworth told me who you were, my first impulse was to hate you. I think if you had come along just then I should have been rather horrid to you. But you were late, and that gave me time to think it over. And then I remembered how nice you had been to me and I felt somehow that – that you must really be quite nice, and it occurred to me that there might be some explanation. And I thought that – perhaps – if you would let me interfere in your private affairs – and if things hadn't gone too far – I might do something to help – try to bring you together, you know.'

She broke off, a little confused, for now that the words were out she was conscious of a return of her former shyness. Even though she was an old friend of Cynthia's, there did seem something insufferably officious in this meddling. And when she saw the look of pain on her companion's face, she regretted that she had spoken. Naturally, she thought, he was offended.

In supposing that Psmith was offended she was mistaken. Internally he was glowing with a renewed admiration for all those beautiful qualities in her which he had detected, before they had ever met, at several yards' range across the street from the window of the Drones Club smoking-room. His look of pain was due to the fact that, having now had time to grapple with the problem, he had decided to dispose of this Cynthia once and for all. He proposed to eliminate her for ever from his life. And the elimination of even such a comparative stranger seemed to him to call for a pained look. So he assumed one.

'That,' he said gravely, 'would, I fear, be impossible. It is like you to suggest it, and I cannot tell you how much I appreciate the kindness which has made you interest yourself in my troubles, but it is too late for any reconciliation. Cynthia and I are divorced.'

For a moment the temptation had come to him to kill the woman off with some wasting sickness, but this he resisted as tending towards possible future complications. He was resolved, however, that there should be no question of bringing them together again.

He was disturbed to find Eve staring at him in amazement.

'Divorced? But how can you be divorced? It's only a few days since you and she were in London together.'

Psmith ceased to wonder that Mr McTodd had had trouble with his wife. The woman was a perfect pest.

'I used the term in a spiritual rather than a legal sense,' he replied. 'True, there has been no actual decree, but we are separated beyond hope of reunion.' He saw the distress in Eve's eyes and hurried on. 'There are things,' he said, 'which it is impossible for a man to overlook, however broad-minded he may be. Love, Miss Halliday, is a delicate plant. It needs tending, nursing, assiduous fostering. This cannot be done by throwing the breakfast bacon at a husband's head.'

'What!' Eve's astonishment was such that the word came out in a startled squeak.

'*In* the dish,' said Psmith sadly.

Eve's blue eyes opened wide.

'*Cynthia* did that!'

'On more than one occasion. Her temper in the mornings was terrible. I have known her lift the cat over two chairs and a settee with a single kick. And all because there were no mushrooms.'

'But – but I can't believe it!'

'Come over to Canada,' said Psmith, 'and I will show you the cat.'

'Cynthia did that! – Cynthia – why, she was always the gentlest little creature.'

'At school, you mean?'

'Yes.'

'That,' said Psmith, 'would, I suppose, be before she had taken to drink.'

'Taken to drink!'

Psmith was feeling happier. A passing thought did come to him that all this was perhaps a trifle rough on the absent Cynthia, but he mastered the unmanly weakness. It was necessary that Cynthia should suffer in the good cause. Already he had begun to detect in Eve's eyes the faint dawnings of an angelic pity, and pity is recognised by all the best authorities as one of the most valuable emotions which your wooer can awaken.

'Drink!' Eve repeated, with a little shudder.

'We lived in one of the dry provinces of Canada, and, as so often happens, that started the trouble. From the moment when she installed a private still her downfall was swift. I have seen her, under the influence of home-brew, rage through the house like a devastating cyclone.... I hate speaking like this of one who was your friend,' said Psmith, in a low, vibrating voice. 'I would not tell these things to anyone but you. The world, of course, supposes that the entire blame for the collapse of our home was mine. I took care that it should be so. The opinion of the world matters little to me. But with you it is different. I should not like you to think badly of me, Miss Halliday. I do not make friends easily – I am a lonely man – but somehow it has seemed to me since we met that you and I might be friends.'

Eve stretched her hand out impulsively.

'Why, of course!'

Psmith took her hand and held it far longer than was strictly speaking necessary.

'Thank you,' he said. 'Thank you.'

He turned the nose of the boat to the shore, and rowed slowly back.

'I have suffered,' said Psmith gravely, as he helped her ashore. 'But, if you will be my friend, I think that I may forget.'

They walked in silence up the winding path to the castle.

§ 6

To Psmith five minutes later, as he sat in his room smoking a cigarette and looking dreamily out at the distant hills, there entered the Hon. Frederick Threepwood, who, having closed the door behind him, tottered to the bed and uttered a deep and discordant groan. Psmith, his mind thus rudely wrenched from pleasant meditations, turned and regarded the gloomy youth with disfavour.

'At any other time, Comrade Threepwood,' he said politely but with firmness, 'certainly. But not now. I am not in the vein.'

'What?' said the Hon. Freddie vacantly.

'I say that at any other time I shall be delighted to listen to your farmyard imitations, but not now. At the moment I am deep in thoughts of my own, and I may say frankly that I regard you as more or less of an excrescence. I want solitude, solitude. I am in a beautiful reverie, and your presence jars upon me somewhat profoundly.'

The Hon. Freddie ruined the symmetry of his hair by passing his fingers feverishly through it.

'Don't *talk* so much! I never met a fellow like you for talking.' Having rumpled his hair to the left, he went through it again and rumpled it to the right. 'I say, do you know what? You've jolly well got to clear out of here quick!' He got up from the bed, and approached the window. Having done which, he bent towards Psmith and whispered in his ear. 'The game's up!'

Psmith withdrew his ear with a touch of hauteur, but he looked at his companion with a little more interest. He had feared, when he saw Freddie stagger in with such melodramatic despair and emit so hollow a groan, that the topic on which he wished to converse was the already exhausted one of his broken heart. It now began to appear that weightier matters were on his mind.

'I fail to understand you, Comrade Threepwood,' he said. 'The last time I had the privilege of conversing with you, you informed me that Susan, or whatever her name is, merely giggled and told you not to be silly when you embraced her. In other words, she is *not* a detective. What has happened since then to get you all worked up?'

'Baxter!'

'What has Baxter been doing?'

'Only giving the whole bally show away to me, that's all,' said Freddie feverishly. He clutched Psmith's arm violently, causing that exquisite to utter a slight moan and smooth out the wrinkles thus created in his sleeve. 'Listen! I've just been talking to the blighter. I was passing the library just now, when he popped out of the door and hauled me in. And, dash it, he hadn't been talking two seconds before I realised that he has seen through the whole dam' thing practically from the moment you got here. Though he doesn't seem to know that I've anything to do with it, thank goodness.'

'I should imagine not, if he makes you his confidant. Why did he do that, by the way? What made him select you as the recipient of his secrets?'

'As far as I can make out, his idea was to form a gang, if you know what I mean. He said a lot of stuff about him and me being the only two able-bodied young men in the place, and we ought to be prepared to tackle you if you started anything.'

'I see. And now tell me how our delightful friend ever happened to begin suspecting that I was not all I seemed to be. I had been flattering myself that I had put the little deception over with complete success.'

'Well, in the first place, dash it, that dam' fellow McTodd – the real one, you know – sent a telegram saying that he wasn't coming. So it seemed rummy to Baxter bang from the start when you blew in all merry and bright.'

'Ah! That was what they all meant by saying they were glad I had come "after all". A phrase which at the moment, I confess, rather mystified me.'

'And then you went and wrote in the Peavey female's autograph-book.'

'In what way was that a false move?'

'Why, that was the biggest bloomer on record, as it has turned out,' said Freddie vehemently. 'Baxter apparently keeps every letter that comes to the place on a file, and he'd skewered McTodd's original letter with the rest. I mean, the one he wrote accepting the invitation to come here. And Baxter compared his handwriting with what you wrote in the Peavey's album, and, of course, they weren't a dam' bit alike. And that put the lid on it.'

Psmith lit another cigarette and drew at it thoughtfully. He realised that he had made a tactical error in underestimating the antagonism of the Efficient One.

'Does he seem to have any idea why I have come to the castle?' he asked.

'Any idea? Why, dash it, the very first thing he said to me was that you must have come to sneak Aunt Connie's necklace.'

'In that case, why has he made no move till to-day? I should have supposed that he would long since have denounced me before as large an audience as he could assemble. Why this reticence on the part of genial old Baxter?'

A crimson flush of chivalrous indignation spread itself over Freddie's face.

'He told me that, too.'

'There seems to have been no reserves between Comrade Baxter and yourself. And very healthy, too, this spirit of confidence. What was his reason for abstaining from loosing the bomb?'

'He said he was pretty sure you wouldn't try to do anything on your own. He thought you would wait till your accomplice arrived. And, damn him,' cried Freddie heatedly, 'do you know who he's got the infernal gall to think is your accomplice? Miss Halliday! Dash him!'

Psmith smoked in thoughtful silence.

'Well, of course, now that this has happened,' said Freddie, 'I suppose it's no good thinking of going on with the thing. You'd better pop off, what? If I were you, I'd leg it to-day and have your luggage sent on after you.'

Psmith threw away his cigarette and stretched himself. During the last few moments he had been thinking with some tenseness.

'Comrade Threepwood,' he said reprovingly, 'you suggest a cowardly and weak-minded action. I admit that the outlook would be distinctly rosier if no such person as Baxter were on the premises, but nevertheless the thing must be seen through to a finish. At least we have this advantage over our spectacled friend, that we know he suspects me and he doesn't know we know. I think that with a little resource and ingenuity we may yet win through.' He turned to the window and looked out. 'Sad,' he sighed, 'that these idyllic surroundings should have become oppressed with a cloud of sinister menace. One thinks one sees a faun popping about in the undergrowth, and on looking more closely perceives that it is in reality a detective with a notebook. What one fancied was the piping of Pan turns out to be a police-whistle, summoning assistance. Still, we must bear these things without wincing. They are our cross. What you have told me will render me, if possible, warier and more snake-like than ever, but my purpose remains firm. The cry goes round the castle battlements "Psmith intends to keep the old flag flying!" So charge off and soothe your quivering ganglions with a couple of aspirins, Comrade Threepwood, and leave me to my thoughts. All will doubtless come right in the future.'

§ 1

FROM out of the scented shade of the big cedar on the lawn in front of the castle Psmith looked at the flower-beds, jaunty and gleaming in the afternoon sun; then he looked back at Eve, incredulity in every feature.

'I must have misunderstood you. Surely,' he said in a voice vibrant with reproach, 'you do not seriously intend to *work* in weather like this?'

'I must. I've got a conscience. They aren't paying me a handsome salary – a fairly handsome salary – to sit about in deck-chairs.'

'But you only came yesterday.'

'Well, I ought to have worked yesterday.'

'It seems to me,' said Psmith, 'the nearest thing to slavery that I have ever struck. I had hoped, seeing that everybody had gone off and left us alone, that we were going to spend a happy and instructive afternoon together under the shade of this noble tree, talking of this and that. Is it not to be?'

'No, it is not. It's lucky you're not the one who's supposed to be cataloguing this library. It would never get finished.'

'And why, as your employer would say, should it? He has expressed the opinion several times in my hearing that the library has jogged along quite comfortably for a great number of years without being catalogued. Why shouldn't it go on like that indefinitely?'

'It's no good trying to tempt me. There's nothing I should like better than to loaf here for hours and hours, but what would Mr Baxter say when he got back and found out?'

'It is becoming increasingly clear to me each day that I stay in this place,' said Psmith moodily, 'that Comrade Baxter is little short of a blister on the community. Tell me, how do you get on with him?'

'I don't like him much.'

'Nor do I. It is on these communities of taste that life-long attachments are built. Sit down and let us exchange confidences on the subject of Baxter.'

Eve laughed.

'I won't. You're simply trying to lure me into staying out here and neglecting my duty. I really must be off now. You have no idea what a lot of work there is to be done.'

'You are entirely spoiling my afternoon.'

'No, I'm not. You've got a book. What is it?'

Psmith picked up the brightly-jacketed volume and glanced at it.

'*The Man with the Missing Toe*. Comrade Threepwood lent it to me. He has a vast store of this type of narrative. I expect he will be wanting you to catalogue his library next.'

'Well, it looks interesting.'

'Ah, but what does it *teach*? How long do you propose to shut yourself up in that evil-smelling library?'

'An hour or so.'

'Then I shall rely on your society at the end of that period. We might go for another saunter on the lake.'

'All right. I'll come and find you when I've finished.'

Psmith watched her disappear into the house, then seated himself once more in the long chair under the cedar. A sense of loneliness oppressed him. He gave one look at *The Man with the missing Toe*, and, having rejected the entertainment it offered, gave himself up to meditation.

Blandings Castle dozed in the midsummer heat like a Palace of Sleep. There had been an exodus of its inmates shortly after lunch, when Lord Emsworth, Lady Constance, Mr Keeble, Miss Peavey, and the Efficient Baxter had left for the neighbouring town of Bridgeford in the big car, with the Hon. Freddie puffing in its wake in a natty two-seater. Psmith, who had been invited to accompany them, had declined on the plea that he wished to write a poem. He felt but a tepid interest in the afternoon's programme, which was to consist of the unveiling by his lordship of the recently completed memorial to the late Hartley Reddish, Esq., J.P., for so many years Member of Parliament for the Bridgeford and Shifley Division of Shropshire. Not even the prospect of hearing Lord Emsworth – clad, not without vain protest and weak grumbling, in a silk hat, morning coat, and spongebag trousers – deliver a speech, had been sufficient to lure him from the castle grounds.

But at the moment when he had uttered his refusal, thereby incurring the ill-concealed envy both of Lord Emsworth and his son Freddie, the latter also an unwilling celebrant, he had supposed that his solitude would be shared by Eve. This deplorable conscientiousness of hers, this morbid craving for work, had left him at a loose end. The time and the place were both above criticism, but, as so often happens in this life of ours, he had been let down by the girl.

But, though he chafed for a while, it was not long before the dreamy peace of the afternoon began to exercise a soothing effect upon him. With the exception of the bees that worked with their usual misguided energy among the flowers and an occasional butterfly which flitted past in the sunshine, all nature seemed to be taking a siesta. Somewhere out of sight a lawn-mower had begun to emphasise the stillness with its musical whir. A telegraph-boy on a red bicycle passed up the drive to the front door, and seemed to have some difficulty in establishing communication with the domestic staff – from which Psmith deduced that Beach, the butler, like a good opportunist, was taking advantage of the absence of authority to enjoy a nap in some distant lair of his own. Eventually a parlourmaid appeared, accepted the telegram and (apparently) a rebuke from the boy, and the bicycle passed out of sight, leaving silence and peace once more.

The noblest minds are not proof against atmospheric conditions of this kind. Psmith's eyes closed, opened, closed again. And presently his regular breathing, varied by an occasional snore, was added to the rest of the small sounds of the summer afternoon.

The shadow of the cedar was appreciably longer when he awoke with that sudden start which generally terminates sleep in a garden-chair. A glance at his watch told him that it was close on five o'clock, a fact which was confirmed a moment later by the arrival of the parlourmaid who had answered the summons of the telegraph-boy. She appeared to be the sole survivor of the little world that had its centre in the servants' hall. A sort of female Casabianca.

'I have put your tea in the hall, sir.'

'You could have performed no nobler or more charitable task,' Psmith assured her; and, having corrected a certain stiffness of limb by means of massage, went in. It occurred to him that Eve, assiduous worker though she was, might have knocked off in order to keep him company.

The hope proved vain. A single cup stood bleakly on the tray. Either Eve was superior to the feminine passion for tea or she was having hers up in the library. Filled with something of the sadness which he had felt at the sight of the toiling bees, Psmith embarked on his solitary meal, wondering sorrowfully at the perverseness which made girls work when there was no one to watch them.

It was very agreeable here in the coolness of the hall. The great door of the castle was open, and through it he had a view of lawns bathed in a thirst-provoking sunlight. Through the green-baize door to his left, which led to the servants' quarters, an occasional sharp giggle gave evidence of the presence of humanity, but apart from that he might have been alone in the world. Once again he fell into a dreamy meditation, and there is little reason to doubt that he would shortly have disgraced himself by falling asleep for the second time in a single afternoon, when he was restored to alertness by the sudden appearance of a foreign body in the open doorway. Against the background of golden light a black figure had abruptly manifested itself.

The sharp pang of apprehension which ran through Psmith's consciousness like an electric shock, causing him to stiffen like some wild creature surprised in the woods, was due to the momentary belief that the new-comer was the local vicar, of whose conversational powers he had had experience on the second day of his visit. Another glance showed him that he had been too pessimistic. This was not the vicar. It was someone whom he had never seen before — a slim and graceful young man with a dark, intelligent face, who stood blinking in the subdued light of the hall with eyes not yet accustomed to the absence of strong sunshine. Greatly relieved, Psmith rose and approached him.

'Hallo!' said the new-comer. 'I didn't see you. It's quite dark in here after outside.'

'The light is pleasantly dim,' agreed Psmith.

'Is Lord Emsworth anywhere about?'

'I fear not. He has legged it, accompanied by the entire household, to superintend the unveiling of a memorial at Bridgeford to — if my memory serves me rightly — the late Hartley Reddish, Esq., J.P., M.P. Is there anything I can do?'

'Well, I've come to stay, you know.'

'Indeed?'

'Lady Constance invited me to pay a visit as soon as I reached England.'

'Ah! Then you have come from foreign parts?'

'Canada.'

Psmith started slightly. This, he perceived, was going to complicate matters. The last thing he desired was the addition to the Blandings circle of one familiar with Canada. Nothing would militate against his peace of mind more than the society of a man who would want to exchange with him views on that growing country.

'Oh, Canada?' he said.

'I wired,' proceeded the other, 'but I suppose it came after everybody had left. Ah, that must be my telegram on that table over there. I walked up from the station.' He was rambling idly about the hall after the fashion of one breaking new ground. He paused at an occasional table, the one where, when taking after-dinner coffee, Miss Peavey was wont to sit. He picked up a book, and uttered a gratified laugh. 'One of my little things,' he said.

'One of what?' said Psmith.

'This book. *Songs of Squalor*. I wrote it.'

'You wrote it!'

'Yes. My name's McTodd. Ralston McTodd. I expect you have heard them speak of me?'

§ 2

The mind of a man who has undertaken a mission as delicate as Psmith's at Blandings Castle is necessarily alert. Ever since he had stepped into the five o'clock train at Paddington, when his adventure might have been said formally to have started, Psmith had walked warily, like one in a jungle on whom sudden and unexpected things might pounce out at any moment. This calm announcement from the slim young man, therefore, though it undoubtedly startled him, did not deprive him of his faculties. On the contrary, it quickened them. His first action was to step nimbly to the table on which the telegram lay awaiting the return of Lord Emsworth, his second was to slip the envelope into his pocket. It was imperative that telegrams signed McTodd should not lie about loose while he was enjoying the hospitality of the castle.

This done, he confronted the young man.

'Come, come!' he said with quiet severity.

He was extremely grateful to a kindly Providence which had arranged that this interview should take place at a time when nobody but himself was in the house.

'You say that you are Ralston McTodd, the author of these poems?'

'Yes, I do.'

'Then what,' said Psmith incisively, 'is a pale parabola of Joy?'

'Er – what?' said the new-comer in an enfeebled voice. There was manifest in his demeanour now a marked nervousness.

'And here is another,' said Psmith. '"The—" Wait a minute, I'll get it soon. Yes. "The sibilant, scented silence that shimmered where we sat." Could you oblige me with a diagram of that one?'

'I – I—What are you talking about?'

Psmith stretched out a long arm and patted him almost affectionately on the shoulder.

'It's lucky you met me before you had to face the others,' he said. 'I fear that you undertook this little venture without thoroughly equipping yourself. They would have detected your imposture in the first minute.'

'What do you mean – imposture? I don't know what you're talking about.'

Psmith waggled his forefinger at him reproachfully.

'My dear comrade, I may as well tell you at once that the genuine McTodd is an old and dear friend of mine. I had a long and entertaining conversation with him only a few days ago. So that, I think we may confidently assert, is that. Or am I wrong?'

'Oh, hell!' said the young man. And, flopping bonelessly into a chair, he mopped his forehead in undisguised and abject collapse.

Silence reigned for a while.

'What,' inquired the visitor, raising a damp face that shone pallidly in the dim light, 'are you going to do about it?'

'Nothing, comrade – by the way, what is your name?'

'Cootes.'

'Nothing, Comrade Cootes. Nothing whatever. You are free to leg it hence whenever you feel disposed. In fact, the sooner you do so, the better I shall be pleased.'

'Say! That's darned good of you.'

'Not at all, not at all.'

'You're an ace—'

'Oh, hush!' interrupted Psmith modestly. 'But before you go tell me one or two things. I take it that your object in coming here was to have a pop at Lady Constance's necklace?'

'Yes.'

'I thought as much. And what made you suppose that the real McTodd would not be here when you arrived?'

'Oh, that was all right. I travelled over with that guy McTodd on the boat, and saw a good deal of him when we got to London. He was full of how he'd been invited here, and I got it out of him that no one here knew him by sight. And then one afternoon I met him in the Strand, all worked up. Madder than a hornet. Said he'd been insulted and wouldn't come down to this place if they came and begged him on their bended knees. I couldn't make out what it was all about, but apparently he had met Lord Emsworth and hadn't been treated right. He told me he was going straight off to Paris.'

'And did he?'

'Sure. I saw him off myself at Charing Cross. That's why it seemed such a cinch coming here instead of him. It's just my darned luck that the first man I run into is a friend of his. How was I to know that he had any friends this side? He told me he'd never been in England before.'

'In this life, Comrade Cootes,' said Psmith, 'we must always distinguish between the Unlikely and the Impossible. It was unlikely, as you say, that you would meet any friend of McTodd's in this out-of-the-way spot; and you rashly ordered your movements on the assumption that it was impossible. With what result? The cry goes round the Underworld, "Poor old Cootes has made a bloomer!"'

'You needn't rub it in.'

'I am only doing so for your good. It is my earnest hope that you will lay this lesson to heart and profit by it. Who knows that it may not be the turning-point in your career? Years hence, when you are a white-haired and opulent man of leisure, having retired from the crook business with a comfortable fortune, you may look back on your experience of to-day and realise that it was the means of starting you on the road to Success. You will lay stress on it when you are interviewed for the *Weekly Burglar* on "How I Began" . . . But, talking of starting on roads, I think that perhaps it would be as well if you now had a dash at the one leading to the railway-station. The household may be returning at any moment now.'

'That's right,' agreed the visitor.

'I think so,' said Psmith. 'I think so. You will be happier when you are away from here. Once outside the castle precincts, a great weight will roll off your mind. A little fresh air will put the roses in your cheeks. You know your way out?'

He shepherded the young man to the door and with a cordial push started him on his way. Then with long strides he ran upstairs to the library to find Eve.

* * * * *

At about the same moment, on the platform of Market Blandings station, Miss Aileen Peavey was alighting from the train which had left Bridgeford some half an hour earlier. A headache, the fruit of standing about in the hot sun, had caused her to forgo the pleasure of hearing Lord Emsworth deliver his speech: and she had slipped back on a convenient train with the intention of lying down and resting. Finding, on reaching Market Blandings, that her head was much better, and the heat of the afternoon being now over, she started to walk to the castle, greatly refreshed by a cool breeze which had sprung up from the west. She left the town at almost the exact time when the disconsolate Mr Cootes was passing out of the big gates at the end of the castle drive.

§ 3

The grey melancholy which accompanied Mr Cootes like a diligent spectre as he began his walk back to the town of Market Blandings, and which not even the delightful evening could dispel, was due primarily, of course, to that sickening sense of defeat which afflicts a man whose high hopes have been wrecked at the very instant when success has seemed in sight. Once or twice in the life of every man there falls to his lot something which can only be described as a soft snap, and it had seemed to Mr Cootes that this venture of his to Blandings Castle came into that category. He had, like most members of his profession, had his ups and downs in the past, but at last, he told himself, the goddess Fortune had handed him something on a plate with watercress round it. Once established in the castle, there would have been a hundred opportunities of achieving the capture of Lady Constance's necklace and it had looked as though all he had to do was to walk in, announce himself, and be treated as the honoured guest. As he slouched moodily between the dusty

hedges that fringed the road to Market Blandings, Edward
Cootes tasted the bitterness that only those know whose plans
have been upset by the hundredth chance.

But this was not all. In addition to the sadness of frustrated
hope, he was also experiencing the anguish of troubled memories. Not only was the Present torturing him, but the Past had
come to life and jumped out and bitten him. A sorrow's crown of
sorrow is remembering happier things, and this was what
Edward Cootes was doing now. It is at moments like this that
a man needs a woman's tender care, and Mr Cootes had lost the
only woman in whom he could have confided his grief, the only
woman who would have understood and sympathised.

We have been introduced to Mr Cootes at a point in his
career when he was practising upon dry land; but that was not
his chosen environment. Until a few months back his business
had lain upon deep waters. The salt scent of the sea was in his
blood. To put it more exactly, he had been by profession a card-
sharper on the Atlantic liners; and it was during this period that
he had loved and lost. For three years and more he had worked in
perfect harmony with the lady who, though she adopted a
variety of names for purposes of travel, was known to her
immediate circle as Smooth Lizzie. He had been the practi-
tioner, she the decoy, and theirs had been one of those ideal
business partnerships which one so seldom meets with in a
world of cynicism and mistrust. Comradeship had ripened into
something deeper and more sacred, and it was all settled
between them that when they next touched New York, Mr
Cootes, if still at liberty, should proceed to the City Hall for a
marriage-licence; when they had quarrelled – quarrelled irrevoc-
ably over one of those trifling points over which lovers do
quarrel. Some absurd dispute as to the proper division of the

quite meagre sum obtained from a cattle millionaire on their last voyage had marred their golden dreams. One word had led to another. The lady, after woman's habit, had the last of the series, and even Mr Cootes was forced to admit that it was a pippin. She had spoken it on the pier at New York, and then passed out of his life. And with her had gone all his luck. It was as if her going had brought a curse upon him. On the very next trip he had had an unfortunate misunderstanding with an irritable gentleman from the Middle West, who, piqued at what he considered – not unreasonably – the undue proportion of kings and aces in the hands which Mr Cootes had been dealing himself, expressed his displeasure by biting off the first joint of the other's right index finger – thus putting an abrupt end to a brilliant career. For it was on this finger that Mr Cootes principally relied for the almost magical effects which he was wont to produce with a pack of cards after a little quiet shuffling.

With an aching sense of what might have been he thought now of his lost Lizzie. Regretfully he admitted to himself that she had always been the brains of the firm. A certain manual dexterity he had no doubt possessed, but it was ever Lizzie who had been responsible for the finer work. If they had still been partners, he really believed that she could have discovered some way of getting round the obstacles which had reared themselves now between himself and the necklace of Lady Constance Keeble. It was in a humble and contrite spirit that Edward Cootes proceeded on his way to Market Blandings.

* * * * *

Miss Peavey, meanwhile, who, it will be remembered, was moving slowly along the road from the Market Blandings end, was finding her walk both restful and enjoyable. There were moments, it has to be recorded, when the society of her hostess and her hostess's relations was something of a strain to Miss Peavey; and she was glad to be alone. Her headache had disappeared, and she revelled in the quiet evening hush. About now, if she had not had the sense to detach herself from the castle platoon, she would, she reflected, be listening to Lord Emsworth's speech on the subject of the late Hartley Reddish, J.P., M.P.: a topic which even the noblest of orators might have failed to render really gripping. And what she knew of her host gave her little confidence in his powers of oratory.

Yes, she was well out of it. The gentle breeze played soothingly upon her face. Her delicately modelled nostrils drank in gratefully the scent from the hedgerows. Somewhere out of sight a thrush was singing. And so moved was Miss Peavey by the peace and sweetness of it all that she, too, began to sing.

Had those who enjoyed the privilege of her acquaintance at Blandings Castle been informed that Miss Peavey was about to sing, they would doubtless have considered themselves on firm ground if called upon to make a conjecture as to the type of song which she would select. Something quaint, dreamy, a little wistful...that would have been the universal guess...some old-world ballad, possibly...

What Miss Peavey actually sang – in a soft, meditative voice like that of a linnet waking to greet a new dawn – was that curious composition known as 'The Beale Street Blues'.

As she reached the last line, she broke off abruptly. She was, she perceived, no longer alone. Down the road toward her, walking pensively like one with a secret sorrow, a man was approaching; and for an instant, as she turned the corner, something in his appearance seemed to catch her by the throat and her breath came sharply.

'Gee!' said Miss Peavey.

She was herself again the next moment. A chance resemblance had misled her. She could not see the man's face, for his head was bent, but how was it possible . . .

And then, when he was quite close, he raised his head, and the county of Shropshire, as far as it was visible to her amazed eyes, executed a sudden and eccentric dance. Trees bobbed up and down, hedgerows shimmied like a Broadway chorus; and from out of the midst of the whirling countryside a voice spoke.

'Liz!'

'Eddie!' ejaculated Miss Peavey faintly, and sat down in a heap on a grassy bank.

§ 4

'Well, for goodness' sake!' said Miss Peavey.

Shropshire had become static once more. She stared at him, wide-eyed.

'Can you tie it!' said Miss Peavey.

She ran her gaze over him once again from head to foot.

'Well, if this ain't the cat's whiskers!' said Miss Peavey. And with this final pronouncement she rose from her bank, somewhat restored, and addressed herself to the task of picking up old threads.

'Wherever,' she inquired, 'did you spring from, Ed?'

There was nothing but affection in her voice. Her gaze was that of a mother contemplating her long-lost child. The past was past and a new era had begun. In the past she had been compelled to describe this man as a hunk of cheese and to express the opinion that his crookedness was such as to enable him to hide at will behind a spiral staircase; but now, in the joy of this unexpected reunion, all these harsh views were forgotten. This was Eddie Cootes, her old side-kick, come back to her after many days, and only now was it borne in upon her what a gap in her life his going had made. She flung herself into his arms with a glad cry.

Mr Cootes, who had not been expecting this demonstration of esteem, staggered a trifle at the impact, but recovered himself sufficiently to return the embrace with something of his ancient warmth. He was delighted at this cordiality, but also surprised. The memory of the lady's parting words on the occasion of their last meeting was still green, and he had not realised how quickly women forget and forgive, and how a sensitive girl, stirred by some fancied injury, may address a man as a pie-faced plugugly and yet retain in her inmost heart all the old love and affection. He kissed Miss Peavey fondly.

'Liz,' he said with fervour, 'you're prettier than ever.'

'Now you behave,' responded Miss Peavey coyly.

The arrival of a baaing flock of sheep, escorted by a priggish dog and followed by a couple of the local peasantry, caused an intermission in these tender exchanges; and by the time the procession had moved off down the road they were in a more suitable frame of mind to converse quietly and in a practical spirit, to compare notes, and to fill up the blanks.

'Wherever,' inquired Miss Peavey again, 'did you spring from, Ed? You could of knocked me down with a feather when I saw you coming along the road. I couldn't have believed it was you, this far from the ocean. What are you doing inland like this? Taking a vacation, or aren't you working the boats any more?'

'No, Liz,' said Mr Cootes sadly. 'I've had to give that up.'

And he exhibited the hiatus where an important section of his finger had been and told his painful tale. His companion's sympathy was balm to his wounded soul.

'The risks of the profession, of course,' said Mr Cootes moodily, removing the exhibit in order to place his arm about her slender waist. 'Still, it's done me in. I tried once or twice, but I couldn't seem to make the cards behave no more, so I quit. Ah, Liz,' said Mr Cootes with feeling, 'you can take it from me that I've had no luck since you left me. Regular hoodoo there's been on me. If I'd walked under a ladder on a Friday to smash a mirror over the dome of a black cat I couldn't have had it tougher.'

'You poor boy!'

Mr Cootes nodded sombrely.

'Tough,' he agreed, 'but there it is. Only this afternoon my jinx gummed the game for me and threw a spanner into the prettiest little scenario you ever thought of. . . . But let's not talk about my troubles. What are you doing now, Liz?'

'Me? Oh, I'm living near here.'

Mr Cootes started.

'Not married?' he exclaimed in alarm.

'No!' cried Miss Peavey with vehemence, and shot a tender glance up at his face. 'And I guess you know why, Ed.'

'You don't mean . . . you hadn't forgotten me?'

'As if I could ever forget you, Eddie! There's only one tintype on *my* mantelpiece.'

'But it struck me . . . it sort of occurred to me as a passing thought that, when we saw each other last, you were a mite peeved with your Eddie . . .'

It was the first allusion either of them had made to the past unpleasantness, and it caused a faint blush to dye Miss Peavey's soft cheek.

'Oh, shucks!' she said. 'I'd forgotten all about that next day. I was good and mad at the time, I'll allow, but if only you'd called me up next morning, Ed . . .'

There was a silence, as they mused on what might have been.

'What are you doing, living here?' asked Mr Cootes after a pregnant pause. 'Have you retired?'

'No, *sir*. I'm sitting in at a game with real worthwhile stakes. But, darn it,' said Miss Peavey regretfully, 'I'm wondering if it isn't too big for me to put through alone. Oh, Eddie, if only there was some way you and me could work it together like in the old days.'

'What is it?'

'Diamonds, Eddie. A necklace. I've only had one look at it so far, but that was enough. Some of the best ice I've saw in years, Ed. Worth every cent of a hundred thousand berries.'

The coincidence drew from Mr Cootes a sharp exclamation. 'A necklace!'

'Listen, Ed, while I slip you the low-down. And, say, if you knew the relief it was to me talking good United States again! Like taking off a pair of tight shoes. I'm doing the high-toned stuff for the moment. Soulful. *You* remember, like I used to pull once or twice in the old days. Just after you and me had that little spat of ours I thought I'd take another trip in the old *Atlantic* – force of habit or something, I guess. Anyway, I sailed, and we weren't two days out from New York when I made the biggest kind of a hit with the dame this necklace belongs to. Seemed to take a shine to me right away . . .'

'I don't blame her!' murmured Mr Cootes devotedly.

'Now don't you interrupt,' said Miss Peavey, administering a gratified slap. 'Where was I? Oh yes. This here now Lady Constance Keeble I'm telling you about . . .'

'What!'

'What's the matter now?'

'Lady Constance Keeble?'

'That's the name. She's Lord Emsworth's sister, who lives at a big place up the road. Blandings Castle it's called. She didn't seem like she was able to let me out of her sight, and I've been with her off and on ever since we landed. I'm visiting at the castle now.'

A deep sigh, like the groan of some great spirit in travail, forced itself from between Mr Cootes's lips.

'Well, wouldn't that jar you!' he demanded of circumambient space. 'Of all the lucky ones! getting into the place like that, with the band playing and a red carpet laid down for you to walk on! Gee, if you fell down a well, Liz, you'd come up with the bucket. You're a human horseshoe, that's what you are. Say, listen. Lemme-tell-ya-sumf'n. Do you know what *I've* been doing this afternoon? Only trying to edge into the dam' place myself and getting the air two minutes after I was past the front door.'

'What! *You*, Ed?'

'Sure. You're not the only one that's heard of that collection of ice.'

'Oh, Ed!' Bitter disappointment rang in Miss Peavey's voice. 'If only you could have worked it! Me and you partners again! It hurts to think of it. What was the stuff you pulled to get you in?'

Mr Cootes so far forgot himself in his agony of spirit as to expectorate disgustedly at a passing frog. And even in this trivial enterprise failure dogged him. He missed the frog, which withdrew into the grass with a cold look of disapproval.

'Me?' said Mr Cootes. 'I thought I'd got it smooth. I'd chummed up with a fellow who had been invited down to the place and had thought it over and decided not to go, so I said to myself what's the matter with going there instead of him. A gink called McTodd this was, a poet, and none of the folks had ever set eyes on him, except the old man, who's too short-sighted to see anyone, so . . .'

Miss Peavey interrupted.

'You don't mean to tell me, Ed Cootes, that you thought you could get into the castle by pretending to be Ralston McTodd?'

'Sure I did. Why not? It didn't seem like there was anything to it. A cinch, that's what it looked like. And the first guy I meet in the joint is a mutt who knows this McTodd well. We had a couple of words, and I beat it. I know when I'm not wanted.'

'But, Ed! Ed! What do you mean? Ralston McTodd is at the castle now, this very moment.'

'How's that?'

'Sure. Been there coupla days and more. Long, thin bird with an eyeglass.'

Mr Cootes's mind was in a whirl. He could make nothing of this matter.

'Nothing like it! McTodd's not so darned tall or so thin, if it comes to that. And he didn't wear no eyeglass all the time I was with him. This . . .' He broke off sharply. 'My gosh! I wonder!' he cried. 'Liz! How many men are there in the joint right now?'

'Only four besides Lord Emsworth. There's a big party coming down for the County Ball, but that's all there is at present. There's Lord Emsworth's son, Freddie . . .'

'What does he look like?'

'Sort of a dude with blond hair slicked back. Then there's Mr Keeble. He's short with a red face.'

'And?'

'And Baxter. He's Lord Emsworth's secretary. Wears spectacles.'

'And that's the lot?'

'That's all there is, not counting this here McTodd and the help.'

Mr Cootes brought his hand down with a resounding report on his leg. The mildly pleasant look which had been a feature of his appearance during his interview with Psmith had vanished now, its place taken by one of an extremely sinister malevolence.

'And I let him shoo me out as if I was a stray pup!' he muttered through clenched teeth. 'Of all the bunk games!'

'What *are* you talking about, Ed?'

'And I thanked him! *Thanked* him!' moaned Edward Cootes, writhing at the memory. 'I thanked him for letting me go!'

'Eddie Cootes, whatever are you...?'

'Listen, Liz.' Mr Cootes mastered his emotion with a strong effort. 'I blew into that joint and met this fellow with the eyeglass, and he told me he knew McTodd well and that I wasn't him. And, from what you tell me, this must be the very guy that's passing himself off as McTodd! Don't you see? This baby must have started working on the same lines I did. Got to know McTodd, found he wasn't coming to the castle, and came down instead of him, same as me. Only he got there first, damn him! Wouldn't that give you a pain in the neck!'

Amazement held Miss Peavey dumb for an instant. Then she spoke.

'The big stiff!' said Miss Peavey.

Mr Cootes, regardless of a lady's presence, went even further in his censure.

'I had a feeling from the first that there was something not on the level about that guy!' said Miss Peavey. 'Gee! He must be after that necklace too.'

'Sure he's after the necklace,' said Mr Cootes impatiently. 'What did you think he'd come down for? A change of air?'

'But, Ed! Say! Are you going to let him get away with it?'

'Am *I* going to let him get away with it!' said Mr Cootes, annoyed by the foolish question. 'Wake me up in the night and ask me!'

'But what are you going to do?'

'Do!' said Mr Cootes. 'Do! I'll tell you what I'm going to ...' He paused, and the stern resolve that shone in his face seemed to flicker. 'Say, what the hell *am* I going to do?' he went on somewhat weakly.

'You won't get anything by putting the folks wise that he's a fake. That would be the finish of him, but it wouldn't get *you* anywhere.'

'No,' said Mr Cootes.

'Wait a minute while I think,' said Miss Peavey.

There was a pause. Miss Peavey sat with knit brows.

'How would it be ...?' ventured Mr Cootes.

'Cheese it!' said Miss Peavey.

Mr Cootes cheesed it. The minutes ticked on.

'I've got it,' said Miss Peavey. 'This guy's ace-high with Lady Constance. You've got to get him alone right away and tell him he's got to get you invited to the place as a friend of his.'

'I knew you'd think of something, Liz,' said Mr Cootes, almost humbly. 'You always were a wonder like that. How am I to get him alone?'

'I can fix that. I'll ask him to come for a stroll with me. He's not what you'd call crazy about me, but he can't very well duck if I keep after him. We'll go down the drive. You'll be in the bushes – I'll show you the place. Then I'll send him to fetch me a wrap or something, and while I walk on he'll come back past where you're hiding, and you jump out at him.'

'Liz,' said Mr Cootes, lost in admiration, 'when it comes to doping out a scheme, you're the snake's eyebrows!'

'But what are you going to do if he just turns you down?'

Mr Cootes uttered a bleak laugh, and from the recesses of his costume produced a neat little revolver.

'*He* won't turn me down!' he said.

§ 5

'Fancy!' said Miss Peavey. 'If I had not had a headache and come back early, we should never have had this little chat!'

She gazed up at Psmith in her gentle, wistful way as they started together down the broad gravel drive. A timid, soulful little thing she looked.

'No,' said Psmith.

It was not a gushing reply, but he was not feeling at his sunniest. The idea that Miss Peavey might return from Bridgeford in advance of the main body had not occurred to him. As he would have said himself, he had confused the Unlikely with the Impossible. And the result had been that she had caught him beyond hope of retreat as he sat in his garden-chair and thought of Eve Halliday, who on their return from the lake had been seized with a fresh spasm of conscience and had gone back to the library to put in another hour's work before dinner. To decline Miss Peavey's invitation to accompany her down the drive in order to see if there were any signs of those who had been doing honour to the late Hartley Reddish, M.P., had been out of the question. But Psmith, though he went, went without pleasure.

Every moment he spent in her society tended to confirm him more and more in the opinion that Miss Peavey was the curse of the species.

'And I have been so longing,' continued his companion, 'to have a nice, long talk. All these days I have felt that I haven't been able to get as *near* you as I should wish.'

'Well, of course, with the others always about . . .'

'I meant in a spiritual sense, of course.'

'I see.'

'I wanted so much to discuss your wonderful poetry with you. You haven't so much as *mentioned* your work since you came here. *Have* you!'

'Ah, but, you see, I am trying to keep my mind off it.'

'Really? Why?'

'My medical adviser warned me that I had been concentrating a trifle too much. He offered me the choice, in fact, between a complete rest and the loony-bin.'

'The *what*, Mr McTodd?'

'The lunatic asylum, he meant. These medical men express themselves oddly.'

'But surely, then, you ought not to *dream* of trying to compose if it is as bad as that? And you told Lord Emsworth that you wished to stay at home this afternoon to write a poem.'

Her glance showed nothing but tender solicitude, but inwardly Miss Peavey was telling herself that *that* would hold him for a while.

'True,' said Psmith, 'true. But you know what Art is. An inexorable mistress. The inspiration came, and I felt that I must take the risk. But it has left me weak, weak.'

'You BIG STIFF!' said Miss Peavey. But not aloud.

They walked on a few steps.

'In fact,' said Psmith, with another inspiration, 'I'm not sure I ought not to be going back and resting now.'

Miss Peavey eyed a clump of bushes some dozen yards farther down the drive. They were quivering slightly, as though they sheltered some alien body; and Miss Peavey, whose temper was apt to be impatient, registered a resolve to tell Edward Cootes that, if he couldn't hide behind a bush without dancing about like a cat on hot bricks, he had better give up his profession and take to selling jellied eels. In which, it may be mentioned, she wronged her old friend. He had been as still as a statue until a moment before, when a large and excitable beetle had fallen down the space between his collar and his neck, an experience which might well have tried the subtlest woodsman.

'Oh, please don't go in yet,' said Miss Peavey. 'It is such a lovely evening. Hark to the music of the breeze in the tree-tops. So soothing. Like a faraway harp. I wonder if it is whispering secrets to the birds.'

Psmith forbore to follow her into this region of speculation, and they walked past the bushes in silence.

Some little distance farther on, however, Miss Peavey seemed to relent.

'You *are* looking tired, Mr McTodd,' she said anxiously. 'I am afraid you really have been overtaxing your strength. Perhaps after all you had better go back and lie down.'

'You think so?'

'I am sure of it. I will just stroll on to the gates and see if the car is in sight.'

'I feel that I am deserting you.'

'Oh, please!' said Miss Peavey deprecatingly.

With something of the feelings of a long-sentence convict unexpectedly released immediately on his arrival in jail, Psmith retraced his steps. Glancing over his shoulder, he saw that Miss Peavey had disappeared round a bend in the drive; and he paused to light a cigarette. He had just thrown away the match and was walking on, well content with life, when a voice behind him said 'Hey!' and the well-remembered form of Mr Edward Cootes stepped out of the bushes.

'See this?' said Mr Cootes, exhibiting his revolver.

'I do indeed, Comrade Cootes,' replied Psmith. 'And, if it is not an untimely question, what is the idea?'

'That,' said Mr Cootes, 'is just in case you try any funny business.' And, replacing the weapon in a handy pocket, he proceeded to slap vigorously at the region between his shoulder blades. He also wriggled with not a little animation.

Psmith watched these manœuvres gravely.

'You did not stop me at the pistol's point merely to watch you go through your Swedish exercises?' he said.

Mr Cootes paused for an instant.

'Got a beetle or something down my back,' he explained curtly.

'Ah? Then, as you will naturally wish to be alone in such a sad moment, I will be bidding you a cordial good evening and strolling on.'

'No, you don't!'

'Don't I?' said Psmith resignedly. 'Perhaps you are right, perhaps you are right.' Mr Cootes replaced the revolver once more. 'I take it, then, Comrade Cootes, that you would have speech with me. Carry on, old friend, and get it off your diaphragm. What seems to be on your mind?'

A lucky blow appeared to have stunned Mr Cootes's beetle, and he was able to give his full attention to the matter in hand. He stared at Psmith with considerable distaste.

'I'm on to you, Bill!' he said.

'My name is not Bill,' said Psmith.

'No,' snapped Mr Cootes, his annoyance by this time very manifest. 'And it's not McTodd.'

Psmith looked at his companion thoughtfully. This was an unforeseen complication, and for the moment he would readily have admitted that he saw no way of overcoming it. That the other was in no genial frame of mind towards him the expression on his face would have showed, even if his actions had not been sufficient indication of the fact. Mr Cootes, having disposed of his beetle and being now at leisure to concentrate his whole attention on Psmith, was eyeing that immaculate young man with a dislike which he did not attempt to conceal.

'Shall we be strolling on?' suggested Psmith. 'Walking may assist thought. At the moment I am free to confess that you have opened up a subject which causes me some perplexity. I think, Comrade Cootes, having given the position of affairs a careful examination, that we may say that the next move is with you. What do you propose to do about it?'

'I'd like,' said Mr Cootes with asperity, 'to beat your block off.'

'No doubt. But ...'

'I'd like to knock you for a goal!'

Psmith discouraged these Utopian dreams with a deprecating wave of the hand.

'I can readily understand it,' he said courteously. 'But, to keep within the sphere of practical politics, what is the actual move which you contemplate? You could expose me, no doubt, to my host, but I cannot see how that would profit you.'

'I know that. But you can remember I've got that up my sleeve in case you try any funny business.'

'You persist in harping on that possibility, Comrade Cootes. The idea seems to be an obsession with you. I can assure you that I contemplate no such thing. What, to return to the point, do you intend to do?'

They had reached the broad expanse opposite the front door, where the drive, from being a river, spread out into a lake of gravel. Psmith stopped.

'You've got to get me into this joint,' said Mr Cootes.

'I feared that that was what you were about to suggest. In my peculiar position I have naturally no choice but to endeavour to carry out your wishes. Any attempt not to do so would, I imagine, infallibly strike so keen a critic as yourself as "funny business". But how can I get you into what you breezily describe as "this joint"?'

'You can say I'm a friend of yours and ask them to invite me.'

Psmith shook his head gently.

'Not one of your brightest suggestions, Comrade Cootes. Tactfully refraining from stressing the point that an instant lowering of my prestige would inevitably ensue should it be supposed that you were a friend of mine, I will merely mention that, being myself merely a guest in this stately home of England, I can hardly go about inviting my chums here for indefinite visits. No, we must find another way. . . . You're sure you want to stay? Quite so, quite so, I merely asked. . . . Now, let us think.'

Through the belt of rhododendrons which jutted out from one side of the castle a portly form at this point made itself visible, moving high and disposedly in the direction of the back premises. It was Beach, the butler, returning from the pleasant ramble in which he had indulged himself on the departure of his employer and the rest of the party. Revived by some gracious hours in the open air, Beach was returning to duty. And with the sight of him there came to Psmith a neat solution of the problem confronting him.

'Oh, Beach,' he called.

'Sir?' responded a fruity voice. There was a brief pause while the butler navigated into the open. He removed the straw hat which he had donned for his excursion, and enfolded Psmith in a pop-eyed but not unkindly gaze. A thoughtful critic of country-house humanity, he had long since decided that he approved of Psmith. Since Lady Constance had first begun to offer the hospitality of the castle to the literary and artistic world, he had been profoundly shocked by some of the rare and curious specimens who had nodded their disordered locks and flaunted their ill-cut evening clothes at the dinner-table over which he presided; and Psmith had come as a pleasant surprise.

'Sorry to trouble you, Beach.'

'Not at all, sir.'

'This,' said Psmith, indicating Mr Cootes, who was viewing the scene with a wary and suspicious eye, an eye obviously alert for any signs of funny business, 'is my man. My valet, you know. He has just arrived from town. I had to leave him behind to attend the bedside of a sick aunt. Your aunt was better when you came away, Cootes?' he inquired graciously.

Mr Cootes correctly interpreted this question as a feeler with regard to his views on this new development, and decided to accept the situation. True, he had hoped to enter the castle in a slightly higher capacity than that of a gentleman's personal gentleman, but he was an old campaigner. Once in, as he put it to himself with admirable common sense, he would be in.

'Yes, sir,' he replied.

'Capital,' said Psmith. 'Capital. Then will you look after Cootes, Beach?'

'Very good, sir,' said the butler in a voice of cordial approval. The only point he had found to cavil at in Psmith had been removed; for it had hitherto pained him a little that a gentleman with so nice a taste in clothes as that dignified guest should have embarked on a visit to such a place as Blandings Castle without a personal attendant. Now all was explained and, as far as Beach was concerned, forgiven. He proceeded to escort Mr Cootes to the rear. They disappeared behind the rhododendrons.

They had hardly gone when a sudden thought came to Psmith as he sat once more in the coolness of the hall. He pressed the bell. Strange, he reflected, how one overlooked these obvious things. That was how generals lost battles.

'Sir?' said Beach, appearing through the green baize door.

'Sorry to trouble you again, Beach.'

'Not at all, sir.'

'I hope you will make Cootes comfortable. I think you will like him. His, when you get to know him, is a very winning personality.'

'He seems a nice young fellow, sir.'

'Oh, by the way, Beach. You might ask him if he brought my revolver from town with him.'

'Yes, sir,' said Beach, who would have scorned to betray emotion if it had been a Lewis gun.

'I think I saw it sticking out of his pocket. You might bring it to me, will you?'

'Very good, sir.'

Beach retired, to return a moment later. On the silver salver which he carried the lethal weapon was duly reposing.

'Your revolver, sir,' said Beach.

'Thank you,' said Psmith.

§ 6

For some moments after the butler had withdrawn in his stately pigeon-toed way through the green-baize door, Psmith lay back in his chair with the feeling that something attempted, something done, had earned a night's repose. He was not so sanguine as to suppose that he had actually checkmated an adversary of Mr Cootes's strenuousness by the simple act of removing a revolver from his possession; but there was no denying the fact that the feel of the thing in his pocket engendered a certain cosy satisfaction. The little he had seen of Mr Cootes had been enough to convince him that the other was a man who was far better off without an automatic pistol. There was an impulsiveness about his character which did not go well with the possession of fire-arms.

Psmith's meditations had taken him thus far when they were interrupted by an imperative voice.

'Hey!'

Only one person of Psmith's acquaintance was in the habit of opening his remarks in this manner. It was consequently no surprise to him to find Mr Edward Cootes standing at his elbow.

'Hey!'

'All right, Comrade Cootes,' said Psmith with a touch of austerity, 'I heard you the first time. And may I remind you that this habit of yours of popping out from unexpected places and saying "Hey!" is one which should be overcome. Valets are supposed to wait till rung for. At least, I think so. I must confess that until this moment I have never had a valet.'

'And you wouldn't have one now if I could help it,' responded Mr Cootes.

Psmith raised his eyebrows.

'Why,' he inquired, surprised, 'this peevishness? Don't you like being a valet?'

'No, I don't.'

'You astonish me. I should have thought you would have gone singing about the house. Have you considered that the tenancy of such a position throws you into the constant society of Comrade Beach, than whom it would be difficult to imagine a more delightful companion?'

'Old stiff!' said Mr Cootes sourly. 'If there's one thing that makes me tired, it's a guy that talks about his darned stomach all the time.'

'I beg your pardon?'

'The Beach gook,' explained Mr Cootes, 'has got something wrong with the lining of his stomach, and if I hadn't made my getaway he'd be talking about it yet.'

'If you fail to find entertainment and uplift in first-hand information about Comrade Beach's stomach, you must indeed be hard to please. I am to take it, then, that you came snorting out here, interrupting my daydreams, merely in order to seek my sympathy?'

Mr Cootes gazed upon him with a smouldering eye.

'I came to tell you I suppose you think you're darned smart.'

'And very nice of you, too,' said Psmith, touched. 'A pretty compliment, for which I am not ungrateful.'

'You got that gun away from me mighty smoothly, didn't you?'

'Since you mention it, yes.'

'And now I suppose you think you're going to slip in ahead of me and get away with that necklace? Well, say, listen, lemme tell you it'll take someone better than a half-baked string-bean like you to put one over on me.'

'I seem,' said Psmith, pained, 'to detect a certain animus creeping into your tone. Surely we can be trade rivals without this spirit of hostility. My attitude towards you is one of kindly tolerance.'

'Even if you get it, where do you think you're going to hide it? And, believe me, it'll take some hiding. Say, lemme tell you something. I'm your valet, ain't I? Well, then, I can come into your room and be tidying up whenever I darn please, can't I? Sure I can. I'll tell the world I can do just that little thing. And you take it from me, Bill . . .'

'You persist in the delusion that my name is William . . .'

'You take it from me, Bill, that if ever that necklace disappears and it isn't me that's done the disappearing, you'll find me tidying up in a way that'll make you dizzy. I'll go through that room of yours with a fine-tooth comb. So chew on that, will you?'

And Edward Cootes, moving sombrely across the hall, made a sinister exit. The mood of cool reflection was still to come, when he would realise that, in his desire to administer what he would have described as a hot one, he had acted a little rashly in putting his enemy on his guard. All he was thinking now was that his brief sketch of the position of affairs would have the effect of diminishing Psmith's complacency a trifle. He had, he flattered himself, slipped over something that could be classed as a jolt.

Nor was he unjustified in this view. The aspect of the matter on which he had touched was one that had not previously presented itself to Psmith: and, musing on it as he resettled himself in his chair, he could see that it afforded food for thought. As regarded the disposal of the necklace, should it ever come into his possession, he had formed no definite plan. He had assumed that he would conceal it somewhere until the first excitement of the chase slackened, and it was only now that he realised the difficulty of finding a suitable hiding-place outside his bedroom. Yes, it was certainly a matter on which, as Mr Cootes had suggested, he would do well to chew. For ten minutes, accordingly, he did so. And – it being practically impossible to keep a good man down – at the end of that period he was rewarded with an idea. He rose from his chair and pressed the bell.

'Ah, Beach,' he said affably, as the green-baize door swung open, 'I must apologise once more for troubling you. I keep ringing, don't I?'

'No trouble at all, sir,' responded the butler paternally. 'But if you were ringing to summon your personal attendant, I fear he is not immediately available. He left me somewhat abruptly a few moments ago. I was not aware that you would be requiring his services until the dressing-gong sounded, or I would have detained him.'

'Never mind. It was you I wished to see. Beach,' said Psmith, 'I am concerned about you. I learn from my man that the lining of your stomach is not all it should be.'

'That is true, sir,' replied Beach, an excited gleam coming into his dull eyes. He shivered slightly, as might a war-horse at the sound of the bugle. 'I do have trouble with the lining of my stomach.'

'Every stomach has a silver lining.'

'Sir?'

'I said, tell me all about it.'

'Well, really, sir...' said Beach wistfully.

'To please me,' urged Psmith.

'Well, sir, it is extremely kind of you to take an interest. It generally starts with a dull shooting pain on the right side of the abdomen from twenty minutes to half an hour after the conclusion of a meal. The symptoms . . .'

There was nothing but courteous sympathy in Psmith's gaze as he listened to what sounded like an eyewitness's account of the San Francisco earthquake, but inwardly he was wishing that his companion could see his way to making it a bit briefer and snappier. However, all things come to an end. Even the weariest river winds somewhere to the sea. With a moving period, the butler finally concluded his narrative.

'Parks' Pepsinine,' said Psmith promptly.

'Sir?'

'That's what you want. Parks' Pepsinine. It would set you right in no time.'

'I will make a note of the name, sir. The specific has not come to my notice until now. And, if I may say so,' added Beach, with a glassy but adoring look at his benefactor, 'I should like to express my gratitude for your kindness.'

'Not at all, Beach, not at all. Oh, Beach,' he said, as the other started to manœuvre towards the door, 'I've just remembered. There was something else I wanted to talk to you about.'

'Yes, sir?'

'I thought it might be as well to speak to you about it before approaching Lady Constance. The fact is, Beach, I am feeling cramped.'

'Indeed, sir? I forgot to mention that one of the symptoms from which I suffer is a sharp cramp.'

'Too bad. But let us, if you do not mind, shelve for the moment the subject of your interior organism and its ailments.

When I say I am feeling cramped, I mean spiritually. Have you ever written poetry, Beach?'

'No, sir.'

'Ah! Then it may be a little difficult for you to understand my feelings. My trouble is this. Out in Canada, Beach, I grew accustomed to doing my work in the most solitary surroundings. You remember that passage in my *Songs of Squalor* which begins "Across the pale parabola of Joy..."?'

'I fear, sir...'

'You missed it? Tough luck. Try to get hold of it some time. It's a bird. Well, that passage was written in a lonely hut on the banks of the Saskatchewan, miles away from human habitation. I am like that, Beach. I need the stimulus of the great open spaces. When I am surrounded by my fellows, inspiration slackens and dies. You know how it is when there are people about. Just as you are starting in to write a nifty, someone comes and sits down on the desk and begins talking about himself. Every time you get going nicely, in barges some alien influence and the Muse goes blooey. You see what I mean?'

'Yes, sir,' said Beach, gaping slightly.

'Well, that is why for a man like me existence in Blandings Castle has its drawbacks. I have got to get a place where I can be alone, Beach – alone with my dreams and visions. Some little eyrie perched on the cliffs of Time.... In other words, do you know of an empty cottage somewhere on the estate where I could betake myself when in the mood and swing a nib without any possibility of being interrupted?'

'A little cottage, sir?'

'A little cottage. With honeysuckle over the door, and Old Mister Moon climbing up above the trees. A cottage, Beach, where I can meditate, where I can turn the key in the door and

bid the world go by. Now that the castle is going to be full of all
these people who are coming for the County Ball, it is imperative that I wangle such a haven. Otherwise, a considerable slab of
priceless poetry will be lost to humanity for ever.'

'You desire,' said Beach, feeling his way cautiously, 'a small
cottage where you can write poetry, sir?'

'You follow me like a leopard. Do you know of such a one?'

'There is an unoccupied gamekeeper's cottage in the west
wood, sir, but it is an extremely humble place.'

'Be it never so humble, it will do for me. Do you think Lady
Constance would be offended if I were to ask for the loan of it for
a few days?'

'I fancy that her ladyship would receive the request with
equanimity, sir. She is used to . . . She is not unaccustomed . . .
Well, I can only say, sir, that there was a literary gentleman
visiting the castle last summer who expressed a desire to take
sun-baths in the garden each morning before breakfast. In the
nood, sir. And, beyond instructing me to warn the maids, her
ladyship placed no obstacle in the way of the fulfilment of his
wishes. So . . .'

'So a modest request like mine isn't likely to cause a heart-
attack? Admirable! You don't know what it means to me to feel
that I shall soon have a little refuge of my own, to which I can
retreat and be in solitude.'

'I can imagine that it must be extremely gratifying, sir.'

'Then I will put the motion before the Board directly Lady
Constance returns.'

'Very good, sir.'

'I should like to splash it on the record once more, Beach, that
I am much obliged to you for your sympathy and advice in this
matter. I knew you would not fail me.'

'Not at all, sir. I am only too glad to have been able to be of assistance.'

'Oh, and, Beach...'

'Sir?'

'Just one other thing. Will you be seeing Cootes, my valet, again shortly?'

'Quite shortly, sir, I should imagine.'

'Then would you mind just prodding him smartly in the lower ribs...'

'Sir?' cried Beach, startled out of his butlerian calm. He swallowed a little convulsively. For eighteen months and more, ever since Lady Constance Keeble had first begun to cast her fly and hook over the murky water of the artistic world and jerk its denizens on to the pile carpets of Blandings Castle, Beach had had his fill of eccentricity. But until this moment he had hoped that Psmith was going to prove an agreeable change from the stream of literary lunatics which had been coming and going all that weary time. And lo! Psmith's name led all the rest. Even the man who had come for a week in April and had wanted to eat jam with his fish paled in comparison.

'Prod him in the ribs, sir?' he quavered.

'Prod him in the ribs,' said Psmith firmly. 'And at the same time whisper in his ear the word "Aha!" '

Beach licked his dry lips.

'Aha, sir?'

'Aha! And say it came from me.'

'Very good, sir. The matter shall be attended to,' said Beach. And with a muffled sound that was half a sigh, half a death-rattle, he tottered through the green-baize door.

§ 1

Breakfast was over, and the guests of Blandings had scattered to their morning occupations. Some were writing letters, some were in the billiard-room: some had gone to the stables, some to the links: Lady Constance was interviewing the housekeeper, Lord Emsworth harrying head-gardener McAllister among the flower-beds: and in the Yew Alley, the dappled sunlight falling upon her graceful head, Miss Peavey walked pensively up and down.

She was alone. It is a sad but indisputable fact that in this imperfect world Genius is too often condemned to walk alone – if the earthier members of the community see it coming and have time to duck. Not one of the horde of visitors who had arrived overnight for the County Ball had shown any disposition whatever to court Miss Peavey's society.

One regrets this. Except for that slight bias towards dishonesty which led her to steal everything she could lay her hands on that was not nailed down, Aileen Peavey's was an admirable character; and, oddly enough, it was the noble side of her nature to which these coarse-fibred critics objected. Of Miss Peavey, the purloiner of other people's goods, they knew nothing; the woman they were dodging was Miss Peavey, the poetess. And it may be mentioned that, however much she might unbend in the presence of a congenial friend like Mr Edward Cootes, she was a perfectly genuine poetess. Those six volumes under her name in the British Museum catalogue were her own genuine and un-aided work: and, though she had been compelled to pay for the production of the first of the series, the other five had been brought out at her publisher's own risk, and had even made a little money.

Miss Peavey, however, was not sorry to be alone: for she had that on her mind which called for solitary thinking. The matter engaging her attention was the problem of what on earth had happened to Mr Edward Cootes. Two days had passed since he had left her to go and force Psmith at the pistol's point to introduce him into the castle: and since that moment he had vanished completely. Miss Peavey could not understand it.

His non-appearance was all the more galling in that her superb brain had just completed in every detail a scheme for the seizure of Lady Constance Keeble's diamond necklace; and to the success of this plot his aid was an indispensable adjunct. She was in the position of a general who comes from his tent with a plan of battle all mapped out, and finds that his army has strolled off somewhere and left him. Little wonder that, as she paced the Yew Alley, there was a frown on Miss Peavey's fair forehead.

The Yew Alley, as Lord Emsworth had indicated in his extremely interesting lecture to Mr Ralston McTodd at the Senior Conservative Club, contained among other noteworthy features certain yews which rose in solid blocks with rounded roof and stemless mushroom finials, the majority possessing arched recesses, forming arbors. As Miss Peavey was passing one of these, a voice suddenly addressed her.

'Hey!'

Miss Peavey started violently.

'Anyone about?'

A damp face with twigs sticking to it was protruding from a near-by yew. It rolled its eyes in an ineffectual effort to see round the corner.

Miss Peavey drew nearer, breathing heavily. The question as to the whereabouts of her wandering boy was solved; but the abruptness of his return had caused her to bite her tongue; and joy, as she confronted him, was blended with other emotions.

'You dish-faced gazooni!' she exclaimed heatedly, her voice trembling with a sense of ill-usage, 'where do you get that stuff, hiding in trees, and barking a girl's head off?'

'Sorry, Liz. I . . .'

'And where,' proceeded Miss Peavey, ventilating another grievance, 'have you been all this darned time? Gosh-dingit, you leave me a coupla days back saying you're going to stick up this bozo that calls himself McTodd with a gat and make him get you into the house, and that's the last I see of you. What's the big idea?'

'It's all right, Liz. He did get me into the house. I'm his valet. That's why I couldn't get at you before. The way the help has to keep itself to itself in this joint, we might as well have been in different counties. If I hadn't happened to see you snooping off by yourself this morning . . .'

Miss Peavey's keen mind grasped the position of affairs.

'All right, all right,' she interrupted, ever impatient of long speeches from others. 'I understand. Well, this is good, Ed.

It couldn't have worked out better. I've got a scheme all doped out, and now you're here we can get busy.'

'A scheme?'

'A pippin,' assented Miss Peavey.

'It'll need to be,' said Mr Cootes, on whom the events of the last few days had caused pessimism to set its seal. 'I tell you that McTodd gook is smooth. He somehow,' said Mr Cootes prudently, for he feared harsh criticism from his lady-love should he reveal the whole truth, 'he somehow got wise to the notion that, as I was his valet, I could go and snoop round in his room, where he'd be wanting to hide the stuff if he ever got it, and now he's gone and got them to let him have a kind of shack in the woods.'

'H'm!' said Miss Peavey. 'Well,' she resumed after a thoughtful pause, 'I'm not worrying about him. Let him go and roost in the woods all he wants to. I've got a scheme all ready, and it's gilt-edged. And, unless you ball up your end of it, Ed, it can't fail to drag home the gravy.'

'Am I in it?'

'You bet you're in it. I can't work it without you. That's what's been making me so darned mad when you didn't show up all this time.'

'Spill it, Liz,' said Mr Cootes humbly. As always in the presence of this dynamic woman, he was suffering from an inferiority complex. From the very start of their combined activities she had been the brains of the firm, he merely the instrument to carry into effect the plans she dictated.

Miss Peavey glanced swiftly up and down the Yew Alley. It was still the same peaceful, lonely spot. She turned to Mr Cootes again, and spoke with brisk decision.

'Now, listen, Ed, and get this straight, because maybe I shan't have another chance of talking to you.'

'I'm listening,' said Mr Cootes obsequiously.

'Well, to begin with, now that the house is full, Her Nibs is wearing that necklace every night. And you can take it from me, Ed, that you want to put on your smoked glasses before you look at it. It's a lalapaloosa.'

'As good as that?'

'Ask me! You don't know the half of it.'

'Where does she keep it, Liz? Have you found that out?' asked Mr Cootes, a gleam of optimism playing across his sad face for an instant.

'No, I haven't. And I don't want to. I've not got time to waste monkeying about with safes and maybe having the whole bunch pile on the back of my neck. I believe in getting things easy. Well, to-night this bimbo that calls himself McTodd is going to give a reading of his poems in the big drawing-room. You know where that is?'

'I can find out.'

'And you better had find out,' said Miss Peavey vehemently. 'And before to-night at that. Well, there you are. Do you begin to get wise?'

Mr Cootes, his head protruding unhappily from the yew tree, would have given much to have been able to make the demanded claim to wisdom, for he knew of old the store his alert partner set upon quickness of intellect. He was compelled, however, to disturb the branches by shaking his head.

'You always were pretty dumb,' said Miss Peavey with scorn. 'I'll say that you've got good solid qualities, Ed – from the neck up. Why, I'm going to sit behind Lady Constance while that goof is shooting his fool head off, and I'm going to reach out and grab that necklace off of her. See?'

'But, Liz' – Mr Cootes diffidently summoned up courage to point out what appeared to him to be a flaw in the scheme – 'if you start any strong-arm work in front of everybody like the way you say, won't they...?'

'No, they won't. And I'll tell you why they won't. They aren't going to see me do it, because when I do it it's going to be good and dark in that room. And it's going to be dark because you'll be somewheres out at the back of the house, wherever they keep the main electric-light works, turning the switch as hard as you can go. See? That's your end of it, and pretty soft for you at that. All you have to do is to find out where the thing is and what you have to do to it to put out all the lights in the joint. I guess I can trust you not to bungle that?'

'Liz,' said Mr Cootes, and there was reverence in his voice, 'you can do just that little thing. But what...?'

'All right, I know what you're going to say. What happens after that, and how do I get away with the stuff? Well, the window'll be open, and I'll just get to it and fling the necklace out. See? There'll be a big fuss going on in the room on account of the darkness and all that, and while everybody's cutting up and what-the-helling, you'll pick up your dogs and run round as quick as you can make it and pouch the thing. I guess it won't be hard for you to locate it. The window's just over the terrace, all smooth turf, and it isn't real dark nights now, and you ought to have plenty of time to hunt around before they can get the lights going again.... Well, what do you think of it?'

There was a brief silence.

'Liz,' said Mr Cootes at length.

'Is it or is it not,' demanded Miss Peavey, 'a ball of fire?'

'Liz,' said Mr Cootes, and his voice was husky with such awe as some young officer of Napoleon's staff might have felt on hearing the details of the latest plan of campaign, 'Liz, I've said it before, and I'll say it again. When it comes to the smooth stuff, old girl, you're the oyster's eye-tooth!'

And, reaching out an arm from the recesses of the yew, he took Miss Peavey's hand in his and gave it a tender squeeze. A dreamy look came into the poetess's fine eyes, and she giggled a little. Dumb-bell though he was, she loved this man.

§ 2

'Mr Baxter!'

'Yes, Miss Halliday?'

The Brains of Blandings looked abstractedly up from his desk. It was only some half-hour since luncheon had finished, but already he was in the library surrounded by large books like a sea-beast among rocks. Most of his time was spent in the library when the castle was full of guests, for his lofty mind was ill-attuned to the frivolous babblings of Society butterflies.

'I wonder if you could spare me this afternoon?' said Eve.

Baxter directed the glare of his spectacles upon her inquisitorially.

'The whole afternoon?'

'If you don't mind. You see, I had a letter by the second post from a great friend of mine, saying that she will be in Market Blandings this afternoon and asking me to meet her there. I must see her, Mr Baxter, *please*. You've no notion how important it is.'

Eve's manner was excited, and her eyes as they met Baxter's sparkled in a fashion that might have disturbed a man made of less stern stuff. If it had been the Hon. Freddie Threepwood, for instance, who had been gazing into their blue depths, that impulsive youth would have tied himself into knots and yapped like a dog. Baxter, the superman, felt no urge towards any such display. He reviewed her request calmly and judicially, and decided that it was a reasonable one.

'Very well, Miss Halliday.'

'Thank you ever so much. I'll make up for it by working twice as hard to-morrow.'

Eve flitted to the door, pausing there to bestow a grateful smile upon him before going out; and Baxter returned to his reading. For a moment he was conscious of a feeling of regret that this quite attractive and uniformly respectful girl should be the partner in crime of a man of whom he disapproved even more than he disapproved of most malefactors. Then he crushed down the weak emotion and was himself again.

Eve trotted downstairs, humming happily to herself. She had expected a longer and more strenuous struggle before she obtained her order of release, and told herself that, despite a manner which seldom deviated from the forbidding, Baxter was really quite nice. In short, it seemed to her that nothing could possibly occur to mar the joyfulness of this admirable afternoon; and it was only when a voice hailed her as she was going through the hall a few minutes later that she realised that she was mistaken. The voice, which trembled throatily, was that of the Hon. Freddie; and her first look at him told Eve, an expert diagnostician, that he was going to propose to her again.

'Well, Freddie?' said Eve resignedly.

The Hon. Frederick Threepwood was a young man who was used to hearing people say 'Well, Freddie?' resignedly when he appeared. His father said it; his Aunt Constance said it; all his other aunts and uncles said it. Widely differing personalities in every other respect, they all said 'Well, Freddie?' resignedly directly they caught sight of him. Eve's words, therefore, and the tone in which they were spoken, did not damp him as they might have damped another. His only feeling was one of solemn gladness at the thought that at last he had managed to get her alone for half a minute.

The fact that this was the first time he had been able to get her alone since her arrival at the castle had caused Freddie a good deal of sorrow. Bad luck was what he attributed it to, thereby giving the object of his affections less credit than was her due for a masterly policy of evasion. He sidled up, looking like a well-dressed sheep.

'Going anywhere?' he inquired.

'Yes. I'm going to Market Blandings. Isn't it a lovely afternoon? I suppose you are busy all the time now that the house is full? Good-bye,' said Eve.

'Eh?' said Freddie, blinking.

'Good-bye. I must be hurrying.'

'Where did you say you were going?'

'Market Blandings.'

'I'll come with you.'

'No, I want to be alone. I've got to meet someone there.'

'Come with you as far as the gates,' said Freddie, the human limpet.

The afternoon sun seemed to Eve to be shining a little less brightly as they started down the drive. She was a kind-hearted girl, and it irked her to have to be continually acting as a black frost in Freddie's garden of dreams. There appeared, however, to be but two ways out of the thing: either she must accept him or he must stop proposing. The first of these alternatives she resolutely declined to consider, and, as far as was ascertainable from his actions, Freddie declined just as resolutely to consider the second. The result was that solitary interviews between them were seldom wholly free from embarrassing developments.

They walked for a while in silence. Then:

'You're dashed hard on a fellow,' said Freddie.

'How's your putting coming on?' asked Eve.

'Eh?'

'Your putting. You told me you had so much trouble with it.'

She was not looking at him, for she had developed a habit of not looking at him on these occasions; but she assumed that the odd sound which greeted her remark was a hollow, mirthless laugh.

'My putting!'

'Well, you told me yourself it's the most important part of golf.'

'Golf! Do you think I have time to worry about golf these days?'

'Oh, how splendid, Freddie! Are you really doing some work of some kind? It's quite time, you know. Think how pleased your father will be.'

'I say,' said Freddie, 'I do think you might marry a chap.'

'I suppose I shall some day,' said Eve, 'if I meet the right one.'

'No, no!' said Freddie despairingly. She was not usually so dense as this. He had always looked on her as a dashed clever girl. 'I mean *me*.'

Eve sighed. She had hoped to avert the inevitable.

'Oh, Freddie!' she exclaimed, exasperated. She was still sorry for him, but she could not help being irritated. It was such a splendid afternoon and she had been feeling so happy. And now he had spoiled everything. It always took her at least half an hour to get over the nervous strain of refusing his proposals.

'I love you, dash it!' said Freddie.

'Well, do stop loving me,' said Eve. 'I'm an awful girl, really. I'd make you miserable.'

'Happiest man in the world,' corrected Freddie devoutly.

'I've got a frightful temper.'

'You're an angel.'

Eve's exasperation increased. She always had a curious fear that one of these days, if he went on proposing, she might say 'Yes' by mistake. She wished that there was some way known to science of stopping him once and for all. And in her desperation she thought of a line of argument which she had not yet employed.

'It's so absurd, Freddie,' she said. 'Really, it is. Apart from the fact that I don't want to marry you, how can you marry anyone – anyone, I mean, who hasn't plenty of money?'

'Wouldn't dream of marrying for money.'

'No, of course not, but...'

'Cupid,' said Freddie woodenly, 'pines and sickens in a gilded cage.'

Eve had not expected to be surprised by anything her companion might say, it being her experience that he possessed a vocabulary of about forty-three words and a sum-total of ideas that hardly ran into two figures; but this poetic remark took her back.

'What!'

Freddie repeated the observation. When it had been flashed on the screen as a spoken sub-title in the six-reel wonder film, 'Love or Mammon' (Beatrice Comely and Brian Fraser), he had approved and made a note of it.

'Oh!' said Eve, and was silent. As Miss Peavey would have put it, it held her for a while. 'What I meant,' she went on after a moment, 'was that you can't possibly marry a girl without money unless you've some money of your own.'

'I say, dash it!' A strange note of jubilation had come into the wooer's voice. 'I say, is that really all that stands between us? Because . . .'

'No, it isn't!'

'Because, look here, I'm going to have quite a good deal of money at any moment. It's more or less of a secret, you know – in fact a pretty deadish secret – so keep it dark, but Uncle Joe is going to give me a couple of thousand quid. He promised me. Two thousand of the crispest. Absolutely!'

'Uncle Joe?'

'*You* know. Old Keeble. He's going to give me a couple of thousand quid, and then I'm going to buy a partnership in a bookie's business and simply coin money. Stands to reason, I mean. You can't help making your bally fortune. Look at all the mugs who are losing money all the time at the races. It's the bookies that get the stuff. A pal of mine who was up at Oxford with me is in a bookie's office, and they're going to let me in if I . . .'

The momentous nature of his information had caused Eve to deviate now from her policy of keeping her eyes off Freddie when in emotional vein. And, if she had desired to check his lecture on finance, she could have chosen no better method than to look at him; for, meeting her gaze, Freddie immediately lost the thread of his discourse and stood yammering. A direct hit from Eve's eyes always affected him in this way.

'Mr Keeble is going to give you two thousand pounds!'

A wave of mortification swept over Eve. If there was one thing on which she prided herself, it was the belief that she was a loyal friend, a staunch pal; and now for the first time she found herself facing the unpleasant truth that she had been neglecting Phyllis Jackson's interests in the most abominable way ever since she had come to Blandings. She had definitely promised Phyllis that she would tackle this stepfather of hers and shame him with burning words into yielding up the three thousand pounds which Phyllis needed so desperately for her Lincolnshire farm. And what had she done? Nothing.

Eve was honest to the core, even in her dealings with herself. A less conscientious girl might have argued that she had had no opportunity of a private interview with Mr Keeble. She scorned to soothe herself with this specious plea. If she had given her mind to it she could have brought about a dozen private interviews, and she knew it. No. She had allowed the pleasant persistence of Psmith to take up her time, and Phyllis and her troubles had been thrust into the background. She confessed, despising herself, that she had hardly given Phyllis a thought.

And all the while this Mr Keeble had been in a position to scatter largess, thousands of pounds of it, to undeserving people like Freddie. Why, a word from her about Phyllis would have . . .

'Two thousand pounds?' she repeated dizzily. 'Mr Keeble!'

'Absolutely!' cried Freddie radiantly. The first shock of looking into her eyes had passed, and he was now revelling in that occupation.

'What for?'

Freddie's rapt gaze flickered. Love, he perceived, had nearly caused him to be indiscreet.

'Oh, I don't know,' he mumbled. 'He's just giving it me, you know, don't you know.'

'Did you simply go to him and ask him for it?'

'Well – er – well, yes. That was about the strength of it.'

'And he didn't object?'

'No. He seemed rather pleased.'

'Pleased!' Eve found breathing difficult. She was feeling rather like a man who suddenly discovers that the hole in his back yard which he has been passing nonchalantly for months is a goldmine. If the operation of extracting money from Mr Keeble was not only easy but also agreeable to the victim...She became aware of a sudden imperative need for Freddie's absence. She wanted to think this thing over.

'Well, then,' said Freddie, 'coming back to it, will you?'

'What?' said Eve, distrait.

'Marry me, you know. What I mean to say is, I worship the very ground you walk on, and all that sort of rot...I mean, and all that. And now that you realise that I'm going to get this couple of thousand...and the bookie's business;...and what not, I mean to say...'

'Freddie,' said Eve tensely, expressing her harassed nerves in a voice that came hotly through clenched teeth, 'go away!'

'Eh?'

'I don't want to marry you, and I'm sick of having to keep on telling you so. Will you please go away and leave me alone?' She stopped. Her sense of fairness told her that she was working off on her hapless suitor venom which should have been expended on herself. 'I'm sorry, Freddie,' she said, softening; 'I didn't mean to be such a beast as that. I know you're awfully fond of me, but really, really I can't marry you. You don't want to marry a girl who doesn't love you, do you?'

'Yes, I do,' said Freddie stoutly. 'If it's you, I mean. Love is a tiny seed that coldness can wither, but if tended and nurtured in the fostering warmth of an honest heart...'

'But, Freddie.'

'Blossoms into a flower,' concluded Freddie rapidly. 'What I mean to say is, love would come after marriage.'

'Nonsense!'

'Well, that's the way it happened in "A Society Mating".'

'Freddie,' said Eve, 'I really don't want to talk any more. Will you be a dear and just go away? I've got a lot of thinking to do.'

'Oh, thinking?' said Freddie, impressed. 'Right ho!'

'Thank you so much.'

'Oh – er – not at all. Well, pip-pip.'

'Good-bye.'

'See you later, what?'

'Of course, of course.'

'Fine! Well, toodle-oo!'

And the Hon. Freddie, not ill-pleased – for it seemed to him that at long last he detected signs of melting in the party of the second part – swivelled round on his long legs and started for home.

§ 3

The little town of Market Blandings was a peaceful sight as it slept in the sun. For the first time since Freddie had left her, Eve became conscious of a certain tranquillity as she entered the old grey High Street, which was the centre of the place's life and thought. Market Blandings had a comforting air of having been exactly the same for centuries. Troubles might vex the generations it housed, but they did not worry that lichened church with its sturdy four-square tower, nor those red-roofed shops, nor the age-old inns whose second storeys bulged so comfortably out over the pavements. As Eve walked in slow meditation towards the 'Emsworth Arms', the intensely respectable hostelry which was her objective, archways met her gaze, opening with a picturesque unexpectedness to show heartening glimpses of ancient nooks all cool and green. There was about the High Street of Market Blandings a suggestion of a slumbering cathedral close. Nothing was modern in it except the moving-picture house – and even that called itself an Electric Theatre, and was ivy-covered and surmounted by stone gables.

On second thoughts, that statement is too sweeping. There was one other modern building in the High Street – Jno. Banks, Hairdresser, to wit, and Eve was just coming abreast of Mr Banks's emporium now.

In any ordinary surroundings these premises would have been a tolerably attractive sight, but in Market Blandings they were almost an eyesore; and Eve, finding herself at the door, was jarred out of her reverie as if she had heard a false note in a solemn anthem. She was on the point of hurrying past, when the door opened and a short, solid figure came out. And at the sight of this short, solid figure Eve stopped abruptly.

It was with the object of getting his grizzled locks clipped in preparation for the County Ball that Joseph Keeble had come to Mr Banks's shop as soon as he had finished lunch. As he emerged now into the High Street he was wondering why he had permitted Mr Banks to finish off the job with a heliotrope-scented hair-wash. It seemed to Mr Keeble that the air was heavy with heliotrope, and it came to him suddenly that heliotrope was a scent which he always found particularly objectionable.

Ordinarily Joseph Keeble was accustomed to show an iron front to hairdressers who tried to inflict lotions upon him; and the reason his vigilance had relaxed under the ministrations of Jno. Banks was that the second post, which arrived at the castle at the luncheon hour, had brought him a plaintive letter from his stepdaughter Phyllis – the second he had had from her since the one which had caused him to tackle his masterful wife in the smoking-room. Immediately after the conclusion of his business deal with the Hon. Freddie, he had written to Phyllis in a vein of optimism rendered glowing by Freddie's promises, assuring her that at any moment he would be in a position to send her the three thousand pounds which she required to clinch the purchase of that dream-farm in Lincolnshire. To this she had replied with thanks. And after that there had been a lapse of days and still he had not made good. Phyllis was becoming worried, and said so in six closely-written pages.

Mr Keeble, as he sat in the barber's chair going over this letter in his mind, had groaned in spirit, while Jno. Banks with gleaming eyes did practically what he liked with the heliotrope bottle. Not for the first time since the formation of their partnership, Joseph Keeble was tormented with doubts as to his wisdom in entrusting a commission so delicate as the purloining of his wife's diamond necklace to one of his nephew Freddie's known feebleness of intellect. Here, he told himself unhappily, was a job of work which would have tested the combined abilities of a syndicate consisting of Charles Peace and the James Brothers, and he had put it in the hands of a young man who in all his life had only once shown genuine inspiration and initiative – on the occasion when he had parted his hair in the middle at a time when all the other members of the Bachelors' Club were brushing it straight back. The more Mr Keeble thought of Freddie's chances, the slimmer they appeared. By the time Jno. Banks had released him from the spotted apron he was thoroughly pessimistic, and as he passed out of the door, 'so perfumed that the winds were love-sick with him', his estimate of his colleague's abilities was reduced to a point where he began to doubt whether the stealing of a mere milk-can was not beyond his scope. So deeply immersed was he in these gloomy thoughts that Eve had to call his name twice before he came out of them.

'Miss Halliday?' he said apologetically. 'I beg your pardon. I was thinking.'

Eve, though they had hardly exchanged a word since her arrival at the castle, had taken a liking to Mr Keeble; and she felt in consequence none of the embarrassment which might have handicapped her in the discussion of an extremely delicate matter with another man. By nature direct and straightforward, she came to the point at once.

'Can you spare me a moment or two, Mr Keeble?' she said. She glanced at the clock on the church tower and saw that she had ample time before her own appointment. 'I want to talk to you about Phyllis.'

Mr Keeble jerked his head back in astonishment, and the world became noisome with heliotrope. It was as if the Voice of Conscience had suddenly addressed him.

'Phyllis!' he gasped, and the letter crackled in his breast-pocket.

'Your stepdaughter Phyllis.'

'Do you know her?'

'She was my best friend at school. I had tea with her just before I came to the castle.'

'Extraordinary!' said Mr Keeble.

A customer in quest of a shave thrust himself between them and went into the shop. They moved away a few paces.

'Of course if you say it is none of my business . . .'

'My dear young lady . . .'

'Well, it *is* my business, because she's my friend,' said Eve firmly. 'Mr Keeble, Phyllis told me she had written to you about buying that farm. Why don't you help her?'

The afternoon was warm, but not warm enough to account for the moistness of Mr Keeble's brow. He drew out a large handkerchief and mopped his forehead. A hunted look was in his eyes. The hand which was not occupied with the handkerchief had sought his pocket and was busy rattling keys.

'I want to help her. I would do anything in the world to help her.'

'Then why don't you?'

'I – I am curiously situated.'

'Yes, Phyllis told me something about that. I can see that it is a difficult position for you. But, Mr Keeble, surely, surely if you can manage to give Freddie Threepwood two thousand pounds to start a bookmaker's business . . .'

Her words were cut short by a strangled cry from her companion. Sheer panic was in his eyes now, and in his heart an overwhelming regret that he had ever been fool enough to dabble in crime in the company of a mere animated talking-machine like his nephew Freddie. This girl knew! And if she knew, how many others knew? The young imbecile had probably babbled his hideous secret into the ears of every human being in the place who would listen to him.

'He told you!' he stammered. 'He t-told you!'

'Yes. Just now.'

'Goosh!' muttered Mr Keeble brokenly.

Eve stared at him in surprise. She could not understand this emotion. The handkerchief, after a busy session, was lowered now, and he was looking at her imploringly.

'You haven't told anyone?' he croaked hoarsely.

'Of course not. I said I had only heard of it just now.'

'You wouldn't tell anyone?'

'Why should I?'

Mr Keeble's breath, which had seemed to him for a moment gone for ever, began to return timidly. Relief for a space held him dumb. What nonsense, he reflected, these newspapers and people talked about the modern girl. It was this very broad-mindedness of hers, to which they objected so absurdly, that made her a creature of such charm. She might behave in certain ways in a fashion that would have shocked her grandmother, but how comforting it was to find her calm and unmoved in the contemplation of another's crime. His heart warmed to Eve.

'You're wonderful!' he said.

'What do you mean?'

'Of course,' argued Mr Keeble, 'it isn't really stealing.'

'What!'

'I shall buy my wife another necklace.'

'You will – what?'

'So everything will be all right. Constance will be perfectly happy, and Phyllis will have her money, and...'

Something in Eve's astonished gaze seemed to smite Mr Keeble.

'Don't you *know*?' he broke off.

'Know? Know what?'

Mr Keeble perceived that he had wronged Freddie. The young ass had been a fool even to mention the money to this girl, but he had at least, it seemed, stopped short of disclosing the entire plot. An oyster-like reserve came upon him.

'Nothing, nothing,' he said hastily. 'Forget what I was going to say. Well, I must be going, I must be going.'

Eve clutched wildly at his retreating sleeve. Unintelligible though his words had been, one sentence had come home to her, the one about Phyllis having her money. It was no time for half-measures. She grabbed him.

'Mr Keeble,' she cried urgently. 'I don't know what you mean, but you were just going to say something which sounded... Mr Keeble, do trust me. I'm Phyllis's best friend, and if you've thought out any way of helping her I wish you would tell me.... You must tell me. I might be able to help...'

Mr Keeble, as she began her broken speech, had been endeavouring with deprecatory tugs to disengage his coat from her grasp. But now he ceased to struggle. Those doubts of Freddie's efficiency, which had troubled him in Jno. Banks's chair, still lingered. His opinion that Freddie was but a broken reed had not changed. Indeed, it had grown. He looked at Eve. He looked at her searchingly. Into her pleading eyes he directed a stare that sought to probe her soul, and saw there honesty, sympathy, and – better still – intelligence. He might have stood and gazed into Freddie's fishy eyes for weeks without discovering a tithe of such intelligence. His mind was made up. This girl was an ally. A girl of dash and vigour. A girl worth a thousand Freddies – not, however, reflected Mr Keeble, that that was saying much. He hesitated no longer.

'It's like this,' said Mr Keeble.

§ 4

The information, authoritatively conveyed to him during breakfast by Lady Constance, that he was scheduled that night to read select passages from Ralston McTodd's *Songs of Squalor* to the entire house-party assembled in the big drawing-room, had come as a complete surprise to Psmith, and to his fellow-guests – such of them as were young and of the soulless sex – as a shock from which they found it hard to rally. True, they had before now gathered in a vague sort of way that he was one of those literary fellows, but so normal and engaging had they found his whole manner and appearance that it had never occurred to them that he concealed anything up his sleeve as lethal as *Songs of Squalor*. Among these members of the younger set the consensus of opinion was that it was a bit thick, and that at such a price even the lavish hospitality of Blandings was scarcely worth having. Only those who had visited the castle before during the era of her ladyship's flirtation with Art could have been described as resigned. These stout hearts argued that while this latest blister was probably going to be pretty bad, he could hardly be worse than the chappie who had lectured on Theosophy last November, and must almost of necessity be better than the bird who during the Shiffley race-week had attempted in a two-hour discourse to convert them to vegetarianism.

Psmith himself regarded the coming ordeal with equanimity. He was not one of those whom the prospect of speaking in public afflicts with nervous horror. He liked the sound of his own voice, and night, when it came, found him calmly cheerful. He listened contentedly to the murmur of the drawing-room filling up as he strolled on the star-lit terrace, smoking a last cigarette before duty called him elsewhere. And when, some few yards away, seated on the terrace wall gazing out into the velvet darkness, he perceived Eve Halliday, his sense of well-being became acute.

All day he had been conscious of a growing desire for another of those cosy chats with Eve which had done so much to make life agreeable for him during his stay at Blandings. Her prejudice – which he deplored – in favour of doing a certain amount of work to justify her salary, had kept him during the morning away from the little room off the library where she was wont to sit cataloguing books; and when he had gone there after lunch he had found it empty. As he approached her now, he was thinking pleasantly of all those delightful walks, those excellent driftings on the lake, and those cheery conversations which had gone to cement his conviction that of all possible girls she was the only possible one. It seemed to him that in addition to being beautiful she brought out all that was best in him of intellect and soul. That is to say, she let him talk oftener and longer than any girl he had ever known.

It struck him as a little curious that she made no move to greet him. She remained apparently unaware of his approach. And yet the summer night was not of such density as to hide him from view – and, even if she could not see him, she must undoubtedly have heard him; for only a moment before he had tripped with some violence over a large flower-pot, one of a row of sixteen which Angus McAllister, doubtless for some good purpose, had placed in the fairway that afternoon.

'A pleasant night,' he said, seating himself gracefully beside her on the wall.

She turned her head for a brief instant, and, having turned it, looked away again.

'Yes,' she said.

Her manner was not effusive, but Psmith persevered.

'The stars,' he proceeded, indicating them with a kindly yet not patronising wave of the hand. 'Bright, twinkling, and – if I may say so – rather neatly arranged. When I was a mere lad, someone whose name I cannot recollect taught me which was Orion. Also Mars, Venus, and Jupiter. This thoroughly useless chunk of knowledge has, I am happy to say, long since passed from my mind. However, I am in a position to state that that wiggly thing up there a little to the right is King Charles's Wain.'

'Yes?'

'Yes, indeed, I assure you.' It struck Psmith that Astronomy was not gripping his audience, so he tried Travel. 'I hear,' he said, 'you went to Market Blandings this afternoon.'

'Yes.'

'An attractive settlement.'

'Yes.'

There was a pause. Psmith removed his monocle and polished it thoughtfully. The summer night seemed to him to have taken on a touch of chill.

'What I like about the English rural districts,' he went on, 'is that when the authorities have finished building a place they stop. Somewhere about the reign of Henry the Eighth, I imagine that the master-mason gave the final house a pat with his trowel and said, "Well, boys, that's Market Blandings." To which his assistants no doubt assented with many a hearty "Grammercy!" and "I'fackins!" these being expletives to which they were much addicted. And they went away and left it, and nobody has touched it since. And I, for one, thoroughly approve. I think it makes the place soothing. Don't you?'

'Yes.'

As far as the darkness would permit, Psmith subjected Eve to an inquiring glance through his monocle. This was a strange new mood in which he had found her. Hitherto, though she had always endeared herself to him by permitting him the major portion of the dialogue, they had usually split conversations on at least a seventy-five–twenty-five basis. And though it gratified

Psmith to be allowed to deliver a monologue when talking with most people, he found Eve more companionable when in a slightly chattier vein.

'Are you coming in to hear me read?' he asked.

'No.'

It was a change from 'Yes,' but that was the best that could be said of it. A good deal of discouragement was always required to damp Psmith, but he could not help feeling a slight diminution of buoyancy. However, he kept on trying.

'You show your usual sterling good sense,' he said approvingly. 'A scalier method of passing the scented summer night could hardly be hit upon.' He abandoned the topic of the reading. It did not grip. That was manifest. It lacked appeal. 'I went to Market Blandings this afternoon, too,' he said. 'Comrade Baxter informed me that you had gone thither, so I went after you. Not being able to find you, I turned in for half an hour at the local moving-picture palace. They were showing Episode Eleven of a serial. It concluded with the heroine, kidnapped by Indians, stretched on the sacrificial altar with the high-priest making passes at her with a knife. The hero meanwhile had started to climb a rather nasty precipice on his way to the rescue. The final picture was a close-up of his fingers slipping slowly off a rock. Episode Twelve next week.'

Eve looked out into the night without speaking.

'I'm afraid it won't end happily,' said Psmith with a sigh. 'I think he'll save her.'

Eve turned on him with a menacing abruptness.

'Shall I tell you why I went to Market Blandings this afternoon?' she said.

'Do,' said Psmith cordially. 'It is not for me to criticise, but as a matter of fact I was rather wondering when you were going to begin telling me all about your adventures. I have been monopolising the conversation.'

'I went to meet Cynthia.'

Psmith's monocle fell out of his eye and swung jerkily on its cord. He was not easily disconcerted, but this unexpected piece of information, coming on top of her peculiar manner, undoubtedly jarred him. He foresaw difficulties, and once again found himself thinking hard thoughts of this confounded female who kept bobbing up when least expected. How simple life would have been, he mused wistfully, had Ralston McTodd only had the good sense to remain a bachelor.

'Oh, Cynthia?' he said.

'Yes, Cynthia,' said Eve. The inconvenient Mrs McTodd possessed a Christian name admirably adapted for being hissed between clenched teeth, and Eve hissed it in this fashion now. It became evident to Psmith that the dear girl was in a condition of hardly suppressed fury and that trouble was coming his way. He braced himself to meet it.

'Directly after we had that talk on the lake, the day I arrived,' continued Eve tersely, 'I wrote to Cynthia, telling her to come here at once and meet me at the "Emsworth Arms" . . .'

'In the High Street,' said Psmith. 'I know it. Good beer.'

'What!'

'I said they sell good beer . . .'

'Never mind about the beer,' cried Eve.

'No, no. I merely mentioned it in passing.'

'At lunch to-day I got a letter from her saying that she would be there this afternoon. So I hurried off. I wanted—' Eve laughed a hollow, mirthless laugh of a calibre which even the Hon. Freddie Threepwood would have found beyond his powers, and he was a specialist – 'I wanted to try to bring you two together. I thought that if I could see her and have a talk with her that you might become reconciled.'

Psmith, though obsessed with a disquieting feeling that he was fighting in the last ditch, pulled himself together sufficiently to pat her hand as it lay beside him on the wall like some white and fragile flower.

'That was like you,' he murmured. 'That was an act worthy of your great heart. But I fear that the rift between Cynthia and myself has reached such dimensions ... '

Eve drew her hand away. She swung round, and the battery of her indignant gaze raked him furiously.

'I saw Cynthia,' she said, 'and she told me that her husband was in Paris.'

'Now, how in the world,' said Psmith, struggling bravely but with a growing sense that they were coming over the plate a bit too fast for him, 'how in the world did she get an idea like that?'

'Do you really want to know?'

'I do, indeed.'

'Then I'll tell you. She got the idea because she had had a letter from him, begging her to join him there. She had just finished telling me this, when I caught sight of you from the inn window, walking along the High Street. I pointed you out to Cynthia, and she said she had never seen you before in her life.'

'Women soon forget,' sighed Psmith.

'The only excuse I can find for you,' stormed Eve in a vibrant undertone necessitated by the fact that somebody had just emerged from the castle door and they no longer had the terrace to themselves, 'is that you're mad. When I think of all you said to me about poor Cynthia on the lake that afternoon, when I think of all the sympathy I wasted on you ... '

'Not wasted,' corrected Psmith firmly. 'It was by no means wasted. It made me love you – if possible – even more.'

Eve had supposed that she had embarked on a tirade which would last until she had worked off her indignation and felt composed again, but this extraordinary remark scattered the thread of her harangue so hopelessly that all she could do was to stare at him in amazed silence.

'Womanly intuition,' proceeded Psmith gravely, 'will have told you long ere this that I love you with a fervour which with my poor vocabulary I cannot hope to express. True, as you are about to say, we have known each other but a short time, as time is measured. But what of that?'

Eve raised her eyebrows. Her voice was cold and hostile.

'After what has happened,' she said, 'I suppose I ought not to be surprised at finding you capable of anything, but – are you really choosing this moment to – to propose to me?'

'To employ a favourite word of your own – yes.'

'And you expect me to take you seriously?'

'Assuredly not. I look upon the present disclosure purely as a sighting shot. You may regard it, if you will, as a kind of formal proclamation. I wish simply to go on record as an aspirant to your hand. I want you, if you will be so good, to make a note of my words and give them a thought from time to time. As Comrade Cootes – a young friend of mine whom you have not yet met – would say, "Chew on them."'

'I . . .'

'It is possible,' continued Psmith, 'that black moments will come to you – for they come to all of us, even the sunniest – when you will find yourself saying, "Nobody loves me!" On such occasions I should like you to add, "No, I am wrong. There *is* somebody who loves me." At first, it may be, that reflection will bring but scant balm. Gradually, however, as the days go by and we are constantly together and my nature unfolds itself before you like the petals of some timid flower beneath the rays of the sun . . .'

Eve's eyes opened wider. She had supposed herself incapable of further astonishment, but she saw that she had been mistaken.

'You surely aren't dreaming of staying on here *now?*' she gasped.

'Most decidedly. Why not?'

'But – but what is to prevent me telling everybody that you are not Mr McTodd?'

'Your sweet, generous nature,' said Psmith. 'Your big heart. Your angelic forbearance.'

'Oh!'

'Considering that I only came here as McTodd – and if you had seen him you would realise that he is not a person for whom the man of sensibility and refinement would lightly allow himself to be mistaken – I say considering that I only took on the job of understudy so as to get to the castle and be near you, I hardly think that you will be able to bring yourself to get me slung out. You must try to understand what happened. When Lord Emsworth started chatting with me under the impression that I was Comrade McTodd, I encouraged the mistake purely with the kindly intention of putting him at his ease. Even when he informed me that he was expecting me to come down to Blandings with him on the five o'clock train, it never occurred to me to do so. It was only when I saw you talking to him in the street and he revealed the fact that you were about to enjoy his hospitality that I decided that there was no other course open to the man of spirit. Consider! Twice that day you had passed out of my life – may I say taking the sunshine with you? – and I began to fear you might pass out of it for ever. So, loath though I was to commit the solecism of planting myself in this happy home under false pretences, I could see no other way. And here I am!'

'You *must* be mad!'

'Well, as I was saying, the days will go by, you will have ample opportunity of studying my personality, and it is quite possible that in due season the love of an honest heart may impress you as worth having. I may add that I have loved you since the moment when I saw you sheltering from the rain under that awning in Dover Street, and I recall saying as much to Comrade Walderwick when he was chatting with me some short time later on the subject of his umbrella. I do not press you for an answer now...'

'I should hope not!'

'I merely say "Think it over." It is nothing to cause you mental distress. Other men love you. Freddie Threepwood loves you. Just add me to the list. That is all I ask. Muse on me from time to time. Reflect that I may be an acquired taste. You probably did not like olives the first time you tasted them. Now you probably do. Give me the same chance you would an olive. Consider, also, how little you actually have against me. What, indeed, does it amount to, when you come to examine it narrowly? All you have against me is the fact that I am not Ralston McTodd. Think how comparatively few people *are* Ralston McTodd. Let your meditations proceed along these lines and...'

He broke off, for at this moment the individual who had come out of the front door a short while back loomed beside them, and the glint of starlight on glass revealed him as the Efficient Baxter.

'Everybody is waiting, Mr McTodd,' said the Efficient Baxter. He spoke the name, as always, with a certain sardonic emphasis.

'Of course,' said Psmith affably, 'of course. I was forgetting. I will get to work at once. You are quite sure you do not wish to hear a scuttleful of modern poetry, Miss Halliday?'

'Quite sure.'

'And yet even now, so our genial friend here informs us, a bevy of youth and beauty is crowding the drawing-room, agog for the treat. Well, well! It is these strange clashings of personal taste which constitute what we call Life. I think I will write a poem about it some day. Come, Comrade Baxter, let us be up and doing. I must not disappoint my public.'

For some moments after the two had left her – Baxter silent and chilly, Psmith, all debonair chumminess, kneading the other's arm and pointing out as they went objects of interest by the wayside – Eve remained on the terrace wall, thinking. She was laughing now, but behind her amusement there was another feeling, and one that perplexed her. A good many men had proposed to her in the course of her career, but none of them had ever left her with this odd feeling of exhilaration. Psmith was different from any other man who had come her way, and difference was a quality which Eve esteemed. . . .

She had just reached the conclusion that life for whatever girl might eventually decide to risk it in Psmith's company would never be dull, when strange doings in her immediate neighbourhood roused her from her meditations.

The thing happened as she rose from her seat on the wall and started to cross the terrace on her way to the front door. She had stopped for an instant beneath the huge open window of the drawing-room to listen to what was going on inside. Faintly, with something of the quality of a far-off phonograph, the sound of Psmith reading came to her; and even at this distance there was a composed blandness about his voice which brought a smile to her lips.

And then, with a startling abruptness, the lighted window was dark. And she was aware that all the lighted windows on that side of the castle had suddenly become dark. The lamp that shone over the great door ceased to shine. And above the hubbub of voices in the drawing-room she heard Psmith's patient drawl.

'Ladies and gentlemen, I think the lights have gone out.'

The night air was rent by a single piercing scream. Something flashed like a shooting star and fell at her feet; and, stooping, Eve found in her hands Lady Constance Keeble's diamond necklace.

§ 5

To be prepared is everything in this life. Ever since her talk with Mr Joseph Keeble in the High Street of Market Blandings that afternoon, Eve's mind had been flitting nimbly from one scheme to another, all designed to end in this very act of seizing the necklace in her hands and each rendered impracticable by some annoying flaw. And now that Fate in its impulsive way had achieved for her what she had begun to feel she could never accomplish for herself, she wasted no time in bewildered inaction. The miracle found her ready for it.

For an instant she debated with herself the chances of a dash through the darkened hall up the stairs to her room. But the lights might go on again, and she might meet someone. Memories of sensational novels read in the past told her that on occasions such as this people were detained and searched....

Suddenly, as she stood there, she found the way. Close beside her, lying on its side, was the flower-pot which Psmith had overturned as he came to join her on the terrace wall. It might have defects as a cache, but at the moment she could perceive none. Most flower-pots are alike, but this was a particularly easily-remembered flower-pot: for in its journeying from the potting shed to the terrace it had acquired on its side a splash of white paint. She would be able to distinguish it from its fellows when, late that night, she crept out to retrieve the spoil. And surely nobody would ever think of suspecting...

She plunged her fingers into the soft mould, and straightened herself, breathing quickly. It was not an ideal piece of work, but it would serve.

She rubbed her fingers on the turf, put the flower-pot back in the row with the others, and then, like a flying white phantom, darted across the terrace and into the house. And so with beating heart, groping her way, to the bathroom to wash her hands.

The twenty-thousand-pound flower-pot looked placidly up at the winking stars.

§ 6

It was perhaps two minutes later that Mr Cootes, sprinting lustily, rounded the corner of the house and burst on to the terrace. Late as usual.

§ 1

THE Efficient Baxter prowled feverishly up and down the yielding carpet of the big drawing-room. His eyes gleamed behind their spectacles, his dome-like brow was corrugated. Except for himself, the room was empty. As far as the scene of the disaster was concerned, the tumult and the shouting had died. It was going on vigorously in practically every other part of the house, but in the drawing-room there was stillness, if not peace.

Baxter paused, came to a decision, went to the wall and pressed the bell.

'Thomas,' he said when that footman presented himself a few moments later.

'Sir?'

'Send Susan to me.'

'Susan, sir?'

'Yes, Susan,' snapped the Efficient One, who had always a short way with the domestic staff. 'Susan, Susan, Susan.... The new parlourmaid.'

'Oh, yes, sir. Very good, sir.'

Thomas withdrew, outwardly all grave respectfulness, inwardly piqued, as was his wont, at the airy manner in which the secretary flung his orders about at the castle. The domestic staff at Blandings lived in a perpetual state of smouldering discontent under Baxter's rule.

'Susan,' said Thomas when he arrived in the lower regions, 'you're to go up to the drawing-room. Nosey Parker wants you.'

The pleasant-faced young woman whom he addressed laid down her knitting.

'Who?' she asked.

'Mister Blooming Baxter. When you've been here a little longer you'll know that he's the feller that owns the place. How he got it I don't know. Found it,' said Thomas satirically, 'in his Christmas stocking, I expect. Anyhow, you're to go up.'

Thomas's fellow-footman, Stokes, a serious-looking man with a bald forehead, shook that forehead solemnly.

'Something's the matter,' he asserted. 'You can't tell me that wasn't a scream we heard when them lights was out. Or,' he added weightily, for he was a man who looked at every side of a question, 'a shriek. It was a shriek or scream. I said so at the time. "There," I said, "listen!" I said. "That's somebody screaming," I said. "Or shrieking." Something's up.'

'Well, Baxter hasn't been murdered, worse luck,' said Thomas. 'He's up there screaming or shrieking for Susan. "Send Susan to me!"' proceeded Thomas, giving an always popular imitation. '"Susan, Susan, Susan." So you'd best go, my girl, and see what he wants.'

'Very well.'

'And, Susan,' said Thomas, a tender note creeping into his voice, for already, brief as had been her sojourn at Blandings, he had found the new parlourmaid making a deep impression on him, 'if it's a row of any kind ...'

'Or description,' interjected Stokes.

'Or description,' continued Thomas, accepting the word, 'if 'e's 'arsh with you for some reason or other, you come right back to me and sob out your troubles on my chest, see? Lay your little 'ead on my shoulder and tell me all about it.'

The new parlourmaid, primly declining to reply to this alluring invitation, started on her journey upstairs; and Thomas, with a not unmanly sigh, resumed his interrupted game of halfpenny nap with colleague Stokes.

* * * * *

The Efficient Baxter had gone to the open window and was gazing out into the night when Susan entered the drawing-room.

'You wished to see me, Mr Baxter?'

The secretary spun round. So softly had she opened the door, and so noiselessly had she moved when inside the room, that it was not until she spoke that he had become aware of her arrival. It was a characteristic of this girl Susan that she was always apt to be among those present some time before the latter became cognisant of the fact.

'Oh, good evening, Miss Simmons. You came in very quietly.'

'Habit,' said the parlourmaid.

'You gave me quite a start.'

'I'm sorry. What was it,' she asked, dismissing in a positively unfeeling manner the subject of her companion's jarred nerves, 'that you wished to see me about?'

'Shut that door.'

'I have. I always shut doors.'

'Please sit down.'

'No, thank you, Mr Baxter. It might look odd if anyone should come in.'

'Of course. You think of everything.'

'I always do.'

Baxter stood for a moment, frowning.

'Miss Simmons,' he said, 'when I thought it expedient to instal a private detective in this house, I insisted on Wragge's sending you. We had worked together before . . .'

'Sixteenth of December, 1918, to January twelve, 1919, when you were secretary to Mr Horace Jevons, the American million-aire,' said Miss Simmons as promptly as if he had touched a spring. It was her hobby to remember dates with precision.

'Exactly. I insisted upon your being sent because I knew from experience that you were reliable. At that time I looked on your presence here merely as a precautionary measure. Now, I am sorry to say . . .'

'Did someone steal Lady Constance's necklace to-night?'

'Yes!'

'When the lights went out just now?'

'Exactly.'

'Well, why couldn't you say so at once? Good gracious, man, you don't have to break the thing gently to me.'

The Efficient Baxter, though he strongly objected to being addressed as 'man', decided to overlook the solecism.

'The lights suddenly went out,' he said. 'There was a certain amount of laughter and confusion. Then a piercing shriek . . .'

'I heard it.'

'And immediately after Lady Constance's voice crying that her jewels had been snatched from her neck.'

'Then what happened?'

'Still greater confusion, which lasted until one of the maids arrived with a candle. Eventually the lights went on again, but of the necklace there was no sign whatever.'

'Well? Were you expecting the thief to wear it as a watch-chain or hang it from his teeth?'

Baxter was finding his companion's manner more trying every minute, but he preserved his calm.

'Naturally the doors were barred and a complete search insti-tuted. And extremely embarrassing it was. With the single exception of the scoundrel who has been palming himself off as McTodd, all those present were well-known members of Society.'

'Well-known members of Society might not object to getting hold of a twenty-thousand-pound necklace. But still, with the McTodd fellow there, you oughtn't to have had far to look. What had he to say about it?'

'He was among the first to empty his pockets.'

'Well, then, he must have hidden the thing somewhere.'

'Not in this room. I have searched assiduously.'

'H'm.'

There was a silence.

'It is baffling,' said Baxter, 'baffling.'

'It is nothing of the kind,' replied Miss Simmons tartly. 'This wasn't a one-man job. How could it have been? I should be inclined to call it a three-man job. One to switch off the lights, one to snatch the necklace, and one to – was that window open all the time? I thought so – and one to pick up the necklace when the second fellow threw it out on to the terrace.'

'Terrace!'

The word shot from Baxter's lips with explosive force. Miss Simmons looked at him curiously.

'Thought of something?'

'Miss Simmons,' said the Efficient One impressively, 'everybody was assembled in here waiting for the reading to begin, but the pseudo-McTodd was nowhere to be found. I discovered him eventually on the terrace in close talk with the Halliday girl.'

'His partner,' said Miss Simmons, nodding. 'We thought so all along. And let me add my little bit. There's a fellow down in the servants' hall that calls himself a valet, and I'll bet he didn't know what a valet was till he came here. I thought he was a crook the moment I set eyes on him. I can tell 'em in the dark. Now, do you know whose valet he is? This McTodd fellow's!'

Baxter bounded to and fro like a caged tiger.

'And with my own ears,' he cried excitedly, 'I heard the Halliday girl refuse to come to the drawing-room to listen to the reading. She was out on the terrace throughout the whole affair. Miss Simmons, we must act! We must act!'

'Yes, but not like idiots,' replied the detective frostily.

'What do you mean?'

'Well, you can't charge out, as you looked as if you wanted to just then, and denounce these crooks where they sit. We've got to go carefully.'

'But meanwhile they will smuggle the necklace away!'

'They won't smuggle any necklace away, not while I'm around. Suspicion's no good. We've made out a nice little case against the three of them, but it's no use unless we catch them with the goods. The first thing we have to do is to find out where they've hidden the stuff. And that'll take patience. I'll start by searching that girl's room. Then I'll search the valet fellow's room. And if the stuff isn't there it'll mean they've hidden it out in the open somewhere.'

'But this McTodd fellow. This fellow who poses as McTodd. He may have it all the while.'

'No. I'll search his room, too, but the stuff won't be there. He's the fellow who's going to get it in the end, because he's got that place out in the woods to hide it in. But they wouldn't have had time to slip it to him yet. That necklace is some-where right here. And if,' said Miss Simmons with grim facetiousness, 'they can hide it from me, they may keep it as a birthday present.'

§ 2

How wonderful, if we pause to examine it, is Nature's inexor-able law of compensation. Instead of wasting time in envy of our mental superiors, we would do well to reflect that these gifts of theirs which excite our wistful jealousy are ever attended by corresponding penalties. To take an example that lies to hand, it was the very fact that he possessed a brain like a buzzsaw that rendered the Efficent Baxter a bad sleeper. Just as he would be dropping off, bing! would go that brain of his, melting the mists of sleep like snow in a furnace.

This was so even when life was running calmly for him and without excitement. To-night, his mind, bearing the load it did, firmly declined even to consider the question of slumber. The hour of two, chiming from the clock over the stables, found him as wide awake as ever he was at high noon.

Lying in bed in the darkness, he reviewed the situation as far as he had the data. Shortly before he retired, Miss Simmons had made her report about the bedrooms. Though subjected to the severest scrutiny, neither Psmith's boudoir nor Cootes's attic nor Eve's little nook on the third floor had yielded up treasure of any description. And this, Miss Simmons held, confirmed her original view that the necklace must be lying concealed in what might almost be called a public spot – on some window-ledge, maybe, or somewhere in the hall. . . .

Baxter lay considering this theory. It did appear to be the only tenable one; but it offended him by giving the search a frivolous suggestion of being some sort of round game like Hunt the Slipper or Find the Thimble. As a child he had held austerely aloof from these silly pastimes, and he resented being compelled to play them now. Still . . .

He sat up, thinking. He had heard a noise.

* * * * *

The attitude of the majority of people towards noises in the night is one of cautious non-interference. But Rupert Baxter was made of sterner stuff. The sound had seemed to come from downstairs somewhere – perhaps from that very hall where, according to Miss Simmons, the stolen necklace might even now be lying hid. Whatever it was, it must certainly not be ignored. He reached for the spectacles which lay ever ready to his hand on the table beside him: then climbed out of bed, and, having put on a pair of slippers and opened the door, crept forth into the darkness. As far as he could ascertain by holding his breath and straining his ears, all was still from cellar to roof; but nevertheless he was not satisfied. He continued to listen. His room was on the second floor, one of a series that ran along a balcony overlooking the hall; and he stood, leaning over the balcony rail, a silent statue of Vigilance.

*****

The noise which had acted so electrically upon the Efficient Baxter had been a particularly noisy noise; and only the intervening distance and the fact that his door was closed had prevented it sounding to him like an explosion. It had been caused by the crashing downfall of a small table containing a vase, a jar of potpourri, an Indian sandalwood box of curious workmanship, and a cabinet-size photograph of the Earl of Emsworth's eldest son, Lord Bosham; and the table had fallen because Eve, *en route* across the hall in quest of her precious flower-pot, had collided with it while making for the front door. Of all indoor sports – and Eve, as she stood pallidly among the ruins, would have been the first to endorse this dictum – the one which offers the minimum of pleasure to the participant is that of roaming in pitch darkness through the hall of a country-house. Easily navigable in the daytime, these places become at night mere traps for the unwary.

Eve paused breathlessly. So terrific had the noise sounded to her guilty ears that every moment she was expecting doors to open all over the castle, belching forth shouting men with pistols. But as nothing happened, courage returned to her, and she resumed her journey. She found the great door, ran her fingers along its surface, and drew the chain. The shooting back of the bolts occupied but another instant, and then she was out on the terrace running her hardest towards the row of flower-pots.

Up on his balcony, meanwhile, the Efficient Baxter was stopping, looking, and listening. The looking brought no results, for all below was black as pitch; but the listening proved more fruitful. Faintly from down in the well of the hall there floated up to him a peculiar sound like something rustling in the darkness. Had he reached the balcony a moment earlier, he would have heard the rattle of the chain and the click of the bolts; but these noises had occurred just before he came out of his room. Now all that was audible was this rustling.

He could not analyse the sound, but the fact that there was any sound at all in such a place at such an hour increased his suspicions that dark doings were toward which would pay for investigation. With stealthy steps he crept to the head of the stairs and descended.

One uses the verb 'descend' advisedly, for what is required is some word suggesting instantaneous activity. About Baxter's progress from the second floor to the first there was nothing halting or hesitating. He, so to speak, did it now. Planting his foot firmly on a golf-ball which the Hon. Freddie Threepwood, who had been practising putting in the corridor before retiring to bed, had left in his casual fashion just where the steps began, he took the entire staircase in one majestic, volplaning sweep. There were eleven stairs in all separating his landing from the landing below, and the only ones he hit were the third and tenth. He came to rest with a squattering thud on the lower landing, and for a moment or two the fever of the chase left him.

The fact that many writers in their time have commented at some length on the mysterious manner in which Fate is apt to perform its work must not deter us now from a brief survey of this latest manifestation of its ingenious methods. Had not his interview with Eve that afternoon so stimulated the Hon. Freddie as to revive in him a faint yet definite desire to putt, there would have been no golf-ball waiting for Baxter on the stairs.

And had he been permitted to negotiate the stairs in a less impetuous manner, Baxter would not at this juncture have switched on the light.

It had not been his original intention to illuminate the theatre of action, but after that Lucifer-like descent from the second floor to the first he was taking no more chances. 'Safety First' was Baxter's slogan. As soon, therefore, as he had shaken off a dazed sensation of mental and moral collapse, akin to that which comes to the man who steps on the teeth of a rake and is smitten on the forehead by the handle, he rose with infinite caution to his feet and, feeling his way down by the banisters, groped for the switch and pressed it. And so it came about that Eve, heading for home with her precious flower-pot in her arms, was stopped when at the very door by a sudden warning flood of light. Another instant, and she would have been across the threshold of disaster.

For a moment paralysis gripped her. The light had affected her like someone shouting loudly and unexpectedly in her ear. Her heart gave one convulsive bound, and she stood frozen. Then, filled with a blind desire for flight, she dashed like a hunted rabbit into the friendly shelter of a clump of bushes.

* * * *

Baxter stood blinking. Gradually his eyes adjusted themselves to the light, and immediately they had done so he was seized by a fresh frenzy of zeal. Now that all things were made visible to him he could see that that faint rustling sound had been caused by a curtain flapping in the breeze, and that the breeze which made the curtain flap was coming in through the open front door.

Baxter wasted no time in abstract thought. He acted swiftly and with decision. Straightening his spectacles on his nose, he girded up his pyjamas and galloped out into the night.

* * * * *

The smooth terrace slept under the stars. To a more poetic man than Baxter it would have seemed to wear that faintly reproachful air which a garden always assumes when invaded at unseemly hours by people who ought to be in bed. Baxter, never fanciful, was blind to this. He was thinking, thinking. That shaking-up on the stairs had churned into activity the very depths of his brain and he was at the fever-point of his reasoning powers. A thought had come like a full-blown rose, flushing his brow. Miss Simmons, arguing plausibly, had suggested that the stolen necklace might be concealed in the hall. Baxter, inspired, fancied not. Whoever it was that had been at work in the hall just now had been making for the garden. It was not the desire to escape which had led him – or her – to open the front door, for the opening had been done before he, Baxter, had come out on to the balcony – otherwise he must have heard the shooting of the bolts. No. The enemy's objective had been the garden. In other words, the terrace. And why? Because somewhere on the terrace was the stolen necklace.

Standing there in the starlight, the Efficient Baxter endeavoured to reconstruct the scene, and did so with remarkable accuracy. He saw the jewels flashing down. He saw them picked up. But there he stopped. Try as he might, he could not see them hidden. And yet that they had been hidden – and that within a few feet of where he was now standing – he felt convinced.

He moved from his position near the door and began to roam restlessly. His slippered feet padded over the soft turf.

* * * * *

Eve peered out from her clump of bushes. It was not easy to see any great distance, but Fate, her friend, was still with her. There had been a moment that night when Baxter, disrobing for bed, had wavered absently between his brown and his lemon-coloured pyjamas, little recking of what hung upon the choice. Fate had directed his hand to the lemon-coloured, and he had put them on; with the result that he shone now in the dim light like the white plume of Navarre. Eve could follow his movements perfectly, and, when he was far enough away from his base to make the enterprise prudent, she slipped out and raced for home and safety. Baxter at the moment was leaning on the terrace wall, thinking, thinking, thinking.

* * * * *

It was possibly the cool air, playing about his bare ankles, that at last chilled the secretary's dashing mood and brought the disquieting thought that he was doing something distinctly dangerous in remaining out here in the open like this. A gang of thieves are ugly customers, likely to stick at little when a valuable necklace is at stake, and it came to the Efficient Baxter that in his light pyjamas he must be offering a tempting mark for any marauder lurking – say in those bushes. And at the thought, the summer night, though pleasantly mild, grew suddenly chilly. With an almost convulsive rapidity he turned to re-enter the house. Zeal was well enough, but it was silly to be rash. He covered the last few yards of his journey at a rare burst of speed.

It was at this point that he discovered that the lights in the hall had been switched off and that the front door was closed and bolted.

§ 3

It is the opinion of most thoughtful students of life that happiness in this world depends chiefly on the ability to take things as they come. An instance of one who may be said to have perfected this attitude is to be found in the writings of a certain eminent Arabian author who tells of a traveller who, sinking to sleep one afternoon upon a patch of turf containing an acorn, discovered when he woke that the warmth of his body had caused the acorn to germinate and that he was now some sixty feet above the ground in the upper branches of a massive oak. Unable to descend, he faced the situation equably. 'I cannot,' he observed, 'adapt circumstances to my will: therefore I shall adapt my will to circumstances. I decide to remain here.' Which he did.

Rupert Baxter, as he stood before the barred door of Blandings Castle, was very far from imitating this admirable philosopher. To find oneself locked out of a country-house at half-past two in the morning in lemon-coloured pyjamas can never be an unmixedly agreeable experience, and Baxter was a man less fitted by nature to endure it with equanimity than most men. His was a fiery and an arrogant soul, and he seethed in furious rebellion against the intolerable position into which Fate had manœuvred him. He even went so far as to give the front door a petulant kick. Finding, however, that this hurt his toes and accomplished no useful end, he addressed himself to the task of ascertaining whether there was any way of getting in – short of banging the knocker and rousing the house, a line of action which did not commend itself to him. He made a practice of avoiding as far as possible the ribald type of young man of which the castle was now full, and he had no desire to meet them at this hour in his present costume. He left the front door and proceeded to make a circuit of the castle walls; and his spirits sank even lower. In the Middle Ages, during that stormy period of England's history when walls were built six feet thick and a window was not so much a window as a handy place for pouring molten lead on the heads of visitors, Blandings had been an impregnable fortress. But in all its career it can seldom have looked more of a fortress to anyone than it did now to the Efficient Baxter.

One of the disadvantages of being a man of action, impervious to the softer emotions, is that in moments of trial the beauties of Nature are powerless to soothe the anguished heart. Had Baxter been of a dreamy and poetic temperament he might now have been drawing all sorts of balm from the loveliness of his surroundings. The air was full of the scent of growing things; strange, shy creatures came and went about him as he walked; down in the woods a nightingale had begun to sing; and there was something grandly majestic in the huge bulk of the castle as it towered against the sky. But Baxter had temporarily lost his sense of smell; he feared and disliked the strange, shy creatures; the nightingale left him cold; and the only thought the towering castle inspired in him was that it looked as if a fellow would need half a ton of dynamite to get into it.

Baxter paused. He was back now near the spot from which he had started, having completed two laps without finding any solution of his difficulties. The idea in his mind had been to stand under somebody's window and attract the sleeper's attention with soft, significant whistles. But the first whistle he emitted had sounded to him in the stillness of early morn so like a steam siren that thereafter he had merely uttered timid, mouse-like sounds which the breezes had carried away the moment they crept out. He proposed now to halt for a while and rest his lips before making another attempt. He proceeded to the terrace wall and sat down. The clock over the stables struck three.

To the restless type of thinker like Rupert Baxter, the act of sitting down is nearly always the signal for the brain to begin working with even more than its customary energy. The relaxed body seems to invite thought. And Baxter, having suspended for the moment his physical activities – and glad to do so, for his slippers hurt him – gave himself up to tense speculation as to the hiding-place of Lady Constance Keeble's necklace. From the spot where he now sat he was probably, he reflected, actually in a position to see that hiding-place – if only, when he saw it, he were able to recognise it for what it was. Somewhere out here – in yonder bushes or in some unsuspected hole in yonder tree – the jewels must have been placed. Or...

Something seemed to go off inside Baxter like a touched spring. One moment, he was sitting limply, keenly conscious of a blister on the sole of his left foot; the next, regardless of the blister, he was off the wall and racing madly along the terrace in a flurry of flying slippers. Inspiration had come to him.

Day dawns early in the summer months, and already a sort of unhealthy pallor had begun to manifest itself in the sky. It was still far from light, but objects hitherto hidden in the gloom had begun to take on uncertain shape. And among these there had come into the line of Baxter's vision a row of fifteen flower-pots.

There they stood, side by side, round and inviting, each with a geranium in its bed of mould. Fifteen flower-pots. There had originally been sixteen, but Baxter knew nothing of that. All he knew was that he was on the trail.

The quest for buried treasure is one which right through the ages has exercised an irresistible spell over humanity. Confronted with a spot where buried treasure may lurk, men do not stand upon the order of their digging; they go at it with both hands. No solicitude for his employer's geraniums came to hamper Rupert Baxter's researches. To grasp the first flowerpot and tilt out its contents was with him the work of a moment. He scrabbled his fingers through the little pile of mould...

Nothing.

A second geranium lay broken on the ground...

Nothing.

A third...

* * * * *

The Efficient Baxter straightened himself painfully. He was unused to stooping, and his back ached. But physical discomfort was forgotten in the agony of hope frustrated. As he stood there, wiping his forehead with an earth-stained hand, fifteen geranium corpses gazed up at him in the growing light, it seemed with reproach. But Baxter felt no remorse. He included all geraniums, all thieves, and most of the human race in one comprehensive black hatred.

All that Rupert Baxter wanted in this world now was bed. The clock over the stables had just struck four, and he was aware of an overpowering fatigue. Somehow or other, if he had to dig through the walls with his bare hands, he must get into the house. He dragged himself painfully from the scene of carnage and blinked up at the row of silent windows above him. He was past whistling now. He stooped for a pebble, and tossed it up at the nearest window.

Nothing happened. Whoever was sleeping up there continued to sleep. The sky had turned pink, birds were twittering in the ivy, other birds had begun to sing in the bushes. All Nature, in short, was waking – except the unseen sluggard up in that room.

He threw another pebble...

* * * *

It seemed to Rupert Baxter that he had been standing there throwing pebbles through a nightmare eternity. The whole universe had now become concentrated in his efforts to rouse that log-like sleeper; and for a brief instant fatigue left him, driven away by a sort of Berserk fury. And there floated into his mind, as if from some previous existence, a memory of somebody once standing near where he was standing now and throwing a flower-pot in at a window at someone. Who it was that had thrown the thing at whom, he could not at the moment recall; but the outstanding point on which his mind focused itself was the fact that the man had had the right idea. This was no time for pebbles. Pebbles were feeble and inadequate. With one voice the birds, the breezes, the grasshoppers, the whole chorus of Nature waking to another day seemed to shout to him, 'Say it with flower-pots!'

§ 4

The ability to sleep soundly and deeply is the prerogative, as has been pointed out earlier in this straightforward narrative of the simple home-life of the English upper classes, of those who do not think quickly. The Earl of Emsworth, who had not thought quickly since the occasion in the summer of 1874 when he had heard his father's footsteps approaching the stable-loft in which he, a lad of fifteen, sat smoking his first cigar, was an excellent sleeper. He started early and finished late. It was his gentle boast that for more than twenty years he had never missed his full eight hours. Generally he managed to get something nearer ten.

But then, as a rule, people did not fling flower-pots through his window at four in the morning.

Even under this unusual handicap, however, he struggled bravely to preserve his record. The first of Baxter's missiles, falling on a settee, produced no change in his regular breathing. The second, which struck the carpet, caused him to stir. It was the third, colliding sharply with his humped back, that definitely woke him. He sat up in bed and stared at the thing.

In the first moment of his waking, relief was, oddly enough, his chief emotion. The blow had roused him from a disquieting dream in which he had been arguing with Angus McAllister about early spring bulbs, and McAllister, worsted verbally, had hit him in the ribs with a spud. Even in his dream Lord Emsworth had been perplexed as to what his next move ought to be; and when he found himself awake and in his bedroom he was at first merely thankful that the necessity for making a decision had at any rate been postponed. Angus McAllister might on some future occasion smite him with a spud, but he had not done it yet.

There followed a period of vague bewilderment. He looked at the flower-pot. It held no message for him. He had not put it there. He never took flower-pots to bed. Once, as a child, he had taken a dead pet rabbit, but never a flower-pot. The whole affair was completely inscrutable; and his lordship, unable to solve the mystery, was on the point of taking the statesmanlike course of going to sleep again, when something large and solid whizzed through the open window and crashed against the wall, where it broke, but not into such small fragments that he could not perceive that in its prime it, too, had been a flower-pot. And at this moment his eyes fell on the carpet and then on the settee; and the affair passed still farther into the realm of the inexplicable. The Hon. Freddie Threepwood, who had a poor singing-voice but was a game trier, had been annoying his father of late by crooning a ballad ending in the words:

> 'It is not raining rain at all:
> It's raining vio-o-lets.'

It seemed to Lord Emsworth now that matters had gone a step farther. It was raining flower-pots.

The customary attitude of the Earl of Emsworth towards all mundane affairs was one of vague detachment; but this phenomenon was so remarkable that he found himself stirred to quite a little flutter of excitement and interest. His brain still refused to cope with the problem of why anybody should be throwing flower-pots into his room at this hour – or, indeed, at any hour; but it seemed a good idea to go and ascertain who this peculiar person was.

He put on his glasses and hopped out of bed and trotted to the window. And it was while he was on his way there that memory stirred in him, as some minutes ago it had stirred in the Efficient Baxter. He recalled that odd episode of a few days back, when that delightful girl, Miss What's-her-name, had informed him that his secretary had been throwing flower-pots at that poet fellow, McTodd. He had been annoyed, he remembered, that Baxter should so far have forgotten himself. Now, he found himself more frightened than annoyed. Just as every dog is permitted one bite without having its sanity questioned, so, if you consider it in a broad-minded way, may every man be allowed to throw one flower-pot. But let the thing become a habit, and we look askance. This strange hobby of his appeared to be growing on Baxter like a drug, and Lord Emsworth did not like it at all. He had never before suspected his secretary of an unbalanced mind, but now he mused, as he tiptoed cautiously to the window, that the Baxter sort of man, the energetic restless type, was just the kind that does go off his head. Just some such calamity as this, his lordship felt, he might have foreseen. Day in, day out, Rupert Baxter had been exercising his brain ever since he had come to the castle – and now he had gone and sprained it. Lord Emsworth peeped timidly out from behind a curtain.

His worst fears were realised. It was Baxter, sure enough; and a tousled, wild-eyed Baxter incredibly clad in lemon-coloured pyjamas.

* * * * *

Lord Emsworth stepped back from the window. He had seen sufficient. The pyjamas had in some curious way set the coping-stone on his dismay, and he was now in a condition approximating to panic. That Baxter should be so irresistibly impelled by his strange mania as actually to omit to attire himself decently before going out on one of these flower-pot-hurling expeditions of his seemed to make it all so sad and hopeless. The dreamy peer was no poltroon, but he was past his first youth, and it came to him very forcibly that the interviewing and pacifying of secretaries who ran amok was young man's work. He stole across the room and opened the door. It was his purpose to put this matter into the hands of an agent. And so it came about that Psmith was aroused some few minutes later from slumber by a touch on the arm and sat up to find his host's pale face peering at him in the weird light of early morning.

'My dear fellow,' quavered Lord Emsworth.

Psmith, like Baxter, was a light sleeper; and it was only a moment before he was wide awake and exerting himself to do the courtesies.

'Good morning,' he said pleasantly. 'Will you take a seat.'

'I am extremely sorry to be obliged to wake you, my dear fellow,' said his lordship, 'but the fact of the matter is, my secretary, Baxter, has gone off his head.'

'Much?' inquired Psmith, interested.

'He is out in the garden in his pyjamas, throwing flower-pots through my window.'

'Flower-pots?'

'Flower-pots!'

'Oh, flower-pots!' said Psmith, frowning thoughtfully, as if he had expected it would be something else. 'And what steps are you proposing to take? That is to say,' he went on, 'unless you wish him to continue throwing flower-pots.'

'My dear fellow...!'

'Some people like it,' explained Psmith. 'But you do not? Quite so, quite so. I understand perfectly. We all have our likes and dislikes. Well, what would you suggest?'

'I was hoping that you might consent to go down – er – having possibly armed yourself with a good stout stick – and induce him to desist and return to bed.'

'A sound suggestion in which I can see no flaw,' said Psmith approvingly. 'If you will make yourself at home in here – pardon me for issuing invitations to you in your own house – I will see what can be done. I have always found Comrade Baxter a reasonable man, ready to welcome suggestions from outside sources, and I have no doubt that we shall easily be able to reach some arrangement.'

He got out of bed, and, having put on his slippers, and his monocle, paused before the mirror to brush his hair.

'For,' he explained, 'one must be natty when entering the presence of a Baxter.'

He went to the closet and took from among a number of hats a neat Homburg. Then, having selected from a bowl of flowers on the mantelpiece a simple white rose, he pinned it in the coat of his pyjama-suit and announced himself ready.

§ 5

The sudden freshet of vicious energy which had spurred the Efficient Baxter on to his recent exhibition of marksmanship had not lasted. Lethargy was creeping back on him even as he stooped to pick up the flower-pot which had found its billet on Lord Emsworth's spine. And, as he stood there after hurling that final missile, he had realised that that was his last shot. If that produced no results, he was finished.

And, as far as he could gather, it had produced no results whatever. No head had popped inquiringly out of the window. No sound of anybody stirring had reached his ears. The place was as still as if he had been throwing marsh-mallows. A weary sigh escaped from Baxter's lips. And a moment later he was reclining on the ground with his head propped against the terrace wall, a beaten man.

His eyes closed. Sleep, which he had been denying to himself for so long, would be denied no more. When Psmith arrived, daintily swinging the Hon. Freddie Threepwood's niblick like a clouded cane, he had just begun to snore.

* * * * *

Psmith was a kindly soul. He did not like Rupert Baxter, but that was no reason why he should allow him to continue lying on turf wet with the morning dew, thus courting lumbago and sciatica. He prodded Baxter in the stomach with the niblick, and the secretary sat up, blinking. And with returning consciousness came a burning sense of grievance.

'Well, you've been long enough,' he growled. Then, as he rubbed his red-rimmed eyes and was able to see more clearly, he perceived who it was that had come to his rescue. The spectacle of Psmith of all people beaming benignly down at him was an added offence. 'Oh, it's you?' he said morosely.

'I in person,' said Psmith genially. 'Awake, beloved! Awake, for morning in the bowl of night has flung the stone that puts the stars to flight; and lo! the hunter of the East has caught the Sultan's turret in a noose of light. The Sultan himself,' he added, 'you will find behind yonder window, speculating idly on your motives for bunging flower-pots at him. Why, if I may venture the question, *did* you?'

Baxter was in no confiding mood. Without replying, he rose to his feet and started to trudge wearily along the terrace to the front door. Psmith fell into step beside him.

'If I were you,' said Psmith, 'and I offer the suggestion in the most cordial spirit of goodwill, I would use every effort to prevent this passion for flinging flower-pots from growing upon me. I know you will say that you can take it or leave it alone; that just one more pot won't hurt you; but can you stop at one? Isn't it just that first insidious flower-pot that does all the mischief? Be a man, Comrade Baxter!' He laid his hand appealingly on the secretary's shoulder. 'The next time the craving comes on you, fight it. Fight it! Are you, the heir of the ages, going to become a slave to a habit? Tush! You know and I know that there is better stuff in you than that. Use your will-power, man, use your will-power.'

Whatever reply Baxter might have intended to make to this powerful harangue – and his attitude as he turned on his companion suggested that he had much to say – was checked by a voice from above.

'Baxter! My dear fellow!'

The Earl of Emsworth, having observed the secretary's awakening from the safe observation-post of Psmith's bedroom, and having noted that he seemed to be exhibiting no signs of violence, had decided to make his presence known. His panic had passed, and he wanted to go into first causes.

Baxter gazed wanly up at the window.

'I can explain everything, Lord Emsworth.'

'What?' said his lordship, leaning farther out.

'I can explain everything,' bellowed Baxter.

'It turns out after all,' said Psmith pleasantly, 'to be very simple. He was practising for the Jerking the Geranium event at the next Olympic Games.'

Lord Emsworth adjusted his glasses.

'Your face is dirty,' he said, peering down at his dishevelled secretary. 'Baxter, my dear fellow, your face is dirty.'

'I was digging,' replied Baxter sullenly.

'What?'

'Digging!'

'The terrier complex,' explained Psmith. 'What,' he asked kindly, turning to his companion, 'were you digging for? Forgive me if the question seems an impertinent one, but we are naturally curious.'

Baxter hesitated.

'What were you digging for?' asked Lord Emsworth.

'You see,' said Psmith. '*He* wants to know.'

Not for the first time since they had become associated, a mad feeling of irritation at his employer's woolly persistence flared up in Rupert Baxter's bosom. The old ass was always pottering about asking questions. Fury and want of sleep combined to dull the secretary's normal prudence. Dimly he realised that he was imparting Psmith, the scoundrel who he was convinced was the ringleader of last night's outrage, valuable information; but anything was better than to have to stand here shouting up at Lord Emsworth. He wanted to get it over and go to bed.

'I thought Lady Constance's necklace was in one of the flower-pots,' he shrilled.

'What?'

The secretary's powers of endurance gave out. This maddening inquisition, coming on top of the restless night he had had, was too much for him. With a low moan he made one agonised leap for the front door and passed through it to where beyond these voices there was peace.

Psmith, deprived thus abruptly of his stimulating society, remained for some moments standing near the front door, drinking in with grave approval the fresh scents of the summer morning. It was many years since he had been up and about as early as this, and he had forgotten how delightful the first beginnings of a July day can be. Unlike Baxter, on whose self-centred soul these things had been lost, he revelled in the soft breezes, the singing birds, the growing pinkness of the eastern sky. He awoke at length from his reverie to find that Lord Emsworth had toddled down and was tapping him on the arm.

'*What* did he say?' inquired his lordship. He was feeling like a man who has been cut off in the midst of an absorbing telephone conversation.

'Say?' said Psmith. 'Oh, Comrade Baxter? Now, let me think. What *did* he say?'

'Something about something being in a flower-pot,' prompted his lordship.

'Ah, yes. He said he thought that Lady Constance's necklace was in one of the flower-pots.'

'What!'

Lord Emsworth, it should be mentioned, was not completely in touch with recent happenings in his home. His habit of going early to bed had caused him to miss the sensational events in the drawing-room: and, as he was a sound sleeper, the subsequent screams – or, as Stokes the footman would have said, shrieks – had not disturbed him. He stared at Psmith, aghast. For a while the apparent placidity of Baxter had lulled his first suspicions, but now they returned with renewed force.

'Baxter thought my sister's necklace was in a flower-pot?' he gasped.

'So I understood him to say.'

'But why should my sister keep her necklace in a flower-pot?'

'Ah, there you take me into deep waters.'

'The man's mad,' cried Lord Emsworth, his last doubts removed. 'Stark, staring mad! I thought so before, and now I'm convinced of it.'

His lordship was no novice in the symptoms of insanity. Several of his best friends were residing in those palatial establishments set in pleasant parks and surrounded by high walls with broken bottles on them, to which the wealthy and aristocratic are wont to retire when the strain of modern life becomes too great. And one of his uncles by marriage, who believed that he was a loaf of bread, had made his first public statement on the matter in the smoking-room of this very castle. What Lord Emsworth did not know about lunatics was not worth knowing.

'I must get rid of him,' he said. And at the thought the fair morning seemed to Lord Emsworth to take on a sudden new beauty. Many a time had he toyed wistfully with the idea of dismissing his efficient but tyrannical secretary, but never before had that sickeningly competent young man given him any reasonable cause to act. Hitherto, moreover, he had feared his sister's wrath should he take the plunge. But now... Surely even Connie, pig-headed as she was, could not blame him for dispensing with the services of a secretary who thought she kept her necklaces in flower-pots, and went out into the garden in the early dawn to hurl them at his bedroom window.

His demeanour took on a sudden buoyancy. He hummed a gay air.

'Get rid of him,' he murmured, rolling the blessed words round his tongue. He patted Psmith genially on the shoulder. 'Well, my dear fellow,' he said, 'I suppose we had better be getting back to bed and seeing if we can't get a little sleep.'

Psmith gave a little start. He had been somewhat deeply immersed in thought.

'Do not,' he said courteously, 'let me keep you from the hay if you wish to retire. To me – you know what we poets are – this lovely morning has brought inspiration. I think I will push off to my little nook in the woods, and write a poem about something.'

He accompanied his host up the silent stairs, and they parted with mutual good will at their respective doors. Psmith, having cleared his brain with a hurried cold bath, began to dress.

As a rule, the donning of his clothes was a solemn ceremony over which he dwelt lovingly; but this morning he abandoned his customary leisurely habit. He climbed into his trousers with animation, and lingered but a moment over the tying of his tie. He was convinced that there was that before him which would pay for haste.

Nothing in this world is sadder than the frequency with which we suspect our fellows without just cause. In the happenings of the night before, Psmith had seen the hand of Edward Cootes. Edward Cootes, he considered, had been indulging in what – in another – he would certainly have described as funny business. Like Miss Simmons, Psmith had quickly arrived at the conclusion that the necklace had been thrown out of the drawing-room window by one of those who made up the audience at his reading: and it was his firm belief that it had been picked up and hidden by Mr Cootes. He had been trying to think ever since where that persevering man could have concealed it, and Baxter had provided the clue. But Psmith saw clearer than Baxter. The secretary, having disembowelled fifteen flower-pots and found nothing, had abandoned his theory. Psmith went further, and suspected the existence of a sixteenth. And he proposed as soon as he was dressed to sally downstairs in search of it.

He put on his shoes, and left the room, buttoning his waist-coat as he went.

§ 6

The hands of the clock over the stables were pointing to half-past five when Eve Halliday, tiptoeing furtively, made another descent of the stairs. Her feelings as she went were very different from those which had caused her to jump at every sound when she had started on this same journey three hours earlier. Then, she had been a prowler in the darkness and, as such, a fitting object of suspicion: now, if she happened to run into anybody, she was merely a girl who, unable to sleep, had risen early to take a stroll in the garden. It was a distinction that made all the difference.

Moreover, it covered the facts. She had not been able to sleep – except for an hour when she had dozed off in a chair by her window; and she certainly proposed to take a stroll in the garden. It was her intention to recover the necklace from the place where she had deposited it, and bury it somewhere where no one could possibly find it. There it could lie until she had a chance of meeting and talking to Mr Keeble, and ascertaining what was the next step he wished taken.

Two reasons had led Eve, after making her panic dash back into the house after lurking in the bushes while Baxter patrolled the terrace, to leave her precious flower-pot on the still of the window beside the front door. She had read in stories of sensation that for purposes of concealment the most open place is the best place: and, secondly, the nearer the front door she put the flower-pot, the less distance would she have to carry it when the time came for its removal. In the present excited condition of the household, with every guest an amateur detective, the spectacle of a girl tripping downstairs with a flower-pot in her arms would excite remark.

Eve felt exhilarated. She was not used to getting only one hour's sleep in the course of a night, but excitement and the reflection that she had played a difficult game and won it against odds bore her up so strongly that she was not conscious of fatigue: and so uplifted did she feel that as she reached the landing above the hall she abandoned her cautious mode of progress and ran down the remaining stairs. She had the sensation of being in the last few yards of a winning race.

* * * * *

The hall was quite light now. Every object in it was plainly visible. There was the huge dinner-gong: there was the long leather settee: there was the table which she had upset in the darkness. And there was the sill of the window by the front door. But the flower-pot which had been on it was gone.

I N any community in which a sensational crime has recently been committed, the feelings of the individuals who go to make up that community must of necessity vary somewhat sharply according to the degree in which the personal fortunes of each are affected by the outrage. Vivid in their own way as may be the emotions of one who sees a fellow-citizen sandbagged in a quiet street, they differ in kind from those experienced by the victim himself. And so, though the theft of Lady Constance Keeble's diamond necklace had stirred Blandings Castle to its depths, it had not affected all those present in quite the same way. It left the house-party divided into two distinct schools of thought – the one finding in the occurrence material for gloom and despondency, the other deriving from it nothing but joyful excitement.

To this latter section belonged those free young spirits who had chafed at the prospect of being herded into the drawing-room on the eventful night to listen to Psmith's reading of *Songs of Squalor*. It made them tremble now to think of what they would have missed, had Lady Constance's vigilance relaxed sufficiently to enable them to execute the quiet sneak for the billiard-room of which even at the eleventh hour they had thought so wistfully. As far as the Reggies, Berties, Claudes, and Archies at that moment enjoying Lord Emsworth's hospitality were concerned the thing was top-hole, priceless, and indisputably what the doctor ordered. They spent a great deal of their time going from one country-house to another, and as a rule found the routine a little monotonous. A happening like that of the previous night gave a splendid zip to rural life. And when they reflected that, right on top of this binge, there was coming the County Ball, it seemed to them that God was in His heaven and all right with the world. They stuck cigarettes in long holders, and collected in groups, chattering like starlings.

The gloomy brigade, those with hearts bowed down, listened to their effervescent babbling with wan distaste. These last were a small body numerically, but very select. Lady Constance might have been described as their head and patroness. Morning found her still in a state bordering on collapse. After breakfast, however, which she took in her room, and which was sweetened by an interview with Mr Joseph Keeble, her husband, she brightened considerably. Mr Keeble, thought Lady Constance, behaved magnificently. She had always loved him dearly, but never so much as when, abstaining from the slightest reproach of her obstinacy in refusing to allow the jewels to be placed in the bank, he spaciously informed her that he would buy her another necklace, just as good and costing every penny as much as the old one. It was at this point that Lady Constance almost seceded from the ranks of gloom. She kissed Mr Keeble gratefully, and attacked with something approaching animation the boiled egg at which she had been pecking when he came in.

But a few minutes later the average of despair was restored by the enrolment of Mr Keeble in the ranks of the despondent. He had gladsomely assumed overnight that one of his agents, either Eve or Freddie, had been responsible for the disappearance of the necklace. The fact that Freddie, interviewed by stealth in his room, gapingly disclaimed any share in the matter had not damped him. He had never expected results from Freddie. But when, after leaving Lady Constance, he encountered Eve and was given a short outline of history, beginning with her acquisition of the necklace, and ending – like a modern novel – on the sombre note of her finding the flower-pot gone, he too sat him down and mourned as deeply as anyone.

Passing with a brief mention over Freddie, whose morose bearing was the subject of considerable comment among the younger set; over Lord Emsworth, who woke at twelve o'clock disgusted to find that he had missed several hours among his beloved flower-beds; and over the Efficient Baxter, who was roused from sleep at twelve-fifteen by Thomas the footman knocking on his door in order to hand him a note from his employer enclosing a cheque, and dispensing with his services; we come to Miss Peavey.

At twenty minutes past eleven on this morning when so much was happening to so many people, Miss Peavey stood in the Yew Alley gazing belligerently at the stemless mushroom finial of a tree about half-way between the entrance and the point where the alley merged into the west wood. She appeared to be soliloquising. For, though words were proceeding from her with considerable rapidity, there seemed to be no one in sight to whom they were being addressed. Only an exceptionally keen observer would have noted a slight significant quivering among the tree's tightly-woven branches.

'You poor bone-headed fish,' the poetess was saying with that strained tenseness which results from the churning up of a generous and emotional nature, 'isn't there anything in this world you can do without tumbling over your feet and making a mess of it? All I ask of you is to stroll under a window and pick up a few jewels, and now you come and tell me...'

'But, Liz!' said the tree plaintively.

'I do all the difficult part of the job. All that there was left for you to handle was something a child of three could have done on its ear. And now...'

'But, Liz! I'm telling you I couldn't find the stuff. I was down there all right, but I couldn't find it.'

'You couldn't find it!' Miss Peavey pawed restlessly at the soft turf with a shapely shoe. 'You're the sort of dumb Isaac that couldn't find a bass-drum in a telephone-booth. You didn't *look*.'

'I did look. Honest, I did.'

'Well, the stuff was there. I threw it down the moment the lights went out.'

'Somebody must have got there first, and swiped it.'

'Who could have got there first? Everybody was up in the room where I was.

'Are you sure?'

'Am I sure? Am I...' The poetess's voice trailed off. She was staring down the Yew Alley at a couple who had just entered. She hissed a warning in a sharp undertone. 'Hsst! Cheese it, Ed. There's someone coming.'

The two intruders who had caused Miss Peavey to suspend her remarks to her erring lieutenant were of opposite sexes – a tall girl with fair hair, and a taller young man irreproachably clad in white flannels who beamed down at his companion through a single eyeglass. Miss Peavey gazed at them searchingly as they approached. A sudden thought had come to her at the sight of them. Mistrusting Psmith as she had done ever since Mr Cootes had unmasked him for the impostor that he was, the fact that they were so often together had led her to extend her suspicion to Eve. If might, of course, be nothing but a casual friendship, begun here at the castle; but Miss Peavey had always felt that Eve would bear watching. And now, seeing them together again this morning, it had suddenly come to her that she did not recall having observed Eve among the gathering in the drawing-room last night. True, there had been many people present, but Eve's appearance was striking, and she was sure that she would have noticed her, if she had been there. And, if she had not been there, why should she not have been on the terrace? Somebody had been on the terrace last night, that was certain. For all her censorious attitude in their recent conversation, Miss Peavey had not really in her heart believed that even a dumb-bell like Eddie Cootes would not have found the necklace if it had been lying under the window on his arrival.

'Oh, good morning, Mr McTodd,' she cooed. 'I'm feeling *so* upset about this terrible affair. Aren't *you*, Miss Halliday?'

'Yes,' said Eve, and she had never said a more truthful word.

Psmith, for his part, was in more debonair and cheerful mood even than was his wont. He had examined the position of affairs and found life good. He was particularly pleased with the fact that he had persuaded Eve to stroll with him this morning and inspect his cottage in the woods. Buoyant as was his temperament, he had been half afraid that last night's interview on the terrace might have had disastrous effects on their intimacy. He was now feeling full of kindliness and goodwill towards all mankind – even Miss Peavey; and he bestowed on the poetess a dazzling smile.

'We must always,' he said, 'endeavour to look on the bright side. It was a pity, no doubt, that my reading last night had to be stopped at a cost of about twenty thousand pounds to the Keeble coffers, but let us not forget that but for that timely interruption I should have gone on for about another hour. I am like that. My friends have frequently told me that when once I start talking it requires something in the nature of a cataclysm to stop me. But, of course, there are drawbacks to everything, and last night's rannygazoo perhaps shook your nervous system to some extent?'

'I was dreadfully frightened,' said Miss Peavey. She turned to Eve with a delicate shiver. 'Weren't *you*, Miss Halliday?'

'I wasn't there,' said Eve absently.

'Miss Halliday,' explained Psmith, 'has had in the last few days some little experience of myself as orator, and with her usual good sense decided not to go out of her way to get more of me than was absolutely necessary. I was perhaps a trifle wounded at the moment, but on thinking it over came to the conclusion that she was perfectly justified in her attitude. I endeavour always in my conversation to instruct, elevate, and entertain, but there is no gainsaying the fact that a purist might consider enough of my chit-chat to be sufficient. Such, at any rate, was Miss Halliday's view, and I honour her for it. But here I am, rambling on again just when I can see that you wish to be alone. We will leave you, therefore, to muse. No doubt we have been interrupting a train of thought which would have resulted but for my arrival in a rondel or a ballade or some other poetic morceau. Come, Miss Halliday. A weird and repellent female,' he said to Eve as they drew out of hearing, 'created for some purpose which I cannot fathom. Everything in this world, I like to think, is placed there for some useful end: but why the authorities unleashed Miss Peavey on us is beyond me. It is not too much to say that she gives me a pain in the gizzard.'

Miss Peavey, unaware of these harsh views, had watched them out of sight, and now she turned excitedly to the tree which sheltered her ally.

'Ed!'

'Hello?' replied the muffled voice of Mr Cootes.

'Did you hear?'

'No.'

'Oh, my heavens!' cried his overwrought partner. 'He's gone deaf now! That girl – you didn't hear what she was saying? She said that she wasn't in the drawing-room when those lights went out. Ed, she was down below on the terrace, that's where she was, picking up the stuff. And if it isn't hidden somewheres in that McTodd's shack down there in the woods I'll eat my Sunday rubbers.'

Eve, with Psmith prattling amiably at her side, pursued her way through the wood. She was wondering why she had come. She ought, she felt, to have been very cold and distant to this young man after what had occurred between them last night. But somehow it was difficult to be cold and distant with Psmith. He cheered her stricken soul. By the time they reached the little clearing and came in sight of the squat, shed-like building with its funny windows and stained door, her spirits, always mercurial, had risen to a point where she found herself almost able to forget her troubles.

'What a horrible-looking place!' she exclaimed. 'Whatever did you want it for?'

'Purely as a nook,' said Psmith, taking out his key. 'You know how the man of sensibility and refinement needs a nook. In this rushing age it is imperative that the thinker shall have a place, however humble, where he can be alone.'

'But you aren't a thinker.'

'You wrong me. For the last few days I have been doing some extremely brisk thinking. And the strain has taken its toll. The fierce whirl of life at Blandings is wearing me away. There are dark circles under my eyes and I see floating spots.' He opened the door. 'Well, here we are. Will you pop in for a moment?'

Eve went in. The single sitting-room of the cottage certainly bore out the promise of the exterior. It contained a table with a red cloth, a chair, three stuffed birds in a glass case on the wall, and a small horsehair sofa. A depressing musty scent pervaded the place, as if a cheese had recently died there in painful circumstances. Eve gave a little shiver of distaste.

'I understand your silent criticism,' said Psmith. 'You are saying to yourself that plain living and high thinking is evidently the ideal of the gamekeepers on the Blandings estate. They are strong, rugged men who care little for the refinements of interior decoration. But shall we blame them? If I had to spend most of the day and night chivvying poachers and keeping an eye on the local rabbits, I imagine that in my off-hours practically anything with a roof would satisfy me. It was in the hope that you might be able to offer some hints and suggestions for small improvements here and there that I invited you to inspect my little place. There is no doubt that it wants doing up a bit, by a woman's gentle hand. Will you take a look round and give out a few ideas? The wall-paper is, I fear, a fixture, but in every other direction consider yourself untrammelled.'

Eve looked about her.

'Well,' she began dubiously, 'I don't think...'

She stopped abruptly, tingling all over. A second glance had shown her something which her first careless inspection had overlooked. Half hidden by a ragged curtain, there stood on the window-sill a large flower-pot containing a geranium. And across the surface of the flower-pot was a broad splash of white paint.

'You were saying...?' said Psmith courteously.

Eve did not reply. She hardly heard him. Her mind was in a confused whirl. A monstrous suspicion was forming itself in her brain.

'You are admiring the shrub?' said Psmith. 'I found it lying about up at the castle this morning and pinched it. I thought it would add a touch of colour to the place.'

Eve, looking at him keenly as his gaze shifted to the flower-pot, told herself that her suspicion had been absurd. Surely this blandness could not be a cloak for guilt.

'Where did you find it?'

'By one of the windows in the hall, more or less wasting its sweetness. I am bound to say I am a little disappointed in the thing. I had a sort of idea it would turn the old homestead into a floral bower, but it doesn't seem to.'

'It's a beautiful geranium.'

'There,' said Psmith, 'I cannot agree with you. It seems to me to have the glanders or something.'

'It only wants watering.'

'And unfortunately this cosy little place appears to possess no water supply. I take it that the late proprietor when in residence used to trudge to the back door of the castle and fetch what he needed in a bucket. If this moribund plant fancies that I am going to spend my time racing to and fro with refreshments, it is vastly mistaken. To-morrow it goes into the dustbin.'

Eve shut her eyes. She was awed by a sense of having arrived at a supreme moment. She had the sensations of a gambler who risks all on a single throw.

'What a shame!' she said, and her voice, though she tried to control it, shook. 'You had better give it to me. I'll take care of it. It's just what I want for my room.'

'Pray take it,' said Psmith. 'It isn't mine, but pray take it. And very encouraging it is, let me add, that you should be accepting gifts from me in this hearty fashion; for it is well known that there is no surer sign of the dawning of the divine emotion – love,' he explained, 'than this willingness to receive presents from the hands of the adorer. I make progress, I make progress.'

'You don't do anything of the kind,' said Eve. Her eyes were sparkling and her heart sang within her. In the revulsion of feeling which had come to her on finding her suspicions unfounded she was aware of a warm friendliness towards this absurd young man.

'Pardon me,' said Psmith firmly. 'I am quoting an established authority – Auntie Belle of *Home Gossip*.'

'I must be going,' said Eve. She took the flower-pot and hugged it to her. 'I've got work to do.'

'Work, work, always work!' sighed Psmith. 'The curse of the age. Well, I will escort you back to your cell.'

'No, you won't,' said Eve. 'I mean, thank you for your polite offer, but I want to be alone.'

'Alone?' Psmith looked at her, astonished. 'When you have the chance of being with *me*? This is a strange attitude.'

'Good-bye,' said Eve. 'Thank you for being so hospitable and lavish. I'll try to find some cushions and muslin and stuff to brighten up this place.'

'Your presence does that adequately,' said Psmith, accompanying her to the door. 'By the way, returning to the subject we were discussing last night, I forgot to mention, when asking you to marry me, that I can do card-tricks.'

'Really?'

'And also a passable imitation of a cat calling to her young. Has this no weight with you? Think! These things come in very handy in the long winter evenings.'

'But I shan't be there when you are imitating cats in the long winter evenings.'

'I think you are wrong. As I visualise my little home, I can see you there very clearly, sitting before the fire. Your maid has put you into something loose. The light of the flickering flames reflects itself in your lovely eyes. You are pleasantly tired after an afternoon's shopping, but not so tired as to be unable to select a card – *any* card – from the pack which I offer...'

'Good-bye,' said Eve.

'If it must be so – good-bye. For the present. I shall see you anon?'

'I expect so.'

'Good! I will count the minutes.'

* * * * *

Eve walked rapidly away. As she snuggled the flower-pot under her arm she was feeling like a child about to open its Christmas stocking. Before she had gone far, a shout stopped her and she perceived Psmith galloping gracefully in her wake.

'Can you spare me a moment?' said Psmith.

'Certainly.'

'I should have added that I can also recite "Gunga-Din". Will you think that over?'

'I will.'

'Thank you,' said Psmith. 'Thank you. I have a feeling that it may just turn the scale.'

He raised his hat ambassadorially and galloped away again.

* * * * *

Eve found herself unable to wait any longer. Psmith was out of sight now, and the wood was very still and empty. Birds twittered in the branches, and the sun made little pools of gold upon the ground. She cast a swift glance about her and crouched down in the shelter of a tree.

The birds stopped singing. The sun no longer shone. The wood had become cold and sinister. For Eve, with a heart of lead, was staring blankly at a little pile of mould at her feet; mould which she had sifted again and again in a frenzied, fruitless effort to find a necklace which was not there.

The empty flower-pot seemed to leer up at her in mockery.

§ 1

B LANDINGS Castle was astir from roof to hall. Lights blazed, voices shouted, bells rang. All over the huge building there prevailed a vast activity like that of a barracks on the eve of the regiment's departure for abroad. Dinner was over, and the Expeditionary Force was making its final preparations before starting off in many motor-cars for the County Ball at Shifley. In the bedrooms on every floor, Reggies, doubtful at the last moment about their white ties, were feverishly arranging new ones; Berties brushed their already glistening hair; and Claudes shouted to Archies along the passages insulting inquiries as to whether they had been sneaking their handkerchiefs. Valets skimmed like swallows up and down corridors, maids fluttered in and out of rooms in aid of Beauty in distress. The noise penetrated into every nook and corner of the house. It vexed the Efficient Baxter, going through his papers in the library preparatory to leaving Blandings on the morrow for ever. It disturbed Lord Emsworth who, stoutly declining to go within ten miles of the County Ball, had retired to his room with a book on Herbaceous Borders. It troubled the peace of Beach the butler, refreshing himself after his activities around the dinner table with a glass of sound port in the housekeeper's room. The only person in the place who paid no attention to it was Eve Halliday.

Eve was too furious to pay attention to anything but her deleterious thoughts. As she walked on the terrace, to which she had fled in quest of solitude, her teeth were set and her blue eyes glowed belligerently. As Miss Peavey would have put it in one of her colloquial moods, she was mad clear through. For Eve was a girl of spirit, and there is nothing your girl of spirit so keenly resents as being made a fool of, whether it be by Fate or by a fellow-human creature. Eve was in the uncomfortable position of having had this indignity put upon her by both. But, while as far as Fate was concerned she merely smouldered rebelliously, her animosity towards Psmith was vivid in the extreme.

A hot wave of humiliation made her writhe as she remembered the infantile guilelessness with which she had accepted the preposterous story he had told her in explanation of his presence at Blandings in another man's name. He had been playing with her all the time – fooling her – and, most unforgivable crime of all, he had dared to pretend that he was fond of her and – Eve's face burned again – to make her – almost – fond of him. How he must have laughed ...

Well, she was not beaten yet. Her chin went up and she began to walk quicker. He was clever, but she would be cleverer. The game was not over ...

'Hallo!'

A white waistcoat was gleaming at her side. Polished shoes shuffled on the turf. Light hair, brushed and brilliantined to the last possible pitch of perfection, shone in the light of the stars. The Hon. Freddie Threepwood was in her midst.

'Well, Freddie?' said Eve resignedly.

'I say,' said Freddie in a voice in which self-pity fought with commiseration for her. 'Beastly shame you aren't coming to the hop.'

'I don't mind.'

'But I do, dash it! The thing won't be anything without you. A bally wash-out. And I've been trying out some new steps with the Victrola.'

'Well, there will be plenty of other girls there for you to step on.'

'I don't *want* other girls, dash them. I want you.'

'That's very nice of you,' said Eve. The first truculence of her manner had softened. She reminded herself, as she had so often been obliged to remind herself before, that Freddie meant well. 'But it can't be helped. I'm only an employée here, not a guest. I'm not invited.'

'I know,' said Freddie. 'And that's what makes it so dashed sickening. It's like that picture I saw once, "A Modern Cinderella". Only there the girl nipped off to the dance – disguised, you know – and had a most topping time. I wish life was a bit more like the movies.'

'Well, it was enough like the movies last night when ... Oh!'

Eve stopped. Her heart gave a sudden jump. Somehow the presence of Freddie was so inextricably associated in her mind with limp proposals of marriage that she had completely forgotten that there was another and a more dashing side to his nature, that side which Mr Keeble had revealed to her at their meeting in Market Blandings on the previous afternoon. She looked at him with new eyes.

'Anything up?' said Freddie.

Eve took him excitedly by the sleeve and drew him farther away from the house. Not that there was any need to do so, for the bustle within continued unabated.

'Freddie,' she whispered, 'listen! I met Mr Keeble yesterday after I had left you, and he told me all about how you and he had planned to steal Lady Constance's necklace.'

'Good Lord!' cried Freddie, and leaped like a stranded fish.

'And I've got an idea,' said Eve.

She had, and it was one which had only in this instant come to her. Until now, though she had tilted her chin bravely and assured herself that the game was not over and that she was not yet beaten, a small discouraging voice had whispered to her all the while that this was mere bravado. What, the voice had asked, are you going to do? And she had not been able to answer it. But now, with Freddie as an ally, she could act.

'Told you all about it?' Freddie was muttering pallidly. He had never had a very high opinion of his Uncle Joseph's mentality, but he had supposed him capable of keeping a thing like that to himself. He was, indeed, thinking of Mr Keeble almost the identical thoughts which Mr Keeble in the first moments of his interview with Eve in Market Blandings had thought of him. And these reflections brought much the same qualms which they had brought to the elder conspirator. Once these things got talked about, mused Freddie agitatedly, you never knew where they would stop. Before his mental eye there swam a painful picture of his Aunt Constance, informed of the plot, tackling him and demanding the return of her necklace. 'Told you all about it?' he bleated, and, like Mr Keeble, mopped his brow.

'It's all right,' said Eve impatiently. 'It's quite all right. He asked me to steal the necklace, too.'

'You?' said Freddie, gaping.

'Yes.'

'My Gosh!' cried Freddie, electrified. 'Then was it you who got the thing last night?'

'Yes it was. But...'

For a moment Freddie had to wrestle with something that was almost a sordid envy. Then better feelings prevailed. He quivered with manly generosity. He gave Eve's hand a tender pat. It was too dark for her to see it, but he was registering renunciation.

'Little girl,' he murmured, 'there's no one I'd rather got that thousand quid than you. If I couldn't have it myself, I mean to say. Little girl...'

'Oh, be quiet!' cried Eve. 'I wasn't doing it for any thousand pounds. I didn't want Mr Keeble to give me money...'

'You didn't want him to give you money!' repeated Freddie wonderingly.

'I just wanted to help Phyllis. She's my friend.'

'Pals, pardner, pals! Pals till hell freezes!' cried Freddie, deeply moved.

'What *are* you talking about?'

'Sorry. That was a sub-title from a thing called "Prairie Nell", you know. Just happened to cross my mind. It was in the second reel where the two fellows are...'

'Yes, yes; never mind.'

'Thought I'd mention it.'

'Tell me...'

'It seemed to fit in.'

'Do *stop*, Freddie!'

'Right-ho!'

'Tell me,' resumed Eve, 'is Mr McTodd going to the ball?'

'Eh? Why, yes, I suppose so.'

'Then, listen. You know that little cottage your father has let him have?'

'Little cottage?'

'Yes. In the wood past the Yew Alley.'

'Little cottage? I never heard of any little cottage.'

'Well, he's got one,' said Eve. 'And as soon as everybody has gone to the ball you and I are going to burgle it.'

'What!'

'Burgle it!'

'Burgle it?'

'Yes, *burgle* it!'

Freddie gulped.

'Look here, old thing,' he said plaintively. 'This is a bit beyond me. It doesn't seem to me to make sense.'

Eve forced herself to be patient. After all, she reflected, perhaps she had been approaching the matter a little rapidly. The desire to beat Freddie violently over the head passed, and she began to speak slowly, and, as far as she could manage it, in words of one syllable.

'I can make it quite clear if you will listen and not say a word till I've done. This man who calls himself McTodd is not Mr McTodd at all. He is a thief who got into the place by saying that he was McTodd. He stole the jewels from me last night and hid them in his cottage.'

'But, I say!'

'Don't interrupt. I know he has them there, so when he has gone to the ball and the coast is clear you and I will go and search till we find them.'

'But, I say!'

Eve crushed down her impatience once more.

'Well?'

'Do you really think this cove has got the necklace?'

'I know he has.'

'Well, then, it's jolly well the best thing that could possibly have happened, because I got him here to pinch it for Uncle Joseph.'

'What!'

'Absolutely. You see, I began to have a doubt or two as to whether I was quite equal to the contract, so I roped in this bird by way of a gang.'

'You got him here? You mean you sent for him and arranged that he should pass himself off as Mr McTodd?'

'Well, no, not exactly that. He was coming here as McTodd anyway, as far as I can gather. But I'd talked it over with him, you know, before that and asked him to pinch the necklace.'

'Then you know him quite well? He is a friend of yours?'

'I wouldn't say that exactly. But he said he was a great pal of Phyllis and her husband.'

'Did he tell you that?'

'Absolutely!'

'When?'

'In the train.'

'I mean, was it before or after you had told him why you wanted the necklace stolen?'

'Eh? Let me think. After.'

'You're sure?'

'Yes.'

'Tell me exactly what happened,' said Eve. 'I can't understand it at all at present.'

Freddie marshalled his thoughts.

'Well, let's see. Well, to start with, I told Uncle Joe I would pinch the necklace and slip it to him, and he said if I did he'd give me a thousand quid. As a matter of fact, he made it two thousand, and very decent of him, I thought it. Is that straight?'

'Yes.'

'Then I sort of got cold feet. Began to wonder, don't you know, if I hadn't bitten off rather more than I could chew.'

'Yes.'

'And then I saw this advertisement in the paper.'

'Advertisement? What advertisement?'

'There was an advertisement in the paper saying if anybody wanted anything done simply apply to this chap. So I wrote him a letter and went up and had a talk with him in the lobby of the Piccadilly Palace. Only, unfortunately, I'd promised the guv'nor I'd catch the twelve-fifty home, so I had to dash off in the middle. Must have thought me rather an ass, it's sometimes occurred to me since. I mean, practically all I said was, "Will you pinch my aunt's necklace?" and then buzzed off to catch the train. Never thought I'd see the man again, but when I got into the five o'clock train – I missed the twelve-fifty – there he was, as large as life, and the guv'nor suddenly trickled in from another compartment and introduced him to me as McTodd the poet. Then the guv'nor legged it, and this chap told me he wasn't really McTodd, only pretending to be McTodd.'

'Didn't that strike you as strange?'

'Yes, rather rummy.'

'Did you ask him why he was doing such an extraordinary thing?'

'Oh, yes. But he wouldn't tell me. And then he asked me why I wanted him to pinch Aunt Connie's necklace, and it suddenly occurred to me that everything was working rather smoothly –

I mean, him being on his way to the castle like that. Right on the spot, don't you know. So I told him all about Phyllis, and it was then that he said that he had been a pal of hers and her husband's for years. So we fixed it up that he was to get the necklace and hand it over. I must say I was rather drawn to the chappie. He said he didn't want any money for swiping the thing.'

Eve laughed bitterly.

'Why should he, when he was going to get twenty thousand pounds' worth of diamonds and keep them? Oh, Freddie, I should have thought that even you would have seen through him. You go to this perfect stranger and tell him that there is a valuable necklace waiting here to be stolen, you find him on his way to steal it, and you trust him implicitly just because he tells you he knows Phyllis – whom he had never heard of in his life till you mentioned her. Freddie, really!'

The Hon. Freddie scratched his beautifully shaven chin.

'Well, when you put it like that,' he said, 'I must own it does sound a bit off. But he seemed such a dashed matey sort of bird. Cheery and all that. I liked the feller.'

'What nonsense!'

'Well, but you liked him, too. I mean to say, you were about with him a goodish lot.'

'I hate him!' said Eve angrily. 'I wish I had never seen him. And if I let him get away with that necklace and cheat poor little Phyllis out of her money, I'll – I'll . . .'

She raised a grimly determined chin to the stars. Freddie watched her admiringly.

'I say, you know, you are a wonderful girl,' he said.

'He *shan't* get away with it, if I have to pull the place down.'

'When you chuck your head up like that you remind me a bit of What's-her-name, the Famous Players star – you know, girl who was in "Wed to a Satyr". Only,' added Freddie hurriedly, 'she isn't half so pretty. I say, I was rather looking forward to that County Ball, but now this has happened I don't mind missing it a bit. I mean, it seems to draw us closer together somehow, if you follow me. I say, honestly, all kidding aside, you think that love might some day awaken in . . .'

'We shall want a lamp, of course,' said Eve.

'Eh?'

'A lamp – to see with when we are in the cottage. Can you get one?'

Freddie reluctantly perceived that the moment for sentiment had not arrived.

'A lamp? Oh, yes, of course. Rather.'

'Better get two,' said Eve. 'And meet me here about half an hour after everybody has gone to the ball.'

§ 2

The tiny sitting-room of Psmith's haven of rest in the woods had never reached a high standard of decorativeness even in its best days; but as Eve paused from her labours and looked at it in the light of her lamp about an hour after her conversation with Freddie on the terrace, it presented a picture of desolation which would have startled the plain-living gamekeeper to whom it had once been a home. Even Freddie, though normally an unobservant youth, seemed awed by the ruin he had helped to create.

'Golly!' he observed. 'I say, we've rather mucked the place up a bit!'

It was no over-statement. Eve had come to the cottage to search, and she had searched thoroughly. The torn carpet lay in a untidy heap against the wall. The table was overturned. Boards had been wrenched from the floor, bricks from the chimney-place. The horsehair sofa was in ribbons, and the one small cushion in the room lay limply in a corner, its stuffing distributed north, south, east and west. There was soot everywhere – on the walls, on the floor, on the fire-place, and on Freddie. A brace of dead bats, the further result of the latter's groping in a chimney which had not been swept for seven months, reposed in the fender. The sitting-room had never been luxurious; it was now not even cosy.

Eve did not reply. She was struggling with what she was fair-minded enough to see was an entirely unjust fever of irritation, with her courteous and obliging assistant as its object. It was wrong, she knew, to feel like this. That she should be furious at her failure to find the jewels was excusable, but she had no possible right to be furious with Freddie. It was not his fault that soot had poured from the chimney in lieu of diamonds. If he had asked for a necklace and been given a dead bat, he was surely more to be pitied than censured. Yet Eve, eyeing his grimy face, would have given very much to have been able to scream loudly and throw something at him. The fact was, the Hon. Freddie belonged to that unfortunate type of humanity which automatically gets blamed for everything in moments of stress.

'Well, the bally thing isn't here,' said Freddie. He spoke thickly, as a man will whose mouth is covered with soot.

'I know it isn't,' said Eve. 'But this isn't the only room in the house.'

'Think he might have hidden the stuff upstairs?'

'Or downstairs.'

Freddie shook his head, dislodging a portion of a third bat.

'Must be upstairs, if it's anywhere. Mean to say, there isn't any downstairs.'

'There's the cellar,' said Eve. 'Take your lamp and go and have a look.'

For the first time in the proceedings a spirit of disaffection seemed to manifest itself in the bosom of her assistant. Up till this moment Freddie had taken his orders placidly and executed them with promptness and civility. Even when the first shower of soot had driven him choking from the fire-place, his manly spirit had not been crushed; he had merely uttered a startled 'Oh, I say!' and returned gallantly to the attack. But now he obviously hesitated.

'Go on,' said Eve impatiently.

'Yes, but, I say, you know...'

'What's the matter?'

'I don't think the chap would be likely to hide a necklace in the cellar. I vote we give it a miss and try upstairs.'

'Don't be silly, Freddie. He may have hidden it any-where.'

'Well, to be absolutely honest, I'd much rather not go into any bally cellar, if it's all the same to you.'

'Why ever not?'

'Beetles. Always had a horror of beetles. Ever since I was a kid.'

Eve bit her lip. She was feeling, as Miss Peavey had so often felt when associated in some delicate undertaking with Edward Cootes, that exasperating sense of man's inadequacy which comes to high-spirited girls at moments such as these. To achieve the end for which she had started out that night she would have waded waist-high through a sea of beetles. But, divining with that sixth sense which tells women when the male has been pushed just so far and can be pushed no farther, that Freddie, wax though he might be in her hands in any other circumstances, was on this one point adamant, she made no further effort to bend him to her will.

'All right,' she said. 'I'll go down into the cellar. You go and look upstairs.'

'No. I say, sure you don't mind?'

Eve took up her lamp and left the craven.

* * * * *

For a girl of iron resolution and unswerving purpose, Eve's inspection of the cellar was decidedly cursory. A distinct feeling of relief came over her as she stood at the top of the steps and saw by the light of the lamp how small and bare it was. For, impervious as she might be to the intimidation of beetles, her armour still contained a chink. She was terribly afraid of rats. And even when the rays of the lamp disclosed no scuttling horrors, she still lingered for a moment before descending. You never knew with rats. They pretended not to be there just to lure you on, and then came out and whizzed about your ankles. However, the memory of her scorn for Freddie's pusillanimity forced her on, and she went down.

The word 'cellar' is an elastic one. It can be applied equally to the acres of bottle-fringed vaults which lie beneath a great pile like Blandings Castle and to a hole in the ground like the one in which she now found herself. This cellar was easily searched. She stamped on its stone flags with an ear strained to detect any note of hollowness, but none came. She moved the lamp so that it shone into every corner, but there was not even a crack in which a diamond necklace could have been concealed. Satisfied that the place contained nothing but a little coal-dust and a smell of damp decay, Eve passed thankfully out.

The law of elimination was doing its remorseless work. It had ruled out the cellar, the kitchen, and the living-room – that is to say, the whole of the lower of the two floors which made up the cottage. There now remained only the rooms upstairs. There were probably not more than two, and Freddie must already have searched one of these. The quest seemed to be nearing its end. As Eve made for the narrow staircase that led to the second floor, the lamp shook in her hand and cast weird shadows. Now that success was in sight, the strain was beginning to affect her nerves.

It was to nerves that in the first instant of hearing it she attributed what sounded like a soft cough in the sitting-room, a few feet from where she stood. Then a chill feeling of dismay gripped her. It could only, she thought, be Freddie, returned from his search; and if Freddie had returned from his search already, what could it mean except that those upstairs rooms, on which she had counted so confidently, had proved as empty as the others? Freddie was not one of your restrained, unemotional men. If he had found the necklace he would have been down-stairs in two bounds, shouting. His silence was ominous. She opened the door and went quickly in.

'Freddie,' she began, and broke off with a gasp.

It was not Freddie who had coughed. It was Psmith. He was seated on the remains of the horsehair sofa, toying with an automatic pistol and gravely surveying through his monocle the ruins of a home.

§ 3

'Good evening,' said Psmith.

It was not for a philosopher like himself to display astonish-ment. He was, however, undeniably feeling it. When, a few minutes before, he had encountered Freddie in this same room, he had received a distinct shock; but a rough theory which would account for Freddie's presence in his home-from-home he had been able to work out. He groped in vain for one which would explain Eve.

Mere surprise, however, was never enough to prevent Psmith talking. He began at once.

'It was nice of you,' he said, rising courteously, 'to look in. Won't you sit down? On the sofa, perhaps? Or would you prefer a brick?'

Eve was not yet equal to speech. She had been so firmly convinced that he was ten miles away at Shifley that his presence here in the sitting-room of the cottage had something of the breath-taking quality of a miracle. The explanation, if she could have known it, was simple. Two excellent reasons had kept Psmith from gracing the County Ball with his dignified support. In the first place, as Shifley was only four miles from the village where he had spent most of his life, he had regarded it as probable, if not certain, that he would have encountered there old friends to whom it would have been both tedious and embarrassing to explain why he had changed his name to McTodd. And secondly, though he had not actually anticipated a nocturnal raid on his little nook, he had thought it well to be on the premises that evening in case Mr Edward Cootes should have been getting ideas into his head. As soon, therefore, as the castle had emptied itself and the wheels of the last car had passed away down the drive, he had pocketed Mr Cootes's revolver and proceeded to the cottage.

Eve recovered her self-possession. She was not a girl given to collapse in moments of crisis. The first shock of amazement had passed; a humiliating feeling of extreme foolishness, which came directly after, had also passed; she was now grimly ready for battle.

'Where is Mr Threepwood?' she asked.

'Upstairs. I have put him in storage for a while. Do not worry about Comrade Threepwood. He has lots to think about. He is under the impression that if he stirs out he will be instantly shot.'

'Oh? Well, I want to put this lamp down. Will you please pick up that table?'

'By all means. But – I am a novice in these matters – ought I not first to say "Hands up!" or something?'

'Will you please pick up that table?'

'A friend of mine – one Cootes – you must meet him some time – generally remarks "Hey!" in a sharp, arresting voice on these occasions. Personally I consider the expression too abrupt. Still, he has had great experience . . . '

'Will you please pick up that table?'

'Most certainly. I take it, then, that you would prefer to dispense with the usual formalities. In that case, I will park this revolver on the mantelpiece while we chat. I have taken a curious dislike to the thing. It makes me feel like Dangerous Dan McGrew.'

Eve put down the lamp, and there was silence for a moment. Psmith looked about him thoughtfully. He picked up one of the dead bats and covered it with his handkerchief.

'Somebody's mother,' he murmured reverently.

Eve sat down on the sofa.

'Mr . . . ' She stopped. 'I can't call you Mr McTodd. Will you please tell me your name?'

'Ronald,' said Psmith. 'Ronald Eustace.'

'I suppose you have a surname?' snapped Eve. 'Or an alias?'

Psmith eyed her with a pained expression.

'I may be hyper-sensitive,' he said, 'but that last remark sounded to me like a dirty dig. You seem to imply that I am some sort of a criminal.'

Eve laughed shortly.

'I'm sorry if I hurt your feelings. There's not much sense in pretending now, is there? What is your name?'

'Psmith. The p is silent.'

'Well, Mr Smith, I imagine you understand why I am here?'

'I took it for granted that you had come to fulfil your kindly promise of doing the place up a bit. Will you be wounded if I say frankly that I preferred it the way it was before? All this may be the last word in ultra-modern interior decoration, but I suppose I am old-fashioned. The whisper flies round Shropshire and adjoining counties, "Psmith is hide-bound. He is not attuned to up-to-date methods." Honestly, don't you think you have rather unduly stressed the bizarre note? This soot...these dead bats...'

'I have come to get that necklace.'

'Ah! The necklace!'

'I'm going to get it, too.'

Psmith shook his head gently.

'There,' he said, 'if you will pardon me, I take issue with you. There is nobody to whom I would rather give that necklace than you, but there are special circumstances connected with it which render such an action impossible. I fancy, Miss Halliday, that you have been misled by your young friend upstairs. No; let me speak,' he said, raising a hand. 'You know what a treat it is to me. The way I envisage the matter is thus. I still cannot understand as completely as I could wish how you come to be mixed up in the affair, but it is plain that in some way or other Comrade Threepwood has enlisted your services, and I regret to be obliged to inform you that the motives animating him in this quest are not pure. To put it crisply, he is engaged in what Comrade Cootes, to whom I alluded just now, would call "funny business".'

'I . . .'

'Pardon me,' said Psmith. 'If you will be patient for a few minutes more, I shall have finished and shall then be delighted to lend an attentive ear to any remarks you may wish to make. As it occurs to me – indeed, you hinted as much yourself just now – that my own position in this little matter has an appearance which to the uninitiated might seem tolerably rummy, I had better explain how I come to be guarding a diamond necklace which does not belong to me. I rely on your womanly discretion to let the thing go no further.'

'Will you please . . .'

'In one moment. The facts are as follows. Our mutual friend Mr Keeble, Miss Halliday, has a stepdaughter who is married to one Comrade Jackson who, if he had no other claim to fame, would go ringing down through history for this reason, that he and I were at school together and that he is my best friend. We two have sported on the green – ooh, a lot of times. Well, owing to one thing and another, the Jackson family is rather badly up against it at the present . . .'

Eve jumped up angrily.

'I don't believe a word of it,' she cried. 'What is the use of trying to fool me like this? You had never heard of Phyllis before Freddie spoke about her in the train . . .'

'Believe me . . .'

'I won't. Freddie got you down here to help him steal that necklace and give it to Mr Keeble so that he could help Phyllis, and now you've got it and are trying to keep it for yourself.'

Psmith started slightly. His monocle fell from its place.

'Is *everybody* in this little plot! Are you also one of Comrade Keeble's corps of assistants?'

'Mr Keeble asked me to try to get the necklace for him.'

Psmith replaced his monocle thoughtfully.

'This,' he said, 'opens up a new line of thought. Can it be that I have been wronging Comrade Threepwood all this time? I must confess that, when I found him here just now standing like Marius among the ruins of Carthage (the allusion is a classical one, and the fruit of an expensive education), I jumped – I may say, sprang – to the conclusion that he was endeavouring to double-cross both myself and the boss by getting hold of the necklace with a view to retaining it for his own benefit. It never occurred to me that he might be crediting me with the same sinful guile.'

Eve ran to him and clutched his arm.

'Mr Smith, is this really true? Are you really a friend of Phyllis?'

'She looks on me as a grandfather. Are *you* a friend of hers?'

'We were at school together.'

'This,' said Psmith cordially, 'is one of the most gratifying moments of my life. It makes us all seem like one great big family.'

'But I never heard Phyllis speak about you.'

'Strange!' said Psmith. 'Strange. Surely she was not ashamed of her humble friend?'

'Her what?'

'I must explain,' said Psmith, 'that until recently I was earning a difficult livelihood by slinging fish about in Billingsgate Market. It is possible that some snobbish strain in Comrade Jackson's bride, which I confess I had not suspected, kept her from admitting that she was accustomed to hob-nob with one in the fish business.'

'Good gracious!' cried Eve.

'I beg your pardon?'

'Smith... Fish business... Why, it was you who called at Phyllis's house while I was there. Just before I came down here. I remember Phyllis saying how sorry she was that we had not met. She said you were just my sort of... I mean, she said she wanted me to meet you.'

'This,' said Psmith, 'is becoming more and more gratifying every moment. It seems to me that you and I were made for each other. I am your best friend's best friend and we both have a taste for stealing other people's jewellery. I cannot see how you can very well resist the conclusion that we are twin-souls.'

'Don't be silly.'

'We shall get into that series of "Husbands and Wives Who Work Together". '

'Where is the necklace?'

Psmith sighed.

'The business note. Always the business note. Can't we keep all that till later?'

'No. We can't.'

'Ah, well!'

Psmith crossed the room, and took down from the wall the case of stuffed birds.

'The one place,' said Eve, with mortification, 'where we didn't think of looking!'

Psmith opened the case and removed the centre bird, a depressed-looking fowl with glass eyes which stared with a haunting pathos. He felt in its interior and pulled out something that glittered and sparkled in the lamp-light.

'Oh!'

Eve ran her fingers almost lovingly through the jewels as they lay before her on the little table.

'Aren't they beautiful!'

'Distinctly. I think I may say that of all the jewels I have ever stolen...'

'HEY!'

Eve let the necklace fall with a cry. Psmith spun round. In the doorway stood Mr Edward Cootes, pointing a pistol.

§ 4

'Hands up!' said Mr Cootes with the uncouth curtness of one who has not had the advantages of a refined home and a nice upbringing. He advanced warily, preceded by the revolver. It was a dainty, miniature weapon, such as might have been the property of some gentle lady. Mr Cootes had, in fact, borrowed it from Miss Peavey, who at this juncture entered the room in a black and silver dinner-dress surmounted by a Rose du Barri wrap, her spiritual face glowing softly in the subdued light.

'Attaboy, Ed,' observed Miss Peavey crisply.

She swooped on the table and gathered up the necklace. Mr Cootes, though probably gratified by the tribute, made no acknowledgement of it, but continued to direct an austere gaze at Eve and Psmith.

'No funny business,' he advised.

'I would be the last person,' said Psmith agreeably, 'to advocate anything of the sort. This,' he said to Eve, 'is Comrade Cootes, of whom you have heard so much.'

Eve was staring, bewildered, at the poetess, who, satisfied with the manner in which the preliminaries had been conducted, had begun looking about her with idle curiosity.

'Miss Peavey!' cried Eve. Of all the events of this eventful night the appearance of Lady Constance's emotional friend in the rôle of criminal was the most disconcerting. 'Miss *Peavey*!'

'Hallo?' responded that lady agreeably.

'I...I...'

'What, I think, Miss Halliday is trying to say,' cut in Psmith, 'is that she is finding it a little difficult to adjust her mind to the present development. I, too, must confess myself somewhat at a loss. I knew, of course, that Comrade Cootes had – shall I say an acquisitive streak in him, but you I had always supposed to be one hundred per cent. soul – and snowy white at that.'

'Yeah?' said Miss Peavey, but faintly interested.

'I imagined that you were a poetess.'

'So I am a poetess,' retorted Miss Peavey hotly. 'Just you start in joshing my poems and see how quick I'll bean you with a brick. Well, Ed, no sense in sticking around here. Let's go.'

'We'll have to tie these birds up,' said Mr Cootes. 'Otherwise we'll have them squealing before I can make a getaway.'

'Ed,' said Miss Peavey with the scorn which her colleague so often excited in her, 'try to remember sometimes that that thing balanced on your collar is a head, not a hubbard squash. And be careful what you're doing with that gat! Waving it about like it was a bouquet or something. How are they going to squeal? They can't say a thing without telling everyone they snitched the stuff first.'

'That's right,' admitted Mr Cootes.

'Well, then, don't come butting in.'

The silence into which this rebuke plunged Mr Cootes gave Psmith the opportunity to resume speech. An opportunity of which he was glad, for, while he had nothing of definitely vital import to say, he was optimist enough to feel that his only hope of recovering the necklace was to keep the conversation going on the chance of something turning up. Affable though his manner was, he had never lost sight of the fact that one leap would take him across the space of floor separating him from Mr Cootes. At present, that small but effective revolver precluded anything in the nature of leaps, however short, but if in the near future anything occurred to divert his adversary's vigilance even momentarily.... He pursued a policy of watchful waiting, and in the meantime started to talk again.

'If, before you go,' he said, 'you can spare us a moment of your valuable time, I should be glad of a few words. And, first, may I say that I cordially agree with your condemnation of Comrade Cootes's recent suggestion. The man is an ass.'

'Say!' cried Mr Cootes, coming to life again, 'that'll be about all from you. If there wasn't ladies present, I'd bust you one.'

'Ed,' said Miss Peavey with quiet authority, 'shut your trap!'

Mr Cootes subsided once more. Psmith gazed at him through his monocle, interested.

'Pardon me,' he said, 'but – if it is not a rude question – are you two married?'

'Eh?'

'You seemed to me to talk to him like a wife. Am I addressing Mrs Cootes?'

'You will be if you stick around a while.'

'A thousand congratulations to Comrade Cootes. Not quite so many to you, possibly, but fully that number of good wishes.'

He moved towards the poetess with extended hand. 'I am thinking of getting married myself shortly.'

'Keep those hands up,' said Mr Cootes.

'Surely,' said Psmith reproachfully, 'these conventions need not be observed among friends? You will find the only revolver I have ever possessed over there on the mantelpiece. Go and look at it.'

'Yes, and have you jumping on my back the moment I took my eyes off you!'

'There is a suspicious vein in your nature, Comrade Cootes,' sighed Psmith, 'which I do not like to see. Fight against it.' He turned to Miss Peavey once more. 'To resume a pleasanter topic, you will let me know where to send the plated fish-slice, won't you?'

'Huh?' said the lady.

'I was hoping,' proceeded Psmith, 'if you do not think it a liberty on the part of one who has known you but a short time, to be allowed to send you a small wedding-present in due season. And one of these days, perhaps, when I too am married, you and Comrade Cootes will come and visit us in our little home. You will receive a hearty, unaffected welcome. You must not be offended if, just before you say good-bye, we count the spoons.'

One would scarcely have supposed Miss Peavey a sensitive woman, yet at this remark an ominous frown clouded her white forehead. Her careless amiability seemed to wane. She raked Psmith with a glittering eye.

'You're talking a dam' lot,' she observed coldly.

'An old failing of mine,' said Psmith apologetically, 'and one concerning which there have been numerous complaints. I see now that I have been boring you, and I hope that you will allow me to express ...'

He broke off abruptly, not because he had reached the end of his remarks, but because at this moment there came from above their heads a sudden sharp cracking sound, and almost simultaneously a shower of plaster fell from the ceiling, followed by the startling appearance of a long, shapely leg, which remained waggling in space. And from somewhere out of sight there filtered down a sharp and agonised oath.

Time and neglect had done their work with the flooring of the room in which Psmith had bestowed the Hon. Freddie Threepwood, and, creeping cautiously about in the dark, he had had the misfortune to go through.

But, as so often happens in this life, the misfortune of one is the good fortune of another. Badly as the accident had shaken Freddie, from the point of view of Psmith it was almost ideal. The sudden appearance of a human leg through the ceiling at a moment of nervous tension is enough to unman the stoutest-hearted, and Edward Cootes made no attempt to conceal his perturbation. Leaping a clear six inches from the floor, he jerked up his head and quite unintentionally pulled the trigger of his revolver. A bullet ripped through the plaster.

The leg disappeared. Not for an instant since he had been shut in that upper room had Freddie Threepwood ceased to be mindful of Psmith's parting statement that he would be shot if he tried to escape, and Mr Cootes's bullet seemed to him a dramatic fulfilment of that promise. Wrenching his leg with painful energy out of the abyss, he proceeded to execute a backward spring which took him to the far wall – at which point, as it was impossible to get any farther away from the centre of events, he was compelled to halt his retreat. Having rolled himself up into as small a ball as he could manage, he sat where he was, trying not to breathe. His momentary intention of explaining through the hole that the entire thing had been a regrettable accident, he prudently abandoned. Unintelligent though he had often proved himself in other crises of his life, he had the sagacity now to realise that the neighbourhood of the hole was unhealthy and should be avoided. So, preserving a complete and unbroken silence, he crouched there in the darkness, only asking to be left alone.

And it seemed, as the moments slipped by, that this modest wish was to be gratified. Noises and the sound of voices came up to him from the room below, but no more bullets. It would be paltering with the truth to say that this put him completely at his ease, but still it was something. Freddie's pulse began to return to the normal.

Mr Cootes's, on the other hand, was beating with a dangerous quickness. Swift and objectionable things had been happening to Edward Cootes in that lower room. His first impression was that the rift in the plaster above him had been instantly followed by the collapse of the entire ceiling, but this was a mistaken idea. All that had occurred was that Psmith, finding Mr Cootes's eye and pistol functioning in another direction, had sprung forward, snatched up a chair, hit the unfortunate man over the head with it, relieved him of his pistol, leaped to the mantelpiece, removed the revolver which lay there, and now, holding both weapons in an attitude of menace, was regarding him censoriously through a gleaming eyeglass.

'No funny business, Comrade Cootes,' said Psmith.

Mr Cootes picked himself up painfully. His head was singing. He looked at the revolvers, blinked, opened his mouth and shut it again. He was oppressed with a sense of defeat. Nature had not built him for a man of violence. Peaceful manipulation of a pack of cards in the smoke-room of an Atlantic liner was a thing he understood and enjoyed: rough-and-tumble encounters were alien to him and distasteful. As far as Mr Cootes was concerned, the war was over.

But Miss Peavey was a woman of spirit. Her hat was still in the ring. She clutched the necklace in a grasp of steel, and her fine eyes glared defiance.

'You think yourself smart, don't you?' she said.

Psmith eyed her commiseratingly. Her valorous attitude appealed to him. Nevertheless, business was business.

'I am afraid,' he said regretfully, 'that I must trouble you to hand over that necklace.'

'Try and get it,' said Miss Peavey.

Psmith looked hurt.

'I am a child in these matters,' he said, 'but I had always gathered that on these occasions the wishes of the man behind the gun were automatically respected.'

'I'll call your bluff,' said Miss Peavey firmly. 'I'm going to walk straight out of here with this collection of ice right now, and I'll bet you won't have the nerve to start any shooting. Shoot a woman? Not you!'

Psmith nodded gravely.

'Your knowledge of psychology is absolutely correct. Your trust in my sense of chivalry rests on solid ground. But,' he proceeded, cheering up, 'I fancy that I see a way out of the difficulty. An idea has been vouchsafed to me. I shall shoot – not you, but Comrade Cootes. This will dispose of all unpleasantness. If you attempt to edge out through that door I shall immediately proceed to plug Comrade Cootes in the leg. At least, I shall try. I am a poor shot and may hit him in some more vital spot, but at least he will have the consolation of knowing that I did my best and meant well.'

'Hey!' cried Mr Cootes. And never, in a life liberally embellished with this favourite ejaculation of his, had he uttered it more feelingly. He shot a feverish glance at Miss Peavey; and, reading in her face indecision rather than that instant acquiescence which he had hoped to see, cast off his customary attitude of respectful humility and asserted himself. He was no caveman, but this was one occasion when he meant to have his own way. With an agonised bound he reached Miss Peavey's side, wrenched the necklace from her grasp and flung it into the enemy's camp. Eve stooped and picked it up.

'I thank you,' said Psmith with a brief bow in her direction.

Miss Peavey breathed heavily. Her strong hands clenched and unclenched. Between her parted lips her teeth showed in a thin white line. Suddenly she swallowed quickly, as if draining a glass of unpalatable medicine.

'Well,' she said in a low, even voice, 'that seems to be about all. Guess we'll be going. Come along, Ed, pick up the Henries.'

'Coming, Liz,' replied Mr Cootes humbly.

They passed together into the night.

§ 5

Silence followed their departure. Eve, weak with the reaction from the complex emotions which she had undergone since her arrival at the cottage, sat on the battered sofa, her chin resting in her hands. She looked at Psmith, who, humming a light air, was delicately piling with the toe of his shoe a funeral mound over the second of the dead bats.

'So that's that!' she said.

Psmith looked up with a bright and friendly smile.

'You have a very happy gift of phrase,' he said. 'That, as you sensibly say, is that.'

Eve was silent for a while. Psmith completed the obsequies and stepped back with the air of a man who has done what he can for a fallen friend.

'Fancy Miss Peavey being a thief!' said Eve. She was somehow feeling a disinclination to allow the conversation to die down, and yet she had an idea that, unless it was permitted to die down, it might become embarrassingly intimate. Subconsciously, she was endeavouring to analyse her views on this long, calm person who had so recently added himself to the list of those who claimed to look upon her with affection.

'I confess it came as something of a shock to me also,' said Psmith. 'In fact, the revelation that there was this other, deeper side to her nature materially altered the opinion I had formed of her. I found myself warming to Miss Peavey. Something that was akin to respect began to stir within me. Indeed, I almost wish that we had not been compelled to deprive her of the jewels.'

'"We"?' said Eve. 'I'm afraid I didn't do much.'

'Your attitude was exactly right,' Psmith assured her. 'You afforded just the moral support which a man needs in such a crisis.'

Silence fell once more. Eve returned to her thoughts. And then, with a suddenness which surprised her, she found that she had made up her mind.

'So you're going to be married?' she said.

Psmith polished his monocle thoughtfully.

'I think so,' he said. 'I think so. What do *you* think?'

Eve regarded him steadfastly. Then she gave a little laugh.

'Yes,' she said, 'I think so, too.' She paused. 'Shall I tell you something?'

'You could tell me nothing more wonderful than that.'

'When I met Cynthia in Market Blandings, she told me what the trouble was which made her husband leave her. What do you suppose it was?'

'From my brief acquaintance with Comrade McTodd, I would hazard the guess that he tried to stab her with the bread-knife. He struck me as a murderous-looking specimen.'

'They had some people to dinner, and there was chicken, and Cynthia gave all the giblets to the guests, and her husband bounded out of his seat with a wild cry, and, shouting "You *know* I love those things better than anything in the world!" rushed from the house, never to return!'

'Precisely how I would have wished him to rush, had I been Mrs McTodd.'

'Cynthia told me that he had rushed from the house, never to return, six times since they were married.'

'May I mention – in passing –' said Psmith, 'that I do not like chicken giblets?'

'Cynthia advised me,' proceeded Eve, 'if ever I married, to marry someone eccentric. She said it was such fun ... Well, I don't suppose I am ever likely to meet anyone more eccentric than you, am I?'

'I think you would be unwise to wait on the chance.'

'The only thing is ...' said Eve reflectively. '"Mrs Smith" ... It doesn't *sound* much, does it?'

Psmith beamed encouragingly.

'We must look into the future,' he said. 'We must remember that I am only at the beginning of what I am convinced is to be a singularly illustrious career. "Lady Psmith" is better ... "Baroness Psmith" better still ... And – who knows? – "The Duchess of Psmith" ...'

'Well, anyhow,' said Eve, 'you were wonderful just now, simply wonderful. The way you made one spring...'

'Your words,' said Psmith, 'are music to my ears, but we must not forget that the foundations of the success of the manœuvre were laid by Comrade Threepwood. Had it not been for the timely incursion of his leg...'

'Good gracious!' cried Eve. 'Freddie! I had forgotten all about him!'

'The right spirit,' said Psmith. 'Quite the right spirit.'

'We must go and let him out.'

'Just as you say. And then he can come with us on the stroll I was about to propose that we should take through the woods. It is a lovely night, and what could be jollier than to have Comrade Threepwood prattling at our side? I will go and let him out at once.'

'No, don't bother,' said Eve.

THE golden stillness of a perfect summer morning brooded over Blandings Castle and its adjacent pleasure-grounds. From a sky of unbroken blue the sun poured down its heartening rays on all those roses, pinks, pansies, carnations, hollyhocks, columbines, larkspurs, London pride and Canterbury bells which made the gardens so rarely beautiful. Flannelled youths and maidens in white serge sported in the shade; gay cries arose from the tennis-courts behind the shrubbery; and birds, bees, and butterflies went about their business with a new energy and zip. In short, the casual observer, assuming that he was addicted to trite phrases, would have said that happiness reigned supreme.

But happiness, even on the finest mornings, is seldom universal. The strolling youths and maidens were happy; the tennis-players were happy; the birds, bees, and butterflies were happy. Eve, walking in pleasant meditation on the terrace, was happy. Freddie Threepwood was happy as he lounged in the smoking-room and gloated over the information, received from Psmith in the small hours, that his thousand pounds was safe. Mr Keeble, writing to Phyllis to inform her that she might clinch the purchase of the Lincolnshire farm, was happy. Even Head-gardener Angus McAllister was as happy as a Scotsman can ever be. But Lord Emsworth, drooping out of the library window, felt only a nervous irritation more in keeping with the blizzards of winter than with the only fine July that England had known in the last ten years.

We have seen his lordship in a similar attitude and a like frame of mind on a previous occasion; but then his melancholy had been due to the loss of his glasses. This morning these were perched firmly on his nose and he saw all things clearly. What was causing his gloom now was the fact that some ten minutes earlier his sister Constance had trapped him in the library, full of jarring rebuke on the subject of the dismissal of Rupert Baxter, the world's most efficient secretary. It was to avoid her compelling eye that Lord Emsworth had turned to the window. And what he saw from that window thrust him even deeper into the abyss of gloom. The sun, the birds, the bees, the butterflies, and the flowers called to him to come out and have the time of his life, but he just lacked the nerve to make a dash for it.

'I think you must be mad,' said Lady Constance bitterly, resuming her remarks and starting at the point where she had begun before.

'Baxter's mad,' retorted his lordship, also re-treading old ground.

'You are too absurd!'

'He threw flower-pots at me.'

'Do please stop talking about those flower-pots. Mr Baxter has explained the whole thing to me, and surely even you can see that his behaviour was perfectly excusable.'

'I don't like the fellow,' cried Lord Emsworth, once more retreating to his last line of trenches – the one line from which all Lady Constance's eloquence had been unable to dislodge him.

There was a silence, as there had been a short while before when the discussion had reached this same point.

'You will be helpless without him,' said Lady Constance.

'Nothing of the kind,' said his lordship.

'You know you will. Where will you ever get another secretary capable of looking after everything like Mr Baxter? You know you are a perfect child, and unless you have someone whom you can trust to manage your affairs I cannot see what will happen.'

Lord Emsworth made no reply. He merely gazed wanly from the window.

'Chaos,' moaned Lady Constance.

His lordship remained mute, but now there was a gleam of something approaching pleasure in his pale eyes; for at this moment a car rounded the corner of the house from the direction of the stables and stood purring at the door. There was a trunk on the car and a suit-case. And almost simultaneously the Efficient Baxter entered the library, clothed and spatted for travel.

'I have come to say good-bye, Lady Constance,' said Baxter coldly and precisely, flashing at his late employer through his spectacles a look of stern reproach. 'The car which is taking me to the station is at the door.'

'Oh, Mr Baxter.' Lady Constance, strong woman though she was, fluttered with distress. 'Oh, Mr Baxter.'

'Good-bye.' He gripped her hand in brief farewell and directed his spectacles for another tense instant upon the sagging figure at the window. 'Good-bye, Lord Emsworth.'

'Eh? What? Oh! Ah, yes. Good-bye, my dear fel—, I mean, good-bye. I – er – hope you will have a pleasant journey.'

'Thank you,' said Baxter.

'But, Mr Baxter,' said Lady Constance.

'Lord Emsworth,' said the ex-secretary icily, 'I am no longer in your employment . . .'

'But, Mr Baxter,' moaned Lady Constance, 'surely...even now...misunderstanding...talk it all over quietly...'

Lord Emsworth started violently.

'Here!' he protested, in much the same manner as that in which the recent Mr Cootes had been wont to say 'Hey!'

'I fear it is too late,' said Baxter, to his infinite relief, 'to talk things over. My arrangements are already made and cannot be altered. Ever since I came here to work for Lord Emsworth, my former employer – an American millionaire named Jevons – has been making me flattering offers to return to him. Until now a mistaken sense of loyalty has kept me from accepting these offers, but this morning I telegraphed to Mr Jevons to say that I was at liberty and could join him at once. It is too late now to cancel this promise.'

'Quite, quite, oh certainly, quite, mustn't dream of it, my dear fellow. No, no, no, indeed no,' said Lord Emsworth with an effervescent cordiality which struck both his hearers as in the most dubious taste.

Baxter merely stiffened haughtily, but Lady Constance was so poignantly affected by the words and the joyous tone in which they were uttered that she could endure her brother's loathly society no longer. Shaking Baxter's hand once more and gazing stonily for a moment at the worm by the window, she left the room.

For some seconds after she had gone, there was silence – a silence which Lord Emsworth found embarrassing. He turned to the window again and took in with one wistful glance the roses, the pinks, the pansies, the carnations, the hollyhocks, the columbines, the larkspurs, the London pride and the Canterbury bells. And then suddenly there came to him the realisation that with Lady Constance gone there no longer existed any reason why he should stay cooped up in this stuffy library on the finest morning that had ever been sent to gladden the heart of man. He shivered ecstatically from the top of his bald head to the soles of his roomy shoes, and, bounding gleefully from the window, started to amble across the room.

'Lord Emsworth!'

His lordship halted. His was a one-track mind, capable of accommodating only one thought at a time – if that, and he had almost forgotten that Baxter was still there. He eyed his late secretary peevishly.

'Yes, yes? Is there anything . . . ?'

'I should like to speak to you for a moment.'

'I have a most important conference with McAllister . . .'

'I will not detain you long. Lord Emsworth, I am no longer in your employment, but I think it my duty to say before I go . . .'

'No, no, my dear fellow, I quite understand. Quite, quite, quite. Constance has been going over all that. I know what you are trying to say. That matter of the flower-pots. Please do not apologise. It is quite all right. I was startled at the time, I own, but no doubt you had excellent motives. Let us forget the whole affair.'

Baxter ground an impatient heel into the carpet.

'I had no intention of referring to the matter to which you allude,' he said. 'I merely wished . . .'

'Yes, yes, of course.' A vagrant breeze floated in at the window, languid with summer scents, and Lord Emsworth, sniffing, shuffled restlessly. 'Of course, of course, of course. Some other time, eh? Yes, yes, that will be capital. Capital, capital, cap—'

The Efficient Baxter uttered a sound that was partly a cry, partly a snort. Its quality was so arresting that Lord Emsworth paused, his fingers on the door-handle, and peered back at him, startled.

'Very well,' said Baxter shortly. 'Pray do not let me keep you. If you are not interested in the fact that Blandings Castle is sheltering a criminal...'

It was not easy to divert Lord Emsworth when in quest of Angus McAllister, but this remark succeeded in doing so. He let go of the door-handle and came back a step or two into the room.

'Sheltering a criminal?'

'Yes.' Baxter glanced at his watch. 'I must go now or I shall miss my train,' he said curtly. 'I was merely going to tell you that this fellow who calls himself Ralston McTodd is not Ralston McTodd at all.'

'Not Ralston McTodd?' repeated his lordship blankly. 'But—' He suddenly perceived a flaw in the argument. 'But he *said* he was,' he pointed out cleverly. 'Yes, I remember distinctly. He said he was McTodd.'

'He is an impostor. And I imagine that if you investigate you will find that it is he and his accomplices who stole Lady Constance's necklace.'

'But, my dear fellow...'

Baxter walked briskly to the door.

'You need not take my word for it,' he said. 'What I say can easily be proved. Get this so-called McTodd to write his name on a piece of paper and then compare it with the signature to the letter which the real McTodd wrote when accepting Lady Constance's invitation to the castle. You will find it filed away in the drawer of that desk there.'

Lord Emsworth adjusted his glasses and stared at the desk as if he expected it to do a conjuring-trick.

'I will leave you to take what steps you please,' said Baxter. 'Now that I am no longer in your employment, the thing does not concern me one way or another. But I thought you might be glad to hear the facts.'

'Oh, I *am*!' responded his lordship, still peering vaguely. 'Oh, I *am*! Oh, yes, yes, yes. Oh, yes, yes . . .'

'Good-bye.'

'But, Baxter . . .'

Lord Emsworth trotted out on to the landing, but Baxter had got off to a good start and was almost out of sight round the bend of the stairs.

'But, my dear fellow . . .' bleated his lordship plaintively over the banisters.

From below, out on the drive, came the sound of an automobile getting into gear and moving off, than which no sound is more final. The great door of the castle closed with a soft but significant bang – as doors close when handled by an untipped butler. Lord Emsworth returned to the library to wrestle with his problem unaided.

He was greatly disturbed. Apart from the fact that he disliked criminals and impostors as a class, it was a shock to him to learn that the particular criminal and impostor then in residence at Blandings was the man for whom, brief as had been the duration of their acquaintance, he had conceived a warm affection. He was fond of Psmith. Psmith soothed him. If he had had to choose any member of his immediate circle for the rôle of criminal and impostor, he would have chosen Psmith last.

He went to the window again and looked out. There was the sunshine, there were the birds, there were the hollyhocks, carnations, and Canterbury bells, all present and correct; but now they failed to cheer him. He was wondering dismally what on earth he was going to do. What *did* one do with criminals and impostors? Had 'em arrested, he supposed. But he shrank from the thought of arresting Psmith. It seemed so deuced unfriendly.

He was still meditating gloomily when a voice spoke behind him.

'Good morning. I am looking for Miss Halliday. You have not seen her by any chance? Ah, there she is down there on the terrace.'

Lord Emsworth was aware of Psmith beside him at the window, waving cordially to Eve, who waved back.

'I thought possibly,' continued Psmith, 'that Miss Halliday would be in her little room yonder' – he indicated the dummy book-shelves through which he had entered. 'But I am glad to see that the morning is so fine that she has given toil the miss-in-baulk. It is the right spirit,' said Psmith. 'I like to see it.'

Lord Emsworth peered at him nervously through his glasses. His embarrassment and his distaste for the task that lay before him increased as he scanned his companion in vain for those signs of villainy which all well-regulated criminals and impostors ought to exhibit to the eye of discernment.

'I am surprised to find you indoors,' said Psmith, 'on so glorious a morning. I should have supposed that you would have been down there among the shrubs, taking a good sniff at a hollyhock or something.'

Lord Emsworth braced himself for the ordeal.

'Er, my dear fellow... that is to say...' He paused. Psmith was regarding him almost lovingly through his monocle, and it was becoming increasingly difficult to warm up to the work of denouncing him.

'You were observing...?' said Psmith.

Lord Emsworth uttered curious buzzing noises.

'I have just parted from Baxter,' he said at length, deciding to approach the subject in more roundabout fashion.

'Indeed?' said Psmith courteously.

'Yes. Baxter has gone.'

'For ever?'

'Er – yes.'

'Splendid!' said Psmith. 'Splendid, splendid.'

Lord Emsworth removed his glasses, twiddled them on their cord, and replaced them on his nose.

'He made . . . He – er – the fact is, he made . . . Before he went Baxter made a most remarkable statement . . . a charge . . . Well, in short, he made a very strange statement about you.'

Psmith nodded gravely.

'I had been expecting something of the kind,' he said. 'He said, no doubt, that I was not really Ralston McTodd?'

His lordship's mouth opened feebly.

'Er – yes,' he said.

'I've been meaning to tell you about that,' said Psmith amiably. 'It is quite true. I am not Ralston McTodd.'

'You – you admit it!'

'I am proud of it.'

Lord Emsworth drew himself up. He endeavoured to assume the attitude of stern censure which came so naturally to him in interviews with his son Frederick. But he met Psmith's eye and sagged again. Beneath the solemn friendliness of Psmith's gaze hauteur was impossible.

'Then what the deuce are you doing here under his name?' he asked, placing his finger in statesmanlike fashion on the very nub of the problem. 'I mean to say,' he went on, making his meaning clearer, 'if you aren't McTodd, why did you come here saying you were McTodd?'

Psmith nodded slowly.

'The point is well taken,' he said. 'I was expecting you to ask that question. Primarily – I want no thanks, but primarily I did it to save you embarrassment.'

'Save me embarrassment?'

'Precisely. When I came into the smoking-room of our mutual club that afternoon when you had been entertaining Comrade McTodd at lunch, I found him on the point of passing out of your life for ever. It seems that he had taken umbrage to some slight extent because you had buzzed off to chat with the florist across the way instead of remaining with him. And, after we had exchanged a pleasant word or two, he legged it, leaving you short one modern poet. On your return I stepped into the breach to save you from the inconvenience of having to return here without a McTodd of any description. No one, of course, could have been more alive than myself to the fact that I was merely a poor substitute, a sort of synthetic McTodd, but still I considered that I was better than nothing, so I came along.'

His lordship digested this explanation in silence. Then he seized on a magnificent point.

'Are you a member of the Senior Conservative Club?'

'Most certainly.'

'Why, then, dash it,' cried his lordship, paying to that august stronghold of respectability as striking a tribute as it had ever received, 'if you're a member of the Senior Conservative, you can't be a criminal. Baxter's an ass!'

'Exactly.'

'Baxter would have it that you had stolen my sister's necklace.'

'I can assure you that I have not got Lady Constance's necklace.'

'Of course not, of course not, my dear fellow. I'm only telling you what that idiot Baxter said. Thank goodness I've got rid of the fellow.' A cloud passed over his now sunny face. 'Though, confound it, Connie was right about one thing.' He relapsed into a somewhat moody silence.

'Yes?' said Psmith.

'Eh?' said his lordship.

'You were saying that Lady Constance had been right about one thing.'

'Oh, yes. She was saying that I should have a hard time finding another secretary as capable as Baxter.'

Psmith permitted himself to bestow an encouraging pat on his host's shoulder.

'You have touched on a matter,' he said, 'which I had intended to broach to you at some convenient moment when you were at leisure. If you would care to accept my services, they are at your disposal.'

'Eh?'

'The fact is,' said Psmith, 'I am shortly about to be married, and it is more or less imperative that I connect with some job which will ensure a moderate competence. Why should I not become your secretary?'

'You want to be my secretary?'

'You have unravelled my meaning exactly.'

'But I've never had a married secretary.'

'I think that you would find a steady married man an improvement on these wild, flower-pot-throwing bachelors. If it would help to influence your decision, I may say that my bride-to-be is Miss Halliday, probably the finest library-cataloguist in the United Kingdom.'

'Eh? Miss Halliday? That girl down there?'

'No other,' said Psmith, waving fondly at Eve as she passed underneath the window. 'In fact, the same.'

'But I like her,' said Lord Emsworth, as if stating an insuperable objection.

'Excellent.'

'She's a nice girl.'

'I quite agree with you.'

'Do you think you could really look after things here like Baxter?'

'I am convinced of it.'

'Then, my dear fellow – well, really I must say...I must say...well, I mean, why shouldn't you?'

'Precisely,' said Psmith. 'You have put in a nutshell the very thing I have been trying to express.'

'But have you had any experience as a secretary?'

'I must admit that I have not. You see, until recently I was more or less one of the idle rich. I toiled not, neither did I – except once, after a bump-supper at Cambridge – spin. My name, perhaps I ought to reveal to you, is Psmith – the p is silent – and until very recently I lived in affluence not far from the village of Much Middlefold in this county. My name is probably unfamiliar to you, but you may have heard of the house which was for many years the Psmith headquarters – Corfby Hall.'

Lord Emsworth jerked his glasses off his nose.

'Corfby Hall! Are you the son of the Smith who used to own Corfby Hall? Why, bless my soul, I knew your father well.'

'Really?'

'Yes. That is to say, I never met him.'

'No?'

'But I won the first prize for roses at the Shrewsbury Flower Show the year he won the prize for tulips.'

'It seems to draw us very close together,' said Psmith.

'Why, my dear boy,' cried Lord Emsworth jubilantly, 'if you are really looking for a position of some kind and would care to be my secretary, nothing could suit me better. Nothing, nothing, nothing. Why, bless my soul . . .'

'I am extremely obliged,' said Psmith. 'And I shall endeavour to give satisfaction. And surely, if a mere Baxter could hold down the job, it should be well within the scope of a Shropshire Psmith. I think so, I think so. . . . And now, if you will excuse me, I think I will go down and tell the glad news to the little woman, if I may so describe her.'

* * * * *

Psmith made his way down the broad staircase at an even better pace than that recently achieved by the departing Baxter, for he rightly considered each moment of this excellent day wasted that was not spent in the company of Eve. He crooned blithely to himself as he passed through the hall, only pausing when, as he passed the door of the smoking-room, the Hon. Freddie Threepwood suddenly emerged.

'Oh, I say!' said Freddie. 'Just the fellow I wanted to see. I was going off to look for you.'

Freddie's tone was cordiality itself. As far as Freddie was concerned, all that had passed between them in the cottage in the west wood last night was forgiven and forgotten.

'Say on, Comrade Threepwood,' replied Psmith; 'and, if I may offer the suggestion, make it snappy, for I would be elsewhere. I have man's work before me.'

'Come over here.' Freddie drew him into a far corner of the hall and lowered his voice to a whisper. 'I say, it's all right, you know.'

'Excellent!' said Psmith. 'Splendid! This is great news. What is all right?'

'I've just seen Uncle Joe. He's going to cough up the money he promised me.'

'I congratulate you.'

'So now I shall be able to get into that bookie's business and make a pile. And, I say, you remember my telling you about Miss Halliday?'

'What was that?'

'Why, that I loved her, I mean, and all that.'

'Ah, yes.'

'Well, look here, between ourselves,' said Freddie earnestly, 'the whole trouble all along has been that she thought I hadn't any money to get married on. She didn't actually say so in so many words, but you know how it is with women – you can read between the lines, if you know what I mean. So now everything's going to be all right. I shall simply go to her and say, "Well, what about it?" and – well, and so on, don't you know?'

Psmith considered the point gravely.

'I see your reasoning, Comrade Threepwood,' he said. 'I can detect but one flaw in it.'

'Flaw? What flaw?'

'The fact that Miss Halliday is going to marry *me*.'

The Hon. Freddie's jaw dropped. His prominent eyes became more prawn-like.

'What!'

Psmith patted his shoulder commiseratingly.

'Be a man, Comrade Threepwood, and bite the bullet. These things will happen to the best of us. Some day you will be thankful that this has occurred. Purged in the holocaust of a mighty love, you will wander out into the sunset, a finer, broader man.... And now I must reluctantly tear myself away. I have an important appointment.' He patted his shoulder once more. 'If you would care to be a page at the wedding, Comrade Threepwood, I can honestly say that there is no one whom I would rather have in that capacity.'

And with a stately gesture of farewell, Psmith passed out on to the terrace to join Eve.

THE END